The Way It Is

Patrick Sanchez

KENSINGTON BOOKS
http://www.kensingtonbooks.com

KENSINGTON BOOKS are published by

Kensington Publishing Corp.
850 Third Avenue
New York, NY 10022

All Kensington titles, imprints and distributed lines are available at special quantity discounts for bulk purchases for sales promotion, premiums, fund raising, educational or institutional use.

Special book excerpts or customized printings can also be created to fit specific needs. For details, write or phone the office of the Kensington Special Sales Manager: Kensington Publishing Corp., 850 Third Avenue, New York, NY, 10022. Attn. Special Sales Department. Phone: 1-800-221-2647.

ISBN 0-7582-0411-6

First Kensington Paperback Printing: October 2003
10 9 8 7 6 5 4 3 2 1

Printed in the United States of America

To my uncle,
Murray Herbert

*May there be long stretches of woods,
teams of hunting beagles, and plenty of
rabbits to chase wherever you are now.*

ACKNOWLEDGMENTS

There are many friends and family members that supported me through the process of moving my first book, *Girlfriends,* off the bookstore shelves and penning this second novel, *The Way It Is.*

My whole-hearted thanks and appreciation to the following:

First and foremost to all the readers who enthusiastically embraced my books, E-mailed me with such positive feedback, and told all your friends about my work. Keep the E-mails coming to *AuthorPatrick@yahoo.com* and please check out my Web site at *www.patrick-sanchez.com.* I also need to thank all the bookstore staff members who welcomed me into their stores to do readings and signings, displayed my posters, and wore my *Girlfriends* buttons. Thanks so much for helping me get the word out!

My parents, Patricia and Guillermo Sanchez: For taking such an interest in my books even if they are a little R-rated for your taste.

My younger sister, Laurie: For being my weeknight dinner partner, telling all your college friends about *Girlfriends,* and posting a *Girlfriends* bumper sticker on your dorm room door.

My two older sisters, Donna and Maria: For inviting me to your book clubs, having a cake made in the image of the *Girlfriends* cover, and helping me spread the word about my books.

My grandmother, Bertha Herbert: For managing to read

Girlfriends after years of declining vision and not being *completely* horrified afterward.

My extended family, Cal, Paul, Freda, Allison, Helen, Caroline, CJ, Tommy, and Anna Maria: For your continued support and enthusiasm for my books.

Brian Reid: For all your support on a daily basis, helping me proofread the final galleys of *The Way It Is,* and, most importantly, for digging out my car after the snow storm in February 2003.

My editor, John Scognamiglio: For encouraging me through the process of writing a second novel, coming up with the title for both my books, taking me to some great New York restaurants, and always listening to what I have to say.

Yvette Chisholm: For supporting me and offering guidance through almost everything I do and for your detailed review of an early draft of *The Way It Is.*

Michelle Kulp and Jenny Veax Meyer: For helping me prepare for my readings, taking an enthusiastic interest in *Girlfriends,* and lending such helpful hands with *The Way It Is.*

Camilla Eriksson: For developing the awesome "*Girlfriends* Holiday Greeting." I'm still amazed that you would be so generous and helpful to someone you have never met or even talked to on the phone. Camilla's fantastic fun pages can be viewed at *www.millan.net*.

Wendy Block at Saks and Robin Highberg at Nordstrom: For enthusiastically helping me navigate the world of women's plus-size fashions.

My agent, Deborah Schneider: For taking me on and answering my endless questions about the publishing industry.

Steve Stark: For all your help during the development of *Girlfriends* and for offering some great insight and ideas for *The Way It Is.*

Hope Winters-Norton: For developing countless marketing materials for my first book, *Girlfriends*. You're the best!

Tony Smith: For helping me pass out *Girlfriends* buttons in the blazing summer heat, hanging a *Girlfriends* poster in your cube at work, being a constant source of promotion for my books, and being my only friend to put a *Girlfriends* bumper sticker on your car.

Tony Curtis and Dan Dycus: For being great friends, promoting my books, and throwing me a wonderful Book Party to launch *Girlfriends* (and for not wearing cologne around me).

Libba Bray: For writing the fantastic jacket copy for *The Way It Is*.

Lori Eisenkraft: For doing a super job copyediting *The Way It Is*.

William Sloan: For crafting a colorful, fun, and eye-catching, cover for *The Way It Is*.

To the Proposal Shop at ValueOptions: Saghi Agha-Khan, Jennifer Bullock, Ed Costas, Laurie Elstone, Lucia Ferguson, Chris Grady, Stephanie Johnson, Hildi Kelsey, Donna Manning, Rabin Massey, Dawn Monk, Rodrigo Peredo, Anne Reins, Jay Reedy, Eric Sanford, Emily Schaneman, Nicki Teale, Roger Williams, and Claudia Winters: For putting up with endless E-mails about my books and helping me reach my ten-year mark with the company with my sanity intact . . . or at least mostly intact.

To the following for helping out by supporting me and just being good friends: Jennifer Amato, Dorothy Barry, Jennifer Carroll, Whitney Clark, Dave Elliott, Jennifer Gauntt, Teresa and Shelly Glaze, Janet Glazier, Mike and Kerri Gray, Scott Kardel, Lyn Laparan, Mary McDonald, Tim McDonald, Andrea Newsome, Cindy Ostrowski, Mark Podrazik, Michael Pfeifer, Jim Palumbo, Angela Perri, Joe Russell, Tasha Tillman, Holly Tracy, Alev Volkan, and Sandy Wells.

The Way It Is

Ruby Waters

"Ruby!" Doris called from the living room to her daughter in the kitchen. "My arm is feeling numb. I think I might be having a stroke," she continued with just a slight hint of panic in her voice.

"Well go have it in the basement, would you? I just vacuumed in there," Ruby replied with an utter lack of enthusiasm. She didn't even look up from the kitchen floor she was mopping.

Doris gradually lifted her elderly frame from the sofa and meandered slowly into the kitchen.

"What are you doing?" she asked, looking at Ruby, already forgetting about her supposedly numb arm. Her words were saying, "What are you doing?" but her tone was saying, "What are you fucking up now?"

"What's it look like I'm doing?" Ruby responded. "I'm mopping the floor."

"Didn't you just mop it an hour ago?"

"As a matter of fact, I did, but that beast of yours peed on it again," Ruby said, nodding her head in Taco's direction. He was sitting almost regally in the kitchen threshold and had been staring intently at Ruby from the moment she grabbed the mop and pail. He seemed to silently mock her for having to clean up after him. Taco was Doris's tiny white Chihuahua. He had pink ears and a pink nose and had been Doris's pride and joy for almost six years. Taco adored Doris and *only* Doris. He hated everyone else and growled viciously at anyone that came within ten feet of his tiny six-pound frame. He hated Ruby as much as anyone, but, having gotten used to her regular visits, she was one of the few guests that Taco would at least tolerate. He and Ruby had developed a sort of understanding. He agreed not to growl at (or attempt to maul) Ruby as long as she made no attempts to pet him, touch him, or otherwise engage him.

"Well, of course he peed on the floor. It's raining outside."

"What?" Ruby replied, halting the mop and looking up from the floor.

"You know Taco doesn't like to go outside when it's raining."

"Well, he'd better learn," Ruby responded before turning her head to Taco. "Did you hear that, Taco?" she said firmly to the dog, who immediately let out a slight growl, warning Ruby to leave him alone.

"Careful on the wet floor, Ruby," Doris said as Ruby returned to her mopping. "If you trip with all that weight you might crack the tile," Doris added with a giggle, as if what she was saying was a good-natured tease, when in fact, it was about the third snide remark Doris had made about Ruby's weight since she arrived a few hours earlier. Ruby had cleaned the bathrooms and the kitchen, changed the sheets, did a little dusting, and ran the vacuum cleaner across the carpet. She made this trek out to LaPlata, Maryland, about once a week to check on her aging mother, help with any paperwork or bills, and keep the house in order. Doris was in her seventies and hadn't fared well since Ruby's father passed away a few years earlier. She suffered from all sorts of vague aches and pains and seemed to be in a rather chronic state of mild depression, about which Doris, of course, would do nothing. If Ruby so much as hinted at Doris trying therapy or taking an antidepressant, she always received the same response. She wasn't "crazy" and she wasn't "going to see any damn two-hundred-dollar-an-hour psychiatrist."

Ruby finished up the mopping and dumped the soiled water down the sink. She watched Doris make her way back to the sofa for the second half of *Wheel of Fortune* while she headed for the bedroom to grab her purse and hit the road. As Ruby threw her bag over her shoulder she couldn't resist checking on *it*—just to make sure that it was still there, waiting for her. She slid open the closet door, rifled past a few blouses and skirts, and found it—Doris's little black dress. Ruby lifted it off the rod and held it out in front of her almost as if it were a wedding dress or some sacred piece of clothing.

"One day," she said quietly to herself. One day she was going to get into that dress. It was one of the most classically beautiful pieces of clothing Ruby had ever seen, and the only designer dress her mother had ever owned. The dress always reminded Ruby of the first time she saw her mother in it. It was New Year's Eve, 1976. She'd never forgotten the moment when Doris emerged from the bedroom in her new black dress from the now defunct department store, Woodward & Lothrop. Her mother was well into her forties by then, but it was one of the first, and best, memories Ruby, who was five at the time, had of Doris. To Ruby, that evening in 1976 was the most beautiful Doris had ever been. Ruby never got to see her mother as a young woman. Doris was in her early forties when Ruby was born—not unusual today, but when Ruby was born in the early seventies, a woman giving birth in her forties was much less common. Doris never talked about why she had Ruby later in life, but Ruby's grandmother had told her that Doris and Ruby's father had tried to have children in their twenties to no avail, eventually resigning to the fact that, for whatever reason, Doris was unable to conceive. Of course, after years of trying to get pregnant, Doris saw no need to use birth control, and life progressed without incident for years until one day in 1970 when Doris was late. She thought it might be early menopause and boy was she shocked when the doctor told her that at forty-one, she was going to have a baby.

Ruby raised the dress in front of her and gave it a long stare. She looked in the mirror and, as usual, focused on her face rather than her body. It wasn't so bad looking at her full cheeks, lined with chin length red hair. She could handle seeing her blue eyes and soft nose. It was her body she couldn't stand to look at. Somehow, she managed to look in the mirror and focus on the dress she held in front of her without looking at her body.

Since she was a little girl, Ruby had silently fantasized about wearing the little black dress despite the fact that, by the time she was ten years old, she was already too large for it. She had not inherited her mother's petite frame or fast metabolism. Instead, Ruby had to settle for the unfortunate genetic propensity to gain weight that she shared with her late father—"the thrifty gene," she'd heard some reporter on television call it. Before the industrial age it was an asset, coming in handy in times when food was scarce, and the ability to store loads of excess fat was essential for survival. But now, in an age of supersizes and value meals it was, at best, a nuisance, and, at worst, a disaster of grand proportions.

Ruby looked at the dress. It was an Oscar de la Renta cocktail dress made of satin with a fine outer layer of chiffon. It was simply elegant with spaghetti straps and intricate beading along the bustline. It made Ruby think of Doris at her happiest and reminded her of a more pleasant time for herself when she spent her days playing on the neighbor's jungle gym or watching *Josie and the Pussycats* rather than constantly obsessing over her weight like she did now as an adult. Her mother's black dress was the catalyst for every diet that Ruby ever went on. She always vowed to, one day, fit into Doris's little black dress.

"What are you doing in there?" Doris called from the living room.

"Just wrapping up," Ruby replied as she gently and reverently placed the dress back in the closet and made her way to the kitchen. She was about to open the back door and put the mop on the deck when she hit a slick spot on the floor and lost her footing. She let out a yelp as she fell face forward toward the floor. She tried to use the back end of the mop as a cane of sorts to stay on her feet. Trying to remain upright, she crashed the wooden rod into the floor, but she slipped onto her belly anyway—one hand still grasping the mop.

"Jesus Christ!" she said to herself, trying to regain some composure and get back on her feet.

"Shit," she said quietly as she lifted herself from the ground and saw what she had done when she jammed the mop handle into the floor. There it was, staring up at her, plain as day—a small crack in the tile. Doris was going to have a field day with that.

"Oh, shut up!" Ruby said to a silent Taco, who had observed the whole spectacle with a condescending look while perched just outside the kitchen.

Games People Play

"Yep! Beer, football, and pussy," Jeremy said to Ruby, who was sitting next to him on the Metro.

"Yeah, I'd have to agree," Ruby replied as she and Jeremy observed a large man with a bit of a potbelly on the other end of the subway car.

Some people read or listened to music to make time pass on their commute. Ruby and Jeremy liked to play "Homo or Hetero," an intricate game of skill in which the players choose an unsuspecting candidate from the crowd and try to figure out what "team" he or she played for. "Beer, football, and pussy," was Jeremy's standard way of saying that their current male selection was straight.

"He was an easy one. He has straight written all over him."

"I don't know. I'm sure there are gay men over thirty who have potbellies and look a little disheveled," Ruby replied.

"Yeah, but we don't claim any of those," Jeremy joked.

"So the gay community is selective now? Only good-looking, fit guys need apply?"

"Absolutely," Jeremy replied with a bit of a chuckle. "And if your body-fat quotient doesn't make the cut, you don't get your card . . . or your free toaster." "Look, he's married," Jeremy added, noting the band on the gentleman's left hand.

"Of course he is. Men can be fat and unattractive and still get married. Women, on the other hand . . ."

Jeremy just offered a slight smile in response. He really couldn't argue with Ruby's point. It did sort of seem that even the most unattractive and socially inept straight man could land a woman. Women just seemed to be more forgiving of imperfections than men. Women were supposed to put up with protruding bellies and receding hairlines, but the moment women's hips started to get a little wide, or fine lines emerged on their faces, their husbands starting hunting for some twenty-five-year-old twinkie with saline tits and hair extensions.

Ruby and Jeremy were on their way back to D.C. from a shopping excursion in the suburbs. Ruby had agreed to help Jeremy find an absolutely gorgeous gown to wear in the annual High Heel Race. Just before Halloween, J.R.'s, a local gay bar, sponsored this event, which originally consisted of a few dozen men in women's clothing and high heels racing down 17th Street. Although a few exuberant drag queens still raced for the win with everything they had, over the years, the event melded into more of a parade or a showcase of sorts. Every year the evening became less and less about the race, and more about a bunch of queens who wanted to try to outdo each other with the most outrageous and extravagant costumes. Jeremy was pulling out all the stops to emerge on top this year and garner the most enthusiastic response from the spectators.

"Sorry we didn't find anything at Bloomingdale's," Ruby said before continuing. "Maybe it was just as well. Do you really want to spend a fortune on a dress you're only going to wear once? Why don't we look at T.J. Maxx or Marshall's or something?"

"T.J. Maxx?" Jeremy said before raising his voice. "Blasphemy!"

"You're only going to be dancing around and lip-syncing to music. I just thought we could find something more reasonable for the parade at . . ."

"Ruby! Do you think Britney Spears buys her costumes at

T.J. Maxx before she dances around and lip-syncs to music? . . . And it's a race, Ruby. Not a parade. There won't be any dancing and singing—just running."

"It's a *parade,* Jeremy, and honey, I hate to be the bearer of bad news, but you ain't exactly Britney Spears."

"Well, of course not. She's the ultimate drag queen."

"Really?"

"Sure. She parades around in fabulous costumes and big hair, has great choreography, and lip-syncs to 'Baby One More Time' and 'Oops, I Did It Again.' You don't get much more drag queen than that."

"And that's why she's your idol?"

"That, and because she fucked Justin Timberlake."

"*Dated* Justin Timberlake," Ruby replied, correcting him. "The fucking part is debatable."

"Yeah, whatever."

The pair laughed as a few of the other passengers watched the gay guy and the fat girl ham it up on the subway—a fag and a tag. Ruby and Jeremy met more than ten years earlier when they were attending George Mason University in Fairfax, Virginia. One might guess it was fate that sat them next to each other on the first day of their freshman year when their professor had the ultra-original idea of each student partnering with the person next to them, quickly interviewing each other, and then telling the class the life story (in one minute or less) of their newfound friend. During the course of their respective interviews Ruby and Jeremy were innately able to relate to each other. As they talked it became clear that they had much in common. Ruby was from an outlying Maryland suburb of D.C. called LaPlata and Jeremy was from Fredericksburg, Virginia, about fifty miles south of D.C. Both towns had now grown into typical suburban communities, but when Ruby and Jeremy were growing up, both LaPlata and Fredricksburg had a little bit of a rural feel. When they started at George Mason in the late eighties it was their first time away from home. Neither of them knew anyone at the school, and they immediately sensed something about each other—they were both outsiders—Ruby, because she was fat, and Jeremy, because he was gay. They were two of society's outcasts who happened to find each other in English composition class. They were never going to be fully embraced by the beautiful people of mainstream society, so they began doing the one thing that fat women and gay men have been doing together since the beginning of time—trashing all the people that shunned them.

Just minutes after meeting they started bantering like old friends. They made fun of the dim-witted story their professor had read at the beginning of class (of which he was the author, of course); trashed a girl on the other side of the room, who was an "obvious whore;" and debated the authenticity of the breasts belonging to some blonde bitch, who was telling her interviewer about her days as a cheerleader at Wakefield High in Arlington. They had such fun during their interview-turned-dish-session, that Jeremy asked Ruby if she wanted to grab some lunch after class.

Ruby was in love with Jeremy from the start. He was handsome with blond hair and brown eyes. He was about five ten or so with a nice average frame. He certainly wasn't buff, or even fit, but he was thin. Ruby was astounded when Jeremy asked her out on what she thought was an actual date. What was a cute thin guy like Jeremy wanting with the likes of her? Ruby couldn't figure it out, and a big part of her didn't want to. She just wanted to enjoy the fact that Jeremy was interested in her. They went to see *Heathers* with Winona Ryder and Christian Slater on their first outing, and then out to dinner at Chi Chi's at Fair Oaks Mall. On their next excursion they went to see *Dead Poet's Society* and then to P.J. Skidoos. The third date was a trip to the multiplex in Merrifield to see *Look Who's Talking* and yet another dinner at Fuddruckers in Annandale. In between outings to the movies and local restaurants they saw each other on campus every day—either in class or during lunch. Over the next few weeks Ruby saw lots of Jeremy, she saw lots of movies, and she saw lots of restaurants. One thing she didn't see, though, was Jeremy's dick. They were spending so much time together and seemed to really be connecting, but there was never any physical intimacy. Ruby figured that, as usual, he wasn't interested in anything romantic with her because she was fat. The thought hadn't even occurred to her that Jeremy was gay. This was the eighties—before *Ellen* and *Will & Grace* had hit the airwaves. Ruby was naïve—she didn't know gay people could look like Jeremy. He didn't have a lisp or a limp wrist. In fact, he looked like someone out of a J. Crew catalog. Although Ruby was disappointed, at the same time it was such a relief when Jeremy finally came out to her a few weeks after they had met. Knowing Jeremy was gay put a whole new kind of ease in their relationship. At least it was her equipment (or lack thereof) that kept Jeremy from putting any moves on her and not her weight.

"Look. Another man on deck! I think this one's a big queen," Jeremy said to Ruby as they watched an attractive thirty-something man in preppy attire board the train with a canvas briefcase over one shoulder and a copy of *The Washington Post* in his hand.

"No, I think you're wrong about this one," Ruby said.

"Ruby, how often am I wrong?"

"Not often," Ruby had to admit. "But this one looks straight to me."

"Are you kidding me?" Jeremy said, looking the man up and down as discreetly as possible. "Banana Republic pants, J-Crew shirt, Timberland boots, socks from Structure, and the belt looks Coach," Jeremy continued. "And I bet the tighty-whities are Calvin Klein." Jeremy had a unique talent for identifying where anyone and everyone bought their clothes. "Now, if he had mixed in a pair of JC Penney socks or Payless shoes with the ensemble, then I might consider him being straight, but . . ."

Ruby laughed as Jeremy cut himself off in mid-sentence, realizing that Ruby had won this round.

"Ha! I win," Ruby said as the two of them watched the gentleman get settled into a seat, sort through his newspaper, and go straight for the *Sports* page.

Fixer-Uppers

The day after the unsuccessful shopping outing with Jeremy, Ruby was on her way home from the bank after making a withdrawal from her savings account. Outwardly, she called it her Christmas Club, but it was actually her "Thin Ruby" account. She'd opened it years ago and had three percent of her paycheck directly deposited into it every two weeks. She also made random deposits into the account when she came into a little extra cash. She had amassed almost three thousand dollars—three thousand dollars that she was going to blow on fancy clothes, makeup, and salon visits as soon as she lost weight.

It pained her to be making a withdrawal from her Thin Ruby account for purposes for which it was not intended. Lately, she was having trouble making ends meet and was forced to tap her Thin Ruby account just to meet her monthly expenses.

Ruby could manage most of her bills. She didn't spend much money on clothes, and Lord knew, she had virtually no social life. Besides her car expenses and her grocery and restaurant bills, she wasn't a big spender. It was really only her mortgage payment that constantly left her strapped for money.

The only thing Ruby had asked for in her divorce settlement with her ex-husband, Warren, the year before was to keep the house—and, oh, how she loved her house. She and Warren had bought the three-bedroom brick row house just before they were married. Ruby fell in love with it the moment she saw it. It was nearly a hundred years old, and, although it had been updated here and there over the years, it was definitely a fixer-upper. That was one of the reasons Ruby liked it so much—it needed work, just like her, and it was also one of the reasons she and Warren could afford it. The house was in the Logan Circle neighborhood of the District, which, until recent years, had always been considered a marginal area of the city. When Ruby and Warren first started looking at real estate, Ruby really had no interest in living in the city—after all, D.C. had only recently started to recover from years of neglect and corruption under a crack-smoking mayor, services like snow plowing and trash collection weren't always reliable, and Lord help you if you had to go to the Department of Motor Vehicles—getting a driver's license renewed was an all-day ordeal, and that was when the computer system was actually up and running. But Warren had grown up in the city, and he sold Ruby on living close to work and being able to take advantage of public transportation, top restaurants, and a multitude of cultural activities.

When Ruby and Warren began looking for a new house in D.C. their realtor kept telling them about Logan Circle and how the whole neighborhood was going through a renaissance—how new shops were opening, how trendy restaurants were starting to sprout up along 14th Street—and, in more of a hushed tone, how white people were starting to move back in.

After realizing that the Dupont Circle and Capitol Hill neighborhoods were out of their price range, Ruby and Warren decided to give Logan Circle a look-see. After shuffling through a few dozen houses, the couple finally settled on Ruby's current residence just off Rhode Island Avenue. It was a classic three-story row house with a kitchen, combined living room/dining room, and a small den on the first floor. The second floor housed two small bedrooms and a full bath, and the third floor was a master suite that spanned the entire length of the house. The day after they closed on their mortgage, Ruby, with limited assistance from Warren, immediately set out to spruce up the place and continued renovating and remodeling for years. She landscaped the tiny front yard with all sorts of flowers and shrubs.

She repainted every room in the house, had the hardwood floors buffed and stained, and hired a contractor to completely update both bathrooms. In a couple more years she hoped to save enough money to have her kitchen completely remodeled, although she had no idea how that would ever happen with the current state of her financial affairs. At this point, she wasn't really sure she could afford to keep the house at all.

As Ruby drove home from the bank she thought about ways to remedy her financial situation. As far as she could tell, she really only had two options if she wanted to keep her house: pick up a second job, or get a roommate. Neither option appealed to her, but she wasn't going to give up her house. She had put so much of herself into the house over the years. It was her little oasis from the harsh world. And the realtor had been right—the neighborhood kept improving after Ruby and Warren moved in. It had become an interesting mix of poor city residents on government assistance, a sizable population of gay men, and an emerging abundance of well-to-do DINK (dual income no kids) straight couples, who bought older homes and spent a fortune renovating them. Some upscale restaurants had opened as well as a few bars and nightclubs, but the neighborhood hadn't really "arrived" until the Fresh Fields organic food market opened on P Street. All of a sudden, everyone in Logan Circle proudly referred to the Fresh Fields when explaining where their home was. People would say things like, "Yes, I live over by the Fresh Fields," or "You know, near the Fresh Fields, that's where I live," as if having an uppity supermarket within walking distance of their home automatically transformed the neighborhood into Bel Air or something. Despite the Fresh Fields and the influx of trendy eateries and hot spots, the neighborhood was still home to its share of riffraff. Hookers still gave blow jobs and dealers still moved crack and ecstasy, only now, they did it in alleys behind restaurants with white tablecloths or stores that sold organic apples and unbleached flour.

As Ruby continued her drive home, she gave the idea of getting a second job brief consideration. There seemed to be a limited number of options when seeking part-time work that would fit around the schedule of her regular job. She wasn't interested in working at a mall or waiting tables, and the idea of telemarketing gave her the creeps—she faced enough rejection in her life without hundreds of people regularly hanging up on her. She also reconsidered getting a roommate to help defray her housing costs. Other than Warren, she hadn't lived with anyone in years and knew it would take some adjusting, but maybe it would be okay if she found the right roommate.

How bad could it be? Ruby thought.

After weighing her options, she decided that looking for a roommate was a lesser evil than getting a second job. Maybe she could run an ad in the *Washington City Paper* or *The Washington Post*. It would be nice if she knew someone who was looking for a place to live, but the only people Ruby socialized with on a regular basis were Jeremy and her mother. Jeremy owned a condo in Arlington, and the idea of Doris living with her made Ruby's heart palpitate. Ruby concluded that she would have to find a roommate the old-fashioned way—by running an ad and sorting through candidates in hopes of not ending up with a total freak for a roommate.

Jumping Aboard the Marriage Train

Ruby was reclining on the sofa, typing on her laptop computer, and half watching a rerun of *Designing Women* on Lifetime. In between giggling at the antics of Suzanne Sugarbaker and Mary Jo Shiveley, Ruby was preparing an ad to run in *The Washington Post* classifieds. She was trying to develop a brief description of the house and what she was looking for in a roommate—and with the price of the ad by the word, Ruby was trying to make it as concise as possible.

> *LOGAN CIRCLE—Seeking prof N/S F, 1BR avail in 3BR TH, Pvt Bath, Avail immed, $800 utils incl. Ask for Ruby.*

As Ruby proofed the draft, and added her phone number, she heard a knock at the door and immediately knew who it was. Only one person had such a slow, deliberate knock.

"Just a sec," Ruby called as she set the laptop aside and made her way to the door.

"Hello, Ruby," Warren said as she opened the door. Just like his knock, his greeting was slow and punctuated. It was never "Hey," or "Hi." It was always "Hello" or something even more formal.

"Warren? What's up?" Ruby replied. She loved saying things like, "What's up?" or sometimes, "How's it hangin'?" to Warren.

It was fun to counter his proper expressions with informal slang. Such behavior annoyed and perplexed Warren, and lately, that was a good thing as far as Ruby was concerned.

"I was in the vicinity and ascertained that it would be advantageous to stop by and collect the last of my belongings."

Ruby paused, as she often did after Warren spoke, to make sense of his words. He loved to spew ostentatious words and stretched out whatever he was saying into inappropriately long sentences. He perpetually sounded like those random bystanders that get interviewed on the news because they happen to be in the area when a manhole explodes or a Starbuck's gets robbed—the ones that desperately try to sound intelligent on the local news by throwing fifty-cent words all over place.

"Oh. Your stuff," Ruby finally concluded. "It's over there yonder," she said, pointing toward the kitchen. Ruby never used the word "yonder" but figured it might annoy Warren, and annoying Warren was such fun.

"Yonder?" Warren questioned.

"In the kitchen. I'll grab it. Be right back," Ruby said, leaving Warren in the entryway to collect a few of his things she'd found while cleaning out the attic a few weeks earlier.

Ruby had met Warren about four years earlier when he started with CrustiCare, the HMO where Ruby had been employed for seven years. Warren was part of the IT support staff and was responsible for things like troubleshooting computer problems and retrieving lost documents for "computer illiterates," as he often referred to Ruby. They met one day when Warren came by her office to fix her ailing computer and update some of her software. While he undertook the rather tedious process of installing a multitude of necessary programs, Ruby had to make do without access to her computer and attempted to pass the idle time with conversation. She was immediately bored by Warren's loquacious manner and his general condescending tone, but she had nothing else to do while he had possession of her keyboard, so she continued to chat with him. After he finished and left her office, Ruby didn't give him another thought. He was just the techie nerd that came to fix her computer, nothing more, nothing less. She was quite surprised when he called her the next day and asked if she would like to "share an evening meal with him." Once Ruby deduced that he was talking about dinner she figured, "What the hell," and agreed to meet him.

Warren's phone call left her with mixed emotions. On one hand, she was excited to be asked on a date, something that hadn't happened in years. On the other hand, the person asking her out didn't really interest her. During their brief interaction Warren seemed rather flat and dull. He certainly wasn't much to look at either. He was also overweight, but, unlike Ruby, his weight was not proportioned evenly across his body. He had a thin face, long skinny arms and legs, and virtually no ass at all. All his fat seemed to congregate in one place—his belly. He looked like an extremely tall pregnant man and his clothing was quite disheveled—as if he had rolled out of bed and thrown on whatever clothes were lying on the floor.

A few days after Warren called, he and Ruby met for dinner at The Village Bistro in Arlington, a restaurant Ruby had suggested they go to—she absolutely loved this wonderful pasta dish they served there—sautéed chicken and apples covered with a delicious cream sauce—heaven, it was pure heaven! Their dinner conversation paralleled their earlier interaction when Warren was fixing Ruby's computer. Warren bored Ruby with talk of his job as a technical support analyst, his high-tech career aspirations, and a persistent rash on his inner thigh that he just couldn't seem to get rid of. As Warren spoke, Ruby assessed that he was pretentious, socially inept, and a total bore. He also had this one habit that annoyed the hell out of her—he wore this pair of big hoot-owl glasses that might have been somewhat in style back when Boy George topped the charts. Every time they slipped forward on his nose he clumsily shoved them back up with his middle finger. He did this every five minutes or so, which amounted to him perpetually flipping the bird at virtually everyone with whom he came into contact.

Ruby sat across from him feeling no interest or chemistry. The only thing she really felt was pity. Warren seemed like such a fish out of water, as if he belonged in some other universe. He had an awkward demeanor and seemed to know little beyond the world of computers. He talked too much about things no one was interested in, and made inappropriate remarks about everything from the waiter to the menu to Ruby. At one point during the meal he elaborated that he had always "possessed a fervent interest in large women" and was immediately attracted to "Ruby's obesity." Under normal circumstances Ruby would have been insulted by such a statement, but coming from Warren it just seemed like an improper comment that might be made by a child or a developmentally disabled adult.

One part of Ruby just wanted to race through the date and get it over with, while another part of her searched long and hard for some redeeming qualities in Warren. She wanted to like him. He was the only guy that had shown any interest in her in years, and he really did seem to have a genuine attraction to her.

Okay, she would think to herself. Let's see . . . He's nice. He knows computers, which could certainly come in handy. He has a strong vocabulary. . . . He met me on time, so he's punctual. . . . Hmmm . . . He's clean. . . .

Despite Ruby's lack of interest, Warren seemed to really enjoy their date, possibly because Ruby allowed him to run his mouth nonstop while she feigned interest. After dinner he walked Ruby to her car, gave her an uninvited clumsy kiss on the lips, and said he would call her.

On the way home from their first date, Ruby gave Warren some detailed consideration. She spent the bulk of her life categorizing herself in relation to others, questioning whether she was superior, equal, or inferior to everyone with whom she came into contact. Generally, she fell into the inferior category as she found most people more attractive and better adjusted than herself. Occasionally, she had a feeling of equality with selected others—like Jeremy, who, although thin and attractive, was gay, which pushed him to the fringe of society with Ruby. And every now and then, Ruby had a feeling of superiority. It didn't surface often, but on the way home from her date with Warren she felt it kick in. Warren seemed to operate in his own world. He didn't even seem to recognize that he was overweight, unattractive, and a bit of an oaf. Sure, Ruby was fat and had issues, but at least she was aware of her faults and in touch with reality.

When Warren called to ask Ruby on a second date she decided she might as well go. If nothing else, it was nice to be pursued by *someone*. They went out a few more times, and Warren began to grow on Ruby. She got past his stodgy demeanor and ungainly looks. She even learned how to tune him out when he began rambling about gigabytes and megahertz, but she never fell in love with him. She fell in love with being in a relationship, she fell in love with saying that she had a boyfriend, and, despite Warren's lack of sexual prowess, she fell in love with sharing a bed with a warm body. In essence, Ruby fell in love with being loved and with not being alone. Even if she didn't love Warren, he loved her, and Ruby thought that might be enough.

They dated for months and Ruby continued to get used to his ramblings about lackluster computer topics and the latest video games. She never did, however, quite get used to some of the totally tactless things that would come out of his mouth. One time after they had made love, he told Ruby that the two of them were "an ideal sexual match." When she asked why, Warren explained that his long slender penis—yes, that's what he said, his "long slender penis"—suited Ruby perfectly. He had heard that obese women such as Ruby—yes, that's how he referred to Ruby, as an "obese woman"—had small vaginas so his svelte member was perfect for her. Again, such a statement from anyone else would have been terribly offensive, but it was what Ruby had come to expect from Warren, and she knew he didn't mean any harm by it. He was just stating what he thought was a fact. She wanted to tell him he was wrong. Ruby didn't believe her vagina was any smaller than that of the general population, and if Warren made himself feel better by referring to his skinny prick as "long and slender," then more power to him. Instead she offered a benign "That's an interesting theory, Warren," in response to his revelation and left it at that.

They dated for eight months before Warren popped the question. Ruby wasn't sure she would ever get married and, despite her lack of any real attraction to Warren, she immediately accepted his marriage proposal. Ruby knew that she was settling, but no one else was knocking at her door, and she figured she had better jump aboard the marriage train while she had the chance.

She remembered Jeremy's reaction when she told him of her plans to marry Warren—the reserved congratulations he offered, the way his eyebrows went up in a "are you sure you're doing the right thing?" kind of way. He never came out and said, "What the fuck are you doing, Ruby? A walking doorknob is more interesting than Warren," but Ruby knew what he was thinking and throughout the whole process of planning the wedding, Ruby sometimes thought the same thing. But she was able to keep her mind off her doubts about the marriage by planning the actual wedding—something Doris was more than happy to assist with. After all, if Doris didn't offer her guidance and recommendations, she was certain Ruby would screw up the whole thing. Unlike Jeremy, Doris was thrilled to hear of Ruby's plans. Actually, she had to fight to keep herself from kneeling on the ground and thanking the Good Lord above for finding someone, anyone, to keep her daughter from becoming a spinster. Ruby had three months to plan the wedding, and Doris was certain that, if nothing else, her planned wedding would motivate Ruby to really lose some weight.

"Why Ruby, I bet you can drop fifty pounds before the big day if you really put your mind to it. Brenda Hill's daughter lost a lot of weight going to Weight Watchers. Maybe you should try that again," Doris said one day as she watched Ruby model a prospective dress at the bridal shop. There were a limited number of wedding gowns in her size, so Ruby didn't have too many to choose from. In fact, when she walked in the door and inquired about dresses, a snooty sales woman took her to the back of store, pointed to a tightly packed rack of gowns, and, as if Ruby was something she had just scraped off her shoe, said, "This is all we have in your size."

Ruby wouldn't admit it to Doris, but she did plan to drop

some weight before her wedding day and ended up buying a fairly simple matte satin dress that was two sizes too small for her. Unfortunately, a week before her wedding day, reality set in, and Ruby rushed to a friend of Doris's, who was handy with a sewing machine, and asked her to let out the dress. Ruby had managed to drop a couple of pounds, but it certainly was not enough to easily fit into the dress she had chosen for her special day. If she hadn't gotten the dress altered, she feared it might have burst at the seams as she walked down the aisle.

When her big day arrived, Ruby was thrilled. Her father had passed away a few years earlier, so Jeremy walked her down the aisle. Ruby didn't have any close female friends, so she dredged up two cousins from North Carolina to be her bridesmaids. She had a lump in her throat as she glided toward the front of the church, making her way to Warren and the priest. It was her day. She was so excited—excited to be proving to everyone that someone wanted to marry her, excited to be having a beautiful wedding, excited to know that all those people who had made fun of her in high school would see her engagement announcement in the local paper . . . and then there was Warren—she looked at him standing at the base of the altar looking like . . . well, looking like *Warren*. She *loved* him—he was good to her and took care of her, but she knew she wasn't, and probably never would be, *in love* with him. As she continued to walk down the aisle she looked away from Warren and tried to focus on something less discerning—maybe the stuffed ham that was going to be served at the reception or the Amaretto wedding cake with butter cream icing waiting to be cut after the ceremony.

Ruby and Warren had a rather uneventful marriage for more than two years. Ruby kept busy renovating the house while Warren spent hours in front of the computer playing games like SimCity and Diablo. They had sex about twice a week, which was more often than Ruby cared to see Warren's "long slender penis," which was another thing about Warren that Ruby never really got used to. His dick wasn't circumcised, which Ruby found quite unsightly. Before Warren, she had had limited sexual experience and had never even seen an uncircumcised cock, not even in a magazine or a movie. The first time she saw Warren naked she wasn't sure if he had a penis or a turkey neck hanging between his legs.

Their relationship was unexciting and a bit glum at times, but it was more than Ruby had ever expected to have. At least she had a husband and wasn't some aging fat girl with sixteen cats. Everything dysfunctionally hummed along for quite a while until the day Warren came home from work and asked Ruby to sit down so he could "converse with her."

Ruby had noticed that Warren seemed to be spending more time away from home. By this time, Warren had gotten a job at a large consulting firm, and he and Ruby were no longer working for the same company. He was leaving earlier for work, getting home later, and occasionally going into the office on weekends, but it didn't really faze Ruby. In fact, she was kind of glad to have him out of the house and out of her hair. Something about watching her husband, a grown man, play computer games for hours saddened her.

With little fanfare, Warren announced that, after much thought, he "needed to request that they terminate their nuptial agreement." Warren had fallen for one of his colleagues who shared his interest in everything technical. He told Ruby he had found someone that "understood" him.

Ruby didn't know how to react when Warren told her the news, so all she said was, "I'm keeping the house," and went upstairs. Warren's confession surprised Ruby and upset her immensely, but not for reasons one might think. She wasn't upset because Warren was having an affair. Quite frankly, she couldn't have cared less. In fact, a part of her was happy that Warren had found someone that "understood" him—Lord knew, Ruby never really had. The idea of a divorce didn't really even faze her. What really affected Ruby was that Warren was dumping her. Who the hell was *he* to dump *her*? She had constantly questioned whether or not she had done the right thing by settling for Warren. The thought never occurred to Ruby that he might have thought he was the one who had settled. Was she that awful she couldn't even hold on to an ungainly, self-proclaimed lover of large women with an unattractive penis? How had it happened? Ruby had been dumped by one of the few individuals to whom she had categorized herself as superior. If anyone was going to do any dumping it should have been Ruby, not Warren. Her lifeless marriage with Warren was more than Ruby had ever thought she would have, and when it ended she lost all hope of having any romance in her life.

Ruby returned from the kitchen with the box of odds and ends Warren had come by to collect.

"Here ya go," she said as she handed the box to Warren.

"Much gratitude," he said as he grabbed the box with one hand and pushed his glasses up on his nose with the middle finger of his other hand. While they were married Ruby mentioned the habit he had with his glasses every now and then. She would try to sound as if she were joking. "You know, you should really push your glasses up with another finger or maybe from the side," she would say with a smile. Warren would laugh with her and agree and then continue to give her the fucking finger day in and day out.

After she said good-bye and closed the door behind Warren she caught the last few minutes of *Designing Women*. It was one of the episodes after Delta Burke had put on so much weight. Ruby hated Delta Burke. She remembered a few years earlier when Delta came out with a clothing line for fat women and wrote a book about how happy she was being a large woman and encouraged others to accept themselves, which was all fine and good. She raved about the pleasures of plus-size and hocked her tacky frocks to fat girls across the country—and then the bitch went and lost weight.

Roomies

"Hey, thanks for coming," Ruby said to Jeremy as he came through the front door of her house. "I'm just not in the mood to deal with these people on my own today."

"No problem," Jeremy replied. "Sorry I'm late. There were all these rowdy straight boys on the Metro. They were going to see some band or something . . . called the Wizards."

"The Wizards are a basketball team, Jeremy, not a band. Ah . . . Michael Jordan? You have heard of him?"

"Of course, he's that sexy Hanes underwear model."

"Yeah, well, he plays a little basketball on the side," Ruby replied with a laugh. "Gosh, Jeremy, you should keep up with sports at least a little bit."

"I keep up with sports just fine."

"Watching men's gymnastics doesn't count, my friend," Ruby joked just before someone knocked at the door.

"Here we go," she said to Jeremy as she reached to open the door.

"Hi. Ruby?" asked the young lady on the other side of the entryway. She was a petite white woman with dated eyeglasses, mousy brown hair, and a pointed nose. Ruby also noted some sort of furry creature shoved under one of her arms.

"Yes," Ruby replied. "Nice to meet you. You must be Suzette?"

"That's right, we spoke on the phone. And this is Miss Kitty,"

Suzette added, nodding her head toward the large cat with long matted fur and a flat angry face. "No!" Suzette said sharply as Ruby reached over to pet the cat, who hissed and swatted her paw at her. "I'm sorry," Suzette added, softening her tone. "Miss Kitty is very temperamental."

Well, Miss Kitty can get her sorry ass out of my house. "You didn't mention a cat on the phone. Is she yours?" Ruby questioned.

"Yes, but don't worry. She's no trouble. May I come in?"

Ruby hesitated for a moment. "Umm . . . sure," she said. "This is my friend Jeremy. He came by to interview perspective roomies with me."

"Hi," Suzette said to Jeremy. "This is the living room?"

"Yes," Ruby said. "Why don't I show you the room for rent upstairs and then we can take a look at the rest of the house," Ruby added, as if she hadn't already made up her mind that Suzette and her mangy beast were not moving into her house.

"Okay, but before we go upstairs, is there a bathroom on this floor?"

"No, but there's one upstairs and on the third floor as well."

"Hmmm . . . Miss Kitty insists on having her own bathroom. She's toilet trained, you know. So if she has ownership of one of the bathrooms that would only leave one for us to share."

"Ah . . . really?" Ruby questioned as she heard Jeremy giggle under his breath.

"May I put Miss Kitty down?" Suzette asked, already lowering the cat to the floor before Ruby had a chance to answer.

"What do you think, Miss Kitty?" Suzette asked the cat, and not in a high patronizing tone like most people spoke to pets. Suzette spoke to Miss Kitty as if she were a married couple from the suburbs touring prospective real-estate buys.

"Yes, that *is* a pretty sofa," Suzette said to the cat as it meandered around the floor in front of the couch. "You like that chair? Yes, it *is* a nice chair."

Suzette, Ruby, and Jeremy watched the cat case the living room. She slowly crawled around the floor checking out the furnishings and poking her head in various spaces as if she were inspecting the place. Eventually Miss Kitty made her way over to Ruby's potted Peace Lily. She sniffed around the plant, scratched at the floor a time or two, and turned around. She then proceeded to raise her tail, cock her ears, and squat toward the plant.

"Miss Kitty! No!" Suzette said as the cat proceeded to take a shit in Ruby's plant.

"Miss Kitty! No!" Jeremy repeated. Half of him was really trying to get the cat to stop defecating in Ruby's living room while the rest was just mocking the cat's peculiar owner.

"Oh my, I'm so sorry."

"Thought she used the toilet?" Ruby responded in a daze, still shocked by the cat's behavior.

"She does. Oh, I assure you, Miss Kitty has excellent bathroom manners. I think this is her way of telling me that she doesn't want to move here. I just don't think this house suits Miss Kitty."

"Damn, and Ruby was so looking forward to having Miss Kitty shit in all her plants," Jeremy offered from the other side of the room.

"Maybe it's best if we go," Suzette said and swooped Miss Kitty up into her arms.

"Ah, yeah, maybe that would be best," Ruby said, looking at the unapologetic cat.

"Here. Take this with you," Jeremy said as he picked up the plant from the floor, held it away from his body like a dirty diaper, and handed it to Suzette.

Suzette accepted the plant without remark and turned to leave.

"Jesus Christ! What a freak!" Ruby said as she closed the door behind Suzette and headed toward the sofa. "Miss Kitty, what do you think? Do you like it here?" Ruby said in a whiney voice, mimicking Suzette's earlier questions. "Bring that damn cat in my house and have it shit in my plant . . ."

"Hey, get this," Jeremy said. "Instead of Miss Kitty, she should be called Miss Shitty," he added, letting out a quick laugh.

"That's a riot, Jeremy. You should write stand-up," Ruby said flatly, not amused by his comment.

"So, who's next?" Jeremy asked as he walked into the kitchen to grab a soda.

"Colleen, I believe her name was. She sounded reasonably normal on the phone . . . a little chatty, but otherwise okay. Hey, as long as she doesn't have a cat with the runs tucked under her arm . . ." Ruby said before another knock at the door interrupted her.

"Hi," Ruby said as she swung the door open to reveal a sharply dressed black woman with big hair and lots of makeup.

"Hi. I'm Colleen. We spoke on the phone earlier about the room?" the woman responded. She was about Ruby's age with large breasts and a thin waist.

"Of course, come in, please."

"Thanks. This is a beautiful house."

"Thank y—" Ruby tried to say before the woman interrupted her.

"Much nicer than the dump I share with my no-good husband . . . who I'm leaving, by the way."

"Gosh. I'm sorry to hear—" Ruby tried to respond, thinking it was odd for someone to divulge such personal information to a complete stranger.

"Why? I'm not. He's a no-good bastard. You wouldn't believe the kind of things he put me through. Lying, cheating, stealing—you name it. Girl, the stories I could tell you. I think he's been plotting to burn the house down . . . with me in it! He wants the insurance money. Some days I fear for my life. Do you know what I'm saying?"

"Ah . . ." Ruby tried to say before Colleen got rolling again.

"It's awful. It will be so nice to get away from him. And this time it's for real. No going back. I wouldn't have gone back the last time, but I missed him. Ya know?"

"Ah, sure . . ."

"Well, to be honest, Rachel . . . It is Rachel, right?

"Ruby."

"Oh yes. Ruby," Colleen replied. "It wasn't really him I missed," she added with a slight grin. "It was his dick—biggest one I've ever seen. His penis is huge. How's a girl supposed to go back to average size cocks once she's had a big one?"

"Um, I don't know . . ."

"But you know, does having a huge penis give him the right to treat me like shit?"

"Did someone say huge penis?" Jeremy said, prompted to come out of the kitchen.

"Jeremy, this is Colleen," Ruby said, glad that someone had shut up the intrusive woman, if only temporarily.

"Hi," Colleen said to Jeremy, before adding, "And yes, it was me that mentioned a huge penis. It belongs to my husband. And it is nice but, you know, it has some kind of skin condition or something. It was all red and inflamed much of the time, so it wasn't very attractive to look at, but, honey, it sure felt good. I always had to make sure the lights were off before he took it out."

"I hear you," Jeremy replied. "Nothing worse than a big penis with a rash."

"You're telling me. I'm the one that put up with that monstrous thing for four years. It's crazy. Just because he has a big dick he thinks he is God's gift to the female species—like he can do whatever he wants with no consequence. I swear, sometimes he barely combs his hair. I think he thinks he just doesn't need too. He goes days without showering. He hasn't worked in months. And the pubic hair! Oh my God, does he have a bush! It's so out of control. Some days it's like a Harlem Globetrotter down there. Remember that Saturday morning cartoon with one of the Globetrotters who pulled all sorts of stuff out of his afro? If I'm ever lost in the Amazon and need someone to pull a life raft out of their bush, he might come in handy, but ya know, what are the chances of that happening? If only he were more like you queer boys," Colleen added, sizing Jeremy up. "I hear you queers keep things all nice and orderly down there."

"Nice and orderly?" Jeremy asked as Ruby watched the two banter about pubic hair in her living room.

"Yeah . . . everything all trimmed and cropped. Straight men could learn a thing or two from you Tootsie Pops."

"Tootsie Pops?"

"Oh, I'm sorry. I didn't mean anything by it. I love me a Tootsie Pop. Remember those commercials with the kid . . . It was a kid wasn't it? . . . Or was it a bird or something, who went around trying to find out how many licks it took to get to the center of a Tootsie Pop? Then that owl chomps down on it after three licks and says 'three!'" Colleen erupted into hysterical laughter while Ruby and Jeremy stared at her in bemusement. "Three? Don't you get it? It takes more than three, but he bit into it . . ."

Ruby and Jeremy forced a slight laugh to appease Colleen, who seemed to finally sense that Ruby and Jeremy were not amused. Maybe she shouldn't have just assumed that Jeremy was gay.

"I'm sorry about the Tootsie Pop remark. Like I said, I didn't mean anything by it. When you asked about my husband, I just assumed you were . . . I mean, you asked about my husband's big dick and . . . You are, aren't you?" she said, eyeing Jeremy.

"Am I gay?" Jeremy responded. "Can I give the Ricky Martin answer?" Jeremy added before delving into his finest Ricky Martin accent. "That information is personal, and I want to keep it just for me. Sexuality is something that each individual should deal with in their own way," Jeremy continued, offering his best impersonation of the Latin singer.

"So, in other words, Jeremy's a big queen," Ruby added. "Now that that's established, would you care to see the room for rent?" Ruby asked, having already decided that she wasn't renting so much as a paddleboat to this loquacious nut. She wasn't about to lease a room in her house to someone who barged in and immediately started talking about her husband's genitals.

"Sure. Lead the way," Colleen replied.

Ruby started up the steps with Colleen following.

"Have you tried the Atkins diet? I lost twelve pounds on it," Colleen said out of the blue as she watched Ruby's large behind swing up the steps in front of her. "You can eat all kinds of stuff . . . bacon, eggs, pork chops . . . as long as it's protein."

"No," Ruby replied, once again stunned by Colleen's candor.

"You should give it a whirl. If not, I know this surgeon who does great liposuction. He could take you down two dress sizes. It's no big deal. I had it done on my stomach a few years ago. They just shove this long stick in your belly and suck all the fat out. I wanted the fat that was taken out of my stomach put in my ass . . . you know . . . so I'd have a big ass like Beyoncé, but he wouldn't do it."

"Really?" Ruby responded. Between dicks with skin conditions, Tootsie Pops, and Beyoncé's ass, she was starting to get a headache.

"Yeah, but just as well I guess. I think Beyoncé's on about thirteen of her fifteen minutes. Have you seen her in those hair color commercials—yeah, like that's her real hair—you know there's some bald-headed girl in Korea wanting her hair back. I bought her last album and . . ."

"This is it," Ruby said, cutting off Colleen in mid-sentence and opening the door to the larger of the two bedrooms on the second floor of her house.

"Hmmm. It's nice. A little bit small, but I could probably make it work."

Colleen took a look around the bedroom and Ruby quickly showed her the bathroom and led her back downstairs with Colleen continuing to chatter.

"Well. I'm definitely interested. Do you have an application for me to fill out?"

"Um . . . not right now. I have your phone number. I'll be in touch when I make a decision," Ruby replied. She didn't mean to project anything, but her tone made it pretty obvious to Colleen that she would not be getting the room.

"Oh God! I'm not getting the room, am I?" Colleen asked with a look a disappointment. "Forgive me if I ran my mouth too much," she added, trying to redeem herself. "I have to learn to keep some things to myself. My friends always say I talk too much. They call me 'Rose,' you know, the character Betty White played on the *Golden Girls* that was always talking about St. Olaf, which is a real place by the way. I saw something about it on *Entertainment Tonight* or something. St. Olaf is an actual city in Minnesota. Isn't that a riot? I love to watch the *Golden Girls*. I'm not sure Lifetime needs to run it six times a day, though. The *Golden Girls* and *Designing Women*, that's all they show on Lifetime. I like the *Golden Girls*, but I'm not a huge fan of *Designing Women*, especially the episodes after Delta Burke and Jean Smart left. You know a lot of people say the show went downhill just because Delta Burke left. But, you know, Jean Smart was pretty important to that show too. Did you ever notice they have a different sofa in every episode? I was watching it the other . . ."

"Okay!" Jeremy said loudly, interrupting Colleen, putting his arm around her shoulder and turning her toward the door. "Thanks for coming by. We'll be in touch."

"Man! I was doing it again, wasn't I? Sometimes it's like I can't control it. I try to remind myself not to talk so much . . ."

"Okay! Great! Thanks for coming. We'll be in touch," Jeremy continued as he ushered her out the door.

"But . . ." Colleen tried to say as Jeremy closed the door.

"Oh my God!" Ruby said. "Thank you. I didn't know how I was going to get rid of her."

"Maybe there's a full moon out tonight or something. Did you run your ad in *The Post* or some Wiccan magazine?

"Maybe a Wiccan magazine would have been a better choice,"

"How many more do you have coming?"

"That was it. I only got six responses and the other four either smoked or had pets or something, so I didn't bother asking them to come see the place," Ruby replied with a sigh and plopped down on the sofa.

"Don't worry," Jeremy said, sitting down next to her. "I'm sure you'll find someone. You'll probably get some more calls next week."

"I hope so. Money is really starting to get tight," Ruby replied, worried that she might have to take even more money out of her Thin Ruby account. She knew it was ridiculous to be so concerned about it. When she opened the account she had intended to have it for only about six months, lose all the weight she had planned on losing, and then withdraw the money to buy a hot new outfit and get her hair done. Five years later she had only succeeded in gaining more weight, but she still held out hope that one day she would be thin, and the more time that went by, the more money she amassed in the account—her Thin Ruby account continued to expand, but, unfortunately, so did her Fat Ruby body. She now had enough to buy several new outfits and get a complete makeover. She figured if she only allowed herself to tap the money when she lost weight it would motivate her to ease up on the Drake's Coffee Cakes and Devil Dogs, and sometimes it did motivate her for a day or two, but eventually her cravings and need for comfort food won out and she returned to her old habits. She hadn't even been trying to diet lately. It wasn't that she had totally given up on the idea of losing weight. It was just something she kept putting off like a visit to the dentist. Every day, when she was tempted by Double Stuff Oreos or marshmallow pies she'd swear that "this time," would be her last binge. She'd start her diet after she finished the box of Pecan Spinwheels or Oatmeal Cream Pies. But the next day her eye would catch the McDonald's sign on the way home from work or the box of Little Debbie Zebra Cakes calling to her from the grocery store shelf, and she'd put the diet off yet again. She really did plan to change her eating habits one day. Really, she did. If only all that damn food just didn't keep getting in the way.

Simone Reyes

My God! Could you possibly take up any more room? Simone thought as she lay in bed next to ah . . . ? ah . . . ? Damn! She couldn't remember his name. She knew it was some waspy Michael/Bill/Tim type name, but she couldn't put her finger on it. It began with an M, didn't it? Or was it a B?

Simone had met ah . . . ? Let's call him Bob. She had met *Bob* at The Front Page in Dupont Circle the night before. Virtually every Friday after she finished up the eleven o'clock news she would stop by The Front Page, which was sort of an official gathering spot for the station's employees. She could always count on a few familiar faces from work for idle chatter, and the staff at the bar adored her. She was friendly with all the bartenders, who loved to tell everyone they knew Simone Reyes. Her late night drinks were usually a nice release from the workweek, and it was fun to socialize with her colleagues outside of work, but the real reason Simone stopped by the bar was to pick up a lay du jour, which was never a problem. Virtually any guy she approached was thrilled to have her company. After all, she had just appeared on the cover of *Washingtonian* magazine with a headline that read "Simone Reyes: D.C.'s Sexiest Newscaster."

Simone had just finished the eleven o'clock telecast and was having a drink with one of the producers when she saw *Bob* on the other side of the bar. He immediately piqued her interest. He was young (and oh, how Simone liked them young) with blond hair, blue eyes, and biceps like a Backstreet Boy. She excused herself from her colleague and went up and introduced herself. Simone wasn't shy about approaching strangers, especially men. She was a celebrity after all—even if no one outside of the D.C. area had ever heard of her. She engaged him in conversation and asked him to join her for a drink, which eventually led back to her place.

Eight hours later the significantly younger man was taking up too much space in her queen-size mahogany sleigh bed.

"Hey, could you scoot over just a tad?" Simone asked, giving *Bob* a nudge. She wanted to squeeze in another five or ten minutes of sleep before she kicked him out and didn't feel like doing it with her ass hanging off the bed. The carpenters were due shortly to begin renovations on her house, and she wanted her gentleman caller gone before they came.

"I think I'm about as far over as I can get," *Bob* replied, still half asleep.

Are you kidding me? You must have, like, three feet over there, Simone thought, giving up on the idea of snoozing a bit longer and sitting up on the edge of the bed. She looked down at the floor, trying to wake up. It was unusual for her to let a guy like *Bob* stay the night. Generally, she got what she wanted and sent her one-night stands packing. Usually a simple "I have an early day tomorrow," or, "If you don't mind, I prefer to sleep alone," was enough to get them on the move. But Simone had had a few too many drinks at the bar. By the time the sex was over, it was nearly four in the morning, and Simone had unwittingly fallen asleep before giving *Bob* his walking papers.

Simone lifted herself from the bed and grabbed a silk robe from the chair next to the dresser. "Rise and shine," she said softly to *Bob*. "I've got to get you out of here before the workmen show up," she continued, trying to sound friendly, but also making it clear that he needed to get his ass out of her bed and out the door.

Bob opened his eyes and sat up on the bed. He grabbed Simone's hand and kissed it.

"Do you really want me to leave right now? Surely we have a

few more minutes," he said, grabbing her hips as she stood in front of him.

"You're sweet," she replied as she lifted his hands from her waist. "Really, you do need to go. I've got three men coming this morning to start on some renovations. It's nearly eight o'clock. They'll be here any minute," Simone said.

Bob raised his eyebrows to show his disappointment and got up from the bed. Simone fidgeted with the sash on her bathrobe as she watched him get dressed. Once *Bob* was fully clothed, she followed him down the steps and opened the front door.

"Can I call you?" he asked. They always asked if they could call her. It was never enough that they got to fuck Simone Reyes, they wanted to date her too.

"I'm really busy for the next few weeks, but maybe I'll look you up sometime," Simone lied.

Bob didn't respond. He just offered a defeated smile and walked out the door.

Simone closed the door behind him and made her way back upstairs. As soon as she walked through her bedroom door she saw *it* on the nightstand. Why hadn't she noticed it before? She must have been slipping. She usually kept an eye out for this sort of thing.

"Oh, no you don't!" she said as she hurriedly walked over to the nightstand and grabbed *Bob*'s watch. She'd had more than one guy try to pull this stunt—leave their watch (or a tie or something) behind, so they had an excuse to come back and see her again.

Simone ran back down the steps and out the door, wearing nothing but a skimpy robe. She saw *Bob* a couple blocks up the street heading toward his car and opened her mouth to call him.

"Shit!" she said out loud as she realized she had forgotten his name.

"Hey," she called toward him, but he didn't turn around.

"Bob?" she called. Damn it! What was his name? Chris, maybe it was Chris.

"Chris," she called, but he still didn't turn around.

Fuck! She was going to have to catch up with him and there

was no time to throw on some clothes. He'd be out of sight by the time she ran upstairs and grabbed some clothes and a pair of shoes. For just a second she weighed her options: Option 1: Simone Reyes being seen chasing a trick down 35th Street in her robe. Option 2: *Bob*, or whatever the hell his name was, having an excuse to show up at her doorstep again.

Simone looked both ways on the sidewalk. After realizing that no one else was in sight, she starting running after *Bob*. As she chased him down, she had visions of a picture of herself sprinting up 35th Street in her robe appearing in *Washingtonian* or making the front page of the *Style* section of *The Washington Post*.

"Hey," she called when she had almost caught up with him. He finally turned around.

"Your watch," she said, trying to catch her breath and handing the cheap Timex to *Bob*.

He just looked at her, huffing and puffing in her robe. "Thanks," he said, giving her a look that said, Freak!

"You're welcome," she replied and turned to walk back to the house, glad to see there was still no activity on the street.

"It's Michael, by the way," he called behind her.

"What?" she said, turning around.

"My name. It's Michael," he repeated before raising his voice. "Bob! Chris!" he called really loud, mimicking Simone's earlier cries and laughing. "And you know what else?" Michael asked and handed the watch back to Simone. "It's not my watch."

Fate Worse Than Death

"Hi, Mom," Ruby said to Doris as she came through the door. She then turned her head toward Taco and said, "Hi, Rat Dog," just to annoy him. Taco ignored her and remained curled up on the sofa next to Doris.

"What's all this?" Ruby asked, pointing toward a pile of clothes Doris had on a chair in the living room.

"Mrs. Jenkins said she was taking a few things to Goodwill and asked if I wanted to donate anything."

"Mrs. Jenkins? Who's that?"

"The woman that moved in across the street a few months ago. She's colored. She's right nice though . . . keeps a clean house."

"Wow. You have quite a lot here," Ruby said, ignoring her mother's comment as she rifled through the pile. She sifted from dress to dress until she came upon a certain little black dress, and her heart started racing.

"You're giving away this one?" Ruby asked, holding up the dress and trying to sound unaffected. "This was your New Year's Eve dress from the seventies."

"Oh, that thing," Doris said. "I haven't worn it in more than twenty years."

"I know. But I think you should keep it, just as a keepsake."

"Ruby, look around you. This place is sky high with keepsakes. I need to get rid of some of this junk."

"Just keep this one dress," Ruby replied. "You looked so pretty in it. It's the only thing you ever owned that wasn't from a discount store." There was no way Ruby was going to say that she wanted Doris to keep the dress so she could wear it one day. The idea of Ruby wearing a sexy size-six dress was so ludicrous, Ruby could barely ponder the thought herself, let alone share it with Doris.

"All right," Doris said. "I can hang on to it."

"Good," Ruby said and took the dress into Doris's bedroom and hung it up. She didn't want to risk leaving it in the living room and having Doris throw it back in with the clothes to be donated.

When she came out of the bedroom she noticed that Doris hadn't done her hair or put on any makeup. "Didn't I tell you I'd be here at seven? You're usually all ready to go when I get here," Ruby said. It was strange for Doris not to be dressed in her Sears Roebuck finest with her hair freshly set when she had plans to leave the house.

"I'm an old lady, Ruby. I don't move as fast as I used to. Let me just put on a little lipstick and brush my hair, and then we can go."

"Okay," Ruby said, just a tad concerned. Even in her seventies, it was rare for Doris to leave the house without ample time spent primping her hair and clothes. Ruby plopped down on the sofa as Doris got up with Taco following. Taco refused to share any piece of furniture with Ruby.

"So how is that hairdresser friend of yours?" Doris said as she walked down the hall.

"Hairdresser? I don't have any hairdresser friends," Ruby replied.

"What's his name . . . Jimmy?"

"Jeremy?" Ruby replied. "He's not a *hairdresser*, Mom. I've told you, he's an accountant for a company downtown."

"Oh yes," Doris called from the bedroom. "Whatever his job, you spend far too much time with him. If you keep it up, people are going to start thinking that you're . . ."

"That I'm what?"

"You know," Doris said, stepping out of the bedroom. "One of those girls . . . you know . . . from *Lebanon*."

Ruby didn't even respond to her mother's comment. Instead, she did what she often did when her mother got on her case about Jeremy, or her weight, or her house in the marginal neighborhood, she changed the subject. "Where do you want to have dinner? I saw a new Italian Place on 301. Why don't we go there?"

"Do we have to go through this every time, Ruby?" Doris said as she walked down the hall. "I'm not eating any of that ethnic stuff."

"Ethnic? It's not like I'm proposing Afghani or Ethiopian. It's spaghetti and lasagna for Christ's sake."

"IHOP," Doris simply responded. There were a limited number of restaurants in which Doris would agree to dine. She generally leaned toward the International House of Pancakes, but every now and then she'd be agreeable to Denny's, Perkins, or Bob Evans. Occasionally, she'd also stop into a McDonald's, which she referred to as "The Hamburger Shop," after a doctor's appointment or a shopping outing to Sears or JC Penney. That had pretty much been the extent of Doris's dining circle her entire life. Doris and Ruby's late father had always been, as Elaine once referred to George on *Seinfeld*, "extremely cautious with money." If it wasn't on sale at Sears or Montgomery Ward, they didn't need it. Ruby was in her late teens before she realized restaurants existed that didn't have pictures of the food on the menu or a senior citizen's discount. As a kid, Ruby remembered spending hours bargain shopping for groceries—being dragged to the Giant to get the best price on a ham, the Grand Union for the sale on canned goods, and the IGA for cheaper produce—all in one outing.

If Doris had any idea about the kind of money Ruby spent, she surely would've had an immediate stroke. Anytime Doris asked Ruby how much she spent on anything from shoes to concert tickets to dinner in a restaurant, Ruby would always cut the amount in half before responding. If she'd spent a hundred dollars on a pair of shoes, she'd tell Doris they had cost fifty, and Doris would still say, "Wow, those are rich girl's shoes!" Then Doris would go into a long spiel about how Ruby needed to save her money, and how she wasn't like those pretty, thin girls who could just get a man to pay their bills. Ruby was going to have to take care of herself.

One time Ruby slipped and mentioned something about leaving a thirty-dollar tip for a waitress in a restaurant downtown, and to this day, Doris still brought it up. "Any woman that leaves a thirty-dollar tip for a waitress ought to have her head examined. Next time, you just leave a dollar and go along. Thirty-dollar tip! Whoever heard of such a thing?"

"Fine," Ruby said in response to Doris's demand to go to IHOP. She walked ahead of her mother, grabbed the door, and held it open for Doris, who seemed to be moving slower than usual. Ruby had to fight her natural instinct to ask her if she was feeling okay. If she did, she would be bombarded with a host of issues from arthritis to osteoporosis to chest pains. Doris was full of complaints, and Lord help the poor soul that was fool enough to inquire as to how she was feeling. Ruby took Doris to the doctor every three months, who refused to validate any of Doris's ailments. He would say that Doris was healthier than he was. Ruby figured it was Doris's way of grieving. When Ruby's father died, Doris never cried or had a breakdown. In fact, she kept telling Ruby to stop crying so much—that her father was in a better place. The only thing that changed about Doris was a slow onslaught of vague aches and pains and a steady increase in her irritability.

It had been almost seven years since Ruby's father died, and Doris wasn't the only one that still missed him terribly. His name was Jack and he had always been the buffer between Ruby and Doris. Being extremely overweight himself, he never said a word about Ruby's weight and had become an expert at changing the subject when Doris brought it up. When Ruby was born she had the faint beginnings of what would later become a full head of vibrant red hair. Jack and Doris had originally planned to name her Kimberly, but, after seeing her baby-fine red hair, Jack insisted that they call her Ruby and later nicknamed her Red. "How's my beautiful little Red?" Ruby remembered him saying almost everyday when he got home from work. He was Ruby's rock and also her partner in crime. When Ruby was a girl, at least once a week, Jack would run some sort of contrived errand with Ruby. Under the pretense of taking her for a haircut or having her tag along to the hardware store, Jack would always manage a quick drive by the TwinKiss Ice Cream Shop for a soft serve cone or McDonald's for a box of McDonaldland Cookies. Wherever they went, they'd eat their treats in the car and toss any remains in the trash before heading home. Jack never told Ruby not to mention their food stops to Doris, but, even from the time she was very little, there was always a sort of understanding between Ruby and Jack that Doris was not to know about their detours. Ruby cherished the time she spent with her father. He was more than willing to let Doris be the disciplinarian, and he often seemed as much a friend to Ruby as a father. It broke her heart when he was diagnosed with lung cancer when she was only twenty-five. He hadn't been feeling well for months, but it wasn't until he could absolutely no longer ignore the symptoms, that he went to see a doctor. Ruby often wondered if he had avoided going to the doctor for the same reason she did—he didn't feel like being harassed about his weight. By the time he was diagnosed, it was really too late to do much more than try to keep him as comfortable as possible until the inevitable happened. It was only two months from the time he got the news of his cancer to the day he died. After he asked her to look after Doris and be patient with her, his last words to Ruby were, "You're beautiful, Red. Don't let anyone tell you otherwise."

It was like Ruby's world had collapsed when Jack passed away. She knew she would miss him terribly, and she was so afraid of life without him—life alone with Doris. How on earth was she going to be able to have a relationship with Doris without Jack around to run interference? She knew she'd manage somehow, but it was going to be so much harder without Jack around to call her Red, tell her she was beautiful, and do his best to keep Doris off her back.

As the women headed to IHOP, Ruby tried to drive slow and steady to keep Doris's comments about her driving to a minimum.

"There's a new four-way stop up there a ways," Doris said. "You have to let folks that get there before you go first. You know how to work it?"

"No, Mother. In my nearly twenty years of driving, I have *never once* encountered a four-way stop."

"Don't get smart with me, Ruby Waters."

"Don't act like I'm an idiot, and I won't get smart with you."

"Are you this crotchety with everyone?" Doris asked.

"I might ask you the same question," Ruby answered, before another car on the road captured Doris's attention.

"Why do the colored people do that to their cars?" Doris said in reference to a souped-up Honda Civic with an extended spoiler on the back.

"Mother, you don't even know if it's black people in that car."

"Yeah, I guess the Mexicans are starting to tacky-up those economy cars as well. Which do you think it is? Blacks or Mexicans?"

Ruby ignored her mother's ridiculous question.

"I bet it's Mexicans," Doris said as Ruby started to approach the suspect vehicle. "You know we have Mexicans in Charles County now. They help fix the roofs and clean the bathrooms and stuff."

"It's a bunch of Chinese boys!" Doris exclaimed as they passed three Korean men in the car next to them.

"See, that's what you get for making stupid assumptions," Ruby said, turning up the radio to try to stifle the conversation.

"Can you turn that down?" Doris said immediately.

"This is Celine Dion. You like Celine."

"Is she that French girl with a neck like a giraffe?"

"She's Canadian."

"I saw her on television. Did you know her husband's big as a house? And he has a girl's name . . . Reneé."

"Yes, as a matter of fact, I did."

"You see, Ruby. Men can get away with that. Women can't. *Men* can be overweight and still get pretty girls, but . . ."

"Pretty girls? You just said she had a neck like a gazelle."

"*Giraffe*. A neck like a *giraffe*. And that doesn't mean she isn't pretty."

Ruby's mother often said things about how overweight men could land attractive, smart women. Doris never came out and said it, but Ruby suspected that her mother was often indirectly referring to her own relationship with Ruby's father. In her prime, Doris was stunningly beautiful, and *she* had married a fat man. Ruby's father was a big guy from the day he and Doris had met and steadily expanded over the course of their marriage. From a young age Ruby noticed the hypocrisy regarding her mother's issues with weight. Doris never nagged Ruby's father about his eating or lack of exercise, but the moment Ruby asked for seconds at the dinner table she was told how "A lady needs to watch her figure." It was as if Doris really thought it was okay for a man to be fat, but it was a fate worse than death for a woman.

Rudy didn't address her mother's last comment. Instead, she huffed in exasperation as she changed the radio station only to hear Stacey Williams, a local deejay on MIX 107.3, doing a commercial for Alase Laser Hair Removal. She was doing one of those deejay infomercials about getting her bikini line treated.

"For Christ sake!" Doris said, listening to the commercial. "On the radio talking about having the hair zapped off her crotch. Why, in my day, she would've been hung from a tree."

When they got to the IHOP, a young Muslim girl wearing a head scarf took them to a large booth by the window.

"Thank you, dear," Doris said to the hostess.

"She'd be so pretty if she'd take that silly thing off her head and put on a little lipstick," Doris added quietly to Ruby as the girl walked away.

"Would you hush and just decide on what you want?" Ruby responded.

"It just seems silly to wear that thing all the time, but I guess it's not as bad as those turbans some of the men wear on their heads. I get so nervous when I see one of them. You know how I hate snakes."

"Snakes?"

"Yeah. They keep snakes up in those turbans, ya know."

"Oh, Mother, they do not! That is so ridiculous," Ruby responded.

"Yes they do."

"I'm *sure*, Mother. They just go about their day with a snake slithering around in their hair. Have you lost your mind?"

"They do. Naomi told me so." Naomi was Doris's beautician. She permed and set half the blue-hairs in Charles County and spread all sorts of nasty gossip and rumors in the process. Doris would question everything she was told by Ruby, her doctor, and Tom Brokaw, but anything Naomi said was taken as indisputable fact.

"It just seems crazy to me. Wearing all that silly stuff on their heads," Doris continued, eyeing the hostess as she walked by to take additional patrons to a table.

"How is it any sillier than your little Catholic rituals? How do you know she isn't over there right now looking at us and saying, 'Look at those Christians. I hear they try to drown their babies at something called a baptism.' "

"What are you doing—speaking out against baptisms! Are you on dope?" Doris said sternly. "All I was saying is that she'd look prettier if she'd take that veil off. It just doesn't look very nice."

"It's called a chador, not a veil. And you know, you didn't look so pretty yourself with that black smudge on the middle of your forehead on Ash Wednesday."

"Hmmm," Doris said, raising her eyebrows and looking up at the ceiling as if she were actually pondering what Ruby said before she started reviewing her menu.

"Have they raised the prices again?" she asked Ruby.

"No. It's the same menu they had last time we were here—the last thirty times."

It wasn't long after Ruby started reviewing the menu that the voices in her head started attacking: *Order a salad, Ruby—yum, get the Rooty Tooty Fresh and Fruity—no, get the grilled chicken breast—oh, Ruby, you're already so fat, what's one more country fried steak going to hurt?*

After Ruby and Doris had perused the menu, a young waitress approached their table to take their order.

"How much is this?" Doris asked, holding up the menu and pointing to one of the platters that was pictured on the cover.

"I think that's six ninety-five."

"Can I get French toast instead of pancakes with it?"

"Sure. It's just a dollar fifty extra."

"A dollar fifty? My goodness. I don't want to buy the whole restaurant. It's just bread dipped in some eggs."

"Give her the French toast," Ruby said, offering an apologetic smile to the waitress. "I'll have the hot roast beef sandwich with mashed potatoes, please."

"Oh, Ruby, you don't want that. Look at all these nice salads on the menu," Doris said in response to Ruby's order.

"I don't want a salad," Ruby said just a tad sharply to Doris before turning back to the waitress. "I think that's it."

"Anything to drink?"

"Water's fine, thanks."

"Okay, your dinners should be out shortly," the waitress said before walking away.

"Now, Ruby, you know gravy is not on your diet."

"I'm not on a diet, Mom," Ruby replied.

"Oh, I thought you were."

"Well, I'm not, and I've got enough on my mind without you harassing me about my weight."

"Is something the matter, dear? Are you on dope?"

"No. I just need to find a housemate to share my place with, and I met a couple candidates the other day, and it was big freak-fest."

"See. This is why I suggested that you go on a diet."

"What?" Ruby asked with a bit of a laugh. It was insulting, but funny at the same time, how Doris always managed to relate everything to Ruby going on diet.

"Maybe you would have had a better chance of keeping your marriage together if you had taken better care of yourself, and your career prospects might be better too. Then you wouldn't have to take in a boarder."

"Oh my God! For your information I was fat when Warren married me, and you know what else, the woman he's seeing now is bigger than I am," Ruby said, even though she had no idea what Warren's current girlfriend looked like.

"Don't get upset, dear," Doris said in the same calm voice she used to say everything. She could be reciting the weather or announcing the death of Ruby's father, and the tone and volume of her voice would be the same. "I only want the best for you. I just want you to be happy."

"I am happy," Ruby lied. "Although I'd be much happier if you'd stop badgering me to lose weight."

Almost as far back as Ruby could remember her mother was on her case to diet. As a kid, Ruby was offered everything from outings to Busch Gardens to swing sets to Parker Brothers' board games to lose weight. Sometimes the bribes worked. She'd drop ten pounds and get that new Atari or mini TV, but within days she would be well on the road to gaining it back.

If it had been up to Doris, there would not have been any junk food in the house at all when Ruby was growing up, but Ruby's father was not about to give up his potato chips or frozen pizzas. Whenever Doris brought things like Twinkies or ice cream home from the grocery store, she would make a special point of saying that such things were for Ruby's father and not for her. If she caught Ruby with any of her father's junk food, Doris would reprimand her and take the food away. "Don't you want to be pretty, dear? That's not going to happen if you eat those Cheetos, now is it?" she would say to Ruby.

Over time, Ruby became a master at sneaking food from the kitchen, hiding it, and eating it out of sight. She learned to arrange the assortment of Twinkies and HoHos in the box so it would appear as if none had been taken. She soon realized it was better to take small amounts from different boxes and bags of food than to take one large amount from any one container—

that way no one would notice anything was missing. When she got a bit older, while Doris was at work, she started baking cakes with the windows open, so Doris wouldn't smell anything when she got home. Ruby would make big fluffy yellow cakes with strawberry icing, thoroughly clean the kitchen after she was done, and then hide the cake in her closet until she had eaten the whole thing. She had food stashed everywhere—under the bed, underneath clothes in her dresser drawers, behind books on the shelf. During dinner with her parents, Ruby would eat a reasonable amount of food, and Doris would praise her for staying on her diet. Ruby would then retreat to her bedroom where she would improvise a sandwich from the bread she had taken from the kitchen earlier in the day and some little jelly and butter containers she'd swiped from a restaurant table when her parents weren't paying attention.

Now, looking across the table at her mother at the IHOP, Ruby almost didn't hear her anymore. She was so used to ignoring Doris's comments about weight and dieting that she had learned to tune them out. Part of Ruby was so angry with her mother for pushing her so hard to lose weight and teaching her to equate thinness and beauty with happiness. But Ruby also knew that in a warped way, Doris harassed Ruby because she wanted her to be happy, and it was inconceivable to Doris that a fat girl could be happy. And, although Ruby would never admit it to Doris, she pretty much agreed. Camryn Manheim could blab all she wanted about being big and beautiful, but in the end, everyone knew she'd rather look like one of her emaciated costars on *The Practice*. It surely would have been easier for Doris to let Ruby eat all she wanted and wash her hands of Ruby's weight issues, but Doris hadn't given up. It had been thirty-two years since Ruby was born, and Doris still found the energy to badger Ruby about her weight every chance she got.

Wanda Johnson

"Do these make my butt look big?" an approaching-middle-age woman asked Wanda as she stared at herself in the three-way mirror.

"Girl, big butts are in this season. We've got women coming in asking for padded panties."

"Oh my God! Then my butt does look big?"

"No, no. Those jeans look great. You actually look quite svelte in them."

"Are you sure? They're a little bit tight."

Well, that's what happens when you try to shove a size fourteen ass into a size twelve pair of jeans. "Absolutely. We have a sweater on sale that would go great with them. Should I grab one for you to try?" Wanda replied.

"Oh no. I just need jeans today," the woman said, stepping back into the dressing room, removing the jeans, and handing them to Wanda who took them over to the register. After the woman was dressed (and had left two other pairs of jeans bunched up on the dressing room floor for Wanda to pick up), she approached the counter and whipped out her Saks charge card.

"That comes to a hundred and thirteen dollars," Wanda said as she put the pants into a small bag.

The woman signed the charge receipt, and as she handed it back to Wanda, she stopped to give her a good once over. "You know what?" the woman asked Wanda, looking at her intently. "You should look into being a large-size model. You're so pretty."

"Thanks," Wanda said. "Actually, I do a little modeling for this store and a few others in the area."

Some women would have been insulted by being told they would make a great *large-size* model, but not Wanda. Ever since Wanda was in high school people had been telling her how attractive she was, and, even as she started to pack on the pounds later in life everyone still swooned over her. They always said the same things about Wanda—"She's big, *but* she's actually very pretty." "Oh, that Wanda Johnson, she's a big girl, *but* she's still quite attractive." "She's fat, *but* she has such a pretty face . . . and dresses so nice. I think she even goes on a fair number of dates."

Virtually everyone that met her seemed so surprised to meet a large woman who was pretty, and confident, and sharply dressed. Wanda was a thirty-five-year-old African-American woman. At five-feet eight-inches tall, she was grossly overweight, as her doctor had told her a few weeks earlier, but she had a beautiful head of relaxed black hair that fell below her shoulders, bright brown eyes, and a killer smile that would make Janet Jackson jealous. Wanda knew she was pretty and had always had a flair for makeup and fashion. She made no apologies for being fat and hadn't been on a diet in years. Whenever she heard friends complaining about their weight and how men were only attracted to thin women, Wanda would say that she was a mass of big black booty, and if a man couldn't handle that much woman, then she didn't need to be bothered with him.

Wanda had always been interested in modeling but had only started pursuing a career on the runway a few years earlier. She had checked into a few local agencies, but they all wanted *her* to pay *them*. The agencies said that if Wanda paid them a substantial fee for training and a portfolio, they might be able to find work for her. The whole thing smelled of scam, so she decided to go a different route. If she couldn't get into the modeling business through an agency, she figured she'd start with the local department stores. Shortly after she moved to the D.C.

area, she started as Christmas help at the Hecht's in Springfield Mall. After the holidays, she was hired full-time and worked there as a sales associate for two years. Working in retail sales wasn't quite the launch pad to stardom Wanda had hoped for. She was able to finagle her way into a couple of local shows, but most of her time was spent ringing up sweaters and handing blouses over the dressing room door to customers. Later, she applied for a sales job at the Saks Fifth Avenue in Chevy Chase where she still worked today. At Saks she was able to make a few more contacts in the local modeling scene and managed to get booked in several local shows. The more shows she booked, the more hectic her schedule became, and it was becoming increasingly difficult for Wanda to manage her sales job, her appearances at local fashion shows, and her packed social calendar. The local shows paid very little, if anything, so until Wanda got a break, she had to keep her job at Saks.

"What happened to your arm?" the woman on the other side of the counter asked Wanda as she took her bag.

"Oh, I fell while I was walking the dog. His leash got wrapped around my legs, and I took a bit of tumble," Wanda lied.

"I thought you fell in the tub," Denise, another Saks associate who was also behind the counter, asked Wanda.

"No. It was the dog," Wanda replied defensively. Shit, had she used the tub excuse? She couldn't remember.

"I thought it was the dog that tripped you when you *supposedly* busted your knee last month."

"It was," Wanda replied, annoyed with Denise's persistence. "And he tripped me again the other day."

"If you say so," Denise responded in a questionable tone. "Funny how the only time we ever hear about this dog is when you call in sick because he's tripped you."

"Hope it gets better soon," Wanda's customer offered, sensing a bit of hostility between Wanda and Denise, before trotting off with her new jeans.

Wanda hadn't cared for Denise from the moment she stepped foot in the store. She hated that Denise was another large, attractive, African-American woman. Wanda was used to being the prettiest fat girl anywhere she went, and she didn't appreciate competition. Wanda hated Denise's deep brown eyes. She hated her perfect, dark brown complexion. She hated her long synthetic braids. But most of all, Wanda hated the fact that Denise was younger. She estimated Denise to be about twenty-five, which gave Wanda a good ten years on her. Wanda was just starting to get attention as a large-size model. She was booking more shows, a small local paper had written a brief feature about her, and she was slated to wear a twelve hundred dollar designer suit in an upcoming Saks show. The last thing she needed was a bitchy twenty-five-year-old nipping at her heels before she had even made it herself.

"Shame about the fashion show," Denise said to Wanda.

"Shame?" Wanda inquired.

"Yeah. You certainly can't be in the show with your arm in a sling."

"Oh. The doctor said I only need it for a few days. I won't have it by the show."

"Really? Isn't that *convenient*," Denise said in a bitchy tone.

Not as convenient as me "accidentally" grabbing that plant holder on your head and twirling your ass out the door. "Yeah, I guess it is," Wanda quietly replied, dismissing Denise's comment before leaving the counter to greet a customer.

Fellow Big Girl

"You sure are getting an early start this year," Ruby said to Jeremy as they got out of the car and walked toward the Saks entrance in Chevy Chase.

"Ruby, Halloween is only three months away. If I don't start looking for an outfit to wear to the drag race now, I'll end up looking like Paul Kipling did last year. You remember him, in that pink, ruffled thing? He was hideous."

"No, actually I don't remember him, so he couldn't have been *that* awful."

"He was truly *hideous*, Ruby. And we're not talking Kathy Lee Gifford–hideous or even Sandra Bernhardt–hideous."

"Oh my! Not . . . ?"

"Yep. Donatella Versace–hideous."

"Oh, wait. He was the one trying to look like Little Bo Peep or Little Miss Muffett or something? He had a parasol and a curly yellow wig . . ."

"And a belly from here to next Tuesday," Jeremy added, interrupting Ruby as they made their way into the store, strolled through to Evening Wear and started scanning the racks. It was so much fun for Ruby to help Jeremy pick out clothes for the annual drag race. He wore a perfect women's size ten. Ruby got to peruse all sorts of clothes she could never wear herself, although she felt a little silly selecting size ten dresses from the racks and holding them up for Jeremy to see. The whole time she was in the store she was afraid someone was going to come up to her and give her directions to Lane Bryant. Ruby even had dreams about horrific department store experiences. She would see herself as a thin attractive woman in the petite department at Nordstrom or Hecht's. She'd grab all sorts of slinky dresses and hold them in front of herself in the mirror. Then she would smile at herself and, just as she was about to head to the dressing room to try on her picks, uniformed guards would appear behind her and shout, "Drop the dresses!" as if Ruby were holding a loaded gun. "Drop the dresses and put your hands in the air . . . slowly . . . slowly," the guards would say as Ruby lowered the dresses to the floor.

"What? What did I do?" Ruby would ask the guards as they handcuffed her.

"No fat girls allowed!" the guards would say, and then Ruby would see her real self, belly, thighs, and all, in the most heinous invention ever made—the department store three-way mirror. It was usually about this time that she woke up, but sometimes she emerged from the dream before the guards came—sometimes she woke up when she was still thin and wore a size six and could confidently look at herself in the mirror. Those dreams—the ones where she woke up while she was still thin were the worst because for a split second when Ruby first awoke from those dreams, she thought she *was* thin, but then she opened her eyes or ran her hand along her stomach and reality set in. God damn fucking reality set in!

"Can I help you with anything?" a very large black woman with one arm in a sling asked Ruby as she browsed the clothing racks. Ruby was immediately intrigued by her. So many of the overweight women she knew had a dowdy hopeless look about them—like because they were fat, there was no point in trying to look good. They always seemed to be in jeans and T-shirts or something equally bland, short wash-and-wear haircuts, and walked around like some sort of victims of the Fat Gods. This woman that stood before Ruby just had a different feel about her. She was dressed in a gorgeous Dana Buchman suit, had a sharp New York haircut, and projected confidence. She was overweight—actually, she was downright fat, but somehow she was utterly beautiful.

"We're actually shopping for him, not me," Ruby said, pointing to Jeremy as she feared that the woman was about to tell her to get her fat ass over to the plus sizes.

"Really?" the saleswoman questioned, although she didn't seem terribly flustered by a man shopping for women's clothing.

"Yeah, I'm looking for a gown to wear in a high heeled race," Jeremy replied, trying to clear up any potential confusion.

"Oh, the one on Seventeenth Street a couple days before Halloween? I went last year. It was loads of fun," the saleswoman replied.

"You did?" Jeremy questioned, although he really wasn't that surprised that she had been to the event. The high heeled race had been gaining more and more notoriety every year. The local news even covered it. It had started years earlier as strictly a gay event, but over time, more and more straight city residents were coming out to see what all the fuss was about and check out all the fabulous men in drag.

"Oh yeah. I went the year before as well. It was a hoot! My name's Wanda, by the way. If you need help finding anything let me know."

"How about a roommate?" Ruby asked facetiously.

"What?"

"Oh, nothing. I was just joking . . . well, not really. I've been trying to rent a room in my house and only freaks have applied."

"Really? Where do you live?"

"Off Rhode Island Avenue in the city . . . Logan Circle area."

"Near the Fresh Fields?"

"Yeah, that's right," Ruby replied.

"Hmmm . . . tell me more. I could be interested."

"You're kidding?"

"No. I live all the way out in Woodbridge. I moved there when I got a job at Hecht's in Springfield. Since I started working here it takes me an hour and half to get to work some days. Logan Circle would be great. I could take the Metro out here."

"You're welcome to come by and see the place. It's a three-story row house. It's about a hundred years old but has lots of updates. I've got a room for rent on the second floor."

"I might just do that. I haven't been in that neighborhood much lately, but I used to go to Weight Watchers meetings on Fourteenth Street."

"In the basement of the National City church? I used to go there too," Ruby responded.

"Notice the key word in both our statements—*used* to go," Wanda said with a laugh.

"Yeah, I've been meaning to go back," Ruby replied.

"Not me. I'm through with that nonsense. I remember when I used to do the Weight Watchers thing. Sometimes I'd alternate."

"Alternate?" Ruby asked.

"Yeah. One week I'd go to Weight Watchers. The next week I'd pig out at the Old Country Buffet, then it was back to Weight Watchers again."

Ruby laughed. "The Old Country Buffet?" she asked, as if she had never heard of the place, which of course was a complete lie. The Old Country Buffet was one of Ruby's favorite bingeing places. Some days she wished there was one closer to her house, and other days she was thankful there wasn't one nearby for fear of going there all the time.

"It's a huge buffet out in Fairfax—vats of the most fattening food you can eat," Wanda responded, not the least bit convinced that Ruby wasn't familiar with the place.

"Really?" Ruby asked.

"You've *really* never been?" Wanda questioned with a telling look—a look that said *liar.*

Ruby laughed "Okay, maybe I've been once or twice."

"Once or twice, eh?"

"Okay, the staff knows me by name, and I have my own table," Ruby joked.

Wanda laughed, and for the next few minutes the girls talked about their experience with Jenny Craig, Pizza Hut's all-you-can-eat lunch buffet, the L.A. Weight Loss program, grilled pound cake brushed with butter, personal fitness trainers, original recipe versus extra crispy, the *Body for Life* program, and where to get the best fast-food milk shakes—Wanda preferred Arby's Jamoca shake while Ruby professed her loyalty to Wendy's Frosties, but only when eaten with Wendy's special deep plastic spoon.

Ruby immediately liked Wanda. She was witty and silly and a fellow big girl. After they finished chatting about all the scam diets and fitness routines they had tried, Ruby scrawled some directions to her house on a slip of paper, and encouraged Wanda to come by and see the place.

"I'd love to see your house," Wanda said, relieved that she might be able to ease her long commute to work.

"Great. Then maybe I'll see you sometime this week. I'd better get back to Jeremy," Ruby replied, nodding in Jeremy's direction. He had lost interest in the girls' conversation and was a few racks down evaluating the merchandise. "Is it okay if he uses the women's dressing room?"

"I won't tell if you won't," Wanda said with a smile. "It was really nice meeting you," she added as Ruby trotted off toward Jeremy, who already had two gowns hanging over his arm.

"What do you think?" he asked Ruby, holding up a short black cocktail dress.

"I don't know, Jeremy. You're so skinny. Black may not be the best color for you," Ruby replied, a bit jealous that Jeremy could wear a sexy black dress and she couldn't. It made her think of Doris's little black dress, and how Ruby had always planned to fit into it one day. Seeing Jeremy hold a slinky black dress in front of him just reminded Ruby of all her failed attempts to lose weight and how lately, she had pretty much stopped trying.

"Why don't you go try those on. Wanda said you could use the women's dressing room," Ruby instructed. "And I'll scope out a couple more and bring them to you."

As Jeremy walked toward the dressing room, Ruby rifled through a few more racks looking for a dress that would flatter him. She eventually found an understated navy blue gown and carried it toward the dressing room for Jeremy to try. It was fun shopping with Jeremy, but at the same time it was a little sad. It made Ruby feel like such a fag hag. Did it get any worse than toting around dresses that she could never fit into for her male best friend?

"God!" Ruby said as she handed the dress to Jeremy. "I'm Margaret Fucking Cho."

Georgetown

"God damn it!" Simone said as she searched through her nightstand to find her earplugs. It was eight-thirty in the morning, and she had just been awakened by hammers and noisy saws. The remodeling men arrived every day between eight and eight-thirty, and it was making Simone crazy. It was generally well after midnight by the time Simone got home from taping the eleven o'clock news and somewhere in the wee hours of the morning before she finally fell asleep. She tried to arrange for the contractor to start after noon, but it would have meant higher costs and a longer delivery time for the renovations on her home.

Every day for the past week she had been cursing herself for buying such an old house in need of major updates. If she had just bought something new in the suburbs, she wouldn't have been trying to sleep in the midst of screeching drills and noisy workmen, but she made her home choice based more on the neighborhood than the house itself—the house was in Georgetown after all. Simone grew up just outside D.C. in Silver Spring, Maryland, and could remember gazing at the grand homes in this exclusive community from the time she was a little girl and her parents took her and her brother into the city for dinner or a visit to a museum. Simone seemed determined to be a raging success from the day she was born, and even as a kid, she knew that Georgetown was the place where people who had made something of themselves (or inherited money from people who had made something of themselves) resided. She could still remember one evening when her mother, who cleaned houses to supplement her father's income, saw Simone staring up at some of the homes on Foxhall Road. "Do you think I could ever live here?" Simone asked her mother. *"Simone, si trabajas fuerte tu puedes hacer lo que quieres. Por eso hemos venido a este pais,"* her mother, who spoke Spanish almost exclusively, replied, which translated to telling Simone she could be whatever she wanted as long as she was willing to work hard enough for it. Simone never forgot those words and still heard her mother's voice every time she felt like giving up.

When Simone first moved back to the D.C. area after working a few years at a local cable channel in Texas, she was living in a modest apartment in Arlington, Virginia, but it wasn't long before she was shopping for houses in Georgetown.

Simone was working at a small station in San Antonio when she was offered the position of anchoring the late news on Channel 6 in Washington, D.C. The job in D.C. didn't pay significantly more than her gig in San Antonio, but she figured it would allow her to be close to her family, and more importantly, introduce her in a major market. She replaced Carol Farnsworth, who, depending on who you believed, either retired of her own volition or was forced out by the station because, after twenty-two years on the air, she had gotten too old to be in front of the camera. Carol was African-American and was, therefore, the black half of the Channel 6 late news team. For decades, in recognition of the District's large African-American population, most of the newscasts in the area were sure to include one white anchor and one black anchor for each newscast; however, once the decision was made that Carol would be replaced, the producers decided to try something different and initiated a search for a Latina newswoman. Through the eighties and nineties the Latino population had exploded in and around the city, and no one in local television seemed to be catering to this audience. Channel 6 planned to be the first.

The producers reviewed countless tapes before they came

upon Simone. Before her tape was over, they knew they had their candidate. At thirty-four, Simone was just old enough to be taken seriously as a newswoman, but still young enough to be the absolute knockout that she was. She had the kind of beauty that wouldn't offend serious news watchers, but would also attract a large male audience who just wanted to see a pretty face and a hot body. Simone was a petite woman with straight brown hair, a slightly olive complexion, brown eyes, and large perky breasts. She had a beautiful smile and seemed to genuinely empathize with the individuals she interviewed.

Simone's parents had immigrated to the States from Bolivia when she was almost two years old. Obviously, Simone was Latina, but, as one of the producers said as they viewed her audition tape, she looked "just Latina enough." The same way news and soap opera producers looked for the whitest black people they could find, they were pleased that, although Simone had an olive complexion and dark hair and eyes, her features were decidedly white. She looked white enough that Caucasians would connect with her, Latinos would certainly tune in to see one of their own anchoring the evening news, and hopefully Simone would win over the African-American and Asian audience with her charm. The producers were sure they had picked a winner, but when they signed her for a modest salary, they had no idea how big of a hit Simone Reyes was going to be.

From the day she first beamed into homes throughout the D.C. area the buzz began. "Did you see that new anchorwoman on Channel 6?" was the question asked around watercoolers all over the Nation's capital the morning after Simone debuted in a low-cut blouse that highlighted her ample cleavage. It wasn't long before she was on the front page of the *Style* section of *The Washington Post* and sporting a Donna Karan suit on the cover of *Washingtonian* magazine. The headlines always read something like "When Did News Become Sexy?" or "Simone Reyes: D.C.'s Sexiest News Anchor Tells Her Story." Channel 6 was mixing sex appeal with serious news and it was working—boy was it working.

Sure, many of the other local anchorwomen were attractive,

or even pretty, but rarely were they considered *sexy*. Only a few weeks after Simone debuted, the eleven o'clock newscast on Channel 6 skyrocketed to number one in the local ratings war, beating every other newscast and even the *Seinfeld* reruns on Channel 5. Everyone was tuning in to see Simone Reyes. If they weren't watching to see the latest news, they were watching to see what Simone was wearing, they were watching to try to figure out if those were her *real* breasts, or, in the case of a few young men, they were watching to jerk off while Simone delivered the latest news about Tony Blair or President Bush.

After six months on the job, Simone hired an agent, who was able to renegotiate her contract, and, days after she received word of her new salary, Simone was driving a Mercedes and looking at houses in Georgetown. When the realtor first showed her current house to Simone, she fell in love with the stone exterior and wrought-iron accents. If only the interior was as tasteful and well maintained as the exterior. The house had been owned by an elderly woman who hadn't redecorated since the seventies. Despite this, Simone was able to see past the harvest gold appliances, fake wood paneling, and shag carpet. As she toured the house, she was already making plans for the renovations she wanted—walls that needed to be torn down, kitchen and bath updates, hardwood floors, the list went on and on.

The house simply had too much potential to turn down, and it was in Georgetown—Georgetown! When Simone announced she was buying a house, everyone asked the same question—where? "*Georgetown*," she loved to say to everyone. There were only a handful of premier addresses in the D.C. area—McLean and Great Falls in Virginia, Chevy Chase, Bethesda, and Potomac in Maryland, and then a few upscale neighborhoods in the District, Georgetown being one of them. When you bought a house in one of these neighborhoods you were not only paying for the land and the housing structure, you were paying for the privilege of being able to have the Georgetown or Chevy Chase zip code printed on your return address labels.

The day Simone signed the mortgage papers, she knew she had months of renovations ahead of her, but it was the happiest day of her life. It was better than her first time on the air as a newswoman, better than seeing herself on the cover of local magazines, even better than renegotiating for a lucrative "well into the six figures" salary to stay at Channel 6. Something about being the owner of a home in Georgetown made her finally feel like she had arrived—the little Latina girl from Silver Spring owned a house in Georgetown.

Simone finally located the earplugs in her nightstand drawer and put them in. As she slipped back under the covers, it suddenly hit her that she wasn't alone. There was a young man in his late twenties with dirty blond hair sleeping soundly next to her, oblivious to the construction noise going on downstairs.

Shit, Simone thought. How was she going to get him out of the house without the workmen seeing him? The lead contractor was always telling her what a big fan he was and how his wife just thought Simone was the "cat's meow." Many of his carpenters and workmen were Hispanic and had told everyone they knew about working in the home of D.C.'s most famous Latina. They were so proud to have one of their own on television who wasn't in a maid's uniform or speaking in some ridiculously overblown Spanish accent on a stupid sitcom. The last thing Simone needed was these men seeing her scoot some young stud out the door early in the morning and spreading the news all over the city.

She grabbed a matchbook she had taken from the bar the night before, opened it, and took a look. "Scott," she said, gently shaking the young man to wake him. She had written his name down on the inside flap of the book as soon as they had gotten home the night before—she wasn't up for a repeat of the *Bob* incident. She met him while she was having lunch at the Café in Nordstrom in Tyson's Corner. He kept staring at her, probably trying to figure out if she was really Simone Reyes. Eventually, Simone smiled at him and said hello, which led to some cross-table conversation. They chatted for a bit before Simone invited him to join her while they finished their lunches. They had a nice conversation, and when Simone had to be on her way, Scott asked if he could call her. As always, Simone said "no" but asked for his number and said she would be in touch. Simone rarely gave her number out to any men. If she did, her phone would ring off the hook twenty-four hours a day.

Simone called Scott a few days later and asked if he'd like to meet her for a drink after work, which in her case, was well after midnight. Some men might have winced at an after-midnight date on a weeknight, but when the date involved Simone, most guys didn't bat an eye. After-work drinks worked best for Simone anyway. It was too late for dinner, so she only had to have a quick drink with her conquests before she took them back to her place. Most of her dates had to get up early in the morning the following day, so it wasn't too difficult to get rid of them right after the sex.

As Scott came to life, she hopped out of bed, hoping he would follow her lead.

"I've got to get moving," Simone said. "I have so much to do today."

Taking her hint, Scott pulled himself from the bed and started to get dressed. Simone slipped on a pair of jeans and a casual shirt, and led him out of the bedroom.

"Listen. I'd prefer the contractors downstairs not see you . . . not good for my reputation, if you know what I mean," Simone said with a smile. "Give me a minute to lure them into the kitchen before you make your exit. Okay?"

"Sure," Scott said. "Can we get together again?"

"We'll see," Simone replied, gave him a quick peck on the cheek, and whisked herself down the steps.

CrustiCare

It was just after nine o'clock when Ruby arrived at the office. She was supposed to be there by nine, but, on a good day, she usually sneaked in around nine-fifteen or nine-thirty. She managed a staff of ten customer service representatives for CrustiCare, an HMO that covered a few hundred thousand people in the Mid-Atlantic area. It was awful telling people the name of her company. CrustiCare sounded like a slang name for a nursing home, or some other place where old people went to die, but Mr. Crusti, who had an ego the size of Jupiter, was the founder, president, and CEO. Of course, he had come up with the name. Ruby had started as a customer service representative herself about seven years earlier and slowly . . . *very* slowly . . . climbed a few ranks to department supervisor.

She pretty much hated her job. She was in that nether world of middle management—the lower end of middle management, which, to Ruby, was the worst place to be. When she was part of plain old front-line staff, she had to work hard, but at least she didn't have to go to any meetings. Now that she was a supervisor, she was expected to attend all sorts of company meetings and still get work done in the meantime. It was the vice presidents of CrustiCare, who didn't have to do any actual work, who had it made. They sat in meetings all day, spouted off their stupid ideas, created a bunch of work for people like Ruby, and went home to their McMansions in McLean.

Just the other day, Ruby spent four hours in a meeting about the company's mission statement. People in the room were all excited about developing a few sentences that were supposed to summarize CrustiCare's mission, as if anyone gave a shit about CrustiCare's mission. Ruby feigned interest in the topic even though she was preoccupied with all the actual work sitting on her desk—work, which some meeting about a retarded statement that was going to hang over the water fountain and mean nothing was keeping her from. The final statement ended up saying something about serving CrustiCare's members with excellence, blah, blah, blah, when it should have said, the mission of CrustiCare, pure and simple, was to make money—as much money as possible any way it could.

On the way to her office, Ruby walked by Alan Parker's cube.

"Good morning," she said in a somewhat hoarse voice. She had just rolled out of bed about an hour earlier and was still trying to wake up. She'd also had a touch of a sore throat for a few days, which she knew she should see a doctor about, but every visit to Dr. Goleman, no matter what it was about, ended with him pestering Ruby about her weight. It didn't matter what Ruby went to see him for—whether it was a sore throat, sinus problems, or bronchitis, he always managed to work in a lecture about her weight and wouldn't let her leave his office without a stack of weight-loss pamphlets and diet brochures. Ruby waited out every illness she had and only went to the doctor under the most dire circumstances. No wonder fat people were at higher risks for health problems. They were all afraid to go to the doctor for fear of being hounded about their weight until things got so bad they absolutely had to go.

"Hi, Ruby," Alan said. "Did you see *Survivor* last night?"

"No. I gave up *Survivor* last season. I've seen enough whores parade around in bikinis for a while."

"Oh, come on. How can you not watch it?" Alan replied, truly surprised that someone could pass up an episode of *Survivor*. Alan was a huge fan of reality TV—*Temptation Island, Big Brother, Fear Factor, The Amazing Race, American Idol*—he watched them all. He and Ruby had been friendly since he started with the company a year earlier. He was a really nice guy with dark brown hair, green eyes, and a bit of belly hanging over his Dockers. Ruby liked Alan, and they had lunch together every now and then, but he never expressed any interest in anything beyond friendship, something Ruby was used to from men, so she never pursued him either.

"How about *The Bachelor*? Did you see it the other day?" Alan asked before Ruby had a chance to answer his first question.

"No. I refuse to watch that show. It would be less degrading to women if they were all bound and gagged and pulled around by their hair. The girls on that show are so pathetic—they're like dogs at the pound yapping and wagging their tails in hopes of someone taking them home," Ruby said, enjoying her feeling of superiority over the wenches on *The Bachelor*. She was dowdy and fat, but at least she wasn't making an ass of herself on national television.

"What? Have you given up all the reality shows?'

"It's not just the reality shows. Actually, I've been kind of over television in general. I haven't been watching much lately," Ruby lied. She watched TV all the time, but didn't care to admit to the hours she often spent in front of reruns or Channel 5 or the old sitcoms on TV Land.

"Not even *Sex and the City*?"

"Well, I still catch that every now and then, although it's starting to get on my nerves. Every time I turn it on the four of them, Carrie, Samantha, Charlotte, and . . . What's the dykey-looking one called?"

"Miranda."

"Oh yeah. They're always at some restaurant eating. Every episode they're meeting for dinner, or chatting over brunch, or having lunch at some outdoor café . . . yeah, like any of them actually eat," Ruby said before she was interrupted by a very distinct smell. "Did Deanna bring those evil things in again?" Ruby asked, sniffing the air as discreetly as possible.

"Yeah, they're on the file cabinet by Preston's office. I think they're still warm," Alan replied, referring to the hot Krispy Kreme doughnuts Deanna had brought into the office.

"Did you have one?" Ruby asked, as if having *one* was really an option.

"No. They're so heavy. They make me sick."

"Of course they make you sick, but it's *so* worth it," Ruby said as she gave Alan a *see ya* kind of look and began her hunt for doughnuts.

Damn that Deanna! Ruby thought as she made her way through the maze of cubicles toward the Krispy Kremes. Not since *Survivor*'s Colby Donaldson had anyone been as annoyingly perfect as Deanna Keys, who lived in Alexandria near a Krispy Kreme bakery, and occasionally brought a few dozen doughnuts into the office to make herself even more popular than she already was. Deanna was blonde, thin, perky, and probably all of twenty-five years old. If that wasn't enough reason for Ruby to hate her, the bitch was also nice.

Ruby never forgot the day a few years earlier when she pleaded with the UPS man to wait just a few minutes longer one evening when she needed to finish up a report that had to be sent overnight to one of the field offices in Pennsylvania. The UPS man insisted that he had to leave and couldn't wait any longer for Ruby to finish the document. He was about to leave when Deanna intervened. She looked up at him from her desk, gave him her trademark puppy dog eyes, and simply said, "Please?"

The UPS man smiled at Deanna and said, "Okay. I can wait a few minutes longer."

Ruby had been grateful for the extra time, but also humiliated by the ease with which Deanna was able to sway him. Ruby always felt fat and inadequate, but around women like Deanna, she felt even *more* fat and inadequate.

Deanna started with the company three years earlier as a customer service representative under Ruby's supervision. Ruby trained and mentored her and, within months, Deanna was promoted above Ruby to a high-level account executive position, traveling all over the East Coast to meet with clients. Ruby had applied for a few account executive openings over the years, but eventually gave up when she realized she had the look of someone CrustiCare preferred to have serve its clients over the telephone rather than in person.

As Ruby got closer to the doughnuts, once again, the voices started: *You turn back around and go to your office, Ruby Waters—oh my God, Ruby, you are going to love those doughnuts!—no doughnuts, Ruby, be strong!—oh, just have a damn doughnut! What's the big deal?*

Ruby was about to reach for a doughnut when Preston DaSilva poked his head out of his office. He was looking for his secretary, who was probably downstairs taking one of her eight daily cigarette breaks.

"Hi, Ruby," he said with his typical bright smile. "Those sure are good, aren't they?"

"Oh. I was just looking. I haven't had a doughnut in years," Ruby lied. She knew Preston didn't believe her, that is, if he cared enough to even bother to think about anything she said. It was a stupid thing for Ruby to say, but she tended to say stupid things around Preston. He was a super-successful sales vice president for the company and was responsible for bringing in more than sixty percent of the company's new business the year before. He was about six feet tall with Mediterranean good looks, a defined chest, and a hard flat stomach. He was unbelievably handsome and was always quite polished in his custom made suits. Looking at Preston, it was so funny to Ruby how the lines between male and female beauty were becoming more and more blurred. Men who were considered attractive seemed to look more and more like women all the time. Just like women, they were slaving at the gym for thin waists and large chests. They were waxing their bodies, coloring their hair, using Rogaine and face creams, and even wearing makeup and having plastic surgery.

"Yeah, I try to avoid them myself," Preston replied, still flashing his Crest Whitening Strips smile. "So, how are you, Ruby? I haven't seen you for a while."

"I'm good," Ruby said, still struggling for words.

"That's great. We should chat some more soon. I wish I had some time now, but I've got to make a phone call," he said and disappeared into his office.

Ruby waited to hear him start his phone call before she stuffed two doughnuts in a napkin and headed to her office, still a bit flustered from the encounter. She didn't see Preston that often. He generally worked from a smaller service center in New York City, where he lived, but he had an office at corporate headquarters in Falls Church, Virginia, where Ruby worked as well.

Preston's sheer charisma and attractiveness made Ruby uneasy, but there was something more about him that ruffled her feathers. She knew it was ridiculous, but whenever she spoke with him, she got the feeling that he was flirting with her. He looked at her differently than other men. Most guys always looked at her face, but Preston seemed to give her a good once over during their conversations with his eyes lingering on her breasts. She knew the idea of Preston being attracted to her was ridiculous, and figured that he looked at all women that way—it was the natural salesman in him. Preston had a way of making *everyone*—from girlfriends to clients to secretaries, feel like they were the *only one*.

"God! No wonder he closes so many deals," Ruby said to herself as she sat down to start on the doughnuts. "If he can make me feel like he's flirting, he can sell matches to the devil himself."

A Place to Live

Certainly not her, Simone thought, looking at Leslie Kurtz, the Channel 6 meteorologist on the other side of the table. And *definitely* not her, Simone surmised, looking at Jennie Sanford, the chubby intern from Georgetown University. Simone was doing what she always did in boring meetings. She was checking out the attendees and making sure no one looked better than she did.

"Hello," Tim Jansen said as he walked in the room to join the meeting. Simone tensed up a bit as he sat down at the table with everyone. Relations with Tim had been somewhat awkward since the Channel 6 Christmas Party last year. The night of the party, Simone had helped herself to a few too many drinks and had shaken up the dance floor with Tim. As the party came to a close, Simone was too inebriated to drive. Rather than taking the Metro or a cab, Simone agreed to let Tim take her home.

Tim wasn't that attractive. He fit the profile of the stereotypical sportscaster—someone who loved to watch sports but was so desperately out of shape he could never actually participate in them. Despite his beer gut, his thinning hair, and, as Simone would later find out, his tiny dick, Simone invited him in for a nightcap to say thanks for taking her home, which, of course, led to the bedroom. Simone had never found Tim attractive but the more she had to drink, the hornier she got, and the more her standards went *whoosh*.

As usual, Simone was just looking for some fun—a roll in the hay. She assumed that's all Tim wanted as well. It wasn't like they had even gone on a date. To Simone, their experience was purely cheap sex. Accordingly, it took her by surprise when a dozen roses arrived at her office the next day. The card read:

> *Last night was very special and such a long time coming.*
> *I look forward to moving to the next level!*
>
> *Love,*
> *Tim*

Very special? Long time coming? The next level? What next level? Simone thought when she read the card. She knew she had to nix whatever Tim was thinking about her, and quickly. She hadn't lost enormous amounts of weight to become the girlfriend of a bald fat guy with a tiny dick. She forced herself into congenial mode, knocked on his office door, and tried to let him down easy. Needless to say, Tim was less than happy. In fact, Simone heard him whisper "slut," under his breath as she walked out the door after giving him the heave-ho.

Simone didn't appreciate Tim calling her a slut, but she understood that he was hurt and angry and, besides, Simone knew that she was, in fact, a slut. When it came to sex, Simone was like a frat boy. She saw men she was attracted to, turned on the charm, and had her way with them. Why shouldn't she? She spent most of her adolescent and young adult years being rejected by men—if they even bothered to notice her at all. She was making up for lost time. So what if she slept with a lot of men? She was careful and was having a good time. At least that's what she told herself. If she'd looked deeper, she would have realized it was more about payback than having a good time. Simone was getting her revenge on all those men that teased her, rejected her, or just plain ignored her when she was fat. When she didn't return calls to her one-night stands, when she scooted them out of bed as soon as the sex was over, even when she was tactfully telling Tim that she wasn't interested in him, she was really getting her revenge. It was her turn to make them feel worthless and unattractive. It was her turn to let them get their hopes up and then knock them down like a sick tree. It was her turn to be the one in control—the one with the power.

Simone would never forget what it was like to be fat. She remembered her troubled childhood, her high school and college years without a single boyfriend, and her early days in journalism when the powers-that-be wouldn't even consider putting her in front of a camera. As hard as she tried, she couldn't put those days behind her.

As she continued to wait for the meeting to start, Simone pulled a compact from her purse and gave herself a quick look. She did this from time to time just to make sure she was still thin, still pretty, still sexy. Once you've been fat you never take being thin for granted. The same way a person who recovers from paralysis is forever grateful for the ability to walk again, Simone relished in every moment of being thin and gorgeous. Every time a man held the door open for her, nervously asked her out on a date, or offered her a sad look of disappointment when she refused to give him her phone number, Simone appreciated her slim figure and ability to make men swoon.

It had been terrible being fat as a kid. She could remember those awful grade school days in gym class when that bitch gym-teacher, Mrs. Locke called two boys to the front of the class, assigned them as team captains, and had them "pick teams" for anything from basketball to soccer to softball games. Each one would take turns picking students from the class to be on his team. David Howell, the class jock, was always the first to be picked. He was usually followed by Chris Wilson, another athletically inclined classmate of Simone's. Gradually the two team captains would work there way through the more capable members of the class. Then they would move on to the students who had little sporting ability but at least wouldn't be a liability to their teams. Eventually a group of "unpicked" stragglers would remain, and the team captains would start rolling their eyes and lifting their noses in disgust as they were forced to choose from these misfits. During virtually every one of these exercises Simone was one of the last three children to be selected. It was so humiliating standing next to Anita Zimmerman, the class intellectual who could spell circles around any of her classmates but ran in fear when a basketball or softball was thrown her way, and Hank Friedman, who was even fatter than Simone and usually had to exit any sporting game after just a few minutes of play due to his chronic asthma.

Simone had to fight back tears as she stood as an undesirable in front of her classmates. She had to pretend like it didn't bother her when one of the team captains grudgingly pointed to her with a snarl, as if she was about to infect his team with some heinous disease. She never forgave the team captains for treating her so badly, but the one she really held a grudge against was Mrs. Locke. The team captains were just boys behaving like boys, but Mrs. Locke was a grown woman, and she was the one that always initiated the hateful process of picking teams. She had to know the effect it had on the self-esteem of students like Simone, and Anita, and Hank. She had to see how awful it was to be the last to be chosen to join the sporting teams. Simone just didn't understand it. Was Mrs. Locke some kind of sick bitch who liked to mentally torture children? To this day Simone had not forgiven that awful woman for putting her through hell once a week during gym class.

Simone fared only somewhat better in high school. She didn't have much of a social circle but at least she wasn't picked on or harassed by the other students. Mostly, she was just ignored. In fact, she was one of those girls that could suddenly transfer to another school and almost no one would have noticed she was gone, which was why it wasn't surprising that she hadn't heard from any of her high school classmates since she came back to D.C. and started topping the ratings charts. Virtually everyone she graduated high school with didn't remember her, and even if they had, they certainly wouldn't have recognized the new Simone—thin, graceful, and a definite head-turner.

"Hi everyone," Steve McFarland said in a chipper voice as he paraded into the room, late as usual. He was the lead producer of the six and eleven o'clock newscasts.

"We have lots to discuss today so get comfortable," he added before beginning to drivel on about the day's top news stories, and the features planned for that evening's telecast. Simone did the best she could to stay alert and pay attention, so she would be knowledgeable about the topics on which she would be speaking during the telecast, but some days it was so hard. Simone had never been interested in hard news, and the stupid local stories they did about some old hag turning one hundred years old or the opening of a new exhibit at the Smithsonian were a total bore.

Simone had never really planned on being an anchorwoman for the local news. Oh, she wanted a career in television, but doing a daily newscast was something she more fell into along the way. Fresh out of college and grossly overweight, Simone landed a paid internship position at a cable station in Philadelphia. She started out answering phones, sending faxes, and fetching chairs and microphones, but Simone was a quick study and slowly began taking on more responsibilities. Eventually she was writing the news, tagging along with camera crews, and taking care of production details. Simone wanted desperately to be in front of the camera, and she knew the only way it was ever going to happen was if she lost weight. You occasionally saw an overweight man forecasting the weather or reviewing the day's sports, but the chance of anyone putting a fat *woman* in front of the camera was unlikely at best. The longer she worked at the station the more her ambition to work in front of the camera intensified.

Of course, Simone had tried diet regimens and fitness programs to get into shape over the years, but it wasn't until she realized that her weight was hampering her career prospects that she developed an unstoppable determination to lose weight. Growing up, she knew she was overweight and considered unattractive by most people, but she always had her intellect, and she counted on it propelling her to success. She may have been fat, but she was going to show everyone that ignored her in school, the boys that wouldn't give her a second look, the girls that disregarded her—she was going to show them that she had made something of herself. She saw how hard her parents had to work just to maintain a barely middle-class standard of living, and she had no intention of repeating their history. When she was in high school and graded tests where handed back, Simone would look at the A's on her papers. Then she'd look around her at the dumb popular girls and the stupid jocks with their C's and D's—she'd look at them, shrugging off their poor grades and thought about how they barely knew that she existed. "But that was okay," Simone would tell herself—they'd be scrubbing her floor one day.

She didn't have a hot body, she didn't have a social life, she didn't have beauty, but she had her career aspirations, and naïve as she was as a young woman, she thought if she combined her innate smarts with hard work that would be enough to get her to the top. When she started at the Philly station she was certain if she worked hard enough she'd climb the media ladder and become a success. She didn't think her weight would matter so much in the adult work world, but it wasn't long before she figured out that she was never going to realize her dreams of fame and fortune if she stayed fat—she would *have* to lose weight if she was going to find her place in the spotlight and she was *determined* to find her place in the spotlight.

After a few years of working behind the scenes, she decided to do whatever it took to lose weight and, like anything Simone set her mind to, she did it. She lost more than a hundred pounds in less than a year, took out a loan to have her breasts lifted and her skin tucked after the weight loss, and charged two designer suits to her ailing credit card. It wasn't long before people started taking notice, and Simone was asked to take a crew and cover a minor story about a family reunion. She did great on her first story, which led to others, and eventually to a full-time reporter position with the station. After another year as a correspondent at the station in Philly, she was offered a better paying job with a larger station in San Antonio, which eventually led her to back to Washington, D.C., where she had grown up.

Simone was good at delivering the news and was happy to be where she was, but it was never her intention to make a life-long career of being a local anchorwoman. She planned to use it as a stepping-stone to bigger things—more interesting things. Who wanted to spend their time reporting on the inches of snow that fell in Alexandria, how students were being barred from local schools because their vaccines were not up-to-date, or manholes exploding in Georgetown? Simone wanted fun, glamour, and excitement. She longed to land a correspondent job on *Access Hollywood* or *Entertainment Tonight*. For heaven's sake, Mary Hart must have been a hundred by now, someone was going to have to replace her eventually. Why couldn't that someone be Simone?

"How are you, Simone?" Leslie asked her as the meeting wrapped up. "You look a little tired."

"Oh, I'm fine. Thanks. I'm just having trouble sleeping. I'm renovating my house, and the contractors start in the wee hours of the morning. I'm actually thinking of trying to find another place to live for a few months. It's getting unbearable at home."

"Really?"

"Well, unbearable might be exaggerating, but the contractors make so much noise, and they have all my furniture covered with drop cloths, and some days, the house is so filled with dust I have trouble breathing."

"Maybe you could move into one of those all-suite hotels like the Marriott Residence Inn or something until the work is done."

"I've been considering it," Simone lied. She couldn't consider a hotel. She couldn't afford a hotel. Even with her considerable salary from Channel 6, between her new house and the renovations, her Mercedes, and the thousands of dollars she spent on clothes and grooming, Simone had racked up so much debt she could barely afford a ham sandwich.

"A friend of mine came to town for an extended period last year and he found a nice place to stay by looking in *The Washington Post*," Leslie offered.

"Really," Simone replied, thinking that it might not be such a bad idea to check the classifieds. It would probably only cost her a few hundred bucks a month to rent a room from someone, and it was only temporary.

"Yeah, actually, I've got today's copy in my bag," Leslie said, rifling through her briefcase and handing a copy of *The Post* to Simone. "Take a look. What do you have to lose?"

"Thanks," Simone said and started flipping through the paper as everyone else left the meeting room. She'd need a place in the city that was close to work, and, of course, she'd have to have her own bathroom. As the meeting room cleared out, Simone scanned the listings and came upon a few that seemed like possibilities. One, in particular, caught her eye. The house was in Logan Circle, which was close to the studio. The ad gave a phone number and said to ask for Ruby. Simone circled the ad. The idea of sharing a house with another woman, like a couple of college girls, didn't exactly thrill Simone, but maybe she would give this Ruby woman a call.

Repressed Minorities

Ruby was in her Saturn SL circling the neighborhood. It pissed her off when she couldn't find any street parking close to home. Sometimes she had to park several blocks from her house. It was one of the drawbacks of living in the city, not to mention that her car had been broken into twice, which was the main reason she hung on to her nine-year-old Saturn—a new car would just attract thieves. She didn't particularly like the car, but she was going through a patriotic phase years ago when she was in the market for a new car, and wanted to buy American. She remembered when she first bought her vehicle, and Saturns were still somewhat of a novelty. When other Saturn owners saw her on the road they would honk and wave at her. Sometimes Ruby would hesitantly wave back. Other times she'd just call them freaks under her breath and ignore them. She even got an invitation to the Saturn Homecoming in Tennessee a few years earlier. She remembered her response when Jeremy asked her if she was going, "Yeah, like I'm going to drive hundreds of miles to eat a damn hot dog in the middle of some muddy field. If I want a hot dog, I'll go to the Weenie Beenie on Shirlington Road like everyone else."

Ruby was getting frustrated. There was no parking in sight, and she was supposed to meet Wanda in just a few minutes to give her a tour of the house. Finally, she saw someone pulling out of a spot on 14th Street. She raced over and flipped her turning signal on and waited while the other car eased out of the space. Just as the other car exited, a young woman in a red Chrysler convertible swooped into the space from behind. Ruby looked back in awe. Who did this bitch think she was? Ruby clearly had dibs on the space. She remained in position with her signal on, figuring that maybe the woman didn't realize Ruby was ahead of her, but soon it became clear that the young lady had made her claim and was not going to give it up. Ruby watched the woman get out of the car. She was a slender black woman with long hair wearing tight jeans and some sort of halter top. As Ruby watched the woman get out of the car she wanted to lay on the horn or get out of the car and tell the woman what she thought of her. Instead, she just said, "Fucking bitch!" within the safety of her closed windows and stomped on the gas to look for another place to park.

Ruby wished she'd had the guts to confront the woman, but confrontation was not something Ruby had ever been good at. She learned a long time ago, that when she stood up for herself she usually got knocked down even farther. It didn't matter what battle Ruby was fighting, someone always managed to come back at her with her weight, particularly when she was younger. If she ever argued with anyone during her school-age years, her opponents never stayed with the topic at hand. They could have been disagreeing over anything from test scores to school projects, but her adversaries would always stray from the issue and say something like, "Who cares what you think, Ruby. All you are is fat!" or "Why don't you go inhale a Twinkie, Ruby and just keep your fat face out of it!" Kids knew where to hit to really hurt someone, and Ruby quickly learned that it was best to keep her mouth shut and fade into the woodwork as best she could.

After Ruby managed to finally park the car about six blocks from the house, she hurried home and tried to straighten up before Wanda got there. She was just about to run the vacuum cleaner when the doorbell rang.

"Hi," Ruby said to Wanda as she opened the door.

Wanda smiled, indicated with her finger that she was still

chewing, and was silent until she swallowed. "Hi. It's great to see you again. Forgive the sandwich," Wanda said as Ruby caught a glimpse of an Italian B.M.T. sub from Subway. "I'm trying to squeeze in some dinner."

"No problem," Ruby replied. "Please. Come in."

"Thank you," Wanda said as she took another bite of her hoagie.

"What happened to your sling?" Ruby asked.

"Oh, I just wear that to work."

"Ah . . . okay," Ruby said, not sure what that was about. "Would you like a tour?"

"Sure," Wanda replied in between attacks on her sandwich and sips on a soda. "Have you had roommates before?"

"Just my ex-husband. I got the house in the divorce, but, unfortunately, I also got the mortgage. Money is starting to get a little tight, so I thought a roommate might be a good idea."

"Girl, I hear you. I live alone right now, but I have to live out in Woodbridge to be able to afford to do that, and, believe it or not, sometimes I miss having roommates," Wanda said as she followed Ruby up the steps. "My friend Kesha says women living together is a recipe for disaster. 'You know women can't get along with each other,' she says. For the most part I think it's nonsense, but sometimes I do think she might be on to something."

"You do?" Ruby asked.

"Well, not really, but look at the music industry and how long any girl groups are able to stay together. If it's a group of guys, they stand a fighting chance. Look how long the Rolling Stones and KISS and Aerosmith have been together. Can you say the same about the Go Gos, the Bangles, the Spice Girls. . . . The Supremes couldn't even check their egos long enough to do a reunion tour and make millions of dollars."

"I never really thought of it that way," Ruby said. Maybe Wanda's friend Kesha was on to something. Why else was Ruby's best friend a gay man?

As they reached the top of the steps, Wanda's mobile phone began chirping from her purse.

"Hello," Ruby heard her say into the phone.

"No, I told you I wouldn't be into work this evening," Wanda responded into the receiver after a pause. "You won't believe this, but I was putting in my contact lens while I was eating a snack . . . a doughnut, and the lens slipped from my hand and landed on the doughnut. Next thing I know, Peepers is eating the doughnut. You know I had to take him to the vet. We're still here now. He's back with the doctor."

Ruby watched as Wanda paused to listen to her caller and then started again. "Okay. Yes, I'll be in tomorrow. Did I say Binkey last time? No, his name is . . .?" Wanda said, looking at Ruby for help. She'd already forgotten what she'd called her fictitious dog only seconds earlier.

"Peepers," Ruby offered.

"Peepers," Wanda said into the phone. "I'll see you tomorrow."

Wanda disconnected her phone. "Thanks."

"You have a dog?" Ruby asked.

"Oh, hell no. I don't even like dogs," Wanda said.

"But you just . . ."

"Oh that. I'm very busy. It's hard to work retail and model. Calling in sick got a little old, so I invented a dog. A nurse friend of mine hooked me up with the sling I've been wearing to work. I figure I have to wear it for a few days to validate my use of sick leave. I may just pop out a kid in a week or two. Kids are a gold mine of not-being-able-to-make-it-to-work excuses."

Ruby laughed. "This is the room I have for rent," she said, leading Wanda into one of two bedrooms on the second floor. "There's a private bath down the hall."

"Great. This is a nice room," Wanda said, before peeking through the blinds and looking out the window. "Is this neighborhood safe?"

Ruby laughed. "Yeah. It's safe. Like anywhere, you have be alert, but I've never felt like I was in any danger."

"That's good. I've heard this is an up-and-coming area," Wanda said, finishing off her sandwich and taking the last sip of her soda.

"Yeah, my property value has skyrocketed since I moved in," Ruby replied, quite taken aback by Wanda's unapologetic eating. Ruby was so used to being ashamed of every morsel of food she put in her mouth, it was strange to see Wanda gobble up a sub right in front of her. Ruby had had plenty of subs in her day, but they were all consumed in the privacy of her car, at home, or, in one instance, a stall in the bathroom of her office building when she didn't want anyone to see her eating for the third time that day.

"You know why your property value keeps going up, don't you?"

"I think the neighborhood's getting trendier, and a lot homes are being renovated . . ."

"And more and more white people, like you, are making it their home," Wanda said, not letting Ruby finish. "That's really what it all comes down to, which is fine by me. Not that I'm thrilled that it takes a white presence to turn a neighborhood around, but at least it brings some retail and value into the neighborhood."

"You think?" Ruby asked,

"Oh yeah. You go into any heavy African-American neighborhood and, unless you want some fried chicken from Popeye's or some crap from a dumpy CVS, you're pretty much out of luck. When I first moved to the area, I lived in Prince George's County in Maryland. Do you know we had some of the highest incomes in the country in P.G. County. We were the most affluent majority African-American county in the U.S., but no retailers wanted to be bothered with us. . . . Can barely get a fast-food burger anywhere in the county."

"Really?" Ruby said, honestly surprised. As a white girl, Ruby did what most white people did, she never gave life from a minority's perspective much thought. She was pretty sure she wasn't racist. She just plain had enough of her own problems to be bothered with the plight of African-Americans or Latinos or whatever. She belonged to her own repressed minority group—fat people.

"Oh yeah. It's a shame really, but that's what's great about this neighborhood. It's diverse. I like that."

"Me, too," Ruby said. "Do you want to see the rest of the place?"

"Sure," Wanda said, rifling through her purse as she followed Ruby. As Ruby walked through the house, she noticed Wanda had pulled a Snickers bar from her purse and was eating away.

"Would you like one?" Wanda said, catching Ruby looking at her candy bar. "I got all kinds." She held open her bag and revealed a mix of goodies—Mars bars, Three Musketeers, Milky Ways.

Before Ruby could answer, the voices were back: *Yeah, a Mars bar, have a Mars bar!—no, Ruby, you're too fat to be taking candy from people!—it doesn't get any better than a Three Musketeers. Pounce on it, baby, while you have the chance!*

"Oh. I better pass. I'm on a diet," Ruby lied, her mouth watering for a taste of Wanda's candy bar. She hadn't really been on a diet in quite some time. If there were some way she could have sneaked a candy bar from Wanda's purse, she'd have done it in a heartbeat, but she never publicly accepted sweets from anyone.

"Me too. It's called the '*girl*, you better eat' diet."

Ruby laughed.

"Sometimes I call it the 'so much food, so little time' diet," Wanda added. "I gave up all that dieting nonsense years ago. You wait. I'm going to be the first famous *real* plus-size model. Not like those size twelve girls who call themselves large-size models. What a joke."

"You're a model?"

"Oh yes . . . well, salesgirl-slash-model."

"Really?" Ruby asked. She did think Wanda was pretty . . . beautiful, in fact, but who was she kidding? This chick was enormous. Of course, Ruby had seen *so-called* plus-size models, but, like Wanda said, they were a joke. Plus-size models were never actually fat. Like Emme, who Ruby had just seen in some magazine posing with the new doll some toy company had made of her. Emme was large. She was a big girl, maybe stocky, but you'd be hard-pressed to call her fat.

"Yes. Plus-size girls like you and me are more and more in demand all the time. The industry is finally starting to realize all American women are not a size four."

"Wow. Have you been in any magazines?" Ruby asked.

"No, not yet. I mostly walk the runway for local department stores, but I'm just starting out. I need to get a little more experience under my belt, and then I'm off to New York to really make it big. You may be able to say you 'knew me when.'"

"I hope so. I'd love to know someone famous."

"Then stick with me, Ruby," Wanda said. "I'll be sure to get you into all the fabulous parties and fashion shows when I hit the big time."

After Ruby finished showing Wanda the house, she got Wanda some coffee, and they sat down in the living room and chatted for a while. Ruby really started to like Wanda. She was so refreshing. She seemed so independent and sure of herself, and, most importantly, she seemed to really like Ruby. When Wanda agreed to take the room, Ruby was thrilled. It would be fun to have a roommate like Wanda.

"Thanks for the tour and the coffee," Wanda said on her way out the door. "I'll be in touch about moving day and all the other details."

"Sure," Ruby replied. "I think we'll be great roommates."

"And great friends," Wanda said. "I think we are going to have a ball together, Ruby Waters," Wanda said and walked out the door.

Going Without

"Just a sec," Ruby called toward the front door as she put the lid back on the jar of peanut butter and shoved the Hershey bar in a drawer in the kitchen. It had only been about a half hour since Wanda had left, and there was someone ringing Ruby's doorbell.

"Who could that be?" Ruby said quietly to herself as she approached the door. Maybe Wanda had forgotten something.

"Hi," said an attractive Latina woman on the other side of the door.

"Hi," Ruby replied, before it hit her. The attractive Latina woman was Simone Reyes, whom Ruby watched almost every night on the late news. What the fuck was Simone Reyes doing at her front door? Had another manhole exploded on the sidewalk? Was there another robbery at Starbuck's? Some news story must have broken in the neighborhood, and Simone was there to get one of those on-the-scene accounts from a local resident, something Ruby had no intention of giving. She wasn't going to be that fat girl everyone saw on the news. She didn't need snide comments made about her all over town.

"I'm Simone," Simone said in response to Ruby's silence. "I called about the room for rent."

Ruby hesitated for a moment. "Oh . . . yes, the room." It was coming back to Ruby now. She remembered talking to *a* Simone (she had no idea it was Simone *Reyes*) a few days earlier when they had scheduled a visit. Somehow, Ruby had forgotten all about it.

"When you said Simone on the phone, I didn't know you meant . . . well, *you*. I watch you on the news all the time," Ruby said, realizing she was coming across as a complete idiot. "When I get a chance, that is," she added, trying to downplay her enthusiasm.

"That's great. I'm glad you like the newscast."

"Please, come in," Ruby said, opening the door wider and feeling silly for taking so long to invite Simone in. "So, you're looking to rent a room?" Ruby questioned. Why on earth was a local celebrity looking for a room to rent?

"Actually, I'm just looking for somewhere to stay for a few months. I'm having some major renovations done on my house, so I'm looking for a place to live until they're finished."

"Oh, great!" Ruby replied, still finding it a bit odd that Simone was looking to share a house with a stranger. Couldn't she stay in a hotel or get a corporate apartment or something? "Can you excuse me for just a second? Please have a seat," Ruby said, gesturing for Simone to sit down on the sofa before she disappeared into the kitchen.

Oh my God! Ruby thought as she quietly dialed the phone. Having Simone in her house was just too exciting to keep to herself.

"Jeremy," Ruby whispered into the phone when his answering machine picked up. "I have three words for you—fuck! fuck! fuck! You will never believe who is sitting in my living room. Call me," she added and hung up the phone. She took a deep breath, tried to calm her nerves, and went back into the living room.

"So, can I give you a quick tour of the place?" Ruby asked, still trying to collect herself as she walked back into the living room.

"Sure," Simone said and got up from the sofa.

"This is the foyer and back here is the den or rec room, or whatever you want to call it." Ruby found herself talking quickly, tripping over her words as she let Simone peek into the small den off the living room. The whole thing seemed surreal—her showing Simone Reyes around her house. "There's a little yard out back with a patio," Ruby added, pointing toward the French doors at the other end of the room.

"Is there off-street parking?" Simone asked.

Damn! Ruby thought. She's not going to want to live here because there's no off-street parking. "I'm afraid there isn't, but I generally don't have much trouble finding parking close to the house," Ruby lied, before she led Simone through the kitchen.

"That's good to know. This kitchen is quite spacious."

"Thanks," Ruby said. "I hope to remodel it over the next year or two."

"Yourself? I can barely screw in a lightbulb without help."

Ruby laughed. "I'll do some things myself, but I'll hire a contractor to do most of it. Do you want to see the upstairs?"

"Sure," Simone said with a smile as Ruby led her toward the stairs. While they were ascending the staircase Ruby suddenly remembered Wanda. Damn! She had already rented the room to Wanda.

Think, Ruby, think! Ruby thought to herself before she had an idea—the house had three bedrooms—maybe she could rent rooms to both Wanda and Simone. She scooted Simone past what was to be Wanda's room, and showed her the adjacent bedroom, which Ruby currently used as a makeshift office.

"This is the room," Ruby said as she opened the door. "Of course, I'll clear everything out if you decide to move in."

Simone barely glanced at the room before she said, "It's very nice, but I think it's a tad small for me."

"Oh?" Ruby said, trying not to show the disappointment in her voice.

"Is that your bedroom?" Simone asked, gesturing down the hall.

"No, that's Wanda's room," Ruby replied as if Wanda had lived there for years.

"Oh. I didn't realize two people lived here. I thought you lived alone."

"Really? I'm sorry. I thought I mentioned on the phone that I was looking to share the house with two roommates. . . . Help me catch up on some bills," Ruby lied. She didn't think it wise to tell the truth—that she had rented a room to Wanda minutes before Simone came to the door.

"Well, you do have a beautiful home," Simone said, even though the house obviously still needed some work. "But living with two other people probably wouldn't work out. I really need a little more privacy than that. It was really a pleasure to meet you, but I'd better get going."

Don't let her leave! Don't let her leave! Ruby thought as she watched Simone head toward the stairs.

"Wait!" Ruby said, hoping she didn't sound as desperate as she thought she did. "Why don't you check out the master suite on the third floor. I'm using it now, but it's too much space for me."

"Master suite?" Simone asked.

"Yes. And it is gorgeous, if I do say so myself."

"Well, okay," Simone said hesitantly as Ruby took her up another flight of steps to her own bedroom.

"This is it," Ruby said. "It's a little disheveled. I wasn't planning to show it today."

"No, it looks great," Simone said, and she really meant it. The room spanned the entire third floor of the house and had lots of light and a private bath. "Gosh, it really is a nice room."

"Yeah, it is," Ruby replied, glad that Simone was expressing some interest, but feeling a little pathetic at the same time—was she really so desperate to have a celebrity live in her house that she was going to give up her own room? It was happening again. She was cheating herself out of something to please someone thinner and prettier—someone Ruby felt was superior.

"You know, I think maybe this could work out," Simone said, expressing some optimism. "Of course, I'd have to pay more rent for this room."

Ruby fought the urge to decline her offer and led Simone back downstairs. They chatted for a few more minutes in the living room, and Simone offered to up her rent payment by two hundred dollars if she could have the master bedroom. Ruby agreed, and the two women worked out a few more details about furniture and moving dates before Simone left.

After she had walked Simone to the door and said good-bye, Ruby was overwhelmed with a multitude of feelings. She had a certain degree of elation that a famous newswoman was going to be living with her, but she also had a sense of remorse giving up her room—actually, it was more a sense of fatigue. She was tired—tired of conceding things that were rightfully hers to people to whom she felt inferior. Somehow she always felt unworthy. She was haunted by memories of going without. She'd never forget the time in third grade when she was in the elementary school cafeteria and picked up the last ice-cream sandwich in the freezer before taking it to the cashier to pay for it.

"Ruby took the last ice-cream sandwich!" Heather Watkins yelled to everyone in line with more disdain than one might think a third grader could conjure up. "She's already so fat! You'd think she could leave something for the rest of us!"

Ruby was so shocked, she didn't know how to respond. "I'm sorry. I don't really want it anyway," she lied and handed the ice-cream sandwich to Heather, who just took it from Ruby's hand and rolled her eyes. That fateful day in third grade was forever burned in Ruby's memory. Even now, at thirty-two years old, she could still see Heather with her golden locks and tiny body calling her fat. It was amazing—she could still feel the pain more than twenty years later, like it had just happened yesterday. The ice-cream sandwich incident was the first time anyone had ever said anything to Ruby about her weight. She had memories of her mother telling her to slow down when she ate her Spaghettios or denying her requests for seconds at the dinner table, and she was aware that her Chubby Grranimals were different from the regular size, but, it wasn't until Heather Watkins shot her little third-grade venom that Ruby really started to realize that something was different about her, that something was wrong with her—that she was fat.

After school that day Ruby went straight for her bedroom mirror when she got off the school bus. She looked herself up and down and gave her eight-year-old body a long stare. For the first time, she could see it. She could see that she was fat. Up until then, she just assumed that she had an average-size body. Before the Heather Watkins incident, even when she looked in the mirror, she saw a normal body. In fact, she really hadn't even known there was a difference between her body and Heather's. She just hadn't seen it until it was viciously brought to her attention.

Ruby often thought about the day Heather Watkins called her fat. It was the day Ruby realized she was different and not part of what society found desirable. Prior to that day, she went through life thinking she was pretty and thin and happy. That day in the third grade came back to her every time she saw young children who were different. She'd see kids in the park or at the mall and wonder when the time would come (or had it come already) that they would realize they were different because they were fat, or because they were Asian or Black or Latino, or that Daddy and Daddy's relationship was frowned upon by thousands. What would be the day that those sweet kids would lose their innocence by way of a Heather Watkins? What would be the day that they realized they were not what society held dear, not what was featured on virtually every television and movie screen? When would the day come that they would realize they were not attractive Caucasian Christian heterosexuals?

As the door shut behind Simone, Ruby thought about the moment more than twenty years ago when she looked at herself in the mirror and cried—the day she gave away something that was rightfully hers, because, next to Heather Watkins, she felt unworthy. And here she was at thirty-two doing it once again—but this time her ice-cream sandwich was her bedroom, and Heather was an anchorwoman from the Channel 6 News.

Ruby didn't know which way to go with her emotions—

should she be thrilled that she'd convinced a local celebrity to move into her home, or should she be upset that the cost of convincing Simone to move in had been giving up her own bedroom? She eventually decided she just wouldn't think about it at all. Instead she turned from the door, walked into the kitchen, and grabbed herself an ice-cream sandwich from the freezer.

Moving Day

Ruby was practically drowning in her own sweat by the time Wanda showed up for moving day. She had talked with her a few days earlier and explained that Simone would be moving in as well. Wanda didn't care about the additional roommate, but she used it as an opportunity to make Ruby lower the rent since she was going to have to share a bathroom.

Ruby had just finished cramming the bulk of her belongings into the smaller of the two rooms on the second level of her house. Jeremy helped with the heavier items. He had to leave for a lunch date before the other girls got there, but he managed to make time to berate Ruby for moving into the smallest bedroom in her own house. Ruby assured Jeremy that she was okay with the arrangement, offering some argument about how the extra money from two roommates would be worth being confined to such a tiny room—especially since Simone only planned to be there for a few months until her renovations were done.

Ruby wanted to jump into the shower and clean up a bit before the other girls arrived to move in their belongings. She was about to head up to the bathroom she would soon cede to Simone when she saw Wanda pull up in a U-Haul.

Ruby gave up on the idea of showering. It was only polite to help the other girls move in, so there wasn't really any point in getting cleaned up anyway.

"Hi," Ruby said to Wanda.

"Hi," Wanda replied, stepping out of the moving truck. As soon as Wanda's feet hit the pavement, the driver of a car behind her U-Haul began honking his horn. There weren't any open spaces in front of Ruby's house, so Wanda had to double-park outside the entrance. The driver of the car wailed on the horn for another second or two. When all the traffic had passed on the other side of the road he pulled up next to the truck and rolled down the window.

"You two heifers want to move that truck!" said a skinny man in a green Honda. "You're blocking half the damn road!"

Ruby stammered for a moment, "Ah . . . sorry . . ." she nervously said, before Wanda maneuvered herself in front of Ruby and cut in, bending over and almost putting her head in the man's car window. "You want to get the fuck out of my face before you're pulling your teeth outta your ass?" Wanda said with a calmness that somehow gave her words more effect than if she had shouted them.

Ruby laughed as the man rolled up his window and was quickly on his way. It was becoming obvious to Ruby that Wanda didn't take shit from anyone. Ruby wouldn't have known what to say to the obnoxious man had Wanda not been there. Chances were, she would have either ignored him or tried to ask for his patience while explaining the moving situation. Either approach probably would have resulted in more names like "heifer," "oinker," "Ms. Piggy," and the recent favorite of nasty thin people, "you fat fuck."

After Wanda gave the Honda driver a piece of her mind, she immediately got down to the business at hand. It was as if the man calling her a heifer hadn't concerned her in the slightest. She just quickly put him in his place and moved on.

"I've got a truck full of stuff. Do you think you can give me a hand? My brother and his friend are supposed to be over later to help me, but they're not the most reliable guys on the planet."

"I'm happy to help," Ruby replied as Wanda slid the back of the truck open.

"Why don't we start with this dresser? It's the heaviest piece."

"Okay," Ruby said as she climbed the ramp into the truck and grabbed one side while Wanda grabbed the other.

"Ready? On three. One. Two. Three," Wanda said as the girls gave it their all and managed to lift the dresser a few inches before slowly hauling it down the ramp.

"Down, down," Wanda said as she and Ruby laid the dresser on the ground. They were both huffing and puffing, and that was just from taking the dresser off the truck.

"How'd you get it in the truck?" Ruby asked.

"Oh. I have a gentleman friend at my old building. He and a friend of his loaded most of my things for me. I guess they think it'll get them in my pants," Wanda said with a laugh.

"Want to give it another try?" Ruby asked.

"Okay. On three again?"

The girls struggled with the dresser once again. Their arms ached as they tried to get it on the sidewalk and take it inside. After another break they were able to get it to the front door. The pair were out of breath and sweating when a perfectly polished silver Mercedes pulled up in front of the house. As Simone hopped out of the car in a pair of beige capri pants and a sleeveless knit top, a large moving van stopped behind her car.

Simone looked at the moving van driver and pointed to Ruby's house before making her way toward Ruby and Wanda.

"Hi," Simone said with a bright smile. She was in full makeup, wearing a pair of Gucci sunglasses, and smelled faintly of Chanel.

"Hi," Ruby said, feeling like a glistening pig next to Simone. "Simone, this is Wanda."

"Hi, Wanda," Simone said, offering another one of her famous smiles.

"It's nice to meet you," Wanda replied. "I love that top. Is that a St. John knit?"

"I think so. It goes with a whole suit, but I just threw it on this morning," Simone replied. "How'd you know?"

"Oh, I work in fashion," Wanda said confidently. "Although I'm sure I don't look like it today."

"Don't be silly," Simone said before turning to Ruby. "Do

you mind if I run upstairs and try to figure out where I want to put everything?"

"No, please go ahead," Ruby replied.

Simone disappeared into the house, and Ruby and Wanda stared at the dresser with apprehension.

"Hey," Wanda said, looking from the dresser to the men sorting Simone's things in the other moving van. "Maybe they'll help us out. They're already here. If I offer to pay them a few bucks, I bet they'll move some of the heavier things for us."

"Doesn't hurt to ask," Ruby said and followed Wanda toward the movers.

"Hi," Wanda said as Ruby lagged behind. Ruby hadn't had good experiences with blue-collar men and didn't want to draw any attention to herself.

"I'm moving in today as well and was wondering if maybe we could cut a deal. Would you guys be willing to move a few of my things for fifty bucks or so?"

"I'm sorry, ma'am," one of the men said. "We've got another job in two hours. I don't think we'll have time."

"Would you have time for, say, a hundred bucks?" Ruby added. She was more than willing to match Wanda's fifty if it meant she didn't have to haul any heavy furniture up the stairs.

"Just don't have the time today, ladies. Sorry," the man said in an "and that's final" sort of tone.

The girls walked back to the house and were about to try to lift the dresser again when Simone reappeared and observed the girls, looking worn-out and clammy. "Were you trying to move this dresser on your own?" she asked. "It looks really heavy."

"Yeah. And this is just the first piece," Wanda replied.

"Oh, no, no, no. Why don't you have my guys move your things in as well?"

"That would be great, but we actually already asked them, and they said they didn't have time," Wanda replied.

"Nonsense," Simone said. "I'll just get them to unload your things as soon as they're done with mine."

"That's sweet of you to offer but . . ."

"I'll be right back," Simone said, taking off her sunglasses, pushing her hair back with them, and approaching the three men behind the moving van. Ruby and Wanda watched her from the front of the house. They couldn't hear what she was saying, but they didn't need to. Her actions said everything. She smiled and cooed at the men, tossed her hair a couple of times, and subtly touched them on their shoulders or arms while she asked the "big strong fellows" if they would mind using "those gorgeous muscles" to help out her friends. Ruby watched Simone with a mixture of relief that she was almost certainly going to persuade the movers to give her and Wanda a hand, and disdain that Simone was so easily able to charm the men with her magnetism and good looks.

"Okay. The guys are going to start on the U-Haul as soon as they have my things moved in," Simone said, returning to the house.

"Wow, thank you," Wanda said. "My back will be forever grateful."

"Yeah. Thanks," Ruby offered.

A few minutes after the movers had hauled everything into the house, Ruby's new roomies were busy unpacking and getting themselves situated. Ruby heard them rumbling upstairs while she tried to mop up all the dirt the movers had tracked in. She couldn't make out what they were saying, but Simone and Wanda seemed to be talking and laughing together as if they were close friends. As she listened to them, it hit her that her house was no longer hers anymore. It belonged to the three of them. She couldn't play her music as loud as she wanted, she couldn't walk around naked, she couldn't—oh God! Ruby thought as it suddenly hit her, she couldn't eat whatever she wanted, whenever she wanted, wherever she wanted—she now had an audience.

"Shit," Ruby said to herself, realizing that she had forgotten to clear out the food in the kitchen before Wanda and Simone arrived. She leaned the mop against the wall and quickly made her way to the kitchen. She pulled some grocery bags from one of the drawers and starting filling them with food. She didn't want the other women to see her bags of Doritos and Chips Ahoy! She selected items from the cabinets and the refrigerator and shoved them in the bags. She'd have to leave the frozen cream puffs and the Klondike Bars in the freezer—there was no way to keep them from melting in her room. Once she had depleted the kitchen of the bulk of its high-calorie, high-fat items, she placed the bags in a large box Wanda had left at the bottom of the stairs and guiltily hauled her booty up the steps. If the girls asked, she'd just say it was knickknacks or something she wanted to store in her bedroom.

On the way to hiding the food, Ruby paused next to Wanda's room, where Simone was seated on the bed chatting while Wanda carefully arranged her clothes in the closest.

"I love that suit," Ruby heard Simone say.

"It's an Eileen Fisher. Got it with my discount at Saks."

"It's gorgeous," Simone replied.

"Girl, I can hook you up with any designer label Saks sells. I'm at the one in Chevy Chase. Come by anytime."

"Absolutely," Simone said as she watched Wanda hang a short red dress in the closet. "Wow. Now that's something else," she added, standing up to get a better look at Wanda's dress.

"Yeah. It's part of Saks's Real Clothes collection. You should see it on me, girl. It looks stunning, if I do say so myself. One of my boyfriends calls it the Red Fox. Every time we go out he wants me to wear 'the Red Fox.'"

"*One* of your boyfriends," Simone asked with a smile. "How many do you have?"

"I'm seeing three or four guys right now. Tom, Leroy, Jackson, and occasionally, I see this guy, Markus, but he's married and lives in Norfolk, so our paths don't cross that often."

"Busy lady."

"Yep. I'll settle down with one guy someday, but I haven't met one that makes the cut, so until then . . ."

"I hear you," Simone said. "It's scary out there."

The whole time Simone and Wanda were bantering in the bedroom, Ruby listened with amazement outside the door. Who was this Wanda chick? She was just as fat as Ruby. What was she doing with designer suits? What was she doing with boyfriends? How was she so comfortable around a beautiful thin woman like Simone? And the thing that really flabbergasted Ruby was when Wanda spoke about herself looking "stunning" in her red dress. Ruby was about the same size as Wanda, and she couldn't remember herself feeling stunning in anything since her first communion dress more than twenty years ago.

Ruby walked past the door with her box of food and smiled at Wanda and Simone. She placed her box in the closet and sat on the bed. Things were uncertain, but Ruby felt just a tad excited—nervous and a bit anxious, but definitely excited. Life was changing—she could feel it. She didn't know how, or even if it would be for better or worse, but somehow, she knew having Wanda and Simone in her house was going to stir up her life.

Girls' Night Out

"Smells *lovely* in here," Simone remarked sarcastically as she, Ruby, and Wanda walked into The Melting Pot in Arlington. The smell of grease steaming from all the fondue pots was quite powerful.

"Grease, baby! That's how you know the food's going to be good," Wanda said with a laugh.

The girls had spent much of the day unpacking and getting settled. By six o'clock, and just three hours after consuming a double-decker peanut butter and jelly sandwich, Wanda announced that she was starving and invited the girls to dinner. She thought it might be nice to have a "let's get acquainted" meal together.

"Hi. Wanda Johnson. I have a reservation for three," Wanda said to the host.

"Follow me, please," the young man replied and led the trio to an isolated booth with high walls and a burner in the middle of the table. "Your server will be right with you," he added as he left menus for the girls.

Ruby sat next to Simone, and Wanda nabbed the other side of the booth for herself.

"Can I start you off with some drinks?" a young male waiter asked after approaching the table.

"Gin and tonic for me please," Simone requested.

"I'm in the mood for something fruity. Do you have daiquiris?" Wanda asked.

"Sure, strawberry, banana . . ."

"Strawberry's good."

"And you ma'am," the waiter said to Ruby.

"House white wine, please," Ruby said. She didn't usually order drinks other than water when she ate out, but she needed something to help her relax. If she ordered a Coke she'd get the *shouldn't you be ordering a diet soda?* look from the waiter, and if she did order a diet soda, she'd get the *yeah, like a diet soda is going to make a difference* look. At least ordering wine would add to the tip, and in the end, that's really what waiters cared about.

"So, what's the deal with this place? They just bring raw meat to the table?" Ruby asked Wanda, the only one of the three that had ever been to The Melting Pot.

"First we get a cheese fondue, and they bring all sorts of things for us to dip in it. Then you get your choice of salads. Then we get a big ole pot of grease to fry up some steak or chicken or shrimp, whatever. Then . . . oh my God! . . . this is the best . . . we get chocolate fondue for dessert!"

"Wow, that's a lot of food," Ruby lied. There'd been occasions in which she had easily consumed more than that in twenty minutes while watching a *Cheers* rerun on Nick at Nite.

"Sure is," Simone added. "I'll never be able to eat all of that."

"Girl, not me. Whatever you don't eat, I will," Wanda said.

"This is confusing to me," Ruby said to Wanda as she reviewed the menu and all the different options. "Too many choices. Why don't you just order for me?"

"Me too," Simone said.

When the waiter returned with their drinks, Wanda placed an order for the whole table: cheddar cheese fondue to start, followed by three chef's salads, a mix of chicken and filet mignon cubes for the main course, and the s'mores chocolate fondue dessert.

"For the chicken and beef, would you prefer to cook with peanut oil or our healthier alternative of beef bouillon?" the waiter asked.

"What? Are you joking me? Bring on the peanut oil," Wanda said without consulting Ruby or Simone.

"Excellent choice. I'll be back shortly," the server said, and disappeared beyond the walls of their booth.

"You two are going to love this, but get comfortable, it's about a three hour ordeal by the time they serve all four courses."

"Well, that will give us plenty of time to get to know each other," Simone said and took a long sip of her gin and tonic. "So, Ruby. How long have you lived in D.C.?"

"Only three years in the city itself, but I've lived in the area my whole life," Ruby replied, hating the way Simone used her name when she was sitting right next to her. Somehow it always seemed condescending and manipulative when people used her name when they spoke directly to her—like they had taken some self-help seminar that taught them that people loved to hear their name and that calling people by name makes them feel important, blah, blah, blah.

"How about you, Wanda?" Simone asked.

"I grew up in Trenton, New Jersey, before I moved here. I was going to move to Arizona—decided to go there after seeing *Waiting to Exhale*, but then I realized anything close to the house Angela Bassett owned in Scottsdale was a fantasy on my salary. I moved here about six years ago," Wanda replied. "And what about you Simone, you little Latina vixen," Wanda added with a smile.

Latina vixen? Ruby thought. Wanda had known Simone for less than a day and was giving her nicknames? It was maddening how Wanda could get so comfortable around people so quickly.

"Gosh. I was born in Bolivia in South America, in a city called Cochabamba. My parents immigrated to the States when I was very little. We lived in New York City for a few years and then moved to Maryland, where I grew up and went to school. I went to the University of Maryland and then moved around a bit working at different television stations after college. I was in San Antonio before I came here and . . ."

"Here we go," the waiter said, interrupting Simone before he started mixing up a pot of shredded cheese, beer, garlic, and a few other goodies. He then placed the pot over the heat and whipped all the ingredients into a creamy blend.

"Careful, it's hot," he said as he set down some cubed bread, vegetables, and sliced apples.

As the waiter trotted away, the girls speared the bread and other fare and started dipping it in the cheese.

Only eat a few bites, Ruby. You don't want Simone and Wanda thinking you're a pig.—Just dive into that pot of cheese like it's a swimming pool and nab all of it for yourself.—No, Ruby! Control yourself!

"So, what do you think?" Wanda asked.

"It's good," Ruby said, trying to hide her enthusiasm. It was a pot of steaming melted cheese—it was fucking fantastic!

"Great," Simone said as she set her elongated dipping fork down on the table after only two bites.

"You're not done?" Wanda asked.

"Oh. I'm just taking a break."

"More for me and Ruby," Wanda replied.

Wanda seemed to be beside herself with pleasure as she dipped into the cheese and consumed her food while Ruby kept silently repeating the same thing over and over again. Slowly, slowly, slowly, she said to herself as she tried to control her actions and eat unhurriedly. When the pot was almost empty, Ruby managed to restrain herself from taking a cube of bread and wiping the pot clean.

When the cheese was finished, the server brought their salads. Wanda and Ruby expertly cleaned their plates as they watched Simone pick out a tomato and a cucumber or two before, once again, putting her fork down and "taking a break."

"Girl, you eat like a bird," Wanda said to Simone.

Simone smiled. "I'm just not that hungry."

Isn't that typical, Ruby thought. The skinny girls *never* get hungry; meanwhile, she was still starving after consuming half a pot of melted cheese and a hearty chef's salad.

"How did you find this place?" Ruby asked Wanda as the server appeared with a spread of raw meat, vegetables, and an array of sauces and started setting everything on the table.

"A date brought me to the one in Rockville last year. He was a dud, but I loved the restaurant."

"Really? What made him a dud?" Ruby asked, curious to hear about any of Wanda's men.

"He was nice to look at but not much going on upstairs. He was tall and lean with a handsome face and a caramel complexion . . ."

"Do people really say that?" Simone asked, interrupting Wanda. "Caramel complexion? I've heard it on the radio, but didn't know anyone really compared skin tone to food."

"Oh yeah. Girl, you've got to get with it. I'm chocolate Easter bunny brown. And you," Wanda said, sizing up Simone, "I'd say you're apple butter or maybe cinnamon toast."

"What about me?" Ruby asked.

"Hmmm. It doesn't really work for white folks. We just lump all of you into vanilla fudge."

"Oh," Ruby said, trying not to sound disappointed. Couldn't she be coconut cake or rice pudding or something?

"So what happened to caramel complexion guy?" Simone asked.

"Gosh. I don't even remember. I think I just never called him back. Oh wait . . . he was my HBO connection. I strung him along until last season's run of *Six Feet Under* was over. Then I gave him the heave-ho. I'm hoping to find another man with premium cable before it starts up again."

"How many guys have you dated?" Ruby asked Wanda. From the way she talked, it sounded like Wanda had dated hundreds of men.

"I lost count after high school, but I'd guess somewhere well into the triple digits. I've slowed down a little these days—only juggling a few men at the moment. The only one I see on a regular basis is Jackson. We were supposed to hook up tonight, but he got called into work."

"Really? What's he do?" Ruby asked.

"Girl, don't start me lying," Wanda said. "All I know is that he does something with computers. He programs them, or installs software . . . or blows them up for all I know. He's tried to explain it to me, but I usually just tune him out when he starts talking about work."

"Yeah, I'm a little technically challenged myself. Thank God for people like Jackson, who keep our computers up and running," Simone said.

"I guess," Wanda replied, as if the thought had never occurred to her. "At least he's employed."

Ruby laughed. "Yes. Employed is good. Not that it matters though, I guess. I don't really care what people do for a living," she added, trying to sound politically correct.

"Really? Not me," Wanda responded. "That's the first thing I ask a guy. I mean, how else am I to know if hooking up with him could ever amount to a Mercedes and a house in Potomac. Employment information is crucial. You never leave a first meeting without finding out his occupation, otherwise you could waste a perfectly good Saturday night with a waiter or parking attendant. Now don't tell me you don't find out what a guy does for a living before agreeing to go out with him?" Wanda asked Ruby.

"I don't. *Really*, I don't," Ruby replied, trying to sound convincing, even though she wasn't *really* lying. She *didn't* inquire about a guy's occupation before dating him but, then again, she didn't date.

"Ruby, you are a brave one. I try to make sure all the guys I date make at least six figures."

It was amazing to Ruby to listen to Wanda. From the way she talked, one might think she looked like Cindy Crawford or Tyra Banks. Wanda talked like she had options, like she had choices in the dating world. Ruby always figured that as a fat girl, she had to take what she could get, but Wanda was just as big as Ruby and, from the way she talked, Wanda had no shortage of suitors.

"What about you, Simone?" Wanda asked. "Don't you think it's important to know what a guy does for a living?"

"Oh, I don't know. I guess it depends on my intentions. If I were looking for a husband, I guess it would certainly be important, but, right now, I'm just having fun. At the moment, the size of his pecs and biceps are more important than the size of his wallet."

"Not to mention the size of certain other body parts," Wanda said with a laugh.

"I hear you. Don't be coming at me with one of those baby carrots," Simone replied, laughing.

The girls were obviously getting more comfortable with each other as the conversation started to turn toward sex—at least Wanda and Simone were getting more comfortable with each other. The more Wanda and Simone talked, the more Ruby felt like an outsider. She just didn't have much to add to the conversation. She hadn't been with a man since Warren, and she wasn't terribly comfortable talking about sex with two women who seemed so experienced. Actually, she wasn't terribly comfortable with them in general. She was starting to feel the way she always did—left out.

"My ex-husband was hung like a light switch," Ruby suddenly blurted out in a desperate effort to rejoin the conversation. She was on her third glass of wine, and her inhibitions were dwindling.

"Really? Is that why you divorced him?" Wanda asked.

"No. I'm not really a size queen—that's what my friend Jeremy calls gay guys that only sleep with well-hung men," Ruby articulated before adding, "Of course, I prefer a big dick, but it's not a deal breaker," Ruby said, hardly believing the words as they came out of her mouth. She almost sounded as if she actually dated and had sex—both of which she hadn't done in years.

"That's a good attitude," Simone said. "I suppose I wouldn't want some guy disregarding me because my boobs are too small."

Ruby laughed at Simone's comment even though she couldn't believe the bitch had the nerve to say that with her two perky D cups plopped on the table.

As the girls continued to chat, Ruby and Wanda feasted, and Simone nibbled a bit here and there. The more they talked, the more Ruby began to realize that her ex-husband Warren was a gold mine of conversation material. When Simone spoke of an old flame with an impotency problem, Ruby countered with how she could never look at Warren when he climaxed—the way he rolled his eyes would just make her laugh. When Wanda talked about a guy that only took her to places for which he had a coupon, Ruby matched her story with the time Warren took her to Taco Bell for their first anniversary. By the time the chocolate fondue arrived, Ruby had forgotten her nervousness, and was just having a good time. Wanda and Simone were including her in the conversation and laughing with her—loving her stories about Warren. He had been a lousy husband and a lousy lay, but, at least for one night at The Melting Pot in Arlington, Warren Waters was finally proving useful.

Thank you, Warren . . . you schmuck, Ruby said silently to herself as the girls divvied up the check and made their way out of the restaurant.

Missed Message

The morning after her evening at The Melting Pot with Wanda and Simone, Ruby reluctantly rolled out of bed after slamming the "off" button on the alarm clock. Now that she was sharing her home with two other women, she figured she'd better put on a bathrobe before heading downstairs to start the coffeemaker. In a morning haze she made her way to the kitchen, plugged in the coffeepot, and starting fumbling with the filters. As she tried to get her morning cup of java going, she noticed the light was blinking on her answering machine.

Why didn't I hear the phone? Ruby thought before realizing that she hadn't checked the machine before going to bed the night before. She pressed the play button and started scooping Maxwell House into the filter.

Beep: "Hello. This message is for Ruby Waters. My name is Florence. It's about eleven-thirty Sunday night. I'm a nurse at Civista hospital in LaPlata. Your mother Doris came to the ER last night with chest pains and difficultly breathing. She was evaluated here, and the doctor arranged for her to be transferred by ambulance to Fairfax Hospital. She should be there any moment. Please call me back as soon as possible." The nurse then left her phone number and hung up.

Ruby dropped the coffee can, her heart starting to palpitate, and hit the "play" button again. She started shaking as she listened to the message again.

"Oh my God!" she said to herself as she ran up the steps, threw a pair of jeans on under her nightshirt, slid her feet into a pair of loafers, and ran back down the steps. She grabbed her keys and raced toward the car. She maneuvered her Saturn through the city in heavy morning traffic until she got to Interstate 66, which would take her out to the hospital. When Ruby hit a rush hour snarl on the highway, she reached over to the passenger seat for her purse.

"Fuck!" she said out loud. She was in such a hurry to leave the house, she'd forgotten her purse, which meant she didn't have her cell phone. As she continued to crawl along the highway—stop and go, stop and go—she thought of Doris and how she constantly badgered Ruby about everything. The more she thought about it the idea of Doris not being around to pester her, to tell her how much better she'd look if she'd lose weight, to complain about the prices at IHOP, terrified Ruby. What would she do? Her father had passed away years ago, and she had no siblings. Doris was the only immediate family she had left. She was critical, stubborn, racist, and quite frequently, could be a royal pain in the ass, but Doris was *Ruby's* royal pain in the ass, and life without her became unthinkable.

Ever since Ruby was a teenager, she and Doris had a relationship reminiscent of Eunice and Mama on *The Carol Burnett Show*, but when push came to shove, they were there for each other. When Ruby came down with the flu a few years earlier, Doris only had to hear how awful she sounded on the phone before showing up at the door with soup, orange juice, and her old standby, Vicks VapoRub. Of course, the entire time she was helping Ruby return to health, she complained about how Ruby kept a dirty home, surmised that Ruby buying a house in such a neighborhood had just been plain foolish, and suggested that if Ruby were thinner, her immune system would be stronger, and she wouldn't have fallen sick in the first place.

When Ruby finally reached the hospital, she checked with the information desk and inquired where to find Doris. After a long wait for an elevator, Ruby found Doris in a recovery room, looking better than she had expected.

"They called you last night. This is the soonest you could get here?" Doris said weakly as she lay on a stretcher with monitors galore.

"I'm so sorry, Mom," Ruby said, and really did mean it. "I was out last night and didn't think to check the machine before I went to bed."

"Were you out with that interior designer friend of yours again?"

"No, Mom. I was out with my new roommates, and you know Jeremy's an accountant," Ruby replied, feeling a wave of relief. Doris couldn't have been that bad off if she was still taking jabs at Jeremy. "What happened?"

"I was washing the floor—you know, you did such a poor job last time you were over, and I really wanted to get it clean," Doris said in a fragile voice. "I just started having pain like I've never had before. I couldn't reach you, so I called Mrs. Jenkins, you know, that nice colored woman across the street, and she called an ambulance. Next thing I know, I'm here and they're shoving tubes in me . . ."

"It's called a cardiac catheter, Doris," said a middle-aged man with white hair and a stethoscope around his neck, who had just appeared in the doorway.

"I'm Dr. Sloan," he said to Ruby.

"This is my daughter, Ruby," Doris said, not wanting to forget her manners, even in a hospital bed. "She'd be right pretty if she'd drop some weight, don't you think?"

"Oh, I think she's pretty just the way she is," the doctor said in a patronizing tone.

Ruby offered an embarrassed smile, and shook hands with the doctor.

"I just got here. I only found out this morning. Is she going to be all right?"

"I expect her to make a full recovery. Your mother had significant plaque buildup in three of her arteries. Early this morning we did an angioplasty procedure to stretch her arteries and increase the blood flow. It's not a terribly invasive procedure, and she should be back on her feet in no time. She's running a slight fever, so we may need to keep her for a day or two, but I think she'll be fine very soon. Someone should probably stay with her for a few days once she's released."

The doctor then asked Doris a few questions about how she was feeling, made a couple of notes in her chart, and told Ruby that a nurse would be by later and could answer any of her questions.

"Thanks, Doctor," Ruby said as he walked off. "Looks like you'll be staying with me and my new roommates for a few days when you get out of here," she added, turning to Doris. She tried to sound upbeat, although the idea of Doris living with her, even for a short time, was already giving her goose bumps.

"I'll be fine on my own," Doris responded.

"I'm sure you would be, but you heard what the doctor said."

"The doctor hasn't seen your house or your neighborhood. Why don't you just stay at my house for a few days—" Doris said, before cutting herself off. Talking about her house had made Doris remember something. "Taco," she said. "Taco's been alone in the house since last night."

Ruby could see her mother's obvious unease and worry about the dog. "Don't worry about Taco. I'll go pick him up."

"But he doesn't like you," Doris responded.

"He doesn't like anyone, Mom. I'm sure I can coax him into the car one way or another. Look, you rest. I need to go make a couple of phone calls to the office and such. Don't worry about the dog. I'll take care of him. Just concentrate on getting well."

"But he doesn't like you," Doris repeated almost silently as she closed her eyes, and Ruby left the room in search of a phone.

True Beauty

Wanda hustled out the door. It was after nine-thirty, and she was supposed to be at the store by ten. She generally took the Metro out to Chevy Chase but, running late as she was, she decided she'd better hop in the car and try to get up Wisconsin Avenue as fast as she could. As she pulled out of her parking space, she dialed her cell phone.

"Hello. Can I have Women's Apparel," she said to the operator at Saks.

"Women's Apparel, Lynn Elliot speaking," Wanda's manager said after she picked up the phone.

"Hi. It's Wanda. There's been an accident on Wisconsin, and we're not moving. I've been sitting here for ten minutes," Wanda lied as she floored it through a yellow light.

"Okay, Wanda," Lynn said in a *yeah, yeah, whatever,* kind of tone. "Get here as soon as you can."

"I will," Wanda replied and hung up the phone. She knew Lynn didn't believe her, and she really didn't care. She had bigger things on her mind than schlepping overpriced designer clothes to people who had more money than brains. She worked at Saks for two reasons—to have the inside track on upcoming fashion shows, and to get her employee perks, which allowed her to afford flattering designer clothes and get free samples of the finest cosmetics. Lately, Wanda was becoming more and more determined to make it as a model and maybe later propel modeling into acting. If Star Jones could land a spot on *The View*, surely Wanda could have a future in the limelight. Wanda idolized Star—she was big and beautiful with no apologies—even if Payless wouldn't show her from the neck down in their shoe commercials. She remembered the first time she saw Star. It was probably sometime in 1997 when she happened upon an early episode of *The View,* and saw this meticulously dressed, enormous black woman with perfect skin, stylish makeup, and more wigs than all three Supremes put together. Wanda had never seen anything like her before. Of course there was Oprah, but Wanda never really saw Oprah as glamorous and Oprah certainly had never been at peace with her size.

When she first saw Star, Wanda was almost thirty and had only been really struggling with her weight for a few years. Wanda had always had full breasts and a big behind, but until her late twenties she'd had a relatively thin waist. It wasn't until sometime after her twenty-fifth birthday that her metabolism slowed down, and the weight began to pile on, which was somewhat disconcerting as Wanda had always been beautiful. When she was a little girl everyone commented on how pretty she was, and by the time she was sixteen, people were stopping in their tracks and turning around to get a second look at Wanda Johnson when she walked by. As she grew into a woman she became more than just pretty—she became a true beauty along the lines of Halle Berry and Vanessa Williams. Wanda tried to stay modest, but she knew the mirror didn't lie, and from a young age, she wanted to put her looks to use and become a model or an actress.

She grew up in a lower-middle-class neighborhood outside Trenton, New Jersey. Her mother died of breast cancer when she was very young, and her father, who never remarried, made ends meet for her and her two younger brothers working for the phone company for nearly twenty years. She'd planned to move to New York as soon as she graduated high school and take the modeling world by storm. She'd even had professional photographs taken and had started sending them to agents. She was set to leave for the Big Apple until three weeks before graduation when she got a call from one of her father's coworkers. He'd collapsed on the job and died of a heart attack. He was only fifty-two years old. He'd provided for Wanda and her brothers when he was alive but left little savings for them after his death. With only a small life insurance payout from the phone company, Wanda was left an orphan at seventeen with two young brothers to look after. She had to put her modeling aspirations aside and see that her brothers made it to school every day and had a roof over their heads. She knew what happened to too many young black men in her neighborhood, and she was determined to see her little brothers make it through school and have futures ahead of them.

She got a job checking groceries at Genuardi's and went straight from high school graduate to pseudo mom. She would have loved to have somehow gotten a start in the fashion world while she took care of her family, but the grocery store paid high union wages while the high-end department stores did not. Her youngest brother was only eight when their father passed away, and it took more than ten years to see him through school.

The entire time she was checking groceries, making lunches, and disciplining her brothers, she had the idea of modeling in the back of her mind. The only problem was that as she continued to work and raise her siblings, she got older and heavier. By the time she was able to let her brothers fend for themselves, she figured she was too old and too fat to be a model. But one day, while watching mid-morning television on a rare day off, she saw Ms. Star Jones on *The View,* and her wheels started turning. If there was room in show business for one fat black woman, there had to be room for another. The more she thought about it, the more confident she became about making it in the modeling industry, but this time, as a large-size model. She started making phone calls, and looking at Web sites, and got the details on the large-size modeling industry. As she did her research she became discouraged to find out that the industry standard for plus-size models ran from about a size ten to a size sixteen. What the fuck was that about? When did a size ten become plus size? Wanda remembered thinking.

She was well beyond a size sixteen and figured she had two choices: either give up the idea of modeling or lose weight, until, that is, she talked with an agent in New York that said, although a size sixteen was generally the maximum for models in New York and L.A., local shows in other cities often hired much larger models.

Wanda was still living in Trenton at the time, but with her brothers out of school, she did a little more research and decided on a move to powerful and wealthy Washington, D.C. She had friends there and knew the city and its suburbs were the home to the likes of Neiman Marcus and Saks and Bloomingdale's. It would be a great place to start in the local modeling scene, get some experience, and make a name for herself . . . and more importantly, lose weight.

When she made the final decision to move she was determined to make it, and when she arrived in D.C., she immediately found work at the Hecht's at Springfield Mall, which at least got her a foot in the door in fashion, but her struggle to lose weight didn't go as well. She tried all sorts of programs and diet plans, but while she was starting and stopping diets and losing a few pounds and gaining them back, a funny thing was happening—she was still getting work in local fashion shows and people were still telling her how beautiful she was. Finally, Wanda said to hell with it and decided she was going to give up dieting and watching what she ate. Her size had never really bothered her anyway. The only problem she really had with being a big woman was that she thought it would keep her from making it as a model, but the more she worked in the industry the less she believed that. She was going to be the first *real* large-size model to make it big—not this size ten to sixteen bullshit. She was going to break the glass ceiling (not to mention the glass walls) and show everyone that a woman of her size could be beautiful and sexy, and walk the runway with the likes of Claudia Schiffer and Naomi Campbell.

Commandeering the Dog

Ruby couldn't remember which key to use, so she tried three different ones before she was finally able to unlock the door to Doris's house. As soon as she swung it open, she saw Taco sitting up on the sofa scowling at her. She wasn't a stranger to him, so he couldn't be bothered to bark at her, which he viciously did to virtually anyone else that walked through the door. Doris was the only person that could pet, pick up, or otherwise interact with Taco, and everyone else was subject to his wrath. He was a tiny dog, barely larger than a squirrel, but when Doris had guests over, she usually had to lock Taco in the bedroom for fear of him attacking her visitors like a rabid raccoon.

Ruby was one of the few people Taco *tolerated*—he didn't like her, but he was used to her presence in the house. As long as she didn't try to touch him, get too close to him, or look at him for an extended period, he mostly ignored her. This arrangement generally worked for both parties, but today Ruby was going to have to approach the dog. Doris was going to be in the hospital overnight, and Ruby had to figure out a way to get Taco back to her house in the city—there was no way she was going to drive forty miles to LaPlata, Maryland, every day to walk and feed the dog while Doris recuperated.

"Hi, Taco," Ruby said in the friendliest tone she could muster.

Taco did not welcome this gesture of goodwill from Ruby.

She had broken their deal. Taco had always agreed to disregard her as long as she never attempted to engage him, but now she was speaking to him! Taco was immediately suspicious. He lifted his head from the sofa, looked at her, and then looked around the room as if he were making sure it was, in fact, *he* to whom Ruby was speaking.

"Hey, boy," Ruby said again in the high-pitched baby voice people often use when talking to animals.

Taco surmised that Ruby was, indeed, talking to him and immediately got to his feet, stretched out his neck, and showed his tiny Chihuahua fangs.

"Now, Taco. Be nice," Ruby said, trying to sound authoritative but friendly at the same time, but Taco was having none of it. He let out a slow growl that forbade Ruby to get any closer.

"Stop this nonsense, Taco. You've got to come home with me," Ruby said as she continued to approach the dog.

Taco responded with a loud bark that essentially said, *Like hell I do!*

As Ruby attempted to reach for the dog, he let out such a sudden and ferocious mixture of growling and barking that she retreated from him for fear of getting mauled.

"Oh, for heaven's sake," Ruby said as she stood back from the growling dog, trying to figure out how she was going to get the little beast in the car and back to her place. If she tried to pick him up, he would probably bite her. She continued to ponder the situation until she spotted an afghan lying on the chair next to the sofa. As Taco continued to anxiously watch her, Ruby reached for the afghan, shook it out, and approached the dog again. She quickly flung the afghan over the dog, and, as soon as the blanket landed, Ruby swooped it underneath Taco, and pulled the ends of the blanket together, creating a little Chihuahua sack. She held the sack with both arms, extending them as far away from her body as possible while Taco furiously squirmed and screeched from inside the blanket.

"Shut up, Taco," Ruby said to the dog as she grabbed his leash from the table, opened the door, and headed outside only to see Mr. Prescott, Doris's neighbor, tending to his flowerbed next door.

"Hello, Mr. Prescott," she said casually to him, trying to look calm and sedate as she walked toward her car—as if it were perfectly normal for a grossly overweight woman to be strolling along with a livid Chihuahua wrapped in an afghan sack.

When Ruby reached the car, she fought the urge to put Taco in the trunk, and opened the car door. After she sat the enraged dog in the back, she made her way to the driver's seat and turned around to look in the back. Taco had ceased barking, and was focusing on trying to make his way out of his crocheted prison. Once he'd maneuvered himself from underneath the blanket, he crawled to the other side of backseat and stood up on his hind legs to try to look out the window. As Ruby backed the car out, Taco began whimpering while frantically pacing back and forth along the backseat.

"It's okay, Taco," Ruby said in a soft voice. He looked so pathetic and lost, Ruby felt sorry for him. She had barely closed her mouth before Taco ceased whimpering and offered Ruby a cautionary growl. Once again, Ruby had broken their agreement and was talking to him, even if it was to comfort him.

"Fine, Rat Dog!" Ruby said, and decided to ignore him. She drove out of her mother's neighborhood, and started to make her way back into the city. If traffic was running smoothly, she could be home in an hour.

Shortly after she pulled away from the house she passed by the former Charles County Community College, which by this time had become the College of Southern Maryland. Every time she drove by the campus, she had flashbacks to the dreadful summer sports camp her parents had forced her to attend at the college when she was a kid.

Ruby could still picture those awful mornings with Doris calling her from the living room to hurry up so she could walk over to the campus for a day spent in the blistering heat. Much of the time, Ruby would call from her bed and say she didn't feel well. Sometimes Doris would let her stay home, but most of the time she harassed Ruby until it was less painful to get out of bed and out the door.

Ruby was always so grateful on the days Doris let her stay home. Of course, Ruby wasn't really sick. She just had no desire to spend eight hours in the blazing sun at the Charles County Community College Sports Camp. Her parents made her go to the stupid day camp two years in a row. Doris professed how good it would be for Ruby to get some exercise and not spend the summer in front of the television.

During her so-called sick days, after Doris had left for work, Ruby would hop out of bed, immediately turn the little plastic wheel on the thermostat to click on the air-conditioning, and make a run for the kitchen. Then she would go back in her bedroom with an array of snacks, turn on the television, and flip the channels. It was the early eighties and cable hadn't come to her neighborhood yet. She would make her way to Channel 7 and crawl back in bed to watch *Good Morning America.* There wasn't much else on that time of day, and there was something about David Hartman and Joan Lunden that was comforting at eight o'clock in the morning. Ruby liked to crank up the air-conditioning, snuggle under a blanket, and watch the news updates and the interviews. When she was twelve years old, watching *Good Morning America* made her feel like a grown-up. Sometimes she'd pour herself a cup of coffee from the pot her mother left on the counter every morning. She barely drank any, but watching the news with a cup of coffee made Ruby feel sophisticated and mature. She couldn't see herself in the mirror from her bed, and when the house was quiet, and her parents were at work, Ruby could sit in bed and pretend she was someone else—maybe Blair Warner or Mallory Keaton—someone thin and pretty with boyfriends galore.

On the days she lost her battle with Doris and ended up having to go to the camp, Ruby would make her way to the gym and walk down the steps to the basketball courts where all the camp attendees congregated first thing in the morning. Spending much of her mornings trying to convince Doris that she was too ill to attend camp often caused her to be a few minutes late.

When she finally got there, the groups had already been quieted down, and lined up in their respective rows, waiting to be herded out to a soccer field or a volleyball court for a day of what, in Ruby's eyes, was pure torture. Ruby always tried to join her group as discreetly as possible, but much of the time, Matthew Green, a wretched little boy that also attended the camp, just wouldn't let that happen. As she tried to quickly join her group, Matthew would almost certainly break the silence with a loud "Mooo." He had perfected it to an art form. He sounded just like a real live cow. Ruby wondered if he hadn't spent time on a farm spying on milk cows, and learning how to imitate their sound with total accuracy.

Ruby did what she always did when Matthew or anyone else did that sort of thing, she pretended not to hear him. She continued to walk and tried to look straight ahead so she wouldn't catch any glimpses of the other kids—some of whom were laughing at her, and others, who offered her looks of pity; she didn't care to see either. One might think that after years of such callous abuse, Ruby might have gotten used to obnoxious mooing or oinking noises, but she never got used to it. It always hurt, as much the first time as the last, but she wasn't going to let Matthew Green see her cry. She wasn't going to be the big fat crybaby. Oh, she would cry, but she refused to do it until she got home, or at least until she could make it to a bathroom stall or the side of a building where no one could see her.

Fashion Sense

"Any luck?" the young wardrobe attendant asked Wanda as she compared two plus-size suits, holding them in front of her as best she could with her arm still supported in her pesky sling.

"I think I'll go with this one," Wanda said, holding up a pant suit by Gianfranco Ferre Forma. "I love his designs—pure class. Let me go try it on."

Wanda was so excited to be one of the featured large-size models in Saks's upcoming show, one of the major shows of the year. Rumor had it that some major New York agents were going to be in the audience. She'd been in the back for almost twenty minutes sorting through a choice of outfits before she finally settled on the Gianfranco Ferre. The show wasn't for almost two weeks, but Wanda needed to select her outfit in advance to make sure it fit.

"Off the hook!" Wanda said out loud as she looked at herself in the mirror. The suit fit her perfectly. It was beige with nicely tailored pants and suede accents on the jacket. She'd even selected a pair of killer shoes to complete the flattering ensemble. The suit looked a bit plain on the hanger, but it had an understated elegance about it once Wanda tried it on. She was going to be stunning in the show.

As Wanda continued to admire herself, she caught a glimpse

of her associate, Denise, in the mirror behind her. Denise had her usual staid demeanor. She was one of those fat people that looked perpetually uncomfortable. She was always hot and constantly complained about the temperature setting in the store. Every now and then, Wanda would see her wiping her brow or fanning herself with a catalog. Wanda figured maybe that was why she was such a bitch—she was persistently overheated.

Wanda and Denise never had any great love for each other. In fact, Denise not only competed with Wanda on the sales floor, she competed with Wanda for spots in every fashion show in town. Wanda didn't bother saying hello as she watched Denise tuck a couple braids behind her ear. A few months earlier, Denise had added one braid of auburn hair to her nest of black strands, and even Wanda had to admit that it did add some style to an otherwise tired look. As usual, Denise had this gaudy Joan Rivers bumblebee pin attached to the lapel of her Anne Klein jacket. A few weeks earlier, Wanda overheard Denise telling a customer all about the silly brooch. She'd rambled on and on about how Joan Rivers professed that a bumblebee was not made to fly—something about the ratio of its body weight to its wingspan should have made it impossible for it to get off the ground. Yet it did; therefore achieving the impossible. Like Joan Rivers, Denise wore the pin as a symbol and a good luck charm. Wanda found the whole thing bizarre. The pin was ugly and why was a sister so enmeshed in the convictions of an old white lady whose skin was pulled so tight she couldn't shut her eyes to go to sleep?

"Miss Johnson?" Denise said to Wanda from behind. She had a hint of attitude in her voice.

"Yes, *Miss* Proctor," Wanda said, turning around. She hated when Denise called her Miss Johnson. Denise did it under the guise of respect, but Wanda knew she just did it to make her feel old.

"May I ask why you're wearing my suit?"

"Your suit?" Wanda questioned as she dramatically looked the suit up and down. "I don't see your name on it."

"Carlos promised me that suit. I picked it out yesterday."

"Carlos promised you the suit for what?" Wanda asked in disbelief.

"For the show next week."

"You're in the show?" Wanda asked with skepticism. Saks generally only featured two large-size models in their seasonal shows. Those two models were generally Wanda and Sarah McHatton, a big-boned white lady who sold Lancome cosmetics at the Tyson's Store. They both had seniority over Denise, so they had right of first refusal for every show. Of course, neither Wanda nor Sarah ever declined a show, which usually left Denise plumb out of luck. Denise had modeled for other stores in the area, but Wanda counted on her seniority keeping Denise out of Saks's shows indefinitely.

"I most certainly am. Carlos told me there was an opening last week."

Carlos managed all of Saks's shows. He picked the models, designed the sets, selected the music, and managed all the little details.

"Whatever. But I'm afraid this suit is mine. I picked it out days ago," Wanda lied. So what if she'd selected the outfit minutes earlier. It was a knockout suit, and she was not going to give it up, especially to the likes of Denise Proctor.

"And those are the shoes I picked out," Denise said with annoyance.

"Sweetie," Wanda replied with a smart smile. "These shoes aren't made for cloven hooves."

"Carlos! Are you back there?" Denise called like a tattletelling child.

"Yes. What is it?" Carlos said, emerging from a makeshift office down the hall.

"That's my suit. And my shoes! Tell her. You were here when I chose them. You told me to come back today to make sure they fit."

Carlos looked confused. "What are you doing here, Wanda?" he asked. "You certainly don't plan on appearing in *my* show with that sling?"

"I'll have the sling off by next Saturday, Carlos."

"Really. When I saw you in that contraption I assumed you wouldn't be available for the show, so I invited Denise to take your place."

"Well, *un*invite her," Wanda said. "I never said I wouldn't be appearing."

Carlos turned to Denise. "If this is the case, Denise, I'm afraid I can no longer offer you a spot on the runway."

"What? No way! You told me you had an opening," Denise snapped before glaring at Wanda, but still speaking to Carlos. "Besides, a woman of *her* advanced years shouldn't be in that suit. It's meant for more of a young, trendy clientele."

"Well, then, it's a shame we don't have any trendy young people available," Wanda replied. "If only the suit were meant for skanky hos, then you'd be perfect!"

"Ladies!" Carlos said. "Another word, and I'll report you both to Personnel. I'm sorry," he added, turning to Denise. "I'm afraid you can't participate in this show. Wanda has seniority, so it really is her call."

"But . . ."

"No buts," Carlos said, like a patronizing father. "End of discussion. Now you two behave," he scolded before heading back to his office.

"So sorry," Wanda said smartly before she turned to go back in the dressing room.

"You will be," Denise replied under her breath as she watched Wanda disappear behind the drawn curtain.

It had been several hours since her incident with Wanda, and Denise was still fuming. She'd managed to get Carlos's home phone number and told him that she *had* to see him. He suggested they talk at the store the next day, but Denise insisted on seeing him that evening. When she arrived at his apartment in Bethesda, she gave herself a quick check in the mirror, stroked her bumblebee pin for good luck, and hopped out of the car.

"Hi," Carlos said, after opening the door.

"Hello," Denise replied, looking down at her blouse, making sure her tits looked okay.

"Please, come in," Carlos said and let Denise follow him to the living room. "I hope this isn't about the fashion show. My hands are tied."

"Well, to be honest," Denise replied, "I was hoping that maybe I could sway you to change your mind and let me appear. This is an important show. New York agents are going to be there. I really need to be in it."

"I wish I could help you, Denise, but we have two outfits in your size. Wanda is wearing one and Sarah is wearing the other."

"What about that great David Dart ensemble I saw? It could be altered to fit me," Denise said.

"What, are you new here?" Carlos asked, looking at Denise like she was a fool. "You must know that we never alter garments for the shows. Models must fit the clothes, not the other way around. We simply don't have an outfit for you, Denise."

"So dump that Wanda heifer, then."

"She has seniority . . ."

"Oh, come on. For me?" Denise said coyly, moving in closer to Carlos, pulling him toward her with his belt. "I'd make it worth your while," she added, feeling him up and starting to unbuckle his belt.

Carlos started laughing as he backed away from her touch. "Are you joking me? I manage women's fashion shows. Did you really think I'd be interested in some nasty hair pie?"

Denise tried to hide her disappointment. Well, she thought, if sex wouldn't get her a spot in the show, she'd use her next most powerful weapon.

"All right, Carlos," she said, reaching into her purse and pulling out her checkbook. "How much is it going to cost me?"

"I can't be bribed, Denise."

"A thousand dollars? Two thousand?"

"Where on earth would a salesgirl at Saks get a couple thousand dollars?"

"Do you think I schlep clothes around Saks for the money? I

don't need any money, Carlos. What I need is a spot in the show."

"Hmm . . ." Carlos said, and paused for a moment. He really didn't understand how someone in the lower levels of retail had two thousand dollars to throw around, but the more he thought about it, the less he cared where the money came from. "Two thousand dollars you say?"

"Make it three," Denise replied with a smile and pulled out a pen.

Chubby Chasers

"I don't know. I just feel sorry for lesbians. I mean, they have no access to dicks," Jeremy said to Ruby and Wanda. The three of them were in Ruby's kitchen trying to pull dinner together. "I mean straight girls have their men's dicks, straight boys have their own dicks, and gay guys, well, we have dicks galore. But lesbians . . ."

"Jeremy. Whatever they don't have, they can always strap on," Wanda said with a laugh as Ruby observed the two of them. Wanda had just met Jeremy only minutes earlier, and was already dishing with him like they were old friends. Wanda's immediate ease with virtually everyone amazed Ruby, and she was a tad jealous over how much Jeremy seemed to be enjoying Wanda's company. As Ruby peeled potatoes over the trash can and made a mental note to limit Jeremy's interaction with Wanda, the voices started:

You're not going to eat any of these potatoes you're peeling.—Okay, maybe one or two bites.—You're going to mostly eat the green beans, maybe a little chicken.—Oh my God, these mashed potatoes are going to be so good. Maybe if I don't eat any green beans, I can have more mashed potatoes.

"Move, doggie," Wanda said to Taco, who was cowering at her feet, hoping some food would drop to the ground. From the time Ruby brought him to her place, he'd kept his distance from her and growled viciously when Jeremy first walked through the door, but for some reason, he seemed to take a liking to Wanda. He had hopped up on the sofa next to her earlier and was now following her all over the kitchen.

It had been a long day, and it was nice to unwind with Jeremy and Wanda. Ruby had spent all morning at the hospital with Doris, trekked out to LaPlata and abducted the dog, and still had to go put a few hours in at the office. By the time she got home, she was exhausted, but pleasantly surprised to see that Jeremy, after hearing of Doris's hospitalization, had stopped by with groceries and plans to make her dinner. Wanda had worked the day shift at Saks, and she and Jeremy had already started putting the meal together when Ruby walked in the door.

"Do we have any mustard?" Wanda asked. "I need to add some to the marinade." Wanda was concocting some sort of mixture to coat the chicken breasts Jeremy had purchased earlier, while Ruby prepared mashed potatoes, and Jeremy snapped green beans.

"In the fridge," Ruby replied.

As Wanda reached for the jar of French's, she caught a glimpse of Simone's personal shelf in the refrigerator. "My God. Look at this," Wanda said, pointing to Simone's stash of yogurt, vegetables, and low-fat condiments. "Jennifer Lopez thinks she's all that," Wanda added, referring to Simone, who had left for the station a couple of hours earlier.

"Really," Ruby added. "If everyone ate the way she did, the Safeway would go out of business."

"I imagine she's perpetually starving," Jeremy said. "But I guess there's so much pressure to be thin in her business."

"What do you say, when she gets home, you and Jeremy hold her down, and I'll force feed her a pizza," Wanda joked to Ruby.

"A pepperoni pizza, large," Ruby replied. "Loaded with cheese."

"Stop it," Wanda said, laughing. "You're going to make me toss this chicken and go looking for some New Jersey Pizza."

"*New Jersey* Pizza?" Ruby questioned, having never heard the term before.

"What is it? Dirty?" Jeremy jabbed from the other side of the counter.

"No," Wanda replied, rolling her eyes. "You know, pizza with the thin crust. I guess most people call it New York style, but since I'm from New Jersey . . ."

"I guess everyone has their favorite kind of pizza and their favorite place to get it—that and hamburgers, everyone claims to know where to get the best hamburger."

"Someone told me that Hamburger Mary's up the street is good," Wanda said.

"No, not Hamburger Mary's. They put their burgers on funky wheat bread. Fuddruckers! Now that's the place for burgers," Ruby replied.

"Obviously, neither of you have been to Five Guys in Alexandria," Jeremy chimed in. "They have the best burgers. I went there with Jorge and Roger last week. And my God, you should have seen that Roger toss back those burgers. He ordered two and then Jorge went back and got him another one."

"Isn't Jorge the one that's always pushing food on Roger?" Ruby asked, remembering an evening she spent with them at The Chop House. They had just gotten out of the Madonna concert at the MCI Center. There were all in a bad mood after watching her "Drowned World" tour—for some bizarre reason Madonna seemed to think people wanted to hear obscure songs like "Candy Perfume Girl" and "Sky Fits Heaven" instead of her hits like "Vogue" or "Like a Virgin"—either that, or she just didn't give a rat's ass what her fans wanted to hear. As they cursed the Material Girl for charging insane amounts of money for her concert tickets and then putting on a show that no one wanted to see, they decided to stop at the Chop House for a quick after-the-concert bite. When they placed their orders, even Ruby was amazed at the amount of food Roger ordered. What was more amazing was that Jorge encouraged him to order even more. "These onion rings look good," she remembered Jorge saying to Roger. "Why don't you get an order of these too. And maybe some of the fried calamari."

"Oh yeah. Jorge is always trying to tempt Roger with desserts and fried food."

"I know I'm not one to talk, but Roger is so grossly overweight. Why does Jorge keep encouraging him to eat more?" Ruby asked. Ruby always prefixed any negative statement about someone else's weight or appearance with "I know I'm not one to talk, but . . ." or something like "I know I need to lose weight myself, but . . ."

"Sounds like Jorge is a chubby chaser," Wanda said.

"Of course he's a chubby chaser. I've known him for twelve years, and I've never seen him date anyone that wasn't enormous."

"Chubby chaser?" Ruby inquired.

"Yeah, you know, someone who only dates fat people. Girl, what I could tell you about my experience with chubby chasers and *chocolate* chubby chasers," Wanda said.

"Chocolate chubby chasers?" Ruby asked again.

"Chubby chasers that are partial to large black women," Wanda said.

"Or large black men," Jeremy corrected.

"Ruby, you've really never heard the term 'chubby chaser' before?" Wanda asked.

"I guess. My ex-husband was one of them, but I had no idea they had an official name."

"They're all over the place. I personally don't care for them," Wanda said. "Of course, I like men to appreciate my size, but I don't want that to be the main reason they're attracted to me. There is so much more to Wanda Johnson than her queen-size panty hose."

"Yeah. I don't think I'd be interested in a guy like that either. I have enough problems trying not to gain any more weight without some man pushing even more food on me," Ruby said, even though the idea of an entire population of men attracted to large women intrigued her immensely. As she started slicing the potatoes, she thought about where she might find some of these men. Did they meet anywhere? Was there a chubby chaser community center? A bar or nightclub they frequented? Then it hit her. Of course! She knew exactly where to find them—where else? The World Wide Web.

Grocery Shopping

Simone pulled her Mercedes into the parking lot of the social Safeway in Georgetown. She reluctantly walked into the grocery store and selected a cart. It was such drudgery—grabbing a cart and pushing it through the aisles like a common housewife. She hated grocery shopping. She seriously doubted Deborah Norville or Leeza Gibbons did their own grocery shopping—one day she wouldn't have to, either.

Simone scooted the metal basket directly toward the produce section and perused the selection of fruits and vegetables. She grabbed a stalk of broccoli and some romaine lettuce and put it in the cart. Then she added a bag of green beans and some cherry tomatoes. When she picked up a bag of baby carrots a small woman on the other side of the produce stand smiled at her. The petite stranger had a large horsey face and mammoth teeth. She had almost certainly recognized Simone from the news and the local magazine covers, and couldn't help but show a little glee. Horsey-Face-Big-Teeth offered a kind of smile that Simone had gotten used to getting from strangers. People were always smiling at her. An hour later they would be able to go home and tell their friends and family that they had seen Simone Reyes in the grocery store. Simone used to smile back at these people—it seemed like the only polite thing to do. At first it was so gratifying. It was what she had always wanted—fame and notoriety, but after several months of people repeatedly walking by her table at local restaurants just to get a look at her, incessant requests for autographs and pictures, and a few unfortunate incidents when she was followed into the ladies' room, Simone stopped making eye contact with strangers. If she didn't make eye contact, she found people were much less likely to bother her. Of course, if someone still directly approached her, Simone was always polite and gracious. She didn't want to let her fans down, and had no intention of getting a Christina Aguilera reputation as an ungrateful bitch—it wouldn't be good for her career.

Simone continued through the produce aisle and made her way to the dairy section where she picked up a few containers of yogurt and cottage cheese. When she left her cart for just a moment to grab some skim milk, Horsey-Face-Big-Teeth quickly walked by Simone's basket and tried to discreetly check out its contents. After all, when she told her friends that she had seen Simone Reyes in the grocery store, they were bound to ask what she had bought. Simone was clearly aware of this, and chose her groceries carefully. When she did her shopping at the Safeway, she filled the cart with all sorts of healthy glamorous foods. Before she put anything in the cart, she thought to herself, would Suzanne Sommers buy this? Would Calista Flockhart put this in her basket? It was a total drag. She had to bypass the Turkey Hill ice cream in favor of the frozen yogurt, and buy whole wheat bread instead of the soft white loaf of Sunbeam that she loved so much.

Simone continued shopping, fully aware that Horsey-Face-Big-Teeth was virtually stalking her, and noting every item she pulled from the shelf. She picked up a couple of Lean Cuisine and Healthy Choice frozen meals from the freezer, grabbed a small container of sorbet, and made her way to the checkout counter.

God! Is there anything more tedious than grocery shopping? Simone thought to herself as she started emptying the contents of her cart onto the conveyer belt. It was maddening to handle groceries so many times—picking them from the shelves, lifting them onto the checkout counter, hauling them out to your car, lugging them from the car to the house, and then removing them from their bags and putting them away, just so they could be handled a few more times at a later date.

Once Simone had emptied her cart, she noticed the man in front of her in line. He was waiting for the cashier to give him a total as his two daughters wreaked havoc on the candy display. Simone had little experience with children, but she guessed the two girls to be about three and five.

"No, Kaley," he said to the younger daughter. "Put that back."

"No!" Kaley replied defiantly while grasping a king-size Butterfinger.

"Can I have some change for the gumball machine?" the older daughter asked.

"No, Haley," the father replied.

Kaley and Haley? Was that on purpose? Simone thought as she observed the father interacting with his children. She guessed him to be a stay-at-home dad. After all, most employed fathers were not at the grocery store with their kids at eleven-thirty in the morning.

"Please," Haley insisted.

"No. You have juice and fruit at home," the father continued, trying to sound firm, but Simone could tell Haley was going to get her change for the gumball machine with just another nudge or two.

Working evenings, Simone ran most of her errands during the day and occasionally ran into this new breed of men—stay-at-home fathers. She did a feature on them for the news a while back. She put on a good facade and told all the house-husbands how she believed staying at home and taking care of kids was as demanding as any job, but in reality, she didn't buy it. In fact, she was totally turned off by these guys. She'd see them in the grocery store or at the mall with one hand on a stroller, and the other grasping the hand of a barely walking toddler. A few weeks earlier she saw one of these fathers in the condiment aisle explaining how to spot values to a toddler barely old enough to speak. "See. The generic peanut butter is seventy-five cents cheaper than the Jif," Simone heard him say to the little boy. As she observed the man showing the kid a coupon and explaining how that would amount to even more savings she couldn't help thinking: Oh, for Christ's sake. Get a job! Ya fuckin' pussy! There was just something so emasculating about a man sorting coupons or pushing a cart through Target, looking for a deal on tampons for his wife.

Simone watched Stay-at-Home Dad cave and give a quarter to Haley and let Kaley put her candy bar on the counter so he could pay for it. She continued to look on as the cashier rang up his total, and stay-at-home dad pulled his checkbook from his back pocket and started patting himself down in search of a pen.

Oh my God! Simone thought to herself, looking at the man. Who writes checks anymore? Do you live in a cave? Did you come here in a horse and buggy? she thought as she grabbed a pen from her own purse, handed it to the man, and smiled, effectively hiding her annoyance.

When Simone had finally charged her groceries to her Visa, she made her way out to the parking lot and loaded the bags in the car. She closed the trunk, turned around, and almost screamed. Horsey-Face-Big-Teeth was standing within inches of her with a pad of yellow stickies and a pen. She had completely startled Simone.

"I'm sorry," Horsey said. "I didn't mean to scare you. I was just hoping to get an autograph. You're Simone Reyes? Right?"

"Of course," Simone said, trying to offer a pleasant smile as she accepted the pad and pen. "Who should I make it out to?"

"Carol," Horsey replied. "I'm such a fan. I never watched the news until I saw you on Channel 6. You always look so pretty . . . and your clothes . . . they dress you in the sharpest clothes."

As Horsey continued to gush, Simone scrawled a quick note

on the pad, shook her hand, and thanked her for her kind words. As soon as Horsey walked off, Simone quickly climbed into the car and took off. She'd had a few determined fans follow her in their cars in the past, and she didn't want to give Horsey the chance.

Once Simone was out of the parking lot she drove up the street a few miles and turned into a 7-Eleven. After she had parked the car, she pulled a floral scarf and a pair of sunglasses from the glove compartment. She put on the sunglasses, wrapped the scarf around her head, hurried into the store, and quickly combed a few of the aisles like a woman on a mission. She raided the Hostess stand, grabbing individual packs of orange cupcakes, fruit pies, and HoHos. She pulled a bag of Funyuns and a cylinder of Pringles from the chips display, and, before heading to the register, she snatched a can of Bush's baked beans from the shelf—her mouth watering with every selection.

"Hi," the cashier said, as Simone dumped her goodies on the counter.

"Hola," Simone replied, pretending not to speak English as the cashier rang up and bagged her items. *"Gracias,"* Simone added after he handed her the bag.

She hustled out of the store, quickly climbed into the car, and drove off. She kept her 7-Eleven buys in the front seat, separate from the healthy items she had just bought from the Safeway. The low-calorie wholesome foods would go in the kitchen for Ruby and Wanda to see, while her 7-Eleven booty would go upstairs in her room.

As Simone headed home, she removed the scarf and sunglasses, and settled in for the ride home. She felt a little ridiculous. After all, she should be able to buy whatever she wanted without any judgment, but she had an image to protect. Simone was determined to be a success and being the darling of Washington, D.C., was not enough. Simone Reyes was going to go national. She hadn't yet figured exactly how or when, but it was going to happen. Simone was going to make it happen. And if becoming a national celebrity meant she had to occasionally don a disguise to buy junk food, then so be it. It would be worth it—one day, when she was sitting across from Barbara Walters or Diane Sawyer, talking about her road to success, it would all be worth it.

RockinRuby

It had only been a day since the evening that Jeremy and Wanda had talked to Ruby about chubby chasers while they prepared dinner, and Ruby was in her bedroom sitting at her computer. It was after eleven P.M., and she had just gotten home from visiting Doris at the hospital and running a few other errands. She was trying to enjoy her last few days before Doris came to stay with her and recuperate from her procedure. Ruby was pointing and clicking her mouse on various Web sites. She had done a Google search on the words "chubby chaser," and the results were overwhelming. Ruby found clothing stores with T-shirts that said "Plump Perfection," a religious site stating that God was a chubby chaser, a "gay chubby chaser playground," the list went on and on, but she couldn't seem to find any interactive sites where she might actually meet men attracted to large women.

Ruby generally didn't spend much time on-line at home. She was reasonably competent on her computer at work, and surfed the Net from time to time to check movie times or book a plane ticket, but that was about it. After her relationship with Warren had gone sour she went through a brief period in which she signed into the AOL chat rooms in hopes of meeting men. She used to log in under the name "RockinRuby." She'd chat with a few guys here and there, but the moment she mentioned her size, virtually every man with whom she chatted would either immediately log off, or doors and phones would suddenly need answering.

Based on her brief experience, she had given up on the whole chat room scene, but after hearing Wanda and Jeremy babble on about these so-called "chubby chasers," Ruby figured there must be a chat room for them. My God! There were chat rooms for Dolly Parton fans, chat rooms for people who worshiped Elvis, chat rooms for people who drove Volkswagen Bugs, there had to be a fucking chat room for men who loved large women.

It was after midnight when Ruby finally stumbled onto a Web site called Big Girls, Don't Cry! It was like the title of the site was speaking to her—not like the song, which seemed to state that big girls, in fact, do not cry. This site seemed to be issuing a request or command—*telling* big girls not to cry. Why should they, when they had this great Web site just for them?

She perused the site and found all sorts of interesting things. There were galleries of pictures of naked or scantily clad overweight women, live streaming peep shows, an on-line store, and, most importantly, an opportunity to chat on-line with men "in your local area." The chat area was organized by areas of the country, which were further subdivided into cities and towns. Ruby clicked on the Washington, D.C. link and counted forty-seven participants. There seemed to be an almost equal mix of men looking to meet large women, and large women looking to meet men. The men had screen names like "Like'emBig" or "BringOnthePounds" while the women had names like "BigBertha" or "RotundRoxanne." From the looks of the site and the screen names of the people involved, it was obvious that this was not a place to start a long-term relationship—it was a place to hook up for sex, which wasn't Ruby's intention, but it couldn't hurt to log on and see what happened.

Ruby filled in the required information and completed an on-line profile. Using her AOL standby, she logged in as RockinRuby, which was of course, completely out of character. Ruby was a lot of things, but "rockin" was not one of them. She had no idea what to say in her profile, but figured it didn't really matter. It wasn't like she was going to run into the epitome of high society in a large woman sex site. After a few moments she settled on the following:

> *RockinRuby: 32-year-old large woman in Logan Circle, red hair, blue eyes, big boobs, looking for whatever . . .*

Somehow, being in the seedy chat room was exciting to Ruby. She had just logged into a world where men were paying a subscription to watch live large woman sex shows, view pictures of fat women in skimpy negligees, and chat with women like her. The whole thing was wonderfully sleazy. It made her feel naughty and mischievous, feelings Ruby was not used to having.

She didn't have the nerve to be the initiator and start a conversation with anyone, so she decided to wait for someone to approach her, which didn't take long. She had only been in the chat room for a minute or two when "LoveLarge" instant-messaged her.

LoveLarge: hi rockinruby

RockinRuby: hi

LoveLarge: sup?

RockinRuby: not much . . . u?

LoveLarge: horny as hell

It was so funny to Ruby. In person, people were afraid to say so much as "boo" to each other, but on-line, a complete stranger had no problem telling her he was "horny as hell." Ruby clicked on LoveLarge's profile. Like hers, it wasn't very detailed. It said little more than that LoveLarge was "looking for a big girl that could handle a big guy."

RockinRuby: me too

Ruby wasn't actually feeling horny, but what else was she supposed to say?

LoveLarge: you have a great profile!

RockinRuby: thanks

LoveLarge: how large, if i may ask?

RockinRuby: oh, quite large

LoveLarge: how large?

RockinRuby: i'm a big girl

LoveLarge: mysterious, eh?

RockinRuby: absolutely

What a riot! Ruby thought. She was "mysterious." She knew nothing about him—what he looked like, how old he was, where he lived, but she was flirting on-line with some guy named LoveLarge. Ruby Waters was flirting! Flirting!

LoveLarge: so what brings you on-line, ruby?

RockinRuby: just bored

LoveLarge: bored? . . . we can fix that. I'm picturing you from your profile and it's totally turning me on.

RockinRuby: thanks

Oh God, that was so lame, Ruby thought. He tells her that she's "totally turning him on," and the best reply she can come up with is "thanks"?

LoveLarge: you're welcome. you're near logan circle?

RockinRuby: yeah

LoveLarge: Alexandria here . . . not far

RockinRuby: no

LoveLarge: what are you looking for?

RockinRuby: whatever . . . any ideas?

LoveLarge: hmm . . . you've got me hot, rockinruby

She'd gotten him hot? *Hot*? Ruby hadn't gotten a man "hot" since she made Warren pull weeds in ninety-eight degree weather a few years earlier.

LoveLarge: i'd love to feel your voluptuous body . . . caress it . . . lick it . . . massage it!

Ruby was starting to throb in places she hadn't felt much more than a tingle in quite some time. This unknown man was making her feel something—something she hadn't really ever felt before. Ruby wasn't positive, but she thought that maybe, just maybe, she was feeling sexy.

LoveLarge: i'd love to meet you

Meet her? YIKES!

RockinRuby: maybe

LoveLarge: how about tonight . . . i could show you a time you'd never forget

Yeah right, Ruby thought. Like I'm going to meet some complete stranger in the middle of the night.

LoveLarge: you could "cum" over here, we could have a few glasses of wine, get to know each other

RockinRuby: maybe

Oh God! Ruby thought as she realized that she might actually be considering meeting this man. It was ridiculous. She didn't know anything about him, but she also hadn't had sex in two years. Maybe this was her moment. As Arsenio Hall used to say, maybe it really was time for her "to get *busy*!"

LoveLarge: well, i'll be on-line for a bit longer if you decide you want to have the night of your life, catch ya later

Shit, she was losing him. If she didn't agree to come over he was going to move on to some other fat girl with the screen name PlumpPenelope or LargeLola. Ruby felt light-headed, and her body got a tad misty as she took a deep breath. She was visibly shaking when she clicked a response on the keys.

RockinRuby: if i'm going to come over, i'll need your address

Channel Surfing

Wanda was upstairs in her bedroom with Taco lying on the floor next to her bed. Ruby had tried to coax him into her room, but he was sticking with Wanda. Wanda wasn't a big fan of dogs and there was no way she was letting him up in the bed with her, but she was willing to tolerate him sleeping on the floor.

Wanda was surfing the channels on her television when she came across an interview with Jill Whelan, the woman who had played Captain Stubing's daughter Vicki on *The Love Boat*. It was a *Lifetime Intimate Portrait* or an *E! True Hollywood Story* or some shit like that. Wanda hated those kinds of shows, but nonetheless, she always got pulled into them. Actually, she didn't so much hate them as much as she feared them. They were always about some washed up celebrity, who, in many cases, was still younger than Wanda when his or her career went south. Every time Wanda turned on one of those biographies, they seemed to showcase some former A-list actress who hadn't been able to land a decent role in years, saying how she was "just focusing on being a mother now," as if she wouldn't sell her first-born into slavery if someone would just cast her in anything other than a late night infomercial. It was funny to Wanda how they always said they were focusing on "motherhood" because, if nothing else, it sounded remotely noble . . . at least more noble than, say, focusing on their car-detailing business, or their new career folding denim at the Gap.

Wanda watched these specials the same way people watched horror movies. They scared her, and made her uneasy, but at the same time, they drew her in and wouldn't let go. They just reminded her how brutal the entertainment industry was, and how one minute you're the hottest ticket in town and next thing you know, the only work you can get is in a Lifetime movie with Tori Spelling and Meredith Baxter. Wanda was already thirty-five and watching these programs made it so much harder to be positive about making it in the modeling business. She had so many things against her—her race, her weight, her age—the list seemed to keep going. But she also had her determination, her charisma, and innate beauty, things she had to keep bringing back to her attention as she watched the Jill Whelan special come to a close with Jill talking about how she hadn't worked much of late because of her commitment to motherhood.

When the credits started rolling on the special, Wanda started clicking on the remote control until she landed on the *Tonight Show*. Jay Leno was interviewing Halle Berry about her latest movie and, of course, they made mention of her 2002 Academy Award. Wanda liked Halle Berry and thought she was beautiful, but it bugged her that when she won for Best Actress, every newscast in town was talking about how she was the first *black* woman to win an Oscar while the camera kept flashing to her *white* mama. Wanda was happy that at least someone who referred to herself as black won the Oscar, but somehow, it was still representative of how far Hollywood hadn't come since the days of Dorothy Dandridge and Lena Horne—that the first black woman to win an Oscar was, in actuality, only half black.

Watching award shows like the Academy Awards, the Emmys, and the Golden Globes always made Wanda sick to her stomach. Minorities were so underrepresented in Hollywood it was ridiculous. This really came to light a year or two earlier when Wanda and some of the other salesgirls at work were playing a little game, trying to decide which actress would play each of them if a movie were to be made about their lives. It was amazing how many actresses the white girls had to pick from—Sarah Smith picked Sela Ward to play her, and Betsy Carter decided on Meg Ryan. Wanda had only a few choices when it came to black actresses, and even fewer when it came to fat black actresses. It was pretty much Oprah Winfrey (who was only fat some of the time) or Star Jones . . . or maybe the Pine-Sol Lady—none of whom could really be considered *movie* stars. Things were even worse for Nora Valdez, who was from Peru. She pretty much had three choices: Salma Hayek, Jennifer Lopez, or Penelope Cruz. And Lord help poor Janice Kim—she was Asian. If Lucy Liu wasn't available, she was just plumb out of luck.

But Wanda didn't let any of Hollywood's racial nonsense deter her dreams. She hadn't let putting her career off for several years to take care of her brothers get in her way. She hadn't let her weight get in her way. She hadn't let countless rejection letters from New York City modeling agencies get in her way. Hell, if Oprah Winfrey could be the richest woman in America, Wanda Johnson could make it as a model.

Preppy White Boys

It was just after midnight when Simone was finally able to get out of the station and head home. She wrapped the news at eleven-thirty, but there was always something to take care of before she could leave. She had to remove her makeup, return the suit to wardrobe, and occasionally tape a voice-over or something before she could make for the exit.

It had been a long day, and Simone was in a hurry to get home and hit the bed. It was only about a fifteen minute drive from the station to Ruby's house. Simone was about half-way there when the car made a loud thud into one of D.C.'s infamous potholes and a loud clank coming out of it.

"Shit!" Simone said as the right side of her Mercedes dropped and started screeching down the road. She hit the brakes and pulled to the side of the road.

"Shit," she said again as she reached in her purse for her cell phone. She rummaged around for a bit, and then remembered she had probably left it on the dressing table in her office. She looked around her. Her tire had bit the dust on 14th Street just a few blocks from the Washington Monument. It wasn't a particularly bad neighborhood, but it was late, and, aside from the occasional passing car, there was no one around.

"Why didn't I spring for the OnStar system?" she muttered to herself as she got out of the car, stepped to the other side, and surveyed the damage. The tire was completely flat. She stood there for a moment, alternating between looking at the tire and looking around her to make sure no midnight derelicts were coming toward her. She was about to step toward the trunk and look for the spare tire, but then decided against it. She wasn't sure she knew how to change a tire, and besides, she just *wasn't* going to change it. Simone Reyes was not going to change her own goddamn tire! There was a big Marriott just a few blocks up the street. She figured she'd just walk to the hotel, call the auto club to come and get the car, and then maybe call Ruby or Wanda to come pick her up. She was about to head in the direction of the hotel when a shiny BMW pulled up behind her.

Simone's heart started racing as she watched the car come to a complete stop, and the driver's door open. Hopefully it was someone wanting to offer assistance—hopefully not someone who wanted to rape and murder her. Simone could do nothing else but look as a young man in a jacket and tie emerged from the car. He was a handsome white guy in a sharp suit and trendy black-rimmed eyeglasses. He had the typical corporate climber hair-cut—clipped short and styled with gel, light eyes, and a hot body. Simone could see his definition, even behind the suit.

"Need some help?" he asked.

Simone took a sigh of relief. "Ah, yeah. I sure do."

"Flat tire?" he said, approaching her and taking a look at the car. "I can change it for you in just a few minutes."

"Oh, would you? I'd so appreciate that," Simone said. "I guess the spare is in the trunk."

Simone opened the trunk for the young man, watched him take off his jacket, roll up his sleeves, and start removing the spare from the back of her car. Simone had always been attracted to the Banana Republic/J. Crew type, and this guy had preppy white boy written all over him. Simone observed while he went to work and actually started to feel aroused as he jacked up the car. A young corporate guy in a tie with his sleeves rolled up doing man's work—it didn't get any sexier than that.

How hot is that? Simone said to herself as she looked on. "Gosh, you really seem to know what you're doing."

"I've always had a knack with cars. This one's a beauty by the way."

He was on his knees with his head about level with her pelvis, and for a minute, Simone thought he was talking about her lower half.

Simone hesitated for a moment. "Oh! The car. Yeah, it's great."

Simone figured he couldn't be more than twenty-five or so. He just had a young look about him.

"I'm Simone, by the way," she said as the young man pulled the flat tire from the car.

"Eric," he replied. "Nice to meet you. What are you doing out so late? All by yourself?"

"Just working late."

"Working late? It's after midnight. You'd better ask for a raise," he replied, taking a quick look at his watch.

Apparently Eric was not a news watcher, or maybe he just didn't recognize Simone at first glance.

"And you?" Simone asked.

"Me what?"

"What are you doing out so late? Wait, don't tell me. Someone else was working late too?"

"Yeah."

"Maybe *you* should ask for a raise."

"I guess we both should," Eric replied before he finished putting on the spare tire and lowered the car back down. "Good as new."

"Thank you so much!"

"Oh, no problem. Drive safely," he said as he tossed the jack back in her trunk, and closed the top.

Drive safely. What a cute thing to say. Simone thought. She didn't know what else to do. She felt like she should offer him a few bucks or something, but from the looks of his own car he certainly didn't need it, and, somehow, asking if there was anything she could do to repay him would have sounded cheap—why not just say, Want to come home and fuck me as a thank-you for changing my tire?

As she watched him walk back to his car, she had a fleeting feeling that she would be an idiot to let him go. She knew that she was probably a good ten years older than him, but walking away with his sleeves rolled up, a loosened tie, and black residue on his hands, he was just so goddamn cute!

"Do you have an early day tomorrow?" she called behind him.

"Umm . . . no," he said, turning around.

"Can I buy you a drink to say thanks?" she said with a smile, actually feeling nervous, which just turned her on even more. It wasn't often that men made Simone anxious. It wasn't that she was afraid Eric might find her too mature or overbearing. She was actually afraid he might just have been too decent to accept a midnight drink invitation.

"Right now?" Eric asked.

"Sure," Simone replied. Of course she meant right now. Now maybe if she hadn't intended on having him in her bed within the next two hours, she may have suggested lunch the following day, or coffee later in the week, but Simone wasn't interested in getting to know Eric or starting a relationship, she was interested in feeling his hard young body on top of her.

"Ah . . . yeah," Eric said with a nervous smile, not at all sure what was in store for him.

LoveLarge

"I can't believe I'm doing this," Ruby said to herself as she ran a comb through her hair, grabbed her purse and her pepper spray key chain, and hurried out the door. She wanted to move fast before she lost her nerve.

Was she insane—going to a complete stranger's house without telling anyone? It felt even more sordid, doing such a thing while her mother recuperated in a hospital bed.

Hookers do it all the time, Ruby thought, trying to reassure herself.

As she drove out to Virginia, she could barely contain herself. It was such a stupid thing to do—driving to a strange man's house in the middle of the night, but at the same time it was an adventure—it was risky and exciting. It almost made her feel like a vixen in a movie or on television—she was just like Cameron Diaz in *The Sweetest Thing*.

She didn't know what to expect from this LoveLarge, and for some odd reason, she didn't really care. It was almost as if it wasn't about him. When she had logged into the chat room earlier that night she didn't have any serious intentions of hooking up with a guy for sex. She knew it wasn't a smart—or safe—thing to do, but something seemed to come over her as LoveLarge talked about showing her a good time . . . about how he wanted to caress and lick her body. He made her feel something she hadn't felt in so long—he made her feel sexy, and

Ruby wasn't ready to give up that feeling just yet. If going to meet a strange man after midnight was what it took to keep that feeling, then so be it.

On the way out to LoveLarge's house she wondered if she was really . . . actually . . . verifiably going to have cheap sex. The whole idea made her feel wonderfully sleazy. It had been about two years since she last got laid, and she'd only had three partners . . . well, two and a half partners over her entire life. Of course, there was Warren with his "long slender penis," and then there was Donald, a nineteen-year-old computer geek who was a student teacher for Ruby's Introduction to Computer Science course her freshman year in college. Donald weighed about a hundred and ten pounds, had an enormous nose, and thick silver-rimmed glasses. Ruby always needed extra help with Computer Science, and Donald seemed to genuinely like her. Being the awkward nerd that he was, one day when they were working on some programming, he randomly put his hand on Ruby's leg, and hurriedly leaned in and started kissing her—all of this from what seemed like out of nowhere. Ruby hadn't been attracted to Donald, but she had never really been kissed before. She wasn't sure how to react, so she let him kiss her; then she let him feel her up and take off her shirt—next thing she knew, Ruby was no longer a virgin. The whole thing only lasted about ten minutes, and Ruby hadn't felt any pain the way she'd read that she would. She left her first sexual experience deciding she had no idea what all the fuss was about. If that was all there was to sex, she could take it or leave it.

Aside from Warren and Donald, her only other sexual partner, if you could call him that, was some frat boy named Harold Swartz she met during her junior year at George Mason University. The whole thing with Harold seemed bizarre from the get-go. Ruby had been studying in the campus library when he approached her and asked if he could share her table, which was odd as there were plenty of vacant tables around. Harold had dark hair and eyes, a lean build, and a smile that knocked Ruby's socks off. He started chatting her up while they were sitting at the table, and later asked her if she'd like to grab some dinner with him. Ruby was thrilled. Up until then, her social life at George Mason had consisted of Jeremy and an occasional meeting of the Psychology Club. She wasn't sure what Harold's intentions were—something didn't seem completely kosher with Harold Swartz—the way he just came up to her table out of the blue and started talking with her. The whole time they talked his tone seemed phony and condescending, but it was so rare—nonexistent in fact—that Ruby was asked to dinner by a man, so she agreed. They went to Brion's at University Mall and talked about majors, and campus life, and anything else Harold could think to bring up. As they talked, Ruby couldn't help but wonder what was up with him. He wasn't a looker, but he could certainly do better than her—did he want her to write a research paper for him, or take a test for him in the Lecture Hall? She was sure he had an ulterior motive, but the more they talked, the more she started to let herself believe that he might have found her attractive. As she got more comfortable she began to tell stories about her family and some of the things she and Jeremy had done over the years. By the time he drove her back to her car on campus, Ruby was reciting the words "Ruby Swartz" in her mind and wondering how Doris would react to her bringing home a Jewish boy. "I'm changing my name to Swartz when we get married, Mother. I don't care what you think," she pictured herself telling Doris after she was engaged.

"Can I kiss you good night?" Harold asked when they pulled up next to her car.

"Sure," Ruby replied, her mouth going dry with excitement.

Harold put his lips on hers, and kissed her briefly before he started nudging her head down toward his crotch. While Ruby resisted and kept kissing him, Harold managed to unzip his pants and pull out his dick. Again, he pushed Ruby's head toward his lap. When she resisted again he said something like, "Come on, suck me off."

Ruby had never had a penis in her mouth before, and as excited as she was to be with Harold, she couldn't bring herself to go down on him. She'd caught a glimpse of his penis. It was oddly shaped with a thin shaft and a big pink head. Ruby was actually afraid she might throw up if she tried to blow him.

"Please!" he begged her.

"Maybe some other time," Ruby replied, now just wanting to get out of the car and go home, away from Harold and his oddly shaped penis.

"Well . . . could you do me a favor, then?" Harold asked.

"What?"

"Can you just lower your head and pretend you're blowing me?"

"What! Why?"

"Just do it, would you?"

"Are you crazy?"

"No, I need to get blown by a fat girl. Come on, what would it hurt to just pretend, so it looks like . . ."

"Is someone watching us?" Ruby asked, looking around outside only to see a carload of frat boys peering at them from the other side of the parking lot.

Ruby started to get out of the car.

"Don't go. Please! I need to do this to get in the fraternity. Come on, I bought you dinner."

Horrified, Ruby ignored him and left the car.

"Cow!" he called behind her. "Ya fucking fat bitch!"

As Ruby drove up to LoveLarge's house in Alexandria, she could still hear those words from Harold Swartz being shouted at her. More than ten years later the sound of his voice yelling "Cow!" was still coming through, loud and clear.

She parked on the street, took a deep breath before getting out of the car, and made her way up the walkway to his house—one half of an old brick duplex in a marginal neighborhood off Duke Street. She rang the doorbell hoping an attractive man would answer. When the door opened, Ruby's sexual fantasy adventures came to an immediate halt. LoveLarge was wearing a pair of polyester boxer shorts and an open robe. He was well into his fifties with an enormous hairy belly, one big eyebrow on his forehead, and a bit of a used-car salesman look. And, Ruby wasn't sure, but he looked like he was wearing a toupee.

"Hi. Ruby?" he asked in a raspy smoker's voice.

"Ah . . . yes," Ruby said, just wanting to run back to her car and go home.

"Hi. I'm Ira. Come in, please," Ira said. "Have a seat. Excuse the mess."

Ira's house smelled of cigarette smoke and litter box. He had old magazines and books stacked against the walls, on the coffee table, on shelves, everywhere. As Ruby walked in, she saw two cats lounging on the back of the sofa, and another licking himself on top of one of the magazine stacks. There was a TV tray at one end of the couch, which had what appeared to be the remains of a Stouffer's lasagna container laying on it.

Yum. Love me some Stouffer's lasagna, Ruby thought as she lowered herself to the sofa, her mind momentarily straying from the relative squalor she had just walked into. She had been seated for just a second when she noticed masses of cat hair collecting on her black pants. Ruby contemplated excuses for getting the hell out of there as she watched Ira stroll over to the couch to join her.

"Can I get you anything?"

Um . . . some Ajax, cat poison, a one-way ticket the hell out of here? "No, thanks."

"My, you're beautiful," Ira said, looking intently at Ruby. "I love the large women."

"Thank you," Ruby said.

"Should we get started?"

"Started?" Ruby asked. She had never hooked up with someone over the Internet before and had no idea how such an encounter was supposed to proceed.

"How about you stand up for me?"

"Okay," Ruby said, thankful to be off the cat-hair couch.

"Now, Ruby. Slowly undress for me," Ira said as he lowered his boxers, exposing his erect self.

Ah, no? Ruby thought, not sure what to do. She just wanted to leave and forget the whole thing. "Um . . . I'm not sure this is going to work," Ruby said. She was trying not to be rude. She knew what it felt like to be rejected, but she wasn't about to strip for this man and his three cats.

"Sure it will. You know what I like?"

Filth? Cats? Bad toupees? "What?"

"I'd like for you to strip for me, and then just shake it all around while I jerk off?"

"Shake it? Shake what?"

"You know, shake your fat around while I stroke my cock. Come on, jiggle for me, Ruby. It really turns me on."

Ruby's mouth dropped with horror at his request and, right then, she noticed a flea climbing up her leg. "I'm sorry. I have to go," Ruby said abruptly, frantically flicking the flea off her leg, grabbing her purse and making a beeline for the door. "I really am sorry," she said just before she closed the door behind her and ran to her car without looking back.

Ruby was thoroughly disgusted—with Ira, the cats, the fleas, and the smell of cigarettes and cat pee, but mostly she was disgusted with herself. What was she thinking, going to meet some freak in the middle of the night? She could have been killed. All she wanted to do was get home and take a shower (and maybe a flea dip), but first she had to make a pit stop—she needed to drop by the Giant and get herself a couple servings of Stouffer's frozen lasagna. Her mouth had been watering for it ever since she had seen the empty container on Ira's TV tray.

Guilty as Charged

Ruby inserted her key in the door and opened it slowly, trying not to make any noise. Her plan was to quietly enter the house, pop her family-size tray of Stouffer's in the microwave, and head upstairs to eat lasagna and watch some late night TV—probably whatever sitcom Nickelodeon was running six or seven times a day—Lord help them if they actually showed a variety of programs.

As she came through the door, Wanda was on the steps with a bag of Oreos in her hand and Taco at her feet. Ruby must have come in just as Wanda was headed upstairs with her late night snack.

"Hi," Ruby said, a bit flustered.

"Hi. Where have you been?"

"Ah . . ." Ruby struggled for something to say. "Um . . . I just ran out to the store," she replied, holding up her plastic grocery bag.

"I heard you step out almost two hours ago. It took you that long to go to the store?" Wanda replied with skepticism.

"Um . . . I ran a couple of other errands. . . ." Ruby said, flushing with embarrassment. She could tell Wanda knew she was lying. Even the dog was looking at her like *you lying bitch*.

"Ruby?" Wanda questioned, hesitating for a moment before she tilted her head, and offered a mischievous smile. "Were you out there gettin' your freak on? Why you little hoochie."

"What? No!" Ruby said, trying not to look so guilty-as-charged. "I was just running some errands. Really!"

"At midnight. What kind of errands were you running at midnight?"

"Just . . ." Ruby tried to respond.

"You can tell me. Come on. Who were you doing the dirty-dirty with?"

"I'm telling you . . ."

"Okay. If you won't tell me his name, at least tell me what's in the bag."

"This?" Ruby said, looking at the bag, embarrassed to be carrying a family-size tray of lasagna. "Just some lasagna for dinner tomorrow night." She wasn't about to admit to her plan of devouring the whole tray over the next few hours.

"Tomorrow night? You're just full of lies tonight. Girl, you know you were planning on eating it tonight. Come on, I'll put these Oreos back, and we'll nuke that lasagna and you can tell me all about *him*."

Ruby laughed nervously. "There is no him," she persisted.

"Okay. Whatever you say," Wanda replied in a questionable tone as the girls made their way to the kitchen.

Between the two of them, Ruby and Wanda polished off the entire tray of lasagna. It was so much fun to eat with Wanda. She was shameless about enjoying her food. After they ate, and Wanda had gone upstairs, Ruby jumped in the shower, cleaned herself up, and headed back to her bedroom. When she sat on the bed, she realized that in her haste to leave to meet LoveLarge, she'd forgotten to log out of the Big Girls, Don't Cry! chat room. It was still up on her monitor, and someone else had tried to start a private chat with her. Ruby had no idea how long the new chat window had been open. The chat initiator could have just instant-messaged her seconds ago, or it could have been hours earlier. The screen name of the man who had paged her was "TravelingMan."

TravelingMan: hi rockinruby . . . how are you?

Her first instinct was to just close up the chat window and shut off the computer. She had to get up early to check on Doris in the hospital. Besides, she didn't want any repeats of the LoveLarge experience. But curiosity got the best of her, and she clicked on his profile:

TravelingMan: nice guy in town on business, attractive, 36, 5'10, 165, fit/lean, interested in meeting large women for a good time

Well, at least his profile sounded good, Ruby thought. She knew it was a bad idea, but, really, what could it hurt to just respond to him? He'd probably paged her hours ago and was gone anyway.

RockinRuby: hi . . . i'm fine . . . u?

TravelingMan: hey . . . thought you were ignoring me

RockinRuby: no . . . just didn't see your page until now

TravelingMan: thanks for responding . . . i liked your profile . . . what brings you on-line?

RockinRuby: actually . . . just getting ready to sign off and go to bed

TravelingMan: bed? already? how about we chat for a bit?

RockinRuby: about?

TravelingMan: hmm . . . maybe about what we might do together if we met up?

RockinRuby: really?

TravelingMan: yeah . . . i love big girls . . . your voluptuous bodies . . . i'd love to show you the time of your life, rockinruby!!!!!

RockinRuby: probably a little late to show me the time of my life tonight . . . maybe the time of my month or week or something

TravelingMan: LOL . . . you're funny, rockinruby . . . it's never too late . . . you're in dc?

RockinRuby: yes . . . logan circle area

TravelingMan: hmmm . . . think i know where that is . . . not from the area, but spend a lot of time here for business. i'm in falls church at the marriott off rte 50

RockinRuby: really? that's close to my office

TravelingMan: hmmm . . . should be easy for us to meet up sometime then

RockinRuby: maybe

TravelingMan: how about we trade pics and if we like what we see, we can talk more about hooking up

Oh no! Ruby thought. The dreaded photograph exchange. She hadn't had good experience sending her picture to guys over the Internet. It usually resulted in them immediately logging off or making up some lame excuse as to why they needed to end the chat. But this situation was a bit different. One, it was a chat room for men attracted to large women such as Ruby, and two, after her experience with LoveLarge, she wasn't really interested in hooking up with anyone anyway, so it wasn't as if she had anything to lose by sending TravelingMan her picture. Ruby agreed to TravelingMan's request, and they exchanged E-mail addresses. While Ruby was composing a new E-mail and attaching her photograph, she got the E-mail from TravelingMan. Eager to see his picture, she minimized the E-mail she was composing and opened his. When she clicked on the attachment and opened TravelingMan's picture her mouth dropped.

"Oh my God!" she said out loud. She couldn't believe it. "No fucking way!" she said as she continued to look at the picture. TravelingMan, the man that wanted to show her the time of her life, was Preston DaSilva, the sales vice president at her company for whom she'd been pining after for years.

Ruby had been rather fatigued up until this point, but now the adrenaline was pumping and she was wired. Preston-Fucking-DaSilva had a thing for fat girls! Ruby wasn't sure what to do, but she knew it wasn't a good idea to send her picture in return. She didn't want Preston to know she was in a late night sex chat room, and she was pretty sure Preston wouldn't want someone from work knowing the same thing about him.

RockinRuby: got your pic . . . very nice . . . but not my type

Ruby couldn't believe what she had written. She had just told Preston DaSilva—gorgeous dynamic Preston DaSilva, that she found him nice, but that he wasn't her type. How she would have loved to go over to his hotel room right then and there, but she knew she had done the right thing. She hated doing it, but at the same time, there was something almost fun about snubbing Preston on-line. She was sure he wasn't used to women rejecting him, and it gave Ruby a small sense of power to know that she just had, even if it was anonymously. She closed the chat window, disconnected from the Internet, and shut down the computer. She leaned back in the chair, her heart pounding with excitement, and smiled. She just couldn't believe that she had run into Preston in a sex chat room. Preston DaSilva was a chubby chaser. Now Ruby just had to figure out how to use that information to her advantage.

Preppy White Boys Part II

"Thank you for the drink," Eric said to Simone. "Or I guess I should say drinks."

Simone and Eric had managed to find a bar that was still open and polished off three glasses of wine each before they made their way back to their cars. They'd relaxed over drinks and gotten to know each other a bit. Eric finally recognized Simone when a waitress asked for her autograph, and the more drinks she got in him, the more Eric's straight white boy demeanor loosened up. Simone learned that he'd graduated college two years earlier, which she figured put him at about twenty-four. He lived in the city and was an account executive for a consulting firm on M Street. She actually found him pretty boring—he seemed most at home talking about the Redskins and the free long distance he got on his mobile phone—but, God! Was he nice to look at!

"Thanks for fixing my car."

"Happy to help. I'm sorry about the flat tire."

"Don't be. The night turned out okay after all," Simone replied.

"Does that mean the night's over?" Eric asked with a nervous laugh, his shoulders tensing up.

"I don't know. Did you have something in mind?" Simone said with a willing smile.

"Um . . ." Eric replied. Even with the booze, he was trembling just a bit. It wasn't every day he hit on a thirty-four-year-old celebrity. "We could go back to my place for one more drink."

"Sure," Simone said, figuring going to his place was probably the best idea. She didn't need Ruby and Wanda hearing her sneak a twenty-four-year-old boy into the house at two in the morning.

Simone followed Eric home in her car, and was actually quite surprised as Eric walked her up the steps to his building. She was expecting a dive typical of men in their twenties, but Eric lived in a fairly upscale building in the Woodley Park neighborhood of D.C. When they got upstairs, and Eric opened the door to his apartment, Simone was quite taken aback. As she stepped inside, she saw a spacious, tastefully decorated living room, not the IKEA fest she had expected from someone in Eric's age group.

"Great place," Simone said while Eric closed the door behind them. As Simone continued to look around something began to concern her. The room was *too* tastefully done. It screamed Pottery Barn—earth tones and dark wood accents, leaning shelves sparsely stacked with books and a couple of knick-knacks, fresh flowers on the end table, and a textured beige accent wall. The place definitely had a woman's touch. Eric was either married or gay.

"Did you decorate the place yourself?" Simone asked, fishing for information.

"No," Eric said without elaborating.

"I didn't think so," Simone said, noticing a woman's scarf on the back of one of the chairs. "And who might this belong to?" she asked, picking up the scarf. "Let me rephrase that. Who, with *hideous* taste, might this belong to?"

Eric started with his trembling again, and seemed to be searching for something to say.

"Eric. If you're involved with someone else, it's not really that big of a deal. I'm not interested in anything long-term," Simone offered, trying to relax him. She really didn't care if he was married or living with someone. She just wanted a piece of ass.

"Really?" Eric said, relaxing more.

"Are you married?" Simone asked.

"Ah . . . sort of."

"That's kind of like sort of pregnant, isn't it? Either you are, or you aren't."

Eric didn't laugh at her joke. "You hit the nail on the head," he said.

"What do you mean?"

"My wife, Cynthia, she got pregnant, so we got married last year. Three weeks after the wedding she miscarried."

"Oh no. I'm sorry," Simone said.

"It's okay. It was actually sort of a mixed blessing. We weren't ready for a kid, and we certainly weren't ready to get married."

"Where is she now? Your wife?"

"She's in Chicago. She travels a lot for work. I think we'll get a divorce sooner or later, but . . . oh, I don't know . . ." Eric said, really starting to look hopeless and sad.

Simone put her arm around him. He looked like he needed some comforting.

"I think she got pregnant on purpose to make me marry her. She was supposed to be on the pill. I shouldn't have trusted her."

"That's terrible," Simone said, leaning in a little closer to let him smell her perfume and feel her breasts against his side. She was trying to stop this little heart-pouring session. She wanted to fuck him, not be his therapist.

"Yeah. It's kind of sucked around here lately."

"Anything I can do to make things better?" Simone asked coyly and leaned in and kissed him.

"Absolutely," he said, his demeanor immediately changing from sad puppy dog to eager wolf hound. All of a sudden Simone was no longer the aggressor. Eric returned her kiss with an intensity that took Simone by surprise. Before she knew it he was working his tongue into her mouth and grabbing her ass. Simone wrapped her arms around him, enjoying the feel of his young chiseled body. And, God, how she loved men in their twenties. Their bodies were so fresh and hard, and they hadn't started losing the hair on their head, while sprouting it everywhere else. Every part of Eric was firm—his chest, his buttocks, and most importantly, his stomach. There was nothing Simone detested more than a protruding beer belly on a man. She couldn't stand it when a man leaned in to kiss her, and she felt his stomach against her body before she felt his lips.

Simone let him unbutton her blouse and started in on his shirt as soon as he was finished with hers. She watched as he lowered his shirt and slipped it off his arms. He had a smooth defined chest that Simone immediately wanted take in her mouth. Eric clumsily released the strap on her bra, helped her slip out of it, and tossed it on the floor before nuzzling his head between her breasts. Simone could feel the stiff brush of a slight five o'-clock shadow starting to fill in on Eric's face as he started to devour her breasts. Simone didn't know how much longer she could stand it. She'd wanted him from the moment he was on his knees, changing her flat tire, and she just couldn't wait any longer. She had to have him inside her now. She started to unbuckle his pants, but, surprisingly, he stopped her. Eric grabbed her hands from his belt and lifted them up over her head, cueing her to just relax and let him go to work.

"Wow!" Eric said. They were both lying completely naked on the living room floor.

Wow is right! No wonder that bitch wife of yours trapped you into marriage, Simone thought before letting out a little laugh. "Yeah, that was really great."

Her sexual experience with Eric had been a wild ride and quite unexpected. He had obviously been nervous and possibly not very experienced, but at the same time he was so enthralled with her body that he made love to her with a passion she was not accustomed to. Simone not only approached *seeking* sex like a man, she usually *had* sex like a man as well. She wasn't terribly interested in long heavy petting sessions—she generally wanted to get right down to business and then be on her way. Most men were happy to oblige when Simone hurried through foreplay, but Eric was having none of it. He kept making her wait. Not only would he not let her take off his pants for quite some time, he kept going at her body with his tongue, from neck to toe, despite her repeated attempts to signal that she was ready to move on. When he was finally naked and had started fucking her, he'd pull out for a few minutes and work his mouth again before going back in—he did this over and over again and, for Simone, it was phenomenal. She had to bite her tongue to keep from begging him to fuck her every time he pulled out.

"You have a beautiful body," Eric said to Simone, turning to lean on one side.

"I might say the same to you," Simone replied and sat up. "I guess I should go. When is your wife due back?"

"Not until Friday evening."

"Really? Well I guess I'd better get going anyway," Simone said, eager to be on her way. She got up from the floor and hunted around for her clothes while Eric did the same. She couldn't help but look at him as she pulled up her panties and started to get dressed. He looked so cute scrounging around the floor with a now flaccid dick, looking for his underwear.

When Simone was fully dressed, Eric approached her in only his boxers, and gave her a long kiss. She could feel him already starting to get hard again—another advantage of twenty-somethings, a short refractory period.

"Can I call you?"

"It's probably not a good idea," Simone replied. "You know, with your wife and all."

"You're probably right, but . . ."

"I really have to go. It must be almost daylight by now."

"Okay," Eric replied and showed her to the door. He kissed her one more time before letting her go and closing the door behind her. As Simone walked toward the elevator, she thought about how incredible the night with Eric had been, and then something occurred to her—maybe Eric being married wasn't such a bad thing. Actually, maybe it was perfect. He could offer her great sex without any of the hassles of a relationship, and she wouldn't have to see him exclusively. She pondered the idea as she approached the elevator, and finally decided to turn around. She walked back to his apartment and knocked on the door.

"Hey," he said with a smile. He was obviously happy to see her again.

"Maybe getting together again isn't such a bad idea," Simone said and handed him her phone number, making him one of a privileged few to whom she divulged her guarded seven digits.

Eric smiled from ear to ear as he looked at the little slip of paper. "Thanks. I'll keep this in a very safe place," he said and stuffed it in the elastic of his shorts.

Beach Food

Ruby was in the elevator on her way up to her office on the eleventh floor. Most days she didn't bother with anything more than a quick shower and a brief run through her hair with a comb, but today she'd gotten up early. She wanted to go to the hospital before work to check on Doris, but she had also arisen early for grooming purposes. She'd blown her hair dry with a curling brush, put on makeup, and dressed in her best Lane Bryant suit. Preston was due in the office today, and she wanted to look good for him. She hadn't seen him since running into him in the Big Girls, Don't Cry! chat room.

Two other women were in the elevator with Ruby and as it began to rise from the lobby, Ruby overheard them chatting. It was almost the end of summer and the skinnier one was talking about her planned trip to Ocean City, Maryland. The petite woman was going on and on about how she was looking forward to soaking up some sun and relaxing on the beach. Ruby was just waiting to hear the scrawny bitch start complaining about how self-conscious she was going to be in her bathing suit the way thin women always did before they put on a bikini that would make Hugh Hefner blush and strutted their fake titties all over the Eastern Seaboard.

Ruby hadn't been to the beach in years. Ever since some teenage boys shouted "beached whale!" behind her while she was sunbathing, she'd been apprehensive about returning. When she did go to the beach she always wore a big T-shirt over her swimsuit. There was no way anyone was going to see her in just a bathing suit. She knew the T-shirt didn't really hide anything, but somehow it made her feel slightly more secure and protected.

Ruby always had a sort of love/hate relationship with the beach. She hated feeling self-conscious and overweight in her bathing suit, and she hated the occasional taunts she'd get, mostly from adolescent boys, but there was one thing Ruby did love about the beach—the food! She could remember when she was a kid and her friends talked about enjoying the ocean, getting tan, walking the boardwalk and, of course, Ruby would agree that those were the best reasons for visiting the shore, but what really got Ruby excited was the anticipation of peanut butter fudge from the Candy Kitchen, caramel popcorn from Dollie's, Grotto Pizza, funnel cake, soft-serve ice cream, Italian water ice, the list went on and on.

From the time Ruby was about ten until she left for college, she and her parents would take an annual trip to Rehoboth Beach, Delaware, about a three-hour drive from the D.C. area. Every day during their vacation Ruby would eat breakfast with her parents before they set up camp on the beach. Then, as her parents read or slept under an umbrella, Ruby would make various excuses about why she needed to go back to their rented house—she had to go to the bathroom or forgot her sunglasses or whatever—but, instead of going back to the house she'd raid the eateries along Rehoboth Avenue. She'd quickly down a funnel cake covered in powdered sugar, then head back to the beach. Then, an hour or so later, she'd excuse herself again and get a couple of slices of Grotto Pizza. She did this every day while they were at the beach, and then ate a big dinner with her parents after the sun went down. During the weeks prior to their vacation Ruby would steal small amounts of money out of her mother's purse to ensure enough cash to meet her vacation feeding needs by the time they made it to the beach.

Ruby knew there was something wrong. She knew she was overweight, and she knew she had no business eating funnel cakes and soft-serve ice cream, but she couldn't help it. It was as if the food was calling to her on the beach. All she could think about while she watched the waves rise on the sand and then drift back into the ocean were the eateries waiting for her to pounce on them.

When the elevator opened on the tenth floor, and the two women stepped out, there was a small Latino man shampooing the carpet, which was shabby and tattered. As the doors closed, Ruby heard one of the women remark to the other, "Why are they cleaning this worn out old carpet. What's the point? It's not like it's going to look any better."

"Yeah, really," the other women replied. "It's like dressing up a fat woman. Why bother?"

Ruby heard the women laugh and wondered if the remark was directed at her. Oddly enough, at that moment, it didn't really bother her that much. She had other things on her mind today—namely Preston DaSilva. She didn't know what she was going to do, but maybe she could somehow get his attention.

When she got out of the elevator, she quickly headed toward her office and checked her E-mail and voice messages. There was nothing urgent, so she started making her way through the maze of cubicles toward Preston's office. She planned to just casually stroll by and see if he was in. As she approached his office door, she heard him on the phone. He was being his usual charismatic self, probably talking to a potential client. Ruby stood outside his door and eavesdropped on the conversation. She was trying to think of some reason to enter his office and say hello. Maybe she could just congratulate him on bringing in the company's latest big account. When she heard him hang up the phone, her heart started to palpitate.

"Go on," she told herself. "Just go in and say hello. What's the worst that can happen?" As she was standing outside Preston's office trying to drum up the nerve to go inside, Alan approached from behind.

"What? No 'good morning?'" Alan asked, noting how Ruby went straight from her desk to Preston's office. Most days, her first stop of the morning was to say hello to Alan and dish about last night's episode of *Friends* or *Will & Grace*.

"Oh, hi," Ruby said to Alan, obviously distracted.

"What are you doing? Why are you hovering outside Preston's office?" he asked.

"I'm not hovering," Ruby lied. "I'm just waiting for him to get off the phone."

Alan paused for a moment and listened. "Sounds like he's off."

"Ah, really?" Ruby said and nervously poked her head in his office. If Alan hadn't come along, she probably would have lost her nerve and just gone back to her desk, but now she had to approach him. "Preston?" she said.

"Yeah?" he replied with a smile.

"Um . . . I just wanted to say congratulations, for . . . um . . . you know, bringing in that big account."

"Well, thank you, Ruby," he replied.

"I guess that's a lot of new revenue for the company," she added, not sure what else to say.

"Yeah. About three million dollars over the next three years."

"Great!" Ruby said, at a loss for anything else to say. "Um . . . guess that's it."

"Okay. Thanks for stopping by."

"Sure," Ruby replied, certain she was red as a lobster. As she came out of his office, Alan was still standing there.

" 'I guess that's a lot of new revenue for the company?' " Alan said, half mimicking Ruby and half asking her what she was up to.

"What? It is a lot of new revenue for the company."

"When did you start caring about company revenue?" Alan asked suspiciously.

"I was just making conversation."

Alan paused for a minute and then, as if a lightbulb had appeared over his head, replied, "You have a thing for Preston."

"What?" Ruby said with a nervous laugh. "I do not."

"You do too. Are you crazy? You know what a dog he is."

"I don't have a thing for him. I just wanted to say hello," Ruby lied, embarrassed that Alan was on to her. "I've got to return some phone calls. I'll catch up with you later," she continued and headed back to her office.

"Damn it!" she said to herself as she walked away. What was she thinking? That she could just saunter into Preston's office and next thing they would be picking out china patterns at Bloomingdale's? She cursed herself for not having a better idea of what to say when she approached him. Alan was right, she had just sounded ridiculous talking about company revenue. Big Fat Ruby had fucked up again. Who was she kidding, anyway? Even if Preston was hot for large women, he probably wouldn't be interested in her. He'd want a girl with more style and charisma. He'd want a girl with charm and grace—not a girl like Ruby.

Model Rivalry

It was just after ten o'clock and Wanda was folding some cashmere sweaters and enjoying the welcome quiet of the early hours at Saks. She hated refolding clothes over and over again. Customers were such pigs. It was a constant struggle for Wanda and the other associates to keep the store in order. She had worked in retail for years, but it still made her hiss inside when she saw some doofy girl stroll by a stack of nicely folded blouses, unravel one of them, hold it up and take a look at it, and then just throw it back on the table like she was at Macy's or something. One would think that customers who could afford to shop at Saks would have better manners, but they didn't behave any better than flea market raiders. They left heaps of garments in the dressing rooms, got makeup stains on the clothes, and you *know* half those nasty bitches didn't keep their undergarments on when they tried on bathing suits. Wanda always thought it would be fun to install cameras in the dressing rooms, and the moment a young lady decided to pull her bikini bottom up over her bare ass, Wanda would rip open the dressing room door and tell them she hoped the swimsuit fit because they had just bought it—"you bare ass it, you buy it!" Wanda pictured telling them.

Wanda liked some aspects of her job. She enjoyed helping the customers put ensembles together, and seeing the latest fashions as soon as they came out, not to mention her employee discount, but lately she wanted out of retail sales more than ever. She was tired of trying to do it all—help customers select clothes, ring up their purchases, stock and tidy shelves and racks, clear dressing rooms. It was too much for the limited staff to do, and still serve the customers properly. She only got into retail as a stepping-stone to modeling, but she was starting to think she was going about it wrong. She was never going to get any serious recognition doing small department store shows. More and more she was thinking that is was time to move to New York City. She had done what she came to D.C. to do. She'd gotten lots of modeling experience under her belt and had made contacts in the industry. Even if her weight put her well above the industry standard for plus-size models, her experience, looks, and determination were bound to propel her ahead. After the big Saks show the following week, she would just get a few more local shows under her belt, and then she'd make her move and take herself, her portfolio, and her wardrobe to the Big Apple.

As Wanda moved on to another stack of sweaters, she saw Denise fanning herself with a Saks catalog as she made her way through the clothing racks. As usual, Denise looked prickly and flushed, but much to Wanda's dismay, she still looked beautiful. Her body was bulky and a tad awkward, but, unlike most large woman, Denise had an unusually thin face that highlighted her high cheekbones. She had on a red skirt with a black jacket, and her single auburn braid hung loose from the rest of her black strands, which were pulled away from her face, and, of course, she had her stupid Joan Rivers bumblebee brooch pinned to her lapel. Wanda didn't care for Denise's braids and she thought the brooch was tacky, but at the same time, she thought it was clever how Denise had developed her own trademarks and made every look her own—sort of like the way Laverne DeFazio slapped the letter L on everything she owned.

Wanda hated Denise, or at least she thought she hated Denise. In reality she more feared her than hated her, mostly because Wanda could see her own determination in Denise. She remembered the first day Denise started with the store—the day she strolled up to Mrs. Elliot, one of the senior managers, dropped her mother's name, and requested an application. Wanda kept her distance from Denise, but she knew a little about her. Denise came from an uppity black family in Fort Washington, Maryland. Her father, who owned a local chain of carpet stores, sat on the schoolboard or the county board or some shit like that, and her mother was a socialite who came to the store on several occasions and dropped a few thousand dollars at a time. Fort Washington was in Prince George's County and home to an abundance of wealthy black families, but its residents were still forced to drive to predominantly white Montgomery County or cross the bridge into Virginia to find any upscale stores, which Denise's mother did fairly regularly. She was well known at Saks, and Denise probably never would have been hired as a sales associate had it not been for her mother's connections. Denise's father's connections also came in handy from time to time, as did his money.

When Wanda was Denise's age she was still living in Trenton, and wearing her fake Gucci hats, and toting a knock-off Louis Vuitton bag. At that time she hadn't even stepped foot in a Saks—she was too busy seeing that her brothers got off to school or working overtime at the supermarket. If it hadn't been for the sudden death of her father, she could have started pursuing her career at Denise's age.

"Hi," Denise said to Wanda, with an unusually pleasant demeanor.

"Hello," Wanda replied, with a chill.

"Sorry to hear about the show," Denise said.

"Sorry about what?"

"That you're not going to be in it."

"Oh, I think you're mistaken. I most certainly am going to be in it."

"Really? Well, I spoke with Carlos earlier, and he assured me that I was in the show, and I was going to wear the Gianfranco Ferre. I think they wanted someone younger, you know, more hip."

"Whatever," Wanda replied, walking away casually, as if she

were not at all worried about what Denise said. But as soon as she was far enough away from Denise, Wanda headed for the cashier station, picked up the phone, and dialed.

"Carlos?" she said into the phone.

"Yes."

"Wanda Johnson here. What's this I hear about Denise taking my place in the show?"

"Oh. I'm sorry, I was going to tell you today. We decided to go with Denise for this particular show."

"So both Denise and I are going to appear?"

Carlos hesitated for a moment. "Ah . . . no, I'm afraid just Denise."

"What! I was slated to be in the show months ago. You can't do this."

"I can do whatever I want, Wanda. It's my show."

Wanda calmed herself down. She knew better than to get on Carlos's bad side. If she did, she'd be blackballed from every show in town. "Well, why don't we both participate?" Wanda asked, trying to hide her anger.

"I'm sorry, Wanda. There are only two large-size modeling slots in the show. Denise is filling one and Sarah McHatton from the Tyson's store is filling the other. I promise we'll put you in the next one."

"Why Sarah? I've been with the store longer," Wanda replied, hearing the desperation in her voice. She hated sucking up to Carlos. He was such a prick.

"We need the diversity," Carlos replied. "We need to have a balance."

"Oh. I get it. It's because Sarah's white," Wanda said, trying to stay cool.

"I'm not confirming or denying anything."

"You don't need to," Wanda said and hung up the phone.

"Fuck!" Wanda said out loud. What had that little Denise bitch done to get Carlos to change his mind? She couldn't have slept with him. Carlos was as queer as colored contact lenses and hair gel. She wasn't sure what Denise had done, but she was going to find out.

Home from the Hospital

"Slow down, Ruby, there's a cop up ahead," Doris said from the passenger side of the car. She'd just been released from the hospital and they were on their way to Ruby's house.

"I see him, Mom. They're there every day."

Ruby and Doris were passing by the Pentagon on their way to Ruby's house and cops were all over the area. Ever since September 11th, policemen parked with their lights flashing on the fringe of every road that went near the Pentagon.

"What are they doing?" Doris asked.

"Guarding the Pentagon, I guess."

"What, like terrorists won't just go blow up some other building?"

"You can't put armed guards at every building in the city, Mom."

"I know. That's why you should move out of the city, Ruby, before those terrorists nuke you."

"Nobody's getting nuked, Mother," Ruby replied, trying to think of something to say to change the subject. Truth was that ever since the attacks on the World Trade Center and the Pentagon, Ruby did get a little nervous living in the nation's capital, probably the mostly likely terrorist target on the planet. She still got slightly anxious every once in a while when she heard planes fly over her house or saw unmarked trucks parked outside. She didn't need Doris increasing her anxiety.

It was so strange how everything changed one day in September 2001, and America became vulnerable. Ruby had no idea why, but her last memory of the days before September 11th was of the 2001 MTV Music Video Awards. Who could have guessed, while they were watching Britney Spears strut around the stage with a python around her neck, that a few days later, passengers jets would be pummeled into buildings? Who also could have guessed that, within days, has-been pop singers, in a last ditch effort to avoid hocking face creams on late night infomercials, would try to revive their ailing careers by sponsoring concert benefits, and hurriedly releasing songs about heroes, and flags, and red-white-and-blue to cash in on the tragedy?

"I'm telling you, Ruby, stay in the ghetto and you're going to get nuked. Nuked! Nuked! Nuked!" Doris said with assurance.

"I'll take my chances. And I'll have you know that houses in the *ghetto*, as you called my neighborhood, are going for more than half a million dollars now." Ruby dreaded the next few days. How on earth was she going to deal with having Doris in her house for an extended stay?

"You should have just taken me home."

Damn right. "The doctor said you needed someone to stay with you for a while."

"So why don't you just stay at my house?"

"Because I have a thing called a job, Mom, and I don't want to spend two hours getting to work in the morning. It will just be for a little while. You can take my room, and I'll sleep in the den, or if you don't want to climb the stairs, you can take the den."

"Those boarders still living with you?"

"Boarders? You mean my housemates? Yes, they're still there. You'll like them. They're both very nice."

When they got in the city, Ruby had a brief stroke of luck and found a parking spot close to the house. She helped Doris out of the car, and took her up the front steps to the house. It was late afternoon. Wanda had just gotten home from work, and Simone was just about to leave for the studio. As Ruby and Doris came through the door, Taco caught a glimpse of them and came running over, his ears perked up and his tail wagging. Ruby had never seen Taco like that before. He was so happy to see Doris, he was almost cute.

"Come here, baby," Doris said and picked Taco up in her arms. He trembled with joy and licked her face. "Did Ruby take good care of you?" she asked as Ruby looked on, watching Doris be more affectionate with Taco than she had ever been with her.

"We spoiled him rotten," Wanda said as she and Simone approached the entryway to say hello.

"Hi," Ruby said to the girls before turning to Doris. "Mom, these are my housemates, Wanda and Simone."

Doris smiled. "Hello," she said.

"So sorry to hear you were in the hospital," Simone said. Doris didn't seem to recognize her from TV, which really shouldn't have been a surprise. Doris was usually in bed by nine o'clock, long before Simone's newscast came on at eleven.

"Oh. I'm a tough old bird, don't worry about me," Doris replied. "A few clogged arteries aren't going to get me down."

"Glad to hear it," Wanda replied.

"Come on, Mom, let's take you in the den and get you settled in," Ruby said to Doris.

"Nice to meet you," Doris said to Simone and Wanda, and slowly followed Ruby toward the small room off the dining area. When they got into the den, Doris closed the door behind them.

"Ruby, you didn't tell me you were renting to a colored girl and a Mexican. My God! It's like the United Nations out there."

"It's African-American, Mother, not colored. And Simone is Bolivian. Didn't you recognize her? She's on TV."

"TV? Is she the one with the famous rear end? The one that was dating that Puff the Magic Dragon fellow."

"No, Mother. That's Jennifer Lopez. Simone anchors the eleven o'clock news on Channel 6."

"Eleven o'clock. I don't remember the last time I was up past nine," Doris said, lowering herself onto the sofa bed and taking a seat. "Don't ever get old, Ruby. Everything goes—your looks, your energy, your health . . ."

"Your health is fine, Mom. The doctor said you'd be back in your garden in no time. And you look great."

"You're sweet, dear. A liar, but sweet," Doris joked with a smile. It was kind of her way of saying thanks to Ruby for taking care of her. She would never actually say thanks, but every once in a while she'd say something nice to Ruby and smile. It was the only thing that kept Ruby going when she was making her weekly trek out to LaPlata to check on Doris, or sitting across from her at IHOP, hearing about the low-calorie items on the menu. Every now and then, she could see the love and accept Doris's warped way of showing it.

"You sure you want to stay in here? You might be more comfortable in my bed and I can sleep down here," Ruby said.

"Yes, I'm sure. I'll be fine here."

"Okay. Why don't you lie down for bit, and I'll get your things out of the car," Ruby said and started to leave the room. "Wanda and I made plans to go to dinner tonight. If you're up to it, you're welcome to come along,"

"Where are you going?"

"Some Ethiopian place on M Street."

"Ethiopian? Ruby, if I wanted dog food, I'd open a can of Alpo." And just like that, Doris's moment of sweetness was over.

"Suit yourself. I'll make you a sandwich before I go," Ruby replied, not really wanting to listen to Doris's mouth during dinner anyway, and headed for the front door. She'd taken the day off to deal with Doris, and go out to her house in LaPlata and collect some clothes for Doris to wear while she stayed with Ruby. Ruby had mostly picked up nightgowns and other low-key clothes, but she couldn't resist grabbing Doris's little black dress. It was the perfect opportunity to get it in her house, and safe from the Salvation Army, Goodwill, or a perfect size six burglar.

As Ruby opened the front door to head back out to the car,

she ran into a skinny effeminate-looking man with spiked hair and leather pants.

"Hi," he said.

"Ah . . . hi," Ruby replied, somewhat startled. Who the hell was he, and what was he doing at her doorstep?

"I'm here for Simone?"

"Oh, sure," Ruby said, and gestured for him to come in. "Simone," Ruby called before Simone appeared behind her.

"Hi, Jasper," Simone said. "Thanks for the lift," she continued, before turning to Ruby. "This is Jasper. He's giving me a ride to the station while I have the Mercedes detailed."

Lord help the princess if she actually took the Metro or a bus somewhere, Ruby thought before responding. "Oh, you work with Simone?" she asked.

"Yes, yes I do," Jasper said, all of a sudden seeming distracted, and looking Ruby up and down. "Turn around for me, would you?" he asked her.

"What?"

"Turn," he said authoritatively.

"Go ahead," Simone encouraged.

"Okay," Ruby said, perplexed, but obliging his request.

"How would you like to be in a commercial?" Jasper asked.

"What? A commercial?"

"Yes. I produce commercials on the side, and I'm developing one for D.C. Slim & Trim Diet Centers . . . Slim & Trim for short. You would be perfect for it."

"Slim & Trim?" Ruby asked.

"They're a new chain of weight loss centers. I think you'd be great in one of their commercials. And besides, it's a great plan. You get a personal coach, dietary recommendations, and prepackaged meals."

"Ah . . . I don't think so."

"Oh, don't be shy. We couldn't pay you very much, but you could join the program for free. We'd take some before shots, and then put you on the Slim & Trim plan, and after a few months, we'd shoot a commercial with the new you."

Ruby was silent for a moment. "Are you serious?"

"I've seen a few of his commercials. He's great. You should do it, Ruby," Simone said.

"Well . . . maybe."

"Here," Jasper said and handed her a business card. "Call me tomorrow if you're interested. We can shoot the before pictures right away, and plan to film the commercial sometime before Christmas."

"Okay. I'll think about it," Ruby said as Simone and Jasper walked off.

Slim & Trim

Ruby was quite anxious as she walked into the small studio in Friendship Heights, almost to the Maryland line. It was all so exciting. After a little prodding from Simone and Wanda, Ruby had called Jasper and agreed to do the Slim & Trim commercial. She would get five hundred dollars and a free six-month membership to the program.

It was so funny that she was going to be in a commercial. Ruby abhorred the whole advertising industry. America was the fattest country on earth, yet virtually every commercial that ran on television and all the ads in magazines featured nothing but thin beautiful people or some emaciated celebrity like Sarah Michelle Gellar or Jennifer Love Hewitt. The whole industry was so ridiculous. It was all lies, and everyone knew it was all lies, yet commercials kept getting progressively more outlandish, making all sorts of promises and stretching the truth to the absolute limit. Did anyone really expect to walk into McDonald's and find a smiling cashier who spoke coherent English? Did anyone actually go into a CVS and sincerely expect them to have their prescription in stock?

As she walked down the hall, Ruby felt a wave of excitement. Something just felt right about the whole thing. How could it not work out? She had the perfect motivation—once she lost weight she'd be on television showing off her new body. If that wasn't enough, the Slim & Trim folks were bound to pay more attention to her than a regular client. After all, they would want her to succeed, and help them bring in business with her success story. She would finally be able spend some of that money in her Thin Ruby account.

As she approached what seemed like a waiting room outside the actual studio, a short plump woman came up to her.

"Ruby Waters?" she asked.

"Yes."

"Hi. I'm Kim, Jasper's assistant. You're here to have some photos taken, right?"

"Yeah."

"Well, come on back and we'll get started."

Kim led Ruby farther down the hall into a small room scattered with a few chairs and backdrops for taking portraits.

"Hi there," said a middle-aged woman fiddling with some camera equipment at a table in the corner. "I'm Sylvia, the photographer. You must be Ruby."

"Yeah. Hi," Ruby said.

"I'm running behind today, so we'll need to hurry. Kim will help you get changed, and then we can get started."

"Changed?" Ruby asked. She had worn a casual cotton dress and figured they would just take her picture in that.

"Yes. Why don't you go in the bathroom and put these on," Kim said, handing a pile of clothes to Ruby. Then we'll do your makeup.

"Okay," Ruby said, taking the clothes and walking into the bathroom. Once she had changed, Ruby took a look at herself in the mirror. Kim had given her a pair of loose-fitting jeans and an enormous flannel shirt, which made her look even fatter than she actually was. Looking in the mirror reminded Ruby of something—she looked like one of those people shown on TV when the news ran stories on obesity in America—random fat people caught on camera, but always shown from only the neck down. Ruby was always afraid she was going to turn on the TV one day, and see her headless body featured during the introduction of some story called something like "America's Expanding Waist Line" or "Out of Control Obesity."

"I'm not sure these fit very well," Ruby said to Kim as she emerged from the bathroom, feeling dumpy and fat. "I don't generally have this problem, but I think these clothes are too big."

"They're supposed to be big," Kim answered, gesturing for Ruby to sit down in a chair with a little makeup mirror sitting next to it. Ruby lowered herself into the chair, and Kim reached for a small tube of some kind of concealor or foundation, and started rubbing it under Ruby's eyes.

"Hmm. I think we need to go darker," Kim said, grabbing another tube. As Kim rubbed the makeup under her eyes, Ruby kept expecting it to fade and blend in with her skin, but it didn't. It remained dark and made Ruby look like she hadn't slept in days.

"Okay," Kim said. "Have a seat in front of the screen and Sylvia can get started."

Ruby felt slovenly as she walked toward the backdrop for her photo session. She knew what they were doing. They wanted to make her look as hideous as possible in the before pictures, so when she lost weight, and shot the after commercial, it would be all the more dramatic. It made sense to her, but seeing herself in the wretched clothes with the circles under her eyes suddenly made her sad. She looked so sloppy and pathetic—almost beyond hope. The excitement she had felt when she walked in the door was gone. Now more than ever she was Fat Ruby and she *hated* Fat Ruby.

"Oh, one more thing," Kim said, handing Ruby a worn baseball cap with the NASCAR logo on it.

Ruby accepted the hat and put it on as she sat down in front of Sylvia.

"Okay, I want you to lounge more. You're sitting up too straight," Sylvia said as she began adjusting the light. Ruby tried to look more relaxed, but apparently it still wasn't enough for Sylvia.

"No. Kind of seep into the chair—like you're a man watching a football game with a can of beer."

"Damn. We should have gotten a can of beer," Kim said to Sylvia.

Thank God for small favors, Ruby thought as she adjusted herself in the chair, and Sylvia began clicking pictures.

Type Versus League

"It was so hot, Ruby!" Jeremy said into the phone. "He was from Honduras and had the cutest accent. He was like twenty-two and gorgeous with that protruding lower lip, like Enrique Iglesias."

"Really? Do you have plans together again?" Ruby asked into the phone. It was almost six o'clock, and she was trying to get her desk cleared off so she could meet Wanda for dinner.

"I seriously doubt it. I wasn't really interested in a relationship anyway."

"I thought you gave up one-night stands, Jeremy?"

"I have, but last night I had to make an exception. Ruby, he was twenty-two. *Twenty-two!* It wasn't like we were going to start dating or something. What do I have in common with a twenty-two-year-old? I knew if I didn't bring him home with me last night it would never happen. I mean, really, what are the chances of me having sex with a twenty-two-year-old again . . . without money changing hands anyway. I needed to seize the opportunity while I could."

"You're a mess, Jeremy. Whatever happened to that Steven guy you were seeing a few weeks ago?" Ruby asked, trying to wrap things up. She figured Wanda was probably already waiting for her in the reception area.

"I'm not sure exactly. He didn't return my last phone call. I think I may have been trying to play out of my league."

"What do you mean? I thought you said he was cute and funny and drove a BMW. He should be *just* your type."

"Oh, he was absolutely my *type*, he was just out of my *league*."

"Type? League? What's the difference?" Ruby asked.

"What's the difference? Ruby, come on, Ricky Martin's my *type*, but he's certainly not in my *league*, Matt Damon's my *type*, but he's not in my *league*, that guy that plays Will on *Will & Grace*, the one with a body like a ballet dancer, he's my *type*, but . . ."

"Okay, I get it, I get it," Ruby said. "Listen, Jeremy. I've got to go, Wanda's probably waiting for me. We're going to the Chart House for dinner," Ruby said, her mouth already watering for some of their cream of crab soup spiked with sherry, maybe followed by the fried coconut shrimp, and finished off with their chocolate lava cake. They were supposed to pick up Doris on the way and get her out of the house for the first time since her procedure, but she had called Ruby a couple hours earlier and just asked her to bring an entrée home. Ruby hated to admit it, but she was so glad when Doris canceled, knowing she would be able to eat whatever she wanted with no comments from her critical mother.

When she finally got off the phone, she shut off her computer, grabbed her purse, and headed for the lobby. On her way down the hall she couldn't stop thinking about what Jeremy had said earlier—about guys that were his type, but out of his league. It made her think of Preston, and how she had been kidding herself—sure Preston was her type, but even if he was attracted to large women, he was still way out of Ruby's league.

As she approached the waiting area, Ruby heard Wanda and another voice, a male voice, coming from the lobby area of her floor. It took Ruby a moment to recognize who the other voice belonged to, but when she did, her heart dropped. It was Preston. As soon as she figured it out, instead of turning the corner into the lobby, Ruby stopped and listened out of sight. Wanda was loudly laughing and carrying on with Preston.

Oh, for Christ's sake, Ruby thought. She's telling him her stupid orange juice story.

"My God. I was at the grocery store, and I just wanted some

regular Minute Maid orange juice, and I couldn't find any. I could find every other kind but what I was looking for. I didn't want country style . . . or pulp free . . . or calcium enriched. I was scuffling through the frozen juice section and finally I just screamed 'All I want is goddamn regular orange juice!'"

"You're a riot!" Preston said, laughing. "Do you work in the building?"

"No. I'm just meeting a friend. I work over in Chevy Chase at Saks."

"Saks. Really? Great ties at Saks," Preston replied, lifting his own and showing it to Wanda. "What do you do there?"

"I'm a model."

You are not a model, Ruby thought. You're a fucking sales clerk.

"A model? Well, I can see why. You're quite striking," Preston replied.

Ruby couldn't let this banter go on any longer. "Hi," she said as she approached the couple, not at all happy with the situation. Ruby had worked with Preston for years and had barely said two words to him. Wanda had met him minutes earlier and was already carrying on with him like they were old friends.

"Hi," Wanda said.

"I see you two have met," Ruby replied, trying to hide her displeasure behind a smile.

"Actually, we haven't been formally introduced," Preston said as he turned to Wanda and stuck out his hand. "DaSilva," Preston said. "Preston DaSilva."

Wanda thought it odd, and a bit arrogant, the way he had introduced himself—with his last name first as if he were Bond. *James* Bond.

"Galore," Wanda replied smartly. "Pussy Galore."

Preston laughed.

"Sorry, couldn't help myself," Wanda said. "Wanda Johnson. It's lovely to meet you."

Ruby could see Wanda turning it on. The way she said, "It's lovely to meet you," like she was a southern belle at her coming out party.

"Are you ready to go?" Ruby asked Wanda abruptly, trying to nix the whole encounter before it went any further.

"Sure," Wanda replied to Ruby, before lifting her eyes back to Preston. "It really was great meeting you."

"Yeah," Preston said before adding, "hey, can I get your phone number and maybe give you a call sometime?"

No! No! No! No! Ruby exclaimed in her head. This couldn't be happening! She tried to look calm as her pulse elevated and her mouth went dry.

"Sure," Wanda said, wrote her number on a slip of paper, and handed it to Preston.

"I'll call you," Preston said as the girls walked off.

"Okay," Wanda replied.

As they walked toward the elevator, Ruby wanted to attack Wanda—right then, right there. She wanted to push her to the ground, rip off her Saks employee discount designer suit, and punch her right in the face. She was so distracted and angry that she didn't even notice Alan as he walked by. She hadn't been paying much attention to him since she encountered Preston in the Big Girls, Don't Cry! chat room. She had been so busy trying to get the courage up to just have a conversation with Preston that she had been unknowingly skipping their morning chats.

"Hey," Alan said with a smile as Ruby and Wanda walked by. Wanda smiled, not knowing who he was, and Ruby, filled with rage, just kept walking.

Cinnamon Rolls

Bitch! Ruby thought as she navigated one of the parking garages at National Airport just outside the city. She was absolutely furious! Wanda must have seen Ruby's distressed state after she had given Preston her phone number. Did she just not care? How could she do that to Ruby?

After she and Wanda had stepped away from Preston and gotten inside the elevator, Ruby claimed she was sick and told Wanda she needed to go straight home rather than out to dinner as they had planned. She couldn't bear sitting across the table from Wanda—that traitor! But, instead of going home, as she had told Wanda, Ruby decided to do what she always did when she was upset—eat!

Who am I kidding? Ruby thought as she tried to find a place to park. The more she thought about it, the more she realized it was herself she was mad at, not Wanda. Wanda or no Wanda, Ruby knew she was never going to get up the nerve to seriously approach Preston.

"I've only had years to do what Wanda did in a few minutes," Ruby said to herself, still trying to find somewhere to park the car in the congested garage. The airport seemed especially busy, and there were no open parking spots in sight. When she finally saw a car pulling out, she put on her signal and waited for the driver to pull out. As the car began to make its way out of the space, a third driver, a young woman in a red convertible, approached and whipped her car right into the space as soon as the other car was out of the way. Ruby was aghast. She was obviously there first and had had her turn signal on.

Ruby watched the sharply dressed black woman put the top up on her car, open the door, and climb onto the concrete. With her right turn signal still blinking, Ruby sat in her car, staring at the woman, taking in her long slender legs and thin waist as she sauntered by Ruby's car as if she weren't there. Once Ruby got a good look at the woman, she couldn't believe what she saw—it was the same woman who had stolen a parking space from Ruby a couple weeks earlier in the city. As she glared at her, Ruby considered pounding on her horn or giving the entitled wench the finger, but she was afraid that would result in being called a wealth of ugly fat names. As usual, Ruby decided it was best not to draw attention to herself. She learned that as a young girl and, as an adult, she still subscribed to the belief that if she didn't draw any attention to herself, there was less chance of someone oinking at her or calling her a heifer.

When Ruby finally came upon an open space, she parked the car and turned the ignition off. Then she inserted the car key into the glove compartment, opened the flap, and pulled out a small, black ring box. She lifted the top to reveal a sparking engagement ring, slipped it on her left hand, and tossed the jewelry box back into the glove compartment. Ruby then got out of the car, opened the trunk, and pulled out an empty business-size suitcase. Finally, with her car parked, an "engagement" ring on her finger, and a suitcase trailing behind her, Ruby entered the terminal from the parking garage and let the moving walkway carry her to the main concourse.

Hmm, Ruby thought to herself as she surveyed the restaurants in the terminal. T.G.I. Friday's or Legal Seafood?

After a moment's thought, she decided on Legal Seafood and made her way through the terminal toward the restaurant. As she walked toward her destination, she passed an elderly gentlemen with a tiny toy poodle. He was sitting on a bench with the dog lying on the floor next to its pet carrier. Ruby smiled at the little dog as she walked, wondering how long the dog was going to be able to stay outside his travel carrier before someone reprimanded the old man.

"One?" the host asked her once Ruby had stepped inside the restaurant.

"Yes," Ruby said, following him to a small table in the corner with her empty suitcase trailing behind her. Ruby sat in the chair with her back to the restaurant. She didn't want to make eye contact with anyone, and besides, it was always embarrassing to have to move tables so she could get between them to the bench seating on other side.

"Are you coming or going?" the host asked as he handed her a menu.

"Huh?" Ruby questioned.

"Traveling? Did you just get in, or are you on your way somewhere?"

"Oh. I'm headed to New York," Ruby lied.

"Great city! Have a safe trip," the host said. "Your waiter will be right with you."

It was the perfect set-up. All Ruby had to do was come to the airport, pull a suitcase behind her, and she could eat in a restaurant alone without feeling totally self-conscious. There was no shame in eating in an *airport* restaurant alone. Everyone would just assume she was a career girl getting ready to leave on a business trip. Ruby had these outings every now and then. Sometimes she'd go to hotel restaurants as well. It was the only way she could have a meal at a sit-down restaurant by herself without feeling like everyone was staring at her and feeling sorry for the poor fat girl who had no one to eat with.

Ruby surveyed the menu and saw all sorts of temptations—crabcakes, fried fish, broiled scallops. As she salivated looking at the menu, she repeated to herself over and over again that she wasn't going to overdo it. She was just going to have a light meal and go home.

Soup, she thought to herself. I'll just have the clam chowder and that will be it.

"Are you ready to order?" a young waiter asked after approaching her table.

"Yes. I just want a bowl of clam chowder and a glass of water please."

As the waiter wrote down her order, Ruby made sure to lift her "engagement" ringed hand to her face as if she were deep in thought—perhaps thinking about her upcoming wedding or her fiancé. She wanted to make sure he noticed it. Ruby may have been fat, she may have been eating alone, but she was engaged . . . someone loved her. . . . At least as far as the waiter at Legal Seafood knew, Ruby was engaged. There was no reason he had to know that Ruby had bought the oversize cubic zirconia ring from a street vendor on K Street a few years earlier. She often wore the thirty-dollar ring when she ate meals alone in a restaurant or went grocery shopping. It was Ruby's way of negating the pity factor—if waiters and grocery store clerks thought she was engaged, maybe she wouldn't get so many looks of sympathy when she ordered two Grand Slams at Denny's or piled boxes of Archway Rocky Road cookies and DiGiorno pizzas on the checkout counter at the grocery store.

"Will that be all?" the waiter asked.

"Um . . . well," Ruby said, eyeing the menu again. *Don't do it, Ruby,* she heard a voice in her head saying. *Only the soup! You said you were only having soup!* "Um, let me have some fried calamari as well."

"Excellent choice," the waiter said and started to walk away.

"Ah!" Ruby called behind him. "You know, let me have a crab roll too, with fries," Ruby added, hearing more voices in her head before the words were even out of her mouth: *You were supposed to only have soup.—Oh, go ahead, Ruby have the calamari.—You keep eating like this, you're going to be fat forever!—You're already so fat, what's it matter if you add a crab roll? I mean, really!—Damn it, Ruby, why did you order all that food!*

Well, what's done is done, Ruby said silently to herself, trying to quiet the contentious voices in her head. She had placed the order. It was too late to change it now. She may as well eat it and enjoy it. Yeah, that's what she may as well do.

When Ruby's soup arrived she felt her mouth watering as she held a spoonful of the creamy chowder up to her lips, blew on it, and waited for it to cool. She could see the steam rising off the spoon and had to fight her urge to slurp it up right then. There was probably only one thing Ruby hated about food—it always arrived too hot and, within minutes, it was too cold. There was such a tiny window when the food was at the perfect temperature—hot and fragrant, but cool enough not to burn your mouth.

The more the soup cooled, the faster Ruby ate it. When she had almost cleaned the bowl, she dumped in an entire package of oyster crackers, stirred them around to coat them with any remaining soup, and then ate every last one.

Shortly after she'd finished her soup, her fried calamari arrived. It, too, came to the table piping hot, and Ruby, after devouring every ring on the plate, started on her crab roll, a mayonnaise crab salad over a toasted buttery bun. Within minutes she had cleared the plate of the crab roll and the accompanying French fries and coleslaw. Ruby was never one to leave food on her plate. It always amazed her when she went out with friends who sent their plates back to the kitchen half full. The idea didn't seem plausible to her. How could they not eat what was on the plate—it was insanity!

"Would you care for any coffee or dessert?" the waiter asked after clearing her plates.

"No, thank you," Ruby replied. She'd already eaten so much, she would be too embarrassed to ask for dessert. Instead she would leave Legal and go to the T.G.I. Friday's farther down the concourse and have dessert there, probably after an order of potato skins with cheese, bacon, and sour cream. She knew it was crazy, potato skins after a three-course meal, but how could she possibly go to T.G.I. Friday's and not have potato skins—

that's what they were known for. It would be like going to the Cheesecake Factory and not having cheesecake, something else Ruby couldn't fathom doing. No, if Ruby was going to T.G.I. Friday's, she had to have potato skins.

After she had paid her bill and gotten up from the table she headed down the terminal toward Friday's. The voices were still going: *Skip Friday's, Ruby. Just go home!—Yum! Potato skins! With extra sour cream. Why did they never bring enough sour cream?—Be strong, Ruby. Say no to potato skins. . . .*

Her mouth was totally ready for cheese and bacon and sour cream when she saw a sign that made her rethink going to Friday's—a sign that said Cinnabon. Suddenly her appetite for potato skins changed to a yearning for those mammoth, dripping-with-goo, cinnamon rolls.

Friday's a distant memory, she hurried toward the Cinnabon sign, and, once again passed the old man with the little poodle, who was still out of its carrier as if it were in a park or something. Ruby again smiled at the dog as she passed by and made her way to the bakery. It was nice to see sweet dogs that behaved themselves—dogs so unlike Taco. As she came through the threshold of the Cinnabon, she wondered if there was any scent more pleasurable than the smell of fresh-baked cinnamon rolls, cream cheese icing, and the aroma of brewing coffee. Clam chowder, calamari, and crab roll already forgotten, she approached the counter.

"May I help you?" asked the clerk.

"Yes. One cinnamon roll and a small cup of coffee."

Ruby again tried to ignore the pesky internal voices as she watched the young man scoop a cinnamon roll, dripping with frosting, from the glass case and place it in a cardboard box. *What the fuck are you doing here? Run! Run from those cinnamon rolls. They're pure evil!—don't fight it, Ruby. What's one cinnamon roll really going to do?—leave! Just leave now, before he hands it to you and it's all over—just have some of the roll. You don't need to eat it all. Have half and throw the other half away.*

"Would you like extra icing?" the young man asked.

Extra icing? Ruby thought. No! No! No! "Ah . . . sure," she responded.

Ruby sat at a little table, opened the box, and immediately went at the roll with a plastic knife and fork. She would only eat half of it. That was the plan—eat half the cinnamon roll and throw the rest away.

She hurriedly cut a chunk out of the roll and put it in her mouth. Heaven! Sweet dough, sprinkled cinnamon, warm sugary icing. It was pure heaven!

Okay. I'm just going to have a couple more bites, she thought to herself as she took another bite and then another.

Okay. I'll leave half the roll here. I've eaten enough, she thought, looking down at what was left of the steaming cinnamon roll.

Okay. Just one more bite, she thought as she cut into it again.

Ruby, leave some of it in the container, a voice in her head said as she kept gobbling up the tasty treat. *If you can just NOT FINISH the entire thing, you'll have victory—you will have beaten the Cinnabon!*

Oh, hell, what's one more bite going to do? another voice said as she finished the last smidgen of the roll.

Staring at the empty container, Ruby felt defeated and exhausted. The cinnamon roll had won. Ruby wasn't able to eat only half or even leave just one bite in the cardboard container. As she wiped her mouth, she tried to not let it bother her. She was starting with Slim & Trim in a few days. Maybe she was entitled to one last binge before starting the program.

Yeah! Ruby thought to herself as she got up from the table and looked at the trays of cinnamon rolls behind the glass. I'm entitled to one last binge!

"Something else?" the young man behind the counter asked.

"Ah . . . yeah. Give me half a dozen, please," Ruby said, pointing to the steaming rolls. "My turn to bring breakfast to work tomorrow," Ruby lied. She wasn't going to share those rolls with anyone in her office. They were all for her. It would be her last eating spree before starting the Slim & Trim program.

When she received her half dozen gooey sweets, she went back into the terminal. She was about to head back to her car when she felt a little embarrassed carrying a six-pack of one of the highest calorie foods on the planet. All she needed was to run into some smart aleck boy with a mess of cinnamon rolls in her hand. Accordingly, she stepped over to one of the benches, unzipped her suitcase, inserted the pack of rolls, and zipped the case back up.

Perfect, she thought as she dragged her bag of cinnamon rolls behind her, nicely concealed in the suitcase. She was almost to the people movers that led to the garage when she ran into the old man with the poodle again. Having passed them twice already, it only seemed polite to stop for a moment and make a quick fuss over the dog.

"What a beautiful dog," Ruby said, bending over slightly to pet it, enjoying her interaction with a dog that actually appreciated her touch and kind words.

"Thank you," the man said. "His name is Bonkers."

"Hi, Bonkers," Ruby said as the dog perked up and let Ruby pet him. "He's adorable," Ruby continued as she scratched behind his ears. Bonkers sat on his hind legs and enjoyed the attention until something suddenly seemed to catch his interest. Out of the blue, as Ruby was petting him, he zipped behind her and started sniffing her suitcase and wagging his tail.

Ruby laughed awkwardly and pulled her suitcase the other way, which just prompted Bonkers to follow. He started scratching at the suitcase, making a determined grunting noise.

"Watcha got in there?" asked the old man. "A bag of Gravy Train?"

"Ah . . . no," Ruby replied and, before the stupid dog damaged her suitcase, Ruby decided to bolt. She offered a last smile to the man, annoyed that he hadn't commanded Bonkers to settle down. She tried to casually walk away, but Bonkers wasn't going to let her go quietly. He started barking and pulling on his leash. Ruby heard the barking behind her and starting walking faster.

"No, Bonkers!" she heard the old man say.

When she turned to take a quick look back, she saw Bonkers fervently pulling on his leash. Suddenly Bonkers didn't look like a sweet little dog. He looked vicious, hungry, and just plain mean—he looked like Taco!

With no intention of sharing her cinnamon rolls with a fucking rabid poodle, Ruby started walking faster. When she looked back again, she saw the old man saying something to an airport employee, probably telling him that Ruby had a bomb or cocaine in her bag.

"Miss?" the man called behind her.

Ruby pretended not to hear and kept walking. She was afraid he'd stop her and ask her to open her bag. She was panicked and couldn't bear the thought of someone checking her bag only to find a half dozen cinnamon rolls. Oh, God! If she let him stop her, she'd be water cooler conversation for every airport employee for weeks. "Did you hear about the obese woman who got caught with the cinnamon rolls?" Ruby pictured everyone saying. Stories like that always spiraled out of control—before she knew it, she'd be the fat girl that robbed the Cinnabon, threatened to eat the clerk himself if he didn't comply with her demands, and tried to get away with hundreds of cinnamon rolls in her suitcase.

Ruby heard the man's shoes clumping behind her, getting faster and faster. She knew it was stupid, but she couldn't help it—she didn't have any other options, so she just started to run down the terminal toward the parking garage. She turned her head and saw that the man was running behind her. In a panic, she let go of the suitcase handle and kept running. When she had made it to the parking garage, she looked behind her again and saw that the man had stopped at the suitcase. Thankful he was no longer chasing her, Ruby hurried to her car and drove off. She quickly made her way to the bottom floor and stopped at the payment booth. Panicked that word would reach the parking garage attendant, Ruby handed him the ticket and a twenty dollar bill. She felt a wave a relief as he gave her some change and opened the bar to let her through.

Fuckers! she thought as she headed for the Interstate. She was so embarrassed by the scene, breathless from the running, and still worried that someone might send the cops after her, but mostly she was just annoyed—annoyed that that fucking Bonkers had cost her a half dozen cinnamon rolls.

Ruthless People

"Hi, there," Simone said to Wanda as she stepped into the house. It was after one in the morning, and Simone was surprised to see that Wanda was still up.

"Watched your newscast tonight. Girl, as always, you were fierce!"

Simone smiled, "Thanks. What are you doing up so late?"

"Just not ready for bed I guess. I don't have to be in until noon tomorrow."

"Ruby in bed?" Simone asked.

"I think so. I haven't seen her since I got home. We were supposed to go to dinner tonight. I went out to her office to meet her, but then she said she felt sick and just wanted to go home."

"Hmm . . . maybe there's something going around. Doris asleep too?"

"Yeah," Wanda said before Simone changed the subject. "Well, I have news!" she said with excitement.

"What?" Wanda asked. "The news lady has news? Do tell."

"I talked with Steve, the producer at Channel 6, about this feature we're doing on plus-size models later this month, and I talked you up big time . . . about all the local shows you've done, and how you'd be great for the story since you live right here in the city, and I think I can arrange it so that you're featured in the story."

"Oh, Simone! Are you kidding me?"

"No. He really seemed excited about the idea. The piece would be about plus-size models in general, but it would focus on you and your story, you know, as an example of the life of a plus-size model."

"Oh my God! That could do wonders for my career. I could tape the broadcast and send it to agents in New York."

"Don't get too excited. It's not a done deal yet. He talked about trying to get Mia Tyler or Kate Dillon, but I made a pretty good argument for focusing on someone local like yourself."

"Oh, come on, Simone. You're the reigning queen of local news. If you can't make it happen, no one can. This calls for a celebration," Wanda said and got up from the sofa to head for the kitchen. "And you know how I like to celebrate?"

"How?"

"With food, silly. Have you eaten?"

"No, but I'm not really hungry," Simone said, following her.

"I've got some cold cuts here," Wanda said, after stepping into the kitchen and opening the refrigerator. "You want to make a sandwich?"

"No, thanks," Simone said, looking over Wanda's shoulder. "I think I'll just have this," she added, taking a prepared salad out of the fridge.

"You seem to eat so healthy all the time. Don't you ever just get a hankering for a meatball sub or a Big Mac?"

Simone laughed. "Oh, I eat stuff like that now and then, but I've got to watch my weight. In my business there's always someone younger and prettier than you trying to push you out of the way."

"I hear you," Wanda said. "This little hussy named Denise is hot on my heels as we speak. She wants to be a plus-size model as well. I think she's, like, all of twenty-five. She even got me axed from the big Saks show this weekend. I'm not sure how she did it."

"It probably involved giving someone a blow job," Simone said.

"I don't know. The show manager's as gay as Target on Sundays."

"Then she probably found some guy to blow him for her," Simone said.

"I wouldn't put it past her."

"You'd better watch her like a hawk. She sounds dangerous—young and determined. Don't let your guard down for a second," Simone advised, speaking to herself as much as Wanda. She knew all about women that were younger and prettier and out to send the older girls to pasture. She knew because she was one of them. It wasn't so long ago that she had engineered a plan to get rid of Gail Moore at Channel 22 in San Antonio before she came back to D.C. Gail was fifty-two and had been anchoring the five o'clock news for fifteen years. She was holding it together pretty well—she kept herself fit and trim, had had her eyes and chin done, and her breasts lifted. All in all, Gail looked smashing for fifty-two, but she was still fifty-two and no match for Simone, who was a mere thirty-one when she was hired as a reporter at Channel 22.

Shortly after Simone started with the station, rumors were flowing that the station's executives were looking to replace Gail. Her ratings had slipped, and they wanted a fresh face—a younger face. Once Simone got wind of this news, she decided she would be Gail's replacement. Simone did all the right things—she kissed up to the station managers, worked hard on her stories, and volunteered to take on extra work. She did everything she could to raise her profile with the decision makers at Channel 22, but it wasn't until the station threw Gail a fifteenth anniversary party that Simone figured out how to really get everyone's attention. A few days before the event, Simone had seen Gail showing her assistant the dress she planned to wear to the party in her honor. Simone had to admit, the woman did have taste. The dress was a red chiffon number adorned with delicate beads. It had a ruffle edge that fell gently below the knees and spaghetti straps that crisscrossed in the back. It was totally sexy without being trashy.

The night of the party Gail looked super in her red dress. Most women her age could never have carried it off, but with the help of some extreme dieting and plastic surgery, Gail would have been able to make it work had it not been for one unfortunate "coincidence." Oops, Simone had "mistakenly" bought the exact same dress and decided to wear it that very night as well—only Simone's dress was two sizes smaller than Gail's to fit Simone's size-six frame. Seeing her dress draped perfectly on the nubile body of a thirty-one-year-old, Gail was mortified. Next to Simone, with her young olive complexion, Gail looked weathered and pasty. She felt like a dried-up old hag wearing the same dress as someone so much younger. And, in reality, next to Simone, Gail did end up looking ridiculous in the risqué dress—sort of like the night Diana Ross wore the same dress as Mariah Carey on *Divas Live*. Diana looked fabulous for someone her age (aside from her hideous Krusty the Klown hair), but next to Mariah, she just looked old and silly.

It was the perfect plan. How better to spark the idea of Simone replacing Gail as the anchor on the five o'clock news—the same way Simone looked so much better in Gail's dress, she would look so much better in Gail's chair behind the news desk. Two short months after her fifteenth anniversary party, Gail was forced out of her job, and Simone was Channel 22's newest anchor. Of course, Simone felt some remorse for what she had done, but Gail was going to go anyway. If Simone hadn't replaced her, it would have just been someone else. Besides, Simone had never forgiven Gail for an incident that had occurred when Simone first joined the station—Simone would never forget it—it was the evening before Simone was due to officially start at Channel 22, and she had stopped by the station's headquarters to drop off some personal items and get her office set up. It was after working hours, so Simone had on a pair of jeans and a T-shirt and her hair pulled back in a ponytail. She was feeling good about starting a new job and wanted her space to be in perfect order for her first day. She was wiping down her desk with some Pledge and a dry rag when Gail walked by, took note of Simone, and poked her head in the office door.

"*Hola,*" she said to Simone in a patronizing tone, before she began to speak very slowly, as if Simone were retarded. "Last night you forgot to empty my trash. Can you be sure to get to it tonight? My office is three doors down." The whole time Gail was speaking to her she made exaggerated hand gestures in case Simone didn't speak English.

Simone was aghast and before she had a chance to say a word, Gail smiled at her and headed back down the hall. The following day, Simone expected an embarrassed apology when she was introduced to Gail as a new correspondent for the station. But with Simone in full makeup, a business suit, and her hair done, Gail didn't even realize she had mistaken her for the cleaning lady the night before. Simone wasn't sure if Gail ever made the connection . . . or, maybe she had, but just didn't want to acknowledge her blunder. It was an honest mistake, and Gail hadn't meant any malice, but at the same time, Simone couldn't help hating her. How dare Gail assume that, just because Simone was Latina and cleaning an office, she was the maid. Gail would never have made such an assumption about a white lady. But as much as Simone disliked Gail for assuming that she was a janitor, she hadn't plotted to replace Gail as the anchor of the San Antonio five o'clock news out of a desire for revenge. She saw it as a necessary move to advance her own career, and her like or dislike for Gail had little to do with the decision. Business was business, and sometimes that meant doing whatever was necessary to get ahead.

Yes, Simone was very aware how ruthless people could be to get what they wanted, and now she was warning Wanda to stay on her toes and watch out for girls like—well, girls like her.

"People can be merciless, Wanda," Simone said. "And this Denise chick sounds like someone who would stop at nothing to get what she wants. My advice to you is to squash her like a bug before she does the same to you."

With that, Simone closed the lid on her salad container, tossed it in the garbage, and said good night to Wanda.

It had been a long day, and her conversation with Wanda just reminded her of how nasty her business could be. Simone knew that one day she would be in Gail's shoes, with some hungry young thang chasing after her job. When she got up to her bedroom, she closed the door and turned on the television. She kicked off her heels and went into the walk-in closet to change into a nightshirt.

After she had changed clothes, she approached the hope chest at the bottom of her bed, hurriedly opened it up, and examined the inventory—Krispy Kreme crullers, moon pies, Pop Tarts, the list went on and on. She rummaged through the goodies and eventually decided on a cylinder of Pringles, a box of Little Debbie Zebra Cakes, and a large can of Bush's baked beans. She tossed the items on the bed, closed the chest, and got up on the mattress.

"Oh yeah!" she said to herself as she opened the can of chips. She pulled them out in groups of five or six and ate clumps of them rather than one chip at a time. The crunchiness, the salt, the rough texture of the chips—they were so good. She finished the can and then grabbed the box of Little Debbie cakes. She opened the package and immediately devoured six of the individual cakes, which made her feel stuffed to the limit. She felt swollen and nauseous when she pulled a manual can opener from the nightstand, attached it to the can of beans, and began cranking open the lid. She put the open can up to her nose and smelled the barbecue sauce with a touch of honey. She grabbed a spoon from her stash of plastic silverware and hurriedly gobbled up the cold beans. When she was finished, almost too stuffed to move, she picked up all the empty boxes, cans, and wrappers and tied them up in small trash bag, which she would stuff in her briefcase in the morning, and drop in a public trash can on the street.

Once she had cleaned up, she lay on the bed and felt the fullness in her belly. She just wanted to revel in it for a few minutes longer. It had been so good—all the food had been so satisfying. A short time later, she got up from the bed, turned up the volume on the television set and went into the bathroom. She opened the lid on the toilet, got down on her knees, and shoved her finger down the back of her throat.

Deserving to Cry

It was nearly eleven o'clock on Friday night, and Ruby was in the living room chatting on the phone with Jeremy. She was seething mad. Doris had just gone to bed after giving Ruby a quick lecture about the perils of eating anything after nine P.M. and, if that wasn't enough, a few hours earlier she had listened from the top of the steps while Wanda chatted on the phone with Preston and made a date to meet him the following week. She couldn't believe that Preston DaSilva was calling her house, but he was calling for Wanda, not her. It had all happened so quickly and right before her eyes.

"Damn it! Why did I ever tell Wanda to meet me at work? If I had just met her at the restaurant, she never would have crossed paths with Preston," Ruby vented into the phone. She knew it wasn't right, but at that moment, she hated Wanda. It was so unfair, why did Wanda have so much charisma and confidence? Ruby was used to men passing her over for thin women, but this time it was a fellow fat girl who had ousted her. She couldn't even compete with someone as big as she was.

"You should tell her how you feel, Ruby. She probably has no idea."

"My God, Jeremy. It was hard enough to admit my feelings about Preston to you. How am I supposed to say anything to Wanda?"

"Easy. Just tell her to lay off your man."

"If only he was my man. God, this sucks!"

"I'm sorry, Ruby. I really think you should talk to her. She seems like a reasonable person. It's better than just sitting around stewing."

"I don't know, maybe."

"I hope you will," Jeremy encouraged before continuing. "Listen, I've got to go. I've got to meet my mother for breakfast tomorrow. I think she's bringing her minister along, you know, to try to convert me or something."

"Oh, you're kidding?"

"No, last week she sent me some info about ex-gays who found salvation through Jesus or something. You'd think she'd get tired of trying to make me straight, but she never seems to give up."

"Don't get me started on mothers who never give up. We'll be on the phone all night. Good luck tomorrow."

"Thanks," Jeremy said. "And, really, talk to Wanda."

"Maybe. Bye, Jeremy," Ruby said and hung up the phone, thinking about how funny it was they both had mothers who badgered them constantly and kept trying to make them into something they would never be. It was strange how they had so much in common—Jeremy was a skinny gay man, and Ruby was a fat straight girl, yet they were treated so similarly by society—as if something was wrong with them, and if they could just see "the light" they would be okay. People were always trying to change them—and always out of some *supposed* higher concern for their greater well-being. The same way the religious right tried to camouflage their fascist ideas behind the Bible and Christianity, Ruby's tormentors hid their agenda with their "selfless concern for the health of fat people"—oh no, it was *never* about looks, or vanity, or not wanting to have an unsightly fat wife by their side . . . or the desire to make billions of dollars off weight loss scams—people were always concerned about the fat girl's health—BULL FUCKING SHIT! Everyone knew that no one gave a rat's ass about the health of fat people—everyone knew what all the husbands were really thinking when they sat next to their obese wives, who were seeking diet help on *The Oprah Winfrey Show*. The husbands would always say something like, "Honey, it's not the way you *look* I care about. It's your *health* that concerns me," when what they were really thinking was: You've gotten so fat, I can't stand to look at you anymore.

The same way the religious right couldn't have really cared less about what the Bible said about Jeremy or how Jesus would have treated homosexuals, skinny fat-hating people had no real interest in the health of the obese. It was just that the Bible and concern for the health of fellow human beings gave their causes some nobility. It beat coming out and saying what they really thought—that they found gay people disgusting and unacceptable because they didn't conform to their idea of what was normal and healthy—that they found fat people disgusting and unacceptable because they didn't conform to their idea of what was normal and healthy.

Yes, Ruby and Jeremy had a lot in common, but over the past few years Ruby watched as gay people gained more and more acceptance. They were being portrayed more realistically on television, states were passing all sorts of favorable legislation, and Vermont was even sanctioning same-sex unions. It had gotten to the point where virtually everyone would think you were crazy if you suggested a gay person try to convert to heterosexuality, yet no one batted an eye when fat people were bombarded with plans and programs promising to change them. Okay, few, if any, had ever really changed from a homosexual to a heterosexual, but when you really thought about it, how many fat people ever really changed to thin people? Ruby could count the number of people she knew who had successfully kept weight off for years on one hand. Maybe, the same way gay people were genetically programmed to be gay, fat people were genetically programmed to be fat—why couldn't anyone accept that? Any reasonable person would look at you in horror if you suggested that a gay person attempt electroshock conversion therapy, yet, those same people would wish their fat friends luck as they were being wheeled off to the operating room to have their gut ripped open and their stomach mutilated and shrunk with staples—all in an effort to conform to what society found normal and attractive. It was craziness—all of it was pure craziness!

Feeling terribly alone and pathetic, Ruby turned on the television to catch Simone's newscast. In a daze she half listened to Simone and her coanchor, Charlie Parker, deliver the latest and greatest about the happenings locally and around the country. It was all of little interest to Ruby until Simone mentioned a recent security scare at National Airport.

"In a bit of strange story," Ruby heard Simone say through the television, "yesterday, a large corridor of Reagan National Airport was sealed off for a brief period due to a suspicious piece of luggage. Late yesterday evening, a Caucasian woman described as heavy-set with red hair and blue eyes abruptly ran from the airport after a canine took an interest in her bag. As she dashed from the terminal to the parking garage, she abandoned her suitcase. The area was later sealed off and a bomb retrieval robot was directed to the luggage. In an odd turn of events, when the bag was opened, the only contents were a six-pack of cinnamon buns from the Cinnabon bakery, which leases space at the airport."

As Simone read from the TelePrompTer, they ran some grainy footage from a security camera at the airport. Ruby was horrified to see her fat self running down the corridor as Simone continued. "The cinnamon rolls have been sent to a lab to be analyzed, and police and airport officials are seeking information anyone might have on the large woman currently being referred to as the Cinnabomber."

As the cameras rolled back from the security footage to Simone and Charlie, Ruby watched them smirk at each other. They usually tried to be professional, but this time, neither Simone nor Charlie tried to conceal their laughter. Charlie could barely keep from cracking up as he went into a story about violence in the Middle East.

Ruby clicked off the TV with her pulse quickening. At least the film from the airport camera was such poor quality no one would be able to recognize her, but somehow that didn't seem to matter. She could *almost* laugh about it—a fat lady, wildly jiggling as she ran through the airport with baked goods in her suitcase—it was funny, really, it was—but not when it was happening to her. She had been the laughingstock of her grade school, the laughingstock of her high school, and now, it had finally happened, she was the laughingstock of the entire Metro area. She was tired of being the butt of jokes. She was tired of being made fun of. She was just plain tired, exhausted, in fact, of being Ruby, Big Fat Ruby! She looked at the blank television screen, and it all came to a head—seeing herself on television, Wanda getting a call from Preston, Simone and Charlie laughing at her on the evening news, even wicked Heather Watkins from the third grade made an entrance in her mind. It was all more than she could handle, and she put her hands to her face and didn't even try to keep from crying. As the tears came, she grabbed a pillow and tried to muffle the sound of her grief—Simone was at work, and Wanda was out, but Doris was in the den, and Ruby didn't want her to hear her wailing. She was too tired to try to fight the tears and just let them flow. It was a different kind of crying from what she had done in a long time. It was the kind of crying when your whole body shakes, a piercing whimpering noise comes from your throat, and you start to lose your breath, but, strangely, something about it felt good. Ruby deserved to cry. At that moment, at eleven-fifteen on a Friday night, after Wanda had gotten a call from a man Ruby had been infatuated with for years, and her obese image had just been strewn across thousands of television sets, Ruby Waters deserved to cry, and she was going to take the time to do it right.

Eventually, her weeping slowed, and she had released a hint of the pain of being Ruby Waters. As she wiped her eyes and blew her nose she heard a faint knock on the door. It was such a quiet tapping, she thought it might be someone at the house next door, but then she recognized the knock—it was slow and deliberate, almost timed to some code or sequence. What was her ex-husband doing at her house so late?

Ruby wiped her eyes again and got up from the sofa and opened the door.

"Hello, Ruby," Warren said.

"Warren. What are you doing here?"

"May I come in?"

"Ah . . . sure."

"Are you well? Your eyes are swollen," Warren said as Ruby closed the door behind him.

"Yeah, just allergies," Ruby lied. "So what's up?"

"I was desirous of someone with whom to converse."

"Um . . ." Ruby hesitated for a moment to decipher Warren's words. "Oh, you want someone to talk to. About what?"

Warren approached the sofa and sat down. "Olga terminated our relationship."

Olga? Ruby thought. You left me for a woman named Olga? What? Is she a hundred? "I'm sorry," Ruby said, and she really was.

"She said I was too rigid, and she needed someone more spontaneous."

"I'm sorry, Warren," Ruby said again. "Maybe it just wasn't meant to be." Ruby put her arm around him. He looked so pathetic and defeated, pretty much the same way Ruby had felt when he knocked on the door.

"I never should have left you," Warren said, looking deeply at Ruby, and then hugging her tightly.

Ruby was shocked by his words and didn't know what to say, so she just hugged him back. They continued to embrace for a moment longer until Warren pulled back just a bit and tried to kiss her. Again, Ruby was shocked and unsure how to react. She wasn't interested in starting something again with Warren, but it had been so long since someone had kissed her that even Warren's lips felt welcome. Preston was chasing Wanda, and she had just been humiliated on the local news, but right then and there, at least someone wanted her. Ruby began returning his kisses, enjoying the comfort and familiarity of Warren's arms, and willingly followed when Warren led her up the steps to her room.

"Shh," she said as she followed him up the steps. "My mother's in the den."

After they had gotten upstairs and Ruby had explained why she was sleeping in the smallest room in her own house, the drudgery of their former sex life began coming back. Warren immediately took off all his clothes and waited on the bed for Ruby to do the same. Just like when they were married, there was no seductive slow removal of clothing. It didn't fit into Warren's efficiency plans. Once Ruby was undressed, she got under the covers with Warren and prepared for the inevitable. Just like he did time and time again when they were married, Warren kissed her for twenty to thirty seconds, fondled and licked her breast for two to three minutes, and then entered her for twenty to thirty thrusts before letting out a long sigh, pulling out, and going to sleep. It was unremarkable and boring, but there was something comforting in the familiarity of it all and, if nothing else, Ruby found some solace in a warm body lying next to her.

As Ruby tried to get comfortable and settle in to go to sleep, she thought about what she had just done. What had driven her to go to bed with Warren? After the divorce she missed a few things about married life—the secure feeling it gave her, the status of being part of a couple, the comfort of having someone to come home to, but one thing she had never missed was the sex with Warren. In fact, she was thankful for never having to sleep with him again, and she was especially grateful to have her Sunday mornings back. Ruby loved to sleep-in on the weekends, but, for some reason Warren was always feeling particularly frisky on Sunday mornings. As they were waking-up, he'd cuddle up next to her and press his erect dick against her thigh. Ruby would try to pretend she was still asleep, but such attempts only prompted Warren to press himself against her harder or start fondling her breasts. Unfortunately, Warren seemed to have more stamina in the mornings and lasted longer inside her. Ruby would never forget those Sunday mornings, with Warren on top of her—she could remember shutting her eyes so he wouldn't make her laugh with the ridiculous expressions that came across his face. All she could think while she lay underneath him, his breath heavy on her shoulder, and his body pumping against her was: My God! Would you fucking come already, so we can go to brunch!

Now, as she lay in bed next to her former husband, Ruby knew that she had made a mistake. As alone as she felt, she didn't feel so alone that she wanted to go back to the monotony of her former marriage. She hoped that Warren hadn't taken their encounter to mean anything more than it was—two people trying to take the edge off their loneliness for one night. As Ruby drifted off to sleep, she hoped to have the dream about hosting Ruby's Deep Fried Party, where everyone brings a dish—anything from broccoli, to potatoes, to cubes of meat, and Ruby shows them that anything—positively *anything* is fantastic when it's deep-fried.

Second Adolescence

Simone and Eric had just had dinner at Odeon, a casual Italian restaurant just off Dupont Circle, and were headed back to Eric's car. It had been an interesting dinner. As usual there was a bit of a hush as Simone entered the restaurant, and diners started less-than-discreetly nudging their companions to turn around to see who had just walked in. By the time Simone and Eric were seated, the restaurant was abuzz with talk of Simone and the young stallion she'd brought through the door with her. It probably wasn't good for her career as a serious newswoman to be seen around town with an obvious boy toy, but then Simone wasn't interested in a career in serious news. In fact, she hoped being seen with a twenty-something stud might spawn a rumor or two and get her some social press, the kind of press that would elevate her celebrity status.

"So? What now?" Eric asked as they walked down Connecticut Avenue and turned onto a side street toward Eric's car.

"Hmm. I'm not sure. It's only nine-thirty. Maybe we could go back to your place for a drink," Simone suggested, hoping to get on with the evening. Having dinner with Eric was more social contact than she had really cared to have with him, and she didn't feel like prolonging the sex any further with drinks at a bar or coffee at some outdoor café. She was horny and wanted a repeat of their last encounter as soon as possible.

"Ah . . ." Eric hesitated for a moment. "My wife's home tonight. She thinks I'm working late. How about your place?"

"Unfortunately my place in under renovation, and I'm staying with friends," Simone replied. She couldn't bear to say she was renting a room in someone's house, like a common boarder.

"Oh yeah, you mentioned that earlier," Eric said as he opened the car door for Simone.

Once they were both in the car, Eric started the ignition and tuned the radio to a jazz station playing romantic music.

"Gosh, I hate to call it a night already," Simone said as she looked over at Eric. He was wearing khaki pants and the sleeves of his polo shirt tightly hugged his biceps. She reached over and put her hand on his leg.

"Maybe we could go to a motel?"

"You better mean *hotel*!" Simone said with a laugh and shook her head. "I don't think that would be a good idea." Simone didn't mind being seen out and about with a guy more than ten years younger than she, but checking into a hotel for a few hours with him might be a bit much, even for her.

Eric looked at Simone and then diverted his eyes out the window. "Well, this street is pretty quiet. I don't see anyone around."

"What are you suggesting?"

"Improvising," Eric said, reaching across Simone's lap, and pressing the recline button on the seat controls.

"What are you doing?" Simone said, even though she knew exactly what he was doing. As the seat lowered, Eric maneuvered on top of her, and Simone could feel his hardness against her thigh. She couldn't believe it. Was she really about to do this? Fuck a guy in the front seat of a car on a public street?

"Wait, Eric," she said, resisting him. She was Simone Fucking Reyes. She didn't have sex in cars like a damn prostitute.

"What?" Eric said as he adjusted himself on top of her and started kissing her neck.

"I don't think . . ."

"Don't think," he said and started breathing a bit heavier and harder. It was happening, the transition that Simone couldn't resist was already happening. Eric was going from straitlaced preppy white boy to hungry animal and there was nothing hotter to Simone. When a guy in Dockers and a polo—a guy who paid his bills on time, and called his mother once a week—started huffing and sighing with pleasure, it was the ultimate turn on. Simone wasn't sure if it was a man's animalistic behavior that aroused her so much, or if she just got off on her own power to make a man drop all thoughts of his stock portfolio or the score of the football game and focus entirely on her. Soon Simone was meeting his lips with hers and letting him undo her blouse like they were a couple of school kids parking after the homecoming dance.

"I can't believe I just did that," Simone said as the two of them tried to reassemble themselves on either side of the car.

"It was great," Eric said, suddenly looking very boyish, like he'd just finished a Happy Meal that came with a Matchbox car.

"God, I hope no one saw," Simone replied as she buttoned her blouse. The sex had been quick, and she didn't even come, but somehow it had still been incredibly hot. Maybe it was the sleaziness of doing it in the front seat of a car or the possibility of being seen—whatever it was, the experience had been a total rush for Simone. They hadn't even gotten completely undressed. Eric never removed his shirt, and lowered his pants only enough to reveal his cock. He unbuttoned Simone's blouse, savagely lowered her panties from underneath her skirt, and started fucking her. It was so untamed and naughty—and, more importantly, it was so high school. Simone felt like she had just had a second adolescence. She was grossly overweight in school and didn't have any boyfriends until after her dramatic weight loss. She didn't get asked to the homecoming dance or the prom and, hence, missed out on the car sex that almost always followed. As she straightened her skirt and tried to tame her hair she felt validated—she felt like the girl she had always wanted to be in high school—the slut that made it in cars with the jocks.

"Can I take you home?" Eric said as he started the car.

"Ah . . ." Simone hesitated for a moment. "You know what?

I think I'll walk," she said and gave him a quick peck on the lips.

"Are you sure?" Eric said.

"Yeah, it's just a few blocks from here," Simone said as she stepped out of the car. "I'll call you," she added before closing the door. She gave Eric a quick wave and turned to walk down the sidewalk—just once, she wanted to do it. She had heard girls talk about it all through college—the walk of shame—the walk home in the predawn hours, from whatever dorm room or frat house in which you had spent the night, trying to slip into your own bed before anyone noticed you had spent the night out. It wasn't the early morning hours, and Simone wasn't in college, but that night she was going to have another rite of passage, she was going to do the notorious "walk of shame" and it was going to feel really good.

Doughnuts!

Ruby inserted the car key into the glove compartment, pulled out her "engagement" ring, and slipped it on her left hand. She opened the door, and the car jiggled as she hoisted her frame from her Saturn, shut the car door, and made her way toward the Shoppers Food Warehouse just outside Washington, D.C., in Falls Church, Virginia. She was on her way to work, but had to make a quick stop before heading to the office.

She grabbed a wide cart, pushed it through the automatic doors, whizzed right through the floral and produce sections, and quickly approached her destination—Mecca . . . the Land of Milk and Honey . . . Paradise—the Shoppers Food Warehouse bakery. Ruby didn't particularly care for the Shoppers Food Warehouse as a place to do general grocery shopping. It was too big, seemed to have a smaller selection than the Giant or the Safeway, and it was often quite crowded, but one thing kept her coming back—the doughnuts! Shoppers had the *best* doughnuts. They were light and fluffy and made fresh every day. They were certainly better than Dunkin Donuts, and maybe, just maybe, they were as good as the melt-in-your-mouth glazed doughnuts sold at the Krispy Kreme shop out on Route 1 in Alexandria. Okay, who was she kidding? Nothing was as good as a Krispy Kreme doughnut, especially when served warm—fresh from the grease, but Ruby didn't have time to go all the way to the Krispy Kreme shop. She needed a doughnut fix, and she needed it right then and there. And she was going to eat her doughnuts with no remorse. When she got up that morning, she had decided that doughnuts were going to be her final binge before starting the Slim & Trim program. She figured she was entitled to them after her plan to consume half a dozen cinnamon rolls was foiled by that pesky poodle at the airport.

Ruby was already salivating as she reached for a cardboard box from the counter, snatched a little plastic sheet from the dispenser, and starting grabbing doughnuts from the showcase—two chocolate frosted, four glazed, two powdered sugar filled with icing, two jelly filled, and two sugar raised. She closed the lid on the box, set it down in the cart, and made her way to the dairy section where she picked up a quart of whole milk and headed straight for the checkout line. As she put the doughnuts and the milk on the conveyer belt she offered a polite greeting to the cashier.

"My turn to pick up breakfast for the office," Ruby lied the same way she had when she'd ordered the cinnamon rolls at the airport. She smiled at the cashier and made sure to lift her engagement-ringed hand to her face

After Ruby paid for her milk and doughnuts, she carried her bag of goodies to the car, lowered herself into the driver's seat, and set the grocery bag on the passenger side. Once she was settled, she started the car and quickly made her way to the other side of the parking lot where there were fewer cars. Ruby steered the car into a space, shifted it into park, and lifted her foot from the brake. She popped an old Wham! cassette into the stereo, turned up the volume, and reached for her food as "Wake Me Up Before You Go Go" streamed from the speakers. She opened the carton of milk and cursed herself for forgetting to get a straw. She lifted the carton to her lips and took a long sip. She then reached for the box of doughnuts, opened it up, and quickly scanned the variety.

"Chocolate!" she said excitedly to herself as she pulled one of the chocolate-iced doughnuts from the box. She was salivating before it reached her mouth and was downright giddy as she began to devour her prize. The doughnut was so light and airy with the perfect complement of chocolate icing. She quickly gobbled it up and hastily reached for a jelly filled. As she consumed her doughnuts she shut her eyes and took deep breaths here and there while she enjoyed the sheer delight of their richness. She had the same look about her that heroin addicts exude just as they begin injecting themselves with a mind-altering drug—the same relief . . . the same elation involved when an irresistible craving is being met—the same feeling around doing something *so* bad that feels *so* good.

When Ruby was about to delve into her third doughnut a car approached her from behind. As the driver pulled into the space next to her, Ruby frantically laid the doughnut back in the box, closed the carton of milk, and sat quietly as if she were just sitting in her car waiting for someone.

As a small man emerged from the car next to her, Ruby was horrified to catch a glimpse of herself in the rearview mirror and see a ring of powdered sugar around her mouth. She quickly wiped her mouth on the sleeve of her shirt—not only had she forgotten to get a straw as she hurried her doughnuts out of the store, she had forgotten to get any napkins. She sat quietly as she watched the man walk past her car. Once he was a safe distance away, Ruby dove back into the box and finished the jelly filled doughnut. She then proceeded to wolf down a sugar raised, a glazed, and the last chocolate frosted. She ate with such enthusiasm and speed it was mere minutes before half the box was empty. There was something almost sexual about the way Ruby binged. She moaned and inhaled deeply, and it wasn't uncommon for her to quietly speak out loud, "Oh God! This is so good! Oh God! Oh God!"

Ruby took another sip of milk and looked at the remaining doughnuts. There were a few glazed, two powdered sugar, and a jelly filled staring up at her. The first six doughnuts had pretty much satiated her appetite. Her stomach no longer had that nagging longing to be filled, but there were still six doughnuts left—six doughnuts calling to her, flaunting their glazed coatings and jelly fillings.

Feeling full and bloated, Ruby polished off a glazed doughnut and looked at the remaining treats in the box. A part of her wanted to finish off the entire dozen even though she really didn't want any more. It just seemed like the right thing to do—to let Fat Ruby stuff herself silly before starting her new life with the Slim & Trim program—her new life as a person with self-control . . . a person losing weight . . . the beginnings of Thin Ruby.

Deciding against consuming the entire box, she closed the lid, got out of the car, and walked the remaining doughnuts over to a trash can in the parking lot. When she reached her destination she stood over the receptacle, not quite ready to do away with her final tastes of sweet goodness. She looked at the trash can and then looked at the doughnuts.

How can you throw away perfectly good doughnuts? said a voice in her head. *Come on, you can finish these off*, the voice added, despite the swollen feeling in her belly.

No! another voice said. *Throw them away, Ruby. Throw them away!*

Ruby stood by the trash can listening to the internal voices, unable to let go of the doughnuts.

"God damn it, Ruby!" she said to herself, lifting her fingers from the box and letting it fall into the garbage can. It took all she had to fight the urge to lift the box back out again and head back to her car.

Feeling as if she had just won a minor victory against Fat Ruby, she removed her "engagement" ring, stuffed it back in the glove compartment, and started the ignition. This was it. She was going to have her first appointment with a Slim & Trim counselor that evening, and it would be a matter of months before she lost substantial weight. It had been awful having the before pictures taken, but it would all be worth it when Ruby starred in the after commercial. Maybe they would even let her wear Doris's little black dress.

As Ruby backed out of the parking space, she thought about how she was going to look wearing a sexy black dress in a major commercial after she lost weight. She ejected the Wham! tape from the stereo and Destiny's Child began to pour from the radio courtesy of Hot 99.5. As "Bootylicious" came from the car speakers, Ruby reached over to turn up the volume. She'd had her last binge and the Slim & Trim program was going to work, she was going to be bootylicious, just like in the song. Oh, she just couldn't wait for it to happen!

The First Time

"*Gracias, Mama,*" Simone said to her mother as she walked from her parents' house with a small cardboard box.

"*Estas muy flaca. Tienes que comer,*" her mother replied. "*Lo hice especialmente para ti.*"

"*Huelen delicioso. Te llamo a fin de semana,*" Simone said and kissed her mother good-bye. "*Te llamo a fin de semana.*"

Simone got in her car, closed the door, and watched her mother slip back into the house after giving Simone a final wave. Her parents lived just twenty minutes outside the city in Silver Spring, Maryland, but Simone only drove out to see them about once a month. She usually dropped by on a Sunday afternoon and picked at whatever her mother had fixed for lunch, caught up on family gossip, and slipped her mother a check for a few hundred dollars. Simone always told her mother that the money was for her and her father, but she knew most of it was sent to her parents' relatives in Bolivia. Simone enjoyed her afternoons with her parents, and they also allowed her to brush up on her Spanish, which was getting worse by the day.

Simone grew up hearing her parents speak Spanish, and it became her first language, but, even as little girl, Simone had a determination that was unusual for young children, and she knew her best chance out of her parents' working class world was to learn to speak English perfectly. She had always been bright and even though she started primary school knowing little English, it wasn't long before she was speaking it as well as any native-born American.

Now, the schools in Silver Spring were full of recent immigrant children whose primary language was Spanish, but in the seventies, Simone was one of only three Latino children in her school. Her entire circle of friends from grade school through college spoke English and only English, and slowly Simone's Spanish began to slip. At thirty-four, she could still carry on a conversation in Spanish, but occasionally she had to stop and think about the translation of certain words and the proper use of others, and it made her parents crazy. They hated that their daughter was losing touch with her Bolivian heritage. They pestered her to visit her homeland, but Simone had never made it a priority. It wasn't that she didn't want to see the beautiful mountains of La Paz or her parents' hometown of Cochabamba, but when it came to spending a few thousands dollars on a vacation, Simone was always swayed toward sunning in Hawaii or cruising the Caribbean rather than getting in touch with her heritage in a developing country. Besides, she figured she'd eventually pitch the idea of some sort of "Going Home" special to Channel 6 and have them foot the bill for her travels to South America.

On her way home from her parents, Simone lifted the foil on the cardboard box and took in the aroma of the Salteñas, a Bolivian delicacy of spicy meat and vegetables baked in a flaky dough. Some people cheated and made them from premade empanada dough, but Simone's mother made the dough and the filling from scratch. It was an all-day job of chopping, stirring, kneading, rolling, and baking, but the final product was always worth it.

The fragrant aroma coming from the box made Simone remember a time several years ago when she was still working on the sidelines of television in Philadelphia and was at home over the holidays visiting her parents. It was Christmas 1996, and Simone came home to a kitchen full of holiday goodies. Her mother had prepared all kinds of Christmas treats, including a Bolivian dessert called *pasteles de navidad con jigote*, which mainly consisted of a sweetened meat mixture that was wrapped in dough, deep fried, and tossed in powdered sugar. This was back when Simone was still grossly overweight, and prior to visiting that particular holiday, Simone had managed one of her longest stints on a diet. She had lost more than fifteen pounds and was starting to feel like there was hope for her getting out of the plus-sizes. She was determined to stay on her diet over the holidays, but when she saw her mother's feast of holiday goodies, she lost control. One evening while her mother was out, she devoured plates of cookies, and *pasteles*, and homemade candies. It was if she had suddenly gone wild and ate and ate until she was beyond full. By the time she was finished she felt terrible . . . awful. She'd done so well on her diet for months and then, in one fell swoop, she threw it all away. She felt hopeless and guilty with her belly full of Christmas desserts. All she could think as she sat in the kitchen, feeling bloated and full, was that if she had the chance again, she would have been strong—she wouldn't have fallen victim to the food. If only there was a way she could get rid of it and not let it add weight to her body. She had never seriously considered the idea of purging before, but, maybe, if she only did it that one time, just to get herself back on track, it would be okay. Yeah, she thought . . . maybe if it was just that one time, it would be okay.

Simone's first bingeing and purging occurrence was supposed to have been a one-time deal, but a few weeks after her first episode, she slipped from her diet regimen again and, just like she had a few days before Christmas, she forced herself to throw-up all the food she had regretted eating. It wasn't long before she was regularly stuffing herself silly and later eliminating what she had eaten by shoving her finger down her throat. It was never easy, but each time she forced herself to vomit, it became more routine. When she first started down this path she had to gag herself time after time to get the job done—she'd shove her finger down her throat, her stomach would contract, and she'd feel that vile heaving sensation, but it wasn't always enough to force up the contents of her stomach. She'd have to keep at it a second time and a third time before she was finally able to rid her body of all those calorie-inlaid foods she had wolfed down only minutes earlier. As time went by, she got better at it—she realized that two fingers did the job better than one and she was eventually able to make herself throw-up more quickly and efficiently.

Over the next few months Simone would alternate between days of healthy low-fat eating and moments of bingeing on thousands of calories in one sitting that she would later purge out of her body. She knew that what she was doing was something she didn't want anyone to know about, but, at the same time, she convinced herself that there really wasn't anything wrong with it. She wasn't depressed or bipolar or schizophrenic—she was just a woman trying to shape herself into something she had always seen as ideal. She certainly didn't have bulimia. Bulimics were these crazy girls that came from homes with fathers that told them how fat they were; bulimics were waif thin with blood-shot eyes and foul-smelling breath; bulimics constantly obsessed about food. Bulimics binged and purged several times a day. Simone only did it once or twice a week. Bulimics binged and purged because they were crazy. Simone didn't binge and purge because she was crazy—she binged and purged to control her weight—there was difference, she convinced herself—really there was. And best of all, it was working. Simone was dropping weight like never before. Her friends and colleagues watched her shrink before their eyes, thinking that all those salads and cups of low-fat yogurt they had been seeing her eat were responsible for her transformation. First, she shed ten pounds, then twenty, then thirty. It wasn't too long before she was almost half her original body weight.

Throughout her radical process of slimming down, the more weight Simone dropped, the more people noticed, and the more her life began to change. Everyone was telling her how good she looked. They were congratulating her as if she was the first woman on the moon. People, men *and* women, were treating her differently—more doors were being held open for her, men were looking at her differently and asking her out on dates, colleagues were paying attention to what she had to say, and talk of promoting her to a reporter position began to be tossed around. But it wasn't enough for Simone to be thin. She wanted to be thin *and* beautiful. As the weight came off, she began racking up huge amounts of debt shopping for new clothes and trying out different haircuts and styles. She spent Saturday after Saturday at the makeup counters at Saks and Neiman Markus determined to find the right cosmetics to make her look her best. She was spending money like crazy, but she was having the time of her life—she was turning heads, people were listening to what she had to say, women were asking her for beauty tips. She had arrived—Simone Reyes had *arrived*.

Delusional Women

"Does this skirt make me look fat?" a young woman asked Wanda as she viewed herself in the mirror outside the dressing room at Saks.

"Skirts don't make people look fat. Fat makes people look fat," Wanda said with a laugh, trying to take the edge off her smart-ass comment. Usually she would just say "No, certainly not," and offer some nonsense about how the skirt shaped the customer's figure, but Wanda was feeling frisky and starting to think her days of kissing up to Saks's shoppers might be almost over. If she could be the star of the Channel 6 feature about large-size models, it would be an enormous boost to her career. A tape of the feature would be a great way to get her foot in the door of a modeling agency.

"Do you have it in a size ten?" the woman, who was already stretching the size twelve skirt, asked.

"Ah . . . for *who*?" Wanda questioned. Again, Wanda would usually have dutifully gotten the size-ten skirt, watched the customer almost burst it at the seams, and ring it up for the delusional woman, who was certain she would eventually lose enough weight to fit into it, but today, Wanda just wasn't in the mood.

"Me," the woman replied sharply.

"Sure, why don't you head back in the dressing room, and I'll go get it for you."

Wanda called it "motivational buying," and she saw it at Saks all the time. Women came in buying clothes anywhere from one to three sizes too small. They would spend a fortune on clothes they were too fat to even try on with some silly hope that if they had the clothes in their closet or hanging on their door staring at them, it would motivate them to stick to their diet and exercise regimens. Unfortunately, most of the women eventually found out that a low-cut Donna Karan blouse and Dolce & Gabbana knee-length skirt weren't enough to cut the cravings for bacon and cheese omelettes and strawberry crepes with homemade chocolate sauce. In the war of silk and chiffon against butter and cream, the butter and cream won almost every time.

As Wanda went to retrieve the skirt, she thought about how glad she was to be at peace with her size. Working in women's apparel, she saw women every day at war with themselves—women with the genes of Kathy Bates and Wynona Judd fighting like mad to look like Gwyneth Paltrow and Julia Roberts, when it just wasn't going to happen.

When Wanda came back into the dressing area, Janice, another sales associate, was pulling discarded items from the dressing stalls.

"Hey, Janice," Wanda said as she handed the skirt over the door to the customer.

"Hi, how are you?" Janice asked.

"I'm fantastic," Wanda replied with a big smile.

"Really? Glad to hear it. What's got you smiling so brightly?"

"Can you keep a secret?"

"Sure,"

"Don't tell anyone, but I think my roommate is going to arrange it so that I'm featured on the Channel 6 news in a story about plus-size models."

"Wow! That's fantastic, Wanda."

"Isn't it? But keep it under wraps for now. I don't want the word to get out until I'm sure it's a go."

"No, problem," Janice said and headed back out to the store to restock the clothes she'd gathered.

"I think I want to go with the size ten," the customer called to Wanda over the dressing room door.

"Sure. If you hand it over to me, I'll meet you at the register."

The woman handed the skirt to Wanda, and she made her way toward the counter.

As Wanda left the dressing area, Denise lowered her feet from the bench in one of the stalls, opened the door, and poked her head out. She had been in the dressing room looking for a scarf a customer had left behind when she overheard Wanda talking to Janice, and lifted herself on a bench so no one would see her legs underneath the door.

"News story?" Denise said to herself, her eyes lighting up as she dialed her cell phone. "Hi, Daddy. Do you know anyone at Channel 6?" she said into the phone. "I need to know the names of some folks in charge of the news features."

Meow

Simone had just come home from the costume store in Arlington and was sorting through the items she had purchased—a headband with cat ears, a fuzzy black tail, and some makeup for drawing whiskers. She figured she'd pair the items with a black lycra bodysuit and some heels to make a sexy cat woman costume. She'd heard Jeremy and Ruby talking about the big High Heel Race on 17th Street, and it sounded like a hoot. Halloween wasn't for almost two months, but Simone was getting her car detailed right next door to the costume store and decided to have a look-see. Ever since she'd lost weight six years earlier, Halloween was Simone's favorite holiday. It was the only day of the year you could dress like a total slut, flaunting every morsel of your sexuality without being considered a complete whore. When she was fat she occasionally participated in Halloween festivities, but it was always in some dowdy witch costume or something more benign. It wasn't until after she had lost all her excess weight that she fell in love with the holiday—maybe because it was late October 1997 that she finally reached her target weight.

She would never forget her first time in the costume store, almost six years earlier, after she had trimmed herself down to a size six. She asked one of the store clerks for some ideas, and he suggested she try on a slinky vampiress costume with a low-cut neckline and a short skirt. As she tried the outfit on the clerk offered her a pair of fishnet hose and spiky black heels. Simone put on the ensemble, and the moment she stepped out of the dressing room and looked in the mirror was a moment she would remember for eternity—it was the first time in her entire life that she looked in the mirror and saw herself as sexy. She had seen the weight loss over the previous months in her face and body. She had slowly been starting to see herself as a pretty girl, but it wasn't until she was dressed in a tight black skirt with fishnet hose that it hit her—not only was she pretty, she was hot—Simone Reyes, who had never had a date in high school and used to hide her body in loose fitting earth-toned clothes was fucking hot! She remembered the sales clerk noting her expression of awe and asking her if she was okay as she looked at herself in the mirror, and she remembered responding, "Oh yeah. I'm pretty damn fine."

As Simone stuffed her bag in the closet, she heard her cell phone ringing in her purse.

"Hello," she said into the phone.

"Hey . . . it's me."

Simone hesitated.

"Eric."

"Hi," Simone said, a bit relieved. She got a little nervous when she didn't recognize male voices on the other end of the phone. She was always afraid some long lost fling was calling to tell her he had gonorrhea or something.

"I think I have to cancel our plans tonight."

"Oh?"

"Yeah, my wife is coming back early. She'll be home tonight."

"Okay," Simone said, annoyed. She'd only seen Eric once since the evening he'd wham-bam-thank-you-ma'am'd her in the car a week earlier. She appreciated that his stupid wife kept him from being too needy and high maintenance, but she was also becoming a real inconvenience. As hot as her sleazy fuck in the front seat of Eric's car was, she had no intention of making it a regular occurrence.

"Unless you want to get together this afternoon for a late lunch or something. Cynthia isn't due back until after ten tonight."

"I can probably do that," Simone replied, knowing that neither one of them had any intention of eating a late lunch.

"I'm working from home today. Why don't you come on over?"

"Okay," Simone said. "I'll see you in a few minutes."

Simone hung up the phone and was about to grab her purse and head out the door when she had an idea. With a grin she ran up the steps, grabbed a black negligee from her dresser, her costume bag from the closet, and scurried down the steps and out the door.

Hopeless

"What's on the menu today?" Marla, one of Ruby's coworkers, asked as she watched Ruby standing by the microwave in the employee lounge at CrustiCare.

"Lean Cuisine Ravioli," Ruby said, pointing to her entrée spinning around in the oven.

"Smells good," Marla noted with a smile and disappeared out the door.

Ruby was going through her typical lunch ritual. She'd nuke a Lean Cuisine or Healthy Choice in the microwave, and consume it with a cup of yogurt or some carrots in the employee lounge while watching *The Young and the Restless* or *All My Children* on the communal television with some coworkers. Then she would do one of two things—either go back to her office, close and lock the door, and consume whatever second lunch she had prepared for herself or leave the building altogether for a Big Mac at McDonald's or a steak and cheese from Jerry's.

She had consumed a half dozen doughnuts just hours earlier, but she was already feeling the familiar pang in her stomach as she watched the little tub of pasta and marinara sauce rotate in the microwave. She pulled the entrée from the oven, gave it a quick look, and wondered how anyone other than Lara Flynn Boyle could possibly make an entire meal out of such a scant amount of food.

There were only about three or four other people in the

lounge, and Ruby really didn't know any of them, so she sat at a small table by herself and watched the last of some scene on *The Young and the Restless*. Once again, Nikki Newman had gotten her hair and makeup done and was dressed to the nines, so she could sit around her ranch house all day and do nothing.

Ruby was only half watching the TV while she scooped the bland ravioli and washed it down with a glass of water. The sound was down rather low, and Ruby was more of an *All My Children* fan anyway, but as she finished off the last of her meal and got up from the table, *The Young and the Restless* flipped to a commercial, and something on the television caught her eye just as she turned to leave.

No! It couldn't be, she thought to herself as she turned back around.

"What the fuck?" she said inaudibly to herself as she looked up at the screen in disbelief. There it was. Right in front of her on the television was this dreadful fat woman with dark circles under her eyes. She was wearing a bulky flannel shirt, baggy jeans, and had a trashy NASCAR hat on her head—it was the before picture of Ruby that had been taken just a few days earlier for Slim & Trim. Ruby moved closer to the set to better hear the sound and get a closer look at herself on the screen. When she got closer to the television she watched as a petite young woman began pushing the poster-size picture of Ruby across the screen, out of the camera's view, as if she were trying to roll a two-ton bolder. "That was me—fat and unhappy, six months ago, before I joined Slim & Trim. But not anymore! Call Slim & Trim and you too can go from this"—the woman, who had an uncanny resemblance to Ruby, only immensely thinner, said before the picture of Ruby was thrown up on the screen again—"to this!" the skinny bitch with a southern accent added after tearing up Ruby's picture and posing her thin shapely frame for the camera.

Ruby was horrified, absolutely horrified! It really was hopeless. She was never going to lose weight. Even the Slim & Trim people were certain of it—so certain they had hired someone to pose as Ruby before even giving her a chance to try. With her eyes starting to well up, she looked around the lounge to see if anyone had made the connection and recognized her. She figured it was quite possible that if she kept her mouth shut, no would notice it was her. After all, she barely looked like herself in the ill-fitting clothes, and between the dark circles painted under her eyes and the baseball cap partially obscuring her face, she was virtually unrecognizable. But it didn't matter to Ruby—so what if no one knew it was her—she knew it—she knew it was her that was so hideous and hopeless, no one was even willing to give her a chance to improve herself. She pictured the Slim & Trim people saying, "Yeah right, like that pathetic cow is ever really going to lose any weight," as they arranged for someone else to pretend to be the thin version of Ruby.

She was so upset, she didn't know what to do. She really wasn't sure she could even move. She actually had had some glimmer of hope that the Slim & Trim program was going to be her answer—that it might be the program that finally worked—the program that finally ridded the world of Fat Ruby. She had felt hopeless about weight loss before, but this time it was different. This time it seemed to finally hit her—she was never going to be Thin Ruby. It had all been a big joke—she had been a big joke.

Ruby managed to keep herself collected long enough to exit the break room and make it back to her office where she tried to fight back tears as she shot off a quick E-mail to her boss, saying she wasn't feeling well and was going home. She grabbed her purse and headed out of the building. She had no idea where she was going, but she knew what she was going to do. If she was never going to be Thin Ruby, she may as well eat . . . and eat and eat!

Yes, Ma'am

Simone didn't feel like being recognized on her way into Eric's building, so she put on her sunglasses and grabbed her scarf from the glove compartment before getting out of the car. Wrapping the scarf around her head as she walked toward the building, Simone reflected on the whole situation with Eric. As far as she knew, she had never been involved with a married man before, and she was beginning to think it wasn't such a good idea after all—sure, she didn't have to worry about him getting all needy and obsessive with her, but at the same time she wasn't thrilled about having to rush over to Eric's in the middle of the day just so they could fuck before his wife got home. Simone was used to being the one in control of her relationships, but with Eric, it was starting to seem like a woman she didn't even know was calling the shots. For Christ's sake, she'd actually gotten laid in the front seat of a car because Eric couldn't take her back to his place. And it wasn't just his wife that was making her rethink the situation—it was his age. Sure, she liked them young, but Eric may have been a bit too young. She was starting to get savvy to his little start and stop way of fucking her. At first she thought it was hot, but when she later realized he was only doing it to keep from ejaculating within ten seconds of entering her it wasn't so sexy anymore. And if that wasn't enough, Eric was obviously not able to wine and dine her in the manner to which she had become accustomed. She didn't understand it: Eric drove a BMW and lived in a nice apartment building in an upscale neighborhood, but, at the same time, he couldn't seem to afford to take Simone to any nice places. Simone was used to her dates taking her to fine restaurants and trendy clubs, but that wasn't the case with Eric. The last time she and Eric went out, he had taken her to the Bennigan's in Falls Church. Simone hadn't been to one of those chain bicycles-on-the-walls restaurants in years and wasn't thrilled to be back. It was a real turnoff to watch Eric snarf down mozzarella sticks and buffalo wings—items that Simone would certainly wolf down herself in the privacy of her bedroom with an open toilet nearby, but wouldn't dream of actually eating in public. She had managed to make it through her Ahi Tuna Steak Salad and a bite of some frozen concoction called Death By Chocolate that Eric had for dessert, but it was when it came time to pay the bill that Simone began to really rethink her relationship with Eric. She was horrified when he reviewed the receipt, whipped out his wallet, and paid the check with . . . oh God, she couldn't bear to think about it—he had paid the bill with . . . with *cash*! Simone hadn't seen a date pick up the tab with cash in years. It was bad enough when it wasn't a gold or platinum Visa that was being set down on the table, but *cash*? Could Simone Reyes really date someone that paid restaurant checks in *cash*?

When Simone got off the elevator, she walked down the hall toward Eric's apartment. She was about to knock when she saw a small note taped to the door. She grabbed the slip of paper, unfolded it, and gave it a quick read.

Simone,

Didn't have anything in the house, so I ran to the store to get some munchies for lunch. Go on in, and I'll be back soon.

Eric

Okay, he had a premature ejaculation problem, paid with cash, and now he was using the word "munchies." It was looking more and more like Simone was going to have to drop Eric by the wayside, but she was already there, so she figured she may as well make the best of it.

She walked in the apartment, set the bag with her lingerie on the floor, and sat down on the sofa. Just as she was getting comfortable she had an idea. She had originally planned to slip into the bathroom after lunch and surprise Eric in her slinky cat woman outfit but decided it would be even better if she got changed before he came home. Besides, Simone was a strong believer in fucking at the *beginning* of a date. It just didn't make sense to her to wait until the end of dates to bed her men. Why wait until after the dinner and a movie when she was tired from a long day. It just seemed logical to get it on at the beginning of a date—when both partners were freshly showered and full of energy.

With a grin on her face Simone got up from the sofa and grabbed her bag. She quickly got undressed, slipped into the lacy black teddy, clipped the cat's tail to her garter belt and placed the kitty ears on her head.

"Damn, you look hot," she said to her reflection in the mirror behind the sofa. As she sat down, she heard Eric coming through the front door. As he walked into the living room Simone turned her head to greet him and offered her best Eartha Kitt, "Meow!"

Eric smiled from ear to ear when he saw Simone on the sofa. "Wow!" he said. "You look amazing."

"Thank you," she replied as Eric continued to approach her with a grin, as if he were about to be the luckiest man alive. He set a couple bags of groceries on the coffee table and tossed a few of the sofa pillows out of his way. Then he sat down on the sofa next to Simone and kissed her on the lips.

"You look so hot," he said as he maneuvered himself on top of her and moved his hand inside her teddy. He was caressing her stomach and working his way up to her breasts when they both heard some keys jingling at the door.

"Shit!" Eric said, hopping up. "She's home early."

"Your wife?" Simone asked, getting up and grabbing her things.

"Hide! Hide!" Eric said in a strong whisper. "Hurry, in here," he continued and opened the door to the coat closet off the living room.

Simone picked up the last of her things, and, feeling utterly ridiculous, scurried into the closet with Eric shutting the door behind her just as Cynthia came through the front door.

"Hi, honey," Cynthia said.

"Hi. You're home early," Eric replied, trying to remain calm. "How was your trip?"

"It was actually quite productive. A few more commissions like the one I landed this week, and I'll be able to move us out to a nice house in the suburbs."

"Great," Simone heard Eric say. He was becoming less and less attractive by the minute. As Simone had suspected, Cynthia was the breadwinner in the marriage. Cynthia was the one that would move them, on her own, to a nice house in the suburbs. Simone was beginning to wonder if Eric had *any* money of his own.

"Did you clean the kitchen and sweep off the balcony like I asked?" Cynthia inquired.

"Yes," Eric replied.

"Yes, what?" Cynthia asked.

"Yes, ma'am."

Oh my God! Simone thought. His wife really is a bitch. She made him call her ma'am. No wonder he was cheating on her. Simone tried to picture what Cynthia looked like—she didn't sound very attractive, and she had the voice of a much older woman. She almost sounded like she was in her fifties.

"What's all this mess?" Simone heard Cynthia ask. "Honestly, Eric," she continued, looking at the food Eric had put on the coffee table, and the pillows scattered on the floor. "I expect you to keep this house in order when I'm out of town."

"I did keep the house in order. I was just getting ready to have some lunch."

Simone was listening from inside the closet, and Eric was sounding more and more pathetic all the time, like a beaten down dog who was so dependent on his master, he didn't dare defy her.

"Who's Simone?" Cynthia asked.

"What?" Eric asked, a hint of panic in his voice. "No one, why?"

"This note," Cynthia said, picking up the note Eric had left Simone earlier from the table. "It's addressed to Simone. We don't know any Simones, other than that bimbo that does the late news."

Bimbo! Simone thought. Who did that bitch think she was, calling her such a thing? Simone's first instinct was to jump out of the closet and defend her honor, but then she looked down at herself, hiding in a married man's closet in little more than a negligee, a pair of heels, and some cat ears—maybe now was not the best time to defend her morality.

"No, no. That's *Simon*," Eric said, trying to sound convincing. "Simon was supposed to come over earlier."

"Simon? Who's Simon?"

"Just a friend from school."

School? Simone thought from inside the closet.

"Have I met him?"

"No, I don't think so,"

"All right, well, I've got a few errands to run. I just wanted to come by and drop off my bags," Cynthia said, grabbing her purse. "I want this place spotless when I get back. Eric, you're eighteen now. You'll be starting community college next week. I'd think I could leave you alone for a few days without the house going to pieces."

"Okay," Eric replied.

"I'll see you in a few hours," Cynthia said. "Now, kiss your mother good-bye."

Eighteen? Mother? Simone thought. What was going on—was she on fucking *Spy TV* or *Invasion of the Hidden Cameras* or something?

When she heard the door close behind Cynthia, she peeked out the closet door, saw that the coast was clear, and came out.

"Eighteen?" she asked Eric.

Eric didn't respond. He just looked at Simone, his face red with embarrassment.

"And Cynthia's not your wife, she's your mother?"

Again, Eric was silent.

"Oh my God! You're eighteen and you live with your mother. Boy, I can pick 'em," Simone said, putting her hand to her forehead.

"Um . . . are you mad?" Eric finally had spoken, and suddenly, Simone could see how obvious it was—how young he really looked.

"I'm . . ." Simone was about to say, "I'm not mad," but instead, she just said, "I'm leaving." She tucked her teddy into her pants and slipped her shirt on over top and headed for the door.

"You never asked how old I was," Eric said behind her.

"No, I didn't," Simone said. She was about to leave but she had to ask. "What were you doing out so late that night you fixed my car—and in a suit and tie, and the BMW."

"I had just finished a performance in the school play. I was Captain von Trapp in our production of *The Sound of Music.* I was on my way home and you had that flat tire. Really, my only intention was to change your flat and be on my way, but then you took an interest in me. I couldn't help myself, so I pretended to be something I'm not."

"And the BMW?"

"It's Mom's . . . I mean Cynthia's."

"What about the story about your wife getting pregnant so you would marry her?"

Looking down at his feet, too embarrassed to look at Simone, Eric replied, "I don't know. I guess I saw something like that on *General Hospital.*"

Simone didn't know what to say. She was still trying to digest the whole thing. She just smiled at Eric. "It's okay," she said. "Now get this place cleaned up before she gets home," she added with a laugh and headed for the door. "Good-bye, Eric," she said as she stepped outside the apartment door and took a deep breath. She was having a bit of an awakening. She'd been fucking a guy who was barely legal and just out of high school—a guy who'd never seen a first-run episode of the *Facts of Life* or played music on a record player.

You've got to get it together, Simone thought to herself as she walked toward the elevator, unaware that she had forgotten to unpin the cat tail from her garter belt. She got all the way to the car before she realized it had been swinging behind her since she left the apartment.

Doughnuts! Part II

Ruby wasn't sure where she was going, or what she was going to do, but what she did know was that, whatever it was, it would involve eating. For the time being, she was just driving with a maze of thoughts running through her head. She thought about how she had just had it—absolutely had it! Something about seeing herself on TV looking so terribly awful seemed to finalize things—Ruby Waters was always going to be Fat Ruby. She had tried so many programs and diets in the past, and all of them had failed, but somehow, it wasn't until she saw herself looking hideous in the Slim & Trim commercial that she felt totally hopeless—like it was finally over—it was time to stop kidding herself and accept the fact that she was always going to be, as the woman in the commercial had referred to her, "fat and unhappy."

She drove up Arlington Boulevard toward the city, keeping her eye out for all the eateries. She saw Celebrity Deli at Loehman's Plaza and thought about one of the sandwiches they served there. It was called the Terminator, and it was a little taste of heaven—hot roast beef with coleslaw, Muenster cheese, and Russian dressing on fried rye bread. She saw the Harvest Moon Chinese restaurant and thought about their all-you-can-eat lunch buffet—all the egg rolls, sweet and sour chicken, and baby spareribs you could snarf. She drove by Bentley's Diner and considered their banana walnut pancakes. She passed by

Chili's and thought about their Awesome Blossom onion loaf and their crispy chicken fingers. But none of the places in view seemed to make the cut. None of them seemed to offer the kind of comfort Ruby needed. She needed a place like Sylvia's in New York, a famous soul food restaurant in Harlem that she and Jeremy had gone to when they visited the city a few years earlier. Ruby could still smell the fragrant corn bread, brought to the table piping hot. She remembered the crispy fried catfish and the creamy macaroni and cheese, the collard greens, and the country gravy. Ruby was seriously considering heading to the airport and booking a flight on the shuttle to New York just to drown her sorrows in a plate of barbecue spareribs at Sylvia's when she passed the Shoppers Food Warehouse she had stopped at earlier that day. *Doughnuts!* she thought. She'd been a fool to throw away those doughnuts. She'd just head back in the store and get another dozen.

Ruby pulled into the shopping center and parked the car. As she hurried toward the grocery store she was in such a daze she didn't even realize that she had ducked under some police tape on her way. When she approached the electronic door, a police officer stopped her.

"Ma'am, didn't you see the police tape?"

Ruby turned and saw the yellow tape strewn along the entryway. "Actually, I didn't."

"The store was robbed earlier. It's going to be closed until we get things settled inside."

"Ah . . . okay," Ruby said, trying to hide her disappointment.

Fighting the urge to beg the officer to let her in or ask him to get her doughnuts for her, Ruby walked back to her car, not the least bit concerned about any robbery. She began making distance calculations in her head. Which was closer? The other Shoppers Food Warehouse at Potomac Yards or the Krispy Kreme doughnut shop in Alexandria? She got in her car, annoyed and upset that she had to go somewhere else for comfort food. She was about to pull out of the parking lot when she remembered the doughnuts she had thrown away earlier in the day. Maybe they were still there.

Ruby pulled the car over toward the wastebasket and got out. She peered down into the trash and saw the discarded box. There they were, as good as new, six donuts. She looked around her to see if anyone was watching and quickly retrieved the box. She walked back to the car, got inside, and closed the door.

What was she doing? Had she really just sorted through the garbage to get something to eat? She wasn't even hungry. She'd already consumed half the box before work and had just finished eating lunch, but, like much of Ruby's eating, it wasn't about being hungry—something no one seemed to understand. People were always telling her to eat less, or eat smaller meals, or take an appetite suppressant to control her hunger, but it wasn't about hunger, it had never really been about hunger—it was about pleasure and escape, the pleasure and escape that food gave her—the taste, the smell, the feeling of fullness, more than anything, it was the comfort. Food comforted her more than *anything,* more than her mother ever had, more than her friends, more than fancy clothes or cars, and certainly more than exercise. Ruby didn't eat because she was hungry. Ruby wasn't even sure she knew what hungry was. She'd never stopped eating long enough to experience it.

The more Ruby thought about the Slim & Trim commercial, and the way she had looked, and how she had rifled through the trash like a drug addict looking for a heroin needle, the more upset she got, which made her want to eat even more. The doughnuts would take the pain the away—they wouldn't take it away permanently, and rationally, Ruby knew that eating them would only make matters worse, but for a brief moment while she ate them, the pain would ease. She could focus on something other than her fat self.

Ruby opened the box and pulled out her first doughnut, a powdery white one stuffed with vanilla cream. She took a big bite and then another and then another.

Positively Shameless

Wanda walked toward the kitchen trying to be as silent as possible. She'd taken her shoes off and was treading lightly in her socks. As she approached the cabinet, she reached up and slowly pulled it open. Quietly, she grabbed the box of TastyKake Krimpets, set it on the counter, and pulled out a plastic packet containing the butterscotch cakes.

Almost home free, she thought to herself as she pulled the plastic apart. This resulted in a soft rustling noise, which was just enough to spark exactly what Wanda was trying to avoid. As soon as she had the wrapper open, she heard Taco's collar tags jingling and his toenails clicking along the wood floor toward her. Ever since Doris came into the house Taco ceased his infatuation with Wanda. He no longer followed her around the house or slept on the floor next to her bed. He wouldn't even come when she called him, but the moment she made the slightest noise opening a package of Krimpets or HoHos, he was at her feet in no time. With the exception of Doris, he mostly ignored or growled at everyone in the house, but the moment anyone was snacking on something of interest to him he appeared out of nowhere, batting his saddest puppy dog eyes.

Wanda didn't care much for dogs, and the idea of having one live among people in the house was absolutely foreign to her. That was one thing about white people that had always struck her as strange—the way they treated their dogs as if they were real members of the family. Wanda had truly been floored one evening when Doris called Taco to come join her up on the sofa. A dog in the house was bad enough, but a dog on the furniture was just bizarre. Dogs belonged outside in their own house or in the garage or the basement. At least Ruby and Doris weren't like some crazy white people Wanda knew who let their dogs eat off their plate or take bites of food off their fork. If that had been the case, Wanda would have just had to move, plain and simple. The idea of sharing her dishes or cutlery with a dog was truly nauseating.

Taco sat at Wanda's feet, looking up at her curiously. He refused to beg or yip—he would not degrade himself with such measures. He seemed to think his sheer presence in the room should have been enough to warrant a taste of Wanda's food. Wanda looked down at the little dog while she munched on her snack and couldn't help but smile at his "so ugly he's cute" little face. It was amusing to her the way dogs were when it came to food—positively shameless. The moment they smelled something fragrant or saw an appetizing treat, they appeared wanting their share and more. It struck Wanda as funny the way people were really the same way. Only people tried to mask their brazen greed for food in front of each other. At least dogs were honest and out-in-the-open about it—unlike so many people Wanda knew—people who would have one doughnut from the counter at work when others were around and then sneak back into the break room when everyone was gone, snatch two more, and wolf them down in a stall in the bathroom. And then there were scavengers from other departments who would just happen to show up at a gathering when word got out that there was going to be free food. Wanda wouldn't see Linda Hawkins for weeks at a time, but the moment someone in Wanda's department brought in fresh baked cookies or cupcakes, Linda some how magically decided that was the day to check in with her friend Wanda.

"Go away, poochie," Wanda said to the dog as she opened a second pack of Krimpets, only exciting Taco further. She was about to start on her second helping when she heard Simone come through the front door and make her way into the kitchen.

"Hey, what's up," Wanda asked.

"Not much. I guess I should head upstairs and get ready for work," Simone said, looking uneasy and distracted. She'd just returned from her encounter with Eric and his mother, and on top of that, on the way home, she got some bad news from her producer.

"You look tired. Things okay?"

"Actually, I have some bad news," Simone said, looking apprehensive.

"What?" Wanda asked.

"You know that feature I was telling you about . . . about the plus-size models? Steve, my producer, called me on my cell a few minutes ago, and they decided to go with another model as the focal point for the story."

"Another model?" Wanda asked, her disappointment showing in her voice.

"Yeah. I'm so sorry. It had nothing to do with you. Rumor has it Steve is dating the model he plans to use—or she's blowing him. I think her name's . . ."

"Don't tell me," Wanda said, interrupting Simone. "Denise. Her name's Denise, isn't it?"

"Yes," Simone said. "I think it is."

"I knew it. That bitch!" Wanda exclaimed, slamming her hand down on the counter. "I knew she'd sink to the lowest levels to fuck with me, but I had no idea . . . How did she know about the news story?"

"I don't know. I've heard rumors last week that they might go with another model . . . something about her having some connections . . . or maybe it was her parents that had some connections to the station. It's all about who you know in this business."

"How could she do this to me? This was my big chance. I've paid my dues. This was going to be my moment. I'll kill her, Simone. I swear, I'll kill her! A sister will put up with a lot of shit, but do not fuck with my time in the limelight!"

"Okay now. No one is killing anyone. Calm down. Maybe I can talk to Steve again . . . see if we can work something out," Simone said trying to offer Wanda some hope, even though she knew using Denise in the feature was a done deal.

"Oh, we'll work something out alright. We'll work something out when I go into work tomorrow and pull each one of her braids out of her scalp, one by one. God, you were so right, Simone. I should have squashed her like a bug while I had the chance!"

Enough!

Before she got out of the car and headed toward her house, Ruby gave herself a look in the rearview mirror, checking her face to make sure there wasn't any powdered sugar or bits of icing around her mouth from her trash can–doughnut binge. As she walked up the sidewalk, she suddenly wished she still lived alone—that her mother would go back to her own house, and Wanda and Simone would move out. The last thing she wanted at that moment was any kind of human interaction. Hoping that the girls were out and Doris might be napping, Ruby inserted her key in the front door.

"Hi," Wanda said as she saw Ruby come in.

"Hi," Ruby replied, trying to keep her head down and make a beeline toward the steps. She figured she must have looked as awful as she felt, and if Wanda got a good look at her, there were bound to be questions—questions Ruby didn't feel like answering. She didn't feel like doing anything except getting under the covers and sleeping as long as she possibly could.

"A Mrs. Jenkins was by earlier and took Doris out to lunch. They should be back in an hour or so."

"Okay," Ruby responded.

"Are you all right?" Wanda asked, sensing something was wrong.

Ruby was about to lie and say "yes," when Simone appeared at the top of the steps.

"Check it out," Simone said. "Look what Doris gave me this morning. She was sorting through some of her clothes and said I could have it."

Ruby looked to the top of the steps and was absolutely horror struck to see Simone in Doris's little black dress, doing a quick twirl to show off her new threads. For a brief moment, Ruby clinched her eyes shut.

Oh, thank God, she thought. It was all a dream—the commercial, the doughnuts in the trash, Simone in her mother's dress . . . it had all been a dream . . . so many terrible things couldn't possibly be happening on the same day. But when Ruby opened her eyes, Simone was still at the top of the steps in Doris's little black dress, she could still feel her stomach bursting with the doughnuts, and the television image of her flannel-clad self was fresh in her memory.

"Are you okay?" Simone asked, looking down at Ruby, whose face was growing redder by the second.

Ruby looked back up at Simone clad in Doris's dress, and it was as if thirty-two years of repressed anger had finally reached its breaking point. She saw Simone in her mother's dress, the dress she had always intended to wear some day. But that wasn't all. She saw those awful women at Slim & Trim handing her oversized clothes and painting dark circles under her eyes. She saw Heather Watkins from the third grade yelling, "God, Ruby's already so fat. You'd think she leave some for the rest of us." She saw Matthew Green and heard him mooing at her as she tried to discreetly walk into the gym at summer camp more than twenty years earlier. She saw her powdered sugar–covered mouth in the rearview mirror of her car. Ruby hurt—she hurt bad! And GOD DAMN IT! SHE WASN'T GOING TO TAKE IT ANYMORE!

"Take it off!" Ruby yelled so fiercely that her voice echoed throughout the house—even Taco ran for cover under the coffee table.

"What?" Simone asked, shocked by Ruby's outburst.

"Take it off!" Ruby demanded again and lunged toward Simone. Ruby screamed with such intensity that Simone, with real fear for her safety, reached for the zipper to begin undoing the dress.

"You skinny bitches have taken things from me my whole life, but you're not taking that dress. It's mine! I know my fat ass can't fit into it, but it's mine, and if you think you're taking it from me, you'd better think again."

"Okay, okay," Simone said, stepping out of the dress and handing it to Ruby, all the while speaking to Ruby as is she were an escaped mental patient with a gun. "Relax, it's okay. I'm taking it off."

"Ruby, what's going on?" Wanda said, getting up from the sofa while Simone, too shocked to say anything further, stood next to her in her slip. "What's the matter, boo?" Wanda continued in a gentle voice, trying to calm Ruby.

"What's the matter? What's the matter!" Ruby shot back. "I'm fat! And I'm fat! And I'm fat! I've always been fat, and I'm always going to be fat! As we speak my grotesque body is being paraded all over television as the before girl for Slim & Trim . . . just the *before* girl. Some perky red-headed coatrack from Kentucky is the after girl. Then I come home and find Penelope Cruz here wearing *my* dress," Ruby said, gesturing toward Simone. She then widened her eyes and shouted in Wanda's direction. "And you! I've been pining for Preston DaSilva for years and you waltz in and bat your eyes at him and two seconds later he's asking you out. And you know what else? I just dug half a dozen doughnuts out of . . ." As upset as Ruby was, she managed not to tell the other girls about digging the doughnuts out of the trash—she was just too ashamed. Instead she walked over to the sofa, sat down, and buried her face in her hands.

"Sweetie," Wanda said as she walked toward Ruby with Simone following. "I had no idea about Preston."

"And I'm sorry about the dress," Simone added. "I swear. I had no idea it meant anything to you."

"I know. I know," Ruby said, wiping her eyes, starting to calm down. "I'm sorry I was such a nut case. I don't know what happened. I just saw you in the dress and lost it. I know it's crazy, but my mother's had that dress since I was a little girl. She looked so beautiful in it, and I guess I've always hoped that . . ." Ruby couldn't say it out loud. It would sound too ridiculous that she thought there was a snowball's chance in hell of her ever fitting into Doris's little black dress.

"You always hoped that one day you would fit into it," Wanda said, completing Ruby's sentence for her.

Ruby just nodded.

"Ruby," Wanda said, sitting down on the sofa next to her and putting her arm around Ruby's shoulder. "You can't base your life and your self worth on a dress, or your weight, or whatever."

"I know," Ruby lied.

"No, I don't think you do," Wanda said. "I've been where you are—constantly reprimanding myself for eating too much, trying scam diets to lose weight, wanting to be thin so bad I could taste it, but when I finally accepted that it wasn't going to happen and learned to like myself instead of my dress size, it changed my life."

Ruby looked at Wanda in disbelief.

"Hey," Wanda said and looked up from Ruby at Simone. "Can you give us a minute?"

"Sure," Simone said. "I really am sorry, Ruby. If there's anything I can do . . ."

Wanda waited for Simone to depart the room before speaking again. "Ruby, do you think I don't know that some people make fun of me because of my size, that countless men won't give me a second look because I'm fat, that the Old Country Buffet bolts the door when I pull up in the parking lot?" Wanda said with a laugh, trying to break some of the tension. "Of course I know, but I choose to focus on the thousands of men that do appreciate my size. I've picked a career that takes advantage of my weight, and I don't let *anyone* walk on me."

"That's you," Ruby said, looking grim and hopeless, but appreciating Wanda's kind words all the same.

"It could be you, too."

"No. No it can't."

"If I can do it, Ruby, anyone . . ."

"Let me ask you something," Ruby said, cutting Wanda off. "Were you fat as a kid?"

"Ah . . . no, not really I guess."

"When did you start putting weight on?"

"Sometime in my late twenties."

"See. That's the difference between you and me, Wanda. I was always fat. I bet you were popular and had boyfriends and never got picked on as a kid. By the time you started putting on weight you already had a positive self-image and inner strength. I, on the other hand, never had a chance. I've been fat since I was a little girl, and my whole life has been shaped by it."

"I guess you're right. We are different, but that doesn't mean anything. The way I see it, us fat girls have three choices. We can keep trying all sorts of plans and programs to lose weight, we can stay fat and miserable, or we can accept ourselves for what we are and choose to be happy. That's just the way it is, Ruby," Wanda said, and got up from the sofa. "Think about it."

Ruby just looked at Wanda as she started to walk away.

"Oh," Wanda added, before reaching the steps. "And about Preston. I'll cancel our date, but only under one condition."

"What?" Ruby asked.

"That you make a serious play for him," Wanda replied before she headed up the stairway.

Fashion Emergency

"The only time I've ever been in a Saks was to look for clothes for Jeremy," Ruby said to Wanda as they parked in front of the Saks Fifth Avenue on Wisconsin Avenue in Chevy Chase. This was a freestanding store, but as she and Wanda walked into the building, Ruby couldn't help but think about the Saks at the Tyson's Galleria, an upscale mall in McLean, Virginia. Ruby noticed that, unlike most department stores, which opened, unobstructed, right into the mall, Saks had closed glass doors partitioning it from the mall's thoroughfare. Those doors had always intimidated Ruby. When she was alone, she was afraid to touch them, much less actually open one and go inside. What business did her overweight middle-class self have in a store like Saks?

As they came through the store entrance, Ruby walked behind Wanda, taking in the opulence of the store—the marble floors, the shiny glass counters, and the racks of overpriced designer clothes. She observed the customers and felt even more out of place. The store was chock-full of wealthy middle-aged white women with highlighted hair and liposuctioned hips.

"I don't think I'd ever get plastic surgery . . . on my face anyway," Wanda said after they passed a shopper with one of those Dixie Carter facelifts—her cheeks pulled so tight one was apt to look behind her and see who was pulling her hair so sadistically hard. "I guess it does make you look younger, but at what cost? I think I'd rather look old than like a mutant from outer space."

"I don't know. My face has never been my problem," Ruby said, looking down at her body.

"Would you stop that," Wanda said. "We're going to find you such a great outfit today, you won't be looking down at your body like that anymore."

Ruby rode the escalator down to the lower level of the store with Wanda, still not convinced she had made the right decision—taking money out of her Thin Ruby account to buy some new clothes for Fat Ruby. It had been a few days since she exploded and nearly mauled Simone over her mother's little black dress. She'd had apologized repeatedly to both Wanda and Simone for her outburst, but a huge part of her really wasn't sorry. In fact, she wasn't sure she'd take back anything she'd said or done that day. Sure, it was inappropriate and crazy. She'd totally overreacted to the situation, but at least, for the first time, she wasn't a doormat. She had said what she felt, taken what was rightfully hers, and it had felt pretty damn good. For the first time in her life she didn't feel like a total victim. Standing up to Simone and Wanda made her realize that everything wrong with her life wasn't just about her weight. It was more about the way she allowed people to treat her. Ruby remembered some self-help guru saying, "People are treated the way they *allow* themselves to be treated," and suddenly it was hitting her that that was true. Sure, people had teased and harassed her because she was fat, but they kept teasing and harassing her because she allowed them to. She wondered what her life would've been like if she had lunged at Heather Watkins in the third grade like she had at Simone a few days earlier instead of conceding to her hateful demands. She thought about what it would have been like if she'd beat the shit out of Harold Swartz, the frat boy that wanted her to blow him so he could get in a fraternity, instead of just getting out of the car. What if she had walked over to Matthew at summer camp while he was mooing at her, and had given him a good swift kick in the nuts?

God! Why had she waited until she was thirty-two years old to stand up for herself?

"Welcome to Salon Z," Wanda said as she and Ruby stepped into Saks's department for plus-size women. Even if they did cram it into the basement of the store, Ruby could see from first glance that it housed some beautiful clothes. Ruby started sorting through the racks—she had no idea so many famous designers made clothes for large women—Anne Klein, Gianfranco Ferre, David Dart, Eileen Fisher, Lafayette, the list went on and on.

"How about this?" Wanda asked, pulling a solid black skirt and a purple suit jacket from the rack.

"Purple?" Ruby said. "I can't wear purple. It's too flashy."

"If you think you're leaving here in something beige or navy blue, you're sadly mistaken. For heaven's sake, Ruby, God gave you curves. Stop dressing out of Eddie Bauer and L.L. Bean and celebrate them," Wanda replied and grabbed another suit off the rack. This one was bright green.

"I think I like the purple one better."

"Yeah, me too," Wanda said before adding, "You see, Ruby, you and me are what they call 'pears' in the fashion world. We're heavier on the bottom than on the top. That's why I picked out the bright jacket and black skirt—this way, we emphasize your smaller half with the purple and minimize your lower half with the black. And look at this," Wanda continued, pointing to the top of the jacket. "The shoulders have a little padding to even out your frame . . . make your waist look smaller."

Ruby took the jacket from Wanda and looked at the price. "Wanda, it's eight hundred dollars!"

"With my discount it will only be five hundred or so."

"Five hundred! I can't buy a suit that costs more than my sofa."

"Ruby, no one ever said looking good was cheap. Now, go try it on," Wanda said with conviction.

"All right," Ruby replied and headed toward the dressing room.

When she had tried the suit on, she stepped out of the dressing room and looked at herself in the mirror. It was surprising what a difference a good suit could make. The cut of the jacket flattered her and the material had a quality look.

"Girl! Off the hook!" Wanda said, coming up behind her. "This didn't take long at all."

"You think?" Ruby questioned.

"Oh yeah. It's a winner."

"I don't know. Five hundred dollars?"

"What else are you going to do with the money, Ruby?"

Wanda's question made Ruby think. Really? What was she going to do with the money? Keep saving it to redo her kitchen, waste it on more junk food, continue hoarding it in hopes of one day becoming thin, so she could spend it on size-six clothes?

"Okay. I'll take it," Ruby said quickly, before she changed her mind.

"Wonderful! Take it off, and I'll take it to the register so we can get my discount."

"Thanks."

"Well, my work here is done. My replacement should be here any minute."

"Your replacement?" Ruby asked.

"Yep," Wanda said. "And here she is," she continued as Simone walked into the dressing area.

"Hi," Ruby said over the dressing room door, surprised to see Simone.

"Hi," Simone replied. "Are you ready?"

"For?"

"Well, you can't wear that new suit without some new makeup and a fresh haircut."

"What?"

"I've got it all taken care of. First we'll go by the Bobbi Brown counter for a makeover, and then I'm taking you to see Alexandre, my hairdresser."

"Seriously?" Ruby asked.

"Of course."

"Wow. You guys are great," Ruby said, truly surprised by

their kindness. For the first time she really started to think of Wanda and Simone as more than just roommates. For the longest time her social circle had revolved around Jeremy, Warren, and the television set, but now maybe she had some new friends.

Hello, Gorgeous!

"Hi," Simone said to the heavily made-up woman behind the Bobbi Brown counter at Saks.

"You're Simone Reyes from the news," the woman said, momentarily taken aback, before returning to professional mode. Sales associates at Saks were not supposed to be giddy around their celebrity customers. "How can I help you?"

"We'd like to purchase some cosmetics for my friend here."

"Hi," Ruby said sheepishly, afraid the salesclerk would be disappointed that she was the customer instead of Simone.

"Sure. My name's Jean. What are you interested in?"

"The works," Simone replied. "Let's start with a moisturizer."

"Great. We have a wonderful hydrating face cream . . ."

"No. She needs the shine-control face gel and some eye cream," Simone said, pointing to some containers under the glass. The makeup artist grabbed the tester items and started applying them to Ruby's face.

"I've never been made up at the counter like this before," Ruby confessed to Simone and Jean. She had always been too intimidated to approach the cosmetics counters at department stores.

"Really?" Jean asked. "Where do you buy your makeup?"

"I don't wear much. I pick up a few things at CVS or Rite Aid, or when I'm buying groceries."

"CVS?" Simone said, looking horrified. "Oh, heaven's no, Ruby. A lady does not buy her mascara and her maxi pads at the same place."

"She's right," Jean said as she grabbed some foundation.

"No," Simone said. "She needs some concealer first."

"Sure," Jean replied and grabbed two little containers. "You're probably an ivory."

"No. Try the porcelain first," Simone said, and she was right. It worked perfectly with Ruby's skin tone.

For the next half hour, Simone directed Jean on exactly how she wanted Ruby made up. She picked out a foundation, eye liner, eye shadow, mascara, blush, lip liner . . . If there was a kind of makeup available, it was on Ruby's face. Jean would make suggestions, but for the most part, Simone ignored them and picked all the shades and colors. Simone obviously knew what she was doing. With each application Ruby saw a new face come into being. When Jean finished up by lightly dusting Ruby's face with powder, Ruby gazed in the mirror in amazement. Her face looked flawless—like Halle Berry or Faith Hill in those cosmetics commercials. There wasn't a wrinkle or blemish to be seen. Her eyes sparkled under seashell cream eye shadow and the snow shimmer wash. Her lips were full and smooth. She was almost unrecognizable.

"Hello gorgeous!" Simone said to Ruby when she turned from the mirror and looked at Simone.

Ruby smiled.

By the time all was said and done, Ruby had spent almost three hundred dollars at the Bobbi Brown counter before being whisked away to Simone's hair salon in Georgetown.

"Mademoiselle Reyes!" Alexandre, one of Georgetown's famous hairdressers, said in a heavy French accent as Simone and Ruby walked through the doors of The Opal Salon on M Street. Rumor had it that Alexandre Boisseau, who claimed to be from Paris, was really Vinnie Santini, and traces of a New Jersey accent occasionally slipped through his French drawl, but, nonetheless, he was a fantastic stylist.

"Alexandre, how nice to see you," Simone said, giving him a kiss on the cheek.

"Are you here for a touch-up *alveady*?" he asked.

"No," Simone replied. "This is my friend Ruby. I was hoping you could fit her in for a haircut and maybe some highlights or . . ."

Before Simone could finish Alexandre approached Ruby and touched her hair with the back of his hand. "Who did *zeese* to you?" he asked with a frown.

"Um . . . Shaheen at the Hair Cuttery," Ruby replied.

"The hair *vhat*-ery?" Alexandre asked with a look of what could only be described as disgust.

"The Hair Cuttery . . . it's on Connecticut Avenue over by the . . ."

"Oh no, no, mademoiselle," Alexandre replied, interrupting her. "I do not *veesh* to know where it is."

"Can you fit her in?" Simone interjected.

"I'm booked solid all day, but for you, Mademoiselle Reyes, I will make room," Alexandre said. He then snapped his fingers, summoning an assistant.

"Prep her for cutting and highlights," he said to the young woman. Then he grabbed Ruby's hand and studied it for a moment before turning back to the assistant. "Manicure. Please!" He then gave Ruby one last look. "And have Yang do *somezing* with those eyebrows," he added before gesturing for Ruby to follow the assistant.

"Thank you, Alexandre. I owe you one," Simone said before turning to Ruby. "You're in good hands . . . the best. I'll see you later."

"Thank you, Simone," Ruby said, suddenly feeling terrible about lunging toward her in a fit of rage a few days earlier. "I'm so sorry about the other day."

"Nonsense," Simone replied. "Believe me, I understand. More than you know, I understand."

And somehow, Ruby sensed that Simone did, in fact, understand.

Pretty

"Not yet! Not yet!" Ruby said, shielding her face with the plastic garment bag that housed her new purple suit jacket and black skirt. She had just come in the front door from her appointment with Alexandre. She raced past Wanda, who was in the living room anxiously awaiting her return. "Let me get the whole ensemble on before you look," she added as she quickly climbed the stairs.

When she got in her bedroom she closed the door and fought the urge to look in the mirror. She didn't want to look until she was in her new suit. She quickly undressed, pulled the suit out of the bag, and slipped into the skirt and jacket. She then rifled through her dresser for a pair of hose, pulled them on, and stepped into a pair of black pumps. She took a mental inventory of herself from head to toe and decided she was ready—ready to give herself a look. She stepped in front of the full-length mirror on the back of the door with her eyes shut and took a deep breath. Once she got in position she opened her eyes.

"Wow," she said, gazing at herself. Quite possibly, she looked the best she had in her entire life. Her new suit was bright and flattering. Alexandre had layered her hair and added some soft highlights, but what was most amazing to Ruby was still her face. Thanks to Simone's makeup expertise her face looked radiant. Looking in the mirror Ruby had the oddest feeling—she could feel her inner self wanting to say that she looked pretty—at that moment, with her new hair, her new clothes, and her new face she wanted to believe that she looked pretty, but Ruby had trouble allowing her mind to even entertain the notion that she looked attractive. When Wanda had first pulled out the purple blazer at Saks, Ruby already heard people making Barney-the-dinosaur jokes behind her back, or nasty bitches saying things like, "You'd think, fat as she is, she'd wear something a bit more subdued," but the more Ruby stared at herself in the mirror the more comfortable she became in the brightly colored suit. It looked good on her and the more she looked at herself the more she realized just that.

She was about to walk downstairs and show off her new look when she remembered a scarf Doris had given her years ago that would go perfectly with the suit. She looked through her dresser and in the closet for the scarf to no avail. Finally, she remembered that she'd left it in the closet of her old bedroom, which, for the time being, belonged to Simone, who had left for work a few hours earlier. Surely she wouldn't mind if Ruby just ran up there and grabbed it.

Ruby climbed the steps to the third story of the house and opened the door to Simone's room. As she stepped inside she couldn't believe how long it had been since she'd been in there, and suddenly she was eager for Simone to move out so she could have it back. She never should have given it up in the first place. She was about to head toward the closet and get her scarf when something on the bed caught her eye. It was a wrapper of some sort. Ruby reached over and picked it up.

What's this? she thought. It didn't have any markings on it, but Ruby was certain it was the white plastic wrapper in which HoHos were sealed. Ruby giggled at the thought of Simone actually eating a HoHo. It just seemed so out of character. She was about to drop the wrapper in the trash and look for her scarf when a thought occurred to her. The wrapper on the bed reminded Ruby of how she often hoarded food in her bedroom, especially when she had been a teenager. She knew it was a silly thought, but what if Simone did the same thing?

No, she couldn't, Ruby said silently to herself as she peeked under the bed, only to find a couple discarded copies of *Vogue* and *Glamour*. She looked in the closet and, although she did find her scarf, there was no sign of any junk food, only some designer suits and fancy shoes.

"Oh well," Ruby thought, grabbing the scarf. She was about to abandon her search and head downstairs when she saw the hope chest at the foot of Simone's bed. She felt like a nosy snoop, but, nonetheless, she bent over and lifted the heavy wooden lid.

"Oh my God!" she said as her eyes caught sight of Simone's stash. Ruby couldn't believe it. Simone's hope chest put Ruby's bottom dresser drawer to shame. It was filled with all sorts of fattening goodies—a box of Frosted Flakes, bags of Kleebler cookies, packaged candy apples, Pop Tarts . . .

She's a fraud! Ruby thought. The skinny little newscaster was a fraud. How did she eat so much junk and stay so thin? Maybe she had a fast metabolism, or maybe she only ate small amounts of all the food she had stored at the foot of her bed . . . or maybe . . . no . . . she wouldn't. Ruby couldn't bring herself to think that maybe Simone was bingeing and purging. But really, if Princess Diana and Paula Abdul did it, why not Simone?

"Ruby?" Ruby heard Wanda calling from the living room. "Come on, let's see you."

Fighting the urge to take a few samples from Simone's chest, Ruby let the lid fall back in place, grabbed her scarf, and hurried down the steps. When she reached the living room Wanda was visibly stunned.

"Ruby, you're beautiful," she said with a huge smile.

"Please," Ruby responded, rolling her eyes.

"No, really, you are. You look fantastic!"

Ruby was about to, once again, deflect Wanda's compliment when Doris came out of the kitchen and caught sight of her.

"Ruby? Is that you?" she asked, as if she really wasn't sure.

"Yes," Ruby said, bracing herself for Doris's criticism—how her new makeup made her look like a painted hooker, how wearing such a bright color was insanity, how cutting her hair was a huge mistake.

Doris looked Ruby up and down and was quiet for a moment before responding. "You look pretty," she said, appearing as surprised to say the words as Ruby was to hear them.

"Pretty?" Wanda questioned. "She looks fabulous!"

"Thank you," Ruby said, looking at Wanda, but she really meant her words for Doris. Doris had never, on any single occasion, told her she looked pretty. Once in a blue moon, she might offer a reserved compliment about Ruby's intelligence, or her ability to bake a killer lemon poppy seed cake, but never before had Doris complimented Ruby's appearance. Never! Okay, so Doris hadn't said she looked beautiful or stunning, but telling Ruby that she looked pretty meant the world to Ruby. If Doris said it, maybe it was true. Maybe it was really true.

"Well, I guess I should hang up this suit so I can wear it to work tomorrow," Ruby said, feeling like a bride who was about to get out of her wedding dress.

"Hang it up?" Wanda replied. "No way, girlfriend! We're hitting the town tonight."

"We are?"

"Oh yes. I have it all arranged. Actually we should get going."

"Where?" Ruby asked.

"You'll see," Wanda said with a mischievous smile. "Go on, get your purse and let's go."

"Um . . . okay. I'll be right back," Ruby said, nervous about whatever Wanda had planned, but the rest of the day had gone so well she was also excited to find out what was in store for her next. When she got upstairs and in her room she closed the door and gave herself another look in the mirror, and just stared at herself for a moment.

"You look . . ." she said, trying to get the words out, but they weren't coming. How could she say it? She'd never said it.

"You look pre . . ." Ruby stumbled again. It was just too

hard to believe. She'd say it and then realize it was all a dream. That it wasn't real.

It was a struggle, and she had to fight like hell to get the words out, but after much hesitation she said it out loud. "You look pretty," she said, repeating Doris's earlier words.

Living Large

"Welcome!" A very large woman in a flashy sequined dress said to Ruby and Wanda as they walked into Club Zei off 14th Street.

"Hi, Itsy," Wanda said to the woman. "This is my friend, Ruby. It's her first time here."

"Well, it's a pleasure to meet you, Ruby. Welcome to Living Large," Itsy, who was by no means *itsy,* said to Ruby.

"Thank you," Ruby said, looking around the club and taking in the scene. She had never seen so many large women in one place . . . well, aside from maybe the Red Lobster on Crabby Mondays.

"What's going on?" Ruby asked Wanda.

"Here," Wanda said and handed Ruby a colorful postcard from a stack on the welcome table. Ruby accepted it and gave it a quick look.

Living Large: A Monthly Social Gathering for Large Women and the Men Who Love Them

"I've never heard of this," Ruby said, putting the card back on the table.

"Oh, we've been around for years. We meet at different restaurants and clubs around the city every month."

Ruby took another look around the room. It was like nothing

she had ever seen before. Fat women everywhere! But they didn't look the way Ruby was used to seeing so many of them. The women at the club were dressed to the nines in designer cocktail dresses and sharp tailored suits. They had trendy haircuts and wore stylish makeup. And what seemed most unusual, at least to Ruby, was that they were comfortably, even confidently socializing with men, all types of men—skinny men, buff men, old men, young men, white men, black men, and yes, fat men. There was almost an even ratio of men to women, and everyone seemed to be having such a good time. Liquor was flowing, music was raging, and the room was abuzz with social chatter.

"Wanda!" a tall black man said from behind.

"Leroy," Wanda replied, after turning around. "How are you?"

"I'm well, but I'll be much better once you introduce me to your fine-looking friend," Leroy responded, which led Ruby to look around her to see who the fine-looking friend was.

"This is my friend, Ruby Waters," Wanda replied.

"Hello, Ruby Waters," Leroy said, sticking out his hand.

"Hi," Ruby replied, still surprised that it was she Leroy had been referring to. She met his hand with hers, thinking he would offer a polite shake. Instead, he gently grasped it, raised it to his lips, and gave it a quick kiss.

"This is her first time here," Wanda said.

"Of course it's her first time. I would have remembered such a beautiful woman if she had been here before."

Ruby was starting to blush.

"Well, we're going to work the room a bit," Wanda said to Leroy.

"Okay, but will you save a dance for me?" Leroy asked Ruby.

"Sure," Ruby replied with a smile. She had never been talked to the way Leroy had spoken to her. That was the way men spoke to Simone or other thin pretty girls. She couldn't believe he had said she was beautiful.

"He's a sweet talker, eh," Ruby said to Wanda as they walked toward the bar.

"Yeah. I think he really liked you. Make sure you get that

dance in with him. He's a player. I wouldn't count on anything long-term with him, but he's a wild ride while it lasts. We had a brief thing last year."

"Really?"

"Yeah and let me tell you, everything they say about brothers . . . it's not true for all of them, but it's true for him."

"You mean?"

"Like a horse," Wanda replied. "I was popping Advil for days afterward."

"Oh my!" Ruby said as Wanda turned toward the bartender.

"Give me a Fat Lady and a Heavy Set," Wanda said.

"A Fat Lady and a Heavy Set? What are those?" Ruby asked.

"I'm not sure, some fruity drinks with rum in them. They're good."

When the bartender came back, Wanda handed Ruby the Fat Lady and kept the Heavy Set for herself. "Watch my drink while I run to the restroom, would you?"

"Sure," Ruby said, not thrilled with the idea of being left standing there by herself. As Wanda trotted off to the ladies' room, Ruby quickly downed her Fat Lady, and just after she asked the bartender for another one, a sharply dressed man with blond hair and beady green eyes approached her.

"Hi, there," he said to Ruby.

"Hi."

"Do want to play the county fair game?"

"The county fair game?" Ruby asked.

"Yeah, you sit on my face, and I guess how much you weigh."

As Ruby just looked at the young man in disbelief, Wanda returned from the bathroom and approached from behind. "Dirk, get out of here!" she said, shooing him away with her hands.

"Did he ask you to play the county fair game?" Wanda asked Ruby, frowning at Dirk as he walked away.

"Yes," Ruby said.

"Most of the guys here are okay, but it does draw the occasional creep. Dirk's here every month looking for someone to 'take to the fair.' He's such an idiot."

"Has anyone ever taken him up on it?"

"I hear Morgan Watts has, but she's nasty. You know how some women just look like their punanies stink to high heaven? Well, that's Morgan Watts. She'd make it with a hound dog if it was willing."

Ruby and Wanda continued to chat and by the time Ruby was on her third Fat Lady, a skinny white man approached them. He appeared to be in his early forties with salt-and-pepper hair.

"Hello," he said to them.

"Hi," the girls replied in unison.

"I'm Carl Beck," he said with a humble expression.

"Wanda," Wanda said before gesturing toward Ruby. "And this is Ruby."

"It's a pleasure to meet you. This is my first time at one of these things."

"Really? Are you enjoying yourself?" Wanda asked.

"Sure, but, gosh, so many gorgeous women in one place. It's overwhelming."

He was corny, but he had a genuiness about him that made it seem like he wasn't just sending a line their way—he really was overwhelmed with all the queen-size beauties.

"Would one of you care to dance?"

"Sure," Wanda said. "Ruby would love to dance," she added and gave Ruby a little nudge in Carl's direction.

Ruby smiled and followed Carl to the dance floor. She had just finished her third drink and had a pretty good buzz going. When they reached the dance floor the Weather Girls' "It's Raining Men" was blaring from the speakers, and Ruby finally noticed that the deejay seemed to be exclusively playing songs by fat women. When they had come in Aretha Franklin's "Freeway" was playing and Wynona Judd's "No One Else on Earth" had just gone off. Ruby hadn't been dancing in years. Even when she did occasionally go to a club when she was younger she was usually the one that stayed on the sidelines watching her friends' purses while they hit the dance floor. She never felt comfortable dancing in public. She loved music, and she loved to move to it—in her room or the shower or the car, but not in public. Even if no one was paying her the least bit of attention she always felt like everyone was staring at the fat girl shaking her blubber all over the place, but on the dance floor at Living Large, Ruby felt different. She felt safe in the company of other big girls and men who were there because they found large women beautiful and sexy. With the help of all the booze she'd just downed, Ruby felt attractive shaking her booty to the Weather Girls. It was fun to watch Carl try to keep rhythm with the music. He obviously suffered from CSBRD (Caucasian Straight Boy Rhythmic Disorder), but there was something cute about the way he couldn't keep time to the music. Suddenly, as the music shifted from the Weather Girls to Chaka Khan, it hit Ruby, and she realized something—she was having fun.

Catholic Popes, Blue Skies, and Bitchy Pop Singers

"Wow! Ruby, you look fantastic," Deanna said as Ruby stepped off the elevator. She'd spent almost two hours getting ready for work that morning—trying to get her hair exactly as Alexandre had fixed it. Simone even got up early to help her with her makeup.

"Thanks," Ruby said with a smile as she made her way to her office. She was hearing it all over the place—everyone was telling her how good she looked—her mother, men at the Living Large gathering, even her dry cleaner commented on Ruby's new look. She'd had such a good time with Wanda the night before, and the Living Large event was a major confidence booster. Ruby and Wanda had stayed at the club until two in the morning. Ruby danced with Carl for quite some time, and then another man asked if he could cut in, and Ruby danced with him. Men bought her drinks and Carl even asked if he could give her a ride home. It had been an amazing night. Ruby Waters had been in demand. She could hardly wait for the event to roll around again next month.

It was so comforting to know that even though most men looked past her because she was fat, there were men who found her gorgeous, and now she knew where to find them. She had actually been tempted to let Carl take her home. He was cute and nice and the idea of going home with someone she'd met at a bar was exciting, but she said no. It was enough that he had wanted to take her home and, besides, the more men catered to her at the Living Large event, the more Ruby thought about one man in particular—Preston DaSilva.

Before Ruby left for work this morning, Wanda had made her promise that she would approach Preston, and Ruby had eventually agreed, but now that it was time to keep her promise, Ruby wasn't sure she could do it. She was feeling better about herself, and obviously Preston was attracted to large women—he'd asked Wanda out, and Ruby had encountered him in an Internet chat room for guys looking to have sex with fat girls, but the idea of hitting on Preston still made her feel panicked and queasy.

As she approached her office, she passed Alan in the hallway. Between her obsession with Preston, and everything else going on her life, she hadn't been stopping by his cube like she used to.

"Hey," he said, before getting a full look at her. "My God, Ruby! Did you go on *Jenny Jones* for a makeover or something?"

Ruby laughed. "No. I just got some new makeup and a haircut, that's all."

Alan was quiet for a moment, just taking her in. "You look amazing," he said.

"Thank you," Ruby replied and, all of a sudden, she realized it—when people gave her compliments, she no longer deflected them, saying things like "No, I don't," or "Oh, please!" She just said "Thank you," and accepted them.

"I haven't seen you in a while. Are things okay?"

"Yeah," Ruby said. "I've just been busy."

"Did you see *American Idol* last night? That one girl, with the snout, who's always bearing her midriff, she was terrible."

"No, I didn't see it," Ruby said, still preoccupied. She was talking to Alan but thinking about Preston.

"How about lunch today?" Alan asked, and right then, Ruby spotted Preston walking behind him in the background.

"Um . . . what?" she said, obviously distracted.

"Lunch? Today? Are you free?"

"Oh. I'm sorry. I can't today."

"Okay," Alan said, looking disappointed, but Ruby didn't notice. She was too busy trying to get up the nerve to approach Preston.

When Alan went back to his cube, Ruby sat down at her desk, leaned back in her chair, took a deep breath, and gave her face a quick check in her compact. Then she got up from her chair with a determined look and headed for Preston's office. She had thought about it on the drive in and knew exactly what she was going to say. She was going to mention to Preston that she was interested in moving into sales and would like to take him to dinner to talk about it. Of course, her interest was in Preston, not a career in sales, but it was the best segue she could think of.

The closer she got to Preston's office, the more her heart began to race. She kept going over what she was going to say and imagined Preston's reaction. Would he happily agree or find a tactful way to decline? She knew the absolute worst he could say was "Fuck off, you fat bitch," and in her heart she knew he was way too polite to say something like that, but it didn't help her anxiety. When she reached his office, tense and faintly perspiring, he wasn't there. She felt an ease come over her, thankful that she could postpone the encounter. At least she could tell Wanda she had tried to approach him. It wasn't her fault he wasn't in his office when she had stopped by.

She was about to turn around when she heard a voice behind her.

"Hello. Did you need something?" Preston asked.

Ruby turned around. "Ah . . . no. I was just . . . ah . . . taking a walk." Fuck! she thought. Fuck! Fuck! Fuck! She had planned what she was going to say to Preston in exact detail and refined and reworked it during the drive to work, and when he approached her all she could say was that she was taking a walk.

"Ruby?" Preston questioned while Ruby stood silently berating herself for such a stupid reply to Preston's question. Who just takes a walk around the office hallway? Stupid! Stupid! Stupid! she thought again.

"Yes?"

"Ah, no," Preston said. "I wasn't asking you a question. I

was just confirming that . . ." Preston hesitated for a moment. "That you were . . . well . . . you. You look so different."

"Thank you. I think," Ruby said. "I just got a new haircut."

"Well, it looks great," he said. "But it seems like more than just a haircut."

"Yeah, well, the suit is new and I got some new makeup."

"No," Preston said. "That's not what I meant. I meant you have a different presence about you—like you're walking taller or more confident or something. Anyway, whatever it is, it suits you."

"Really?"

"Yeah . . . hey," Preston said, stumbling for just a moment, like he was the one at a loss for words. "I guess this is sort of coming out of the blue, but would you like to go to dinner or have a drink together sometime?"

Is the Pope Catholic? Is the sky blue? Is Diana Ross a bitch? "Sure," Ruby said, trying to hide her elation.

"Maybe tomorrow night?"

"Okay," Ruby said, not sure she could wait that long.

"Great. Then it's a date," Preston said and headed back into his office.

Ruby stood outside Preston's office for a moment, almost unable to move. She couldn't help but smile while she thought about what Preston had said—about her seeming more confident, and on the way back to her desk, she noticed that she was looking straight ahead as she walked instead of down at the floor.

After work, Ruby hurried to her car and made a beeline to Saks Fifth Avenue. She had called Wanda immediately after Preston had asked her out, and suddenly it hit her that she needed something to wear. Wanda agreed to help her pick out another outfit. When she got to the store, she hurried inside and didn't even notice that the glass doors at the entrance no longer intimidated her. She just pulled them open and walked in.

"Can I help you?" an attractive large black woman asked her. She looked incredibly familiar to Ruby, but Ruby couldn't remember where she had seen her. It was something about the woman's single auburn braid and the hideous bumblebee pin she had on her jacket. Ruby had seen her before, but she couldn't remember where.

"Hi. I'm looking for Wanda Johnson."

"Oh," the woman said, and rolled her eyes. "She's over there."

"Thanks," Ruby said and headed in Wanda's direction.

"Hi!" Ruby said with a smile that said *He asked me out! He fucking asked me out!*

Wanda smiled. "So let's find you something fabulous to wear tomorrow night."

Just then the woman that had directed Ruby to Wanda walked by and offered a scowl in Wanda's direction.

"Who is that? She kind of rolled her eyes at me when I said I was looking for you."

"That's Denise Proctor. She's the bitch that sucked someone's cock to get me axed from the Channel 6 feature on plus-size models."

"Really? She looks familiar to me," Ruby said. She couldn't place exactly where she had seen Denise before, but for some reason Ruby sensed that whatever encounter she had had with her, it wasn't good. "Gosh. I know her from somewhere," Ruby said.

"Maybe you were at the same Satan worship service," Wanda replied with a giggle.

Ruby laughed. "I'll remember eventually," she said and followed Wanda to pick out yet another outfit.

Sex Object

Ruby had been on pins and needles all day. Wanda had helped her select an attractive Lafayette black pantsuit the night before. It was a bit too formal to wear to the office, but Ruby assumed she and Preston would go out right after work, and she didn't want to change clothes right before they left—it would make her seem too eager. Not that she wasn't eager, she just didn't want to appear too ecstatic about their date.

She'd avoided him all day. She'd stayed in her office as much as possible. For some reason she didn't want to see him until their date officially began. She had no idea what to say to him if she happened to pass him in the hall. She was about to run to the bathroom and check her hair and makeup when her phone rang.

"Ruby Waters," she said into the phone.

"So you ready for the big date?" Jeremy asked.

"As ready as I'll ever be, I guess. I'm so nervous."

"Don't be nervous. Just slam a few gin and tonics as soon as you get to the restaurant."

"Sounds like a good idea," Ruby replied before adding in a bit of a panic, "My God, Jeremy! What am I going to talk about with Preston?"

"Just fawn over him. Ask him about his family and his job. People love to talk about themselves. If you play it right, you won't have to talk at all. He'll spend the evening talking about himself."

"I hope so. I'm just so nervous. He's so good-looking. I'm afraid everyone is going to be looking at us, wondering what a guy like him is doing with a girl like me."

"He's going to be with you because he thinks you're hot. Who cares what everyone else thinks?"

"I know they're all going to think 'Who's the cute gay guy with the fat girl?' People always think that when they see an attractive man with a fat woman."

"So what if people think you're his beard. They aren't the ones that are going to be sucking his cock at the end of the night."

"Jeremy!" Ruby said, as if the thought had never occurred to her.

"Oh please! Don't play little Miss Virgin with me. I know you want to lay him."

Ruby was blushing on the other end of the phone. "So I should just blow him in public, so people don't think he's a gay guy with a fat wife of convenience?"

"No, you should stop worrying about what people think. Besides, no one's interested in gay people trying to pass themselves off as straight anymore. The new thing is straight people trying to pass themselves off as gay."

"What?"

"Oh yeah. It's all the rage, with women anyway."

"That's ridiculous."

"Really? Ah, Anne Heche? Julie Cypher?"

"What about them?"

"What about them? They came to the other side for a *vacation,* and then decided they needed a stiff dick and left poor Ellen and Melissa alone with their vibrators."

"Hmmm," Ruby replied, considering what Jeremy had just said. "Why only women?"

"I don't know. But it's not that uncommon to see women switching teams—going from 'straight' to 'gay' back to 'straight' again. You never see men do it."

"Sex is different for women, Jeremy. God, you men will do it with anything you're attracted too. Sex is so physical for you guys—gay or straight. I think it's more mental for us women. Maybe some girls can get their sexual needs met with another woman even if they're not really gay . . . hell, what do I know?"

"I think you're right. For us men, it's all about dicks and pussy . . ."

"Jeremy! Must you be so vulgar? I'm at work," Ruby said as if she hadn't been thinking about Preston's dick and her own pussy for half the day.

"It's the truth. If men need pussy, men *need* pussy. And if men need dick, men *need* dick. Yep, dicks and pussy . . ."

"You forgot titties," Ruby argued.

"What?"

"For straight men, it's not just about pussy. It's about titties too."

"I guess. Anyway, I think you'd be pretty hard-pressed to find a straight guy pretending to be gay. But straight women pretending to be lesbians, it's not that uncommon."

"Whatever, Jeremy. I'd better get moving. We can debate faux lesbians later," Ruby replied.

"Okay. I have to go watch some football game with Gary anyway."

"*You* are watching a football game? What? Is Patti LaBelle doing the half-time show?"

"Very funny. No, Gary likes football. At least he says he does, but I think it's because he's so closeted. He figures two guys at a sporting event won't attract any attention."

"Attention?"

"Yeah, you know. He doesn't want anyone to know he's gay. We're not like lesbians. They can be so much more discreet. Woman can go shopping or out to dinner and no one thinks anything. If two men do anything besides go to a ball game together you might as well have 'I'm a big fag' written on your forehead."

"The things you'll put up with for a piece of ass," Ruby said to Jeremy as she whirled around in her chair to see Preston standing in her doorway.

"You got to do what . . ."

"Jeremy, I have to go," Ruby said, startled to see Preston standing there.

"Is he there?"

"Bye," Ruby said and hung up the phone. Shit! Had Preston heard her talking about pieces of ass? God, she hoped he hadn't been standing there to hear about bogus lesbians and stiff dicks.

"Hi. I can come back if you're busy," Preston said, still lingering in the doorway.

"No, no. I'm just getting ready to go."

"I thought maybe we could have a drink over at my hotel across the street."

"Sure," Ruby said, shutting down her computer and gathering her purse. As she got up from her chair, her heart was racing, and she was afraid he would notice her shaking. She began to wish she had sneaked a few drinks before the date instead of waiting until they got to the bar.

Ruby and Preston walked across the street to the Marriott and sat at a small table in the lounge. As soon as they were seated, a young waitress approached them.

"What can I get for you?"

"Do you like wine?" Preston asked Ruby.

"Sure," Ruby lied. She didn't care for wine. She could deal with a glass of chardonnay or pinot grigio every now and then, but she couldn't stand red wine.

Preston gave the wine list a quick review. "Bring us a bottle of the Clos du Val."

"I think you'll like it," Preston said to Ruby as the waitress walked away.

"I'm sure I will," she said. She had never heard of it, and was hoping it was a white wine.

"So how was your day?"

"Busy," Ruby replied. "I had two reps out sick today so the phones were crazy." Ruby felt silly talking about her job supervising the customer service department. She was sure it paled in comparison to Preston's glamorous world of sales and marketing. "How about you? Any exciting sales prospects in the pipeline?"

"Yes. I'm actually about to close a deal with a big employer in Baltimore. If all goes well, we should have a signed contract by the end of the week."

"Congratulations," Ruby replied, not sure what to say next. *Ask him about himself,* she heard Jeremy telling her in her head. "So how long have you been in sales?"

"Almost twenty years. I was a born salesman. My parents always said I could sell ice cubes to Eskimos if I wanted to."

Ruby laughed and was about to inquire about his family as Jeremy had suggested when the wine arrived. It was in a dark bottle, which was a bad sign. The waitress presented the wine to Preston. He gave her the okay and she removed the cork. She handed the cork to Preston and poured a small amount of wine into his glass.

Shit! Ruby thought. It was red.

Preston felt the cork and swirled the wine around in his glass for a moment before taking a sip. It all seemed so sophisticated to Ruby. She was used to Miller Lites and Coronas, or frozen daiquiris and margaritas.

"It's fine," he said.

When the waitress had filled both glasses, Ruby took a sip. Red wine always burned the back of her throat, and she tried not to wince as she swallowed. She didn't like it, but she needed something to relax her, so she took another sip and another. They talked some more about Preston's family and how he grew up in Connecticut, where he went to college, what it was like for him to travel all the time for work, and his marketing philosophy. Jeremy had been right. All Ruby needed to do was ask questions. It was so simple. She kept asking, and Preston kept talking and talking. Ruby wasn't even annoyed that he never stopped to ask anything about her. She was just happy that there were no uncomfortable lulls in the conversation.

They were halfway through their second bottle of wine when Preston reached across the table and set his hand on hers.

"I'm having a good time," he said with a smile.

"Me too," Ruby added and downed some more wine. It was

going straight to her head. She felt high—high from the wine, high from being on a date with Preston DaSilva.

"It's getting late," Preston said, looking at his watch. "If you want, maybe we could go up to my room and have another bottle of wine up there . . . or some other cocktails if you want."

"Okay," Ruby said and took yet another sip of her wine. She was drunk, but not drunk enough that her heart didn't start to palpitate wildly when Preston asked her up to his room. This was their first date, and it wasn't even really a date—it was a drink after work. It was clear that this was how Preston had planned it. How convenient to have their date in the lounge at his hotel. Ruby knew that going up to his room was a bad idea, but she didn't care. This was her chance to have sex with someone for whom she had pined for years. Suppose he got hit by a bus the next day and she hadn't fucked him? How could she live with herself?

When they got up to Preston's suite, Ruby was amazed at the opulence. It consisted of two exquisitely furnished rooms—a sitting room and a bedroom. The company wouldn't let her give her employees anything more than a three on their performance reviews to keep raises down, and yet they were putting Preston up in a two-room suite on the concierge level.

"Have a seat," Preston said and gestured for Ruby to sit down on the sofa. "Can I fix you a drink?"

"Okay," Ruby said. "How about a gin and tonic?"

Between the two of them they'd had a bottle of wine each. Actually, Ruby was downing the wine so quickly she may have had most of both bottles, but she didn't care. She was in a hotel room with Preston.

Preston raided the minibar and fixed drinks for him and Ruby. He laid them on the coffee table and sat down next to her.

"Are you comfortable?" he asked.

"Very," Ruby lied. Even with her system filled with booze she was still nervous, but at least she wasn't shaking anymore.

"Is there anything I can do to make you more comfortable?" Preston said before leaning in and giving her a kiss.

"No. I'm fine," she replied before Preston kissed her again. He took Ruby totally by surprise. She hadn't expected him to move so quickly, but she tried to return his kisses the best she could. She hadn't kissed anyone since Warren, but Preston was so taken with her, she just let his lips guide hers.

Ruby had never felt a man kiss her with such intensity. Preston kissed her so hard and so fast it left her almost breathless. He wrapped his arms around her and seemed to want to feel every inch of her. He went up and down her sides, firmly massaging her with his hands. He seemed totally enthralled with her body. It was something Ruby had never experienced before. He loved her body—he was captivated by it.

Preston unbuttoned Ruby's suit jacket and helped it fall off her shoulders. He released the clasp on her bra and practically ripped it off her. Tightly squeezing her buttocks, he nuzzled his head between her breasts as Ruby lay in a mixed state of pleasure and disbelief. She was in such flux it was several minutes before she was aware of what Preston's body felt like. As he devoured her breasts, an awareness of Preston's solid, defined build came over Ruby, and she started unbuttoning his shirt. Once she had his shirt off him he pressed his bare chest against hers. His body was so hard, his pecs felt like a thick board against her bosom. It was all just too unbelievable. Ruby Waters, Big Fat Ruby Waters, was a sex object—a sex object to an inarguably gorgeous and successful man.

Milking the Cow for Free

Ruby walked back to her car from the hotel by herself, feeling like she was positively glowing. She hadn't had sex with anyone since Warren, and her experience with him seemed like a trip to the dentist in comparison to her evening with Preston. Preston had made her feel sexy and attractive. He ravished her body and seemed to truly think she was beautiful.

As she got in her car she thought about Preston and what would happen next. Did he think she was a total slut? How could she be a slut? She'd been with less men her whole life than most woman were with in a month. She probably should have played a little harder to get, but Preston was obviously enamored with her—surely, he would ask her out again. God! What would everyone think when Ruby showed up at events on the arm of Preston DaSilva? She pictured the thin girls staring at them in disbelief and trying to lure Preston away with their perky little tits and tiny behinds. She imagined herself telling the skinny bitches that Preston needed a woman with some meat on her bones, and they had better head to the Dairy Queen if they ever intended to land a man like him.

As she drove home, she wanted to call Preston on the cell phone and tell him what a wonderful time she had. She just wanted to hear his voice again. She loved him. Yes, she knew it was ridiculous, but she loved him. She loved the way he looked, the way he smiled, the way he thought she was beautiful, the way he made love to her like she was a sex goddess.

"Ruby DaSilva," she said out loud. "Ruby DaSilva," she said again, as she started looking for an open McDonald's or Burger King. She hadn't eaten since long before her date with Preston and she was starving.

When Ruby got home she hurried up the front steps and rushed inside.

"Where have you been?" Doris asked Ruby as she came through the door. "It's after two in the morning. I was worried sick. I even called Jimmy, that florist friend of yours, and he didn't know where you were."

"Jeremy," Ruby corrected. "I've told you a hundred times, he's a . . ."

"I told you she would be home late, Doris," Wanda said, appearing from the kitchen and interrupting Ruby. "She was working late," she added, making sure Ruby knew what Wanda had told Doris about her extended absence from the house.

"Yeah, Mom. I was at work," Ruby said, feeling silly lying to her mother. She was over thirty years old for Christ's sake.

"Couldn't you have called? What's going on? Are you on dope?"

"No, Mother, I'm not on dope. I'm sorry," Ruby said, feeling some modicum of comfort knowing that Doris was worried about her. "I guess I'm not used to letting anyone know when I'm going to be home late."

"Honestly," Doris said and walked toward the den to go to bed. "I think it's time for me to go back to my house."

"So?" Wanda asked, once Doris had closed the door to the den.

Ruby smiled from ear to ear. She had been hoping Wanda was still up. She was dying to tell someone about her evening.

"That good?"

"Fan-fucking-tastic," Ruby said.

"You little vixen. Tell me all about it."

"Oh, Wanda. It was incredible. We went for a drink at his hotel and . . ."

"Whoa. Wait a minute. A drink at his hotel? He didn't even take you to dinner?"

"No, we just had some wine in the hotel lounge."

Wanda raised her eyebrow like she disapproved—like Ruby was letting Preston milk the cow for free.

"I had way too much to drink," Ruby continued. "Eventually, we went up to his room and then . . . well . . . it was incredible."

"I'm so glad you had a good time, but next time, make him buy a girl a meal first or at least take you to a movie or something."

"Yeah, you're right, but I just couldn't resist," Ruby replied, really starting to question if she had done the right thing by sleeping with Preston so quickly, hoping she hadn't blown the chance of anything long-term with him. But, tonight, she wasn't going to think about that, she was just going to bask in the glow of feeling pretty and sexy.

"So how are you?" she asked Wanda, trying to sway the conversation in another direction. She didn't want to hear anymore from Wanda about how she gave the goodies away too soon.

"Okay, still bummed about missing out on the news feature to that awful Denise."

"Yeah, she did seem pretty nasty," Ruby said, remembering how Denise had rolled her eyes at her when she asked for Wanda at Saks the day before. And then, she had a flash of recognition—Ruby remembered where she had seen Denise.

"Oh my God!" Ruby said.

"What?" Wanda asked.

"I remember where I saw Denise."

"Where?"

"You are not going to believe this."

"What?" Wanda said, getting impatient.

"If I'm right, and I'm certain I am, she's hiding something. Oh my God!"

"Really? What? Did she used to be a hooker? Oh, please tell me she used to be a hooker."

"No," Ruby said, laughing at Wanda's guess.

"She's a man? Is she really a man?"

"No. Worse," Ruby replied. "Much worse!"

Depressed

Ruby was at her desk eyeing the Lenny Kravitz CD she had purchased three days earlier. She was at the Target at Potomac Yards when she saw it, and it reminded her of Preston and how much he said he liked Lenny's music the night they'd gone for a drink. She still wasn't sure if she would keep it for herself or give it to Preston as a gift, so she hadn't removed the plastic from the case yet. As she looked at the cover, she thought about her evening with Preston almost a week earlier. She remembered him talking about Lenny Kravitz, what a fan he was, and how eager he was to get tickets to his concert when he came to town.

Ruby smiled when she thought of Preston at a Lenny Kravitz concert—how, like most straight white boys, he'd probably sit in his chair the entire time and barely so much as tap his foot to the beat all the while, professing what a good time he was having. That was something Ruby never understood about men—their relationship with music. She knew of so many guys who professed to love music and owned hundreds of CDs, but whenever she observed them listening to them, they did little more than sit still or barely tap their foot. She wondered if, in private, with the door closed and the blinds shut, they ever cranked up the music and boogied like they were Michael Jackson. Maybe it had something to do with what Jeremy called the straight boy fun deficiency—how being gay was a struggle, but there were times when Jeremy actually felt sorry for straight boys—how they were so afraid of being perceived as gay they would deny themselves so many things. Lord help them if they ever actually allowed themselves to really move to music, admitted to wanting to go see a movie tagged as a "chick flick," or, God forbid, admitted that another man was good-looking.

Ruby set the CD down and checked her E-mail for the fourth time that morning. Why hadn't Preston responded to any of her E-mails? She'd E-mailed the day after their encounter to say that she had a good time and E-mailed him again a few days later just to say hi. He was traveling all week, but she knew he always had a laptop and access to E-mail.

The more time that passed without any word from Preston, the more worried Ruby became. She never should have slept with him so early. She should have played hard to get or at least not-so-fucking-easy to get. Maybe she was just another notch in his bedpost. Or had she been so awful in the sack that Preston was avoiding her for that reason? The way he was moaning and panting when he fucked her, he seemed to be having as good a time as she was, but Lord knew, Ruby wasn't terribly experienced. Surely, he knew she was nervous. She'd be better next time when she was more relaxed and at ease with Preston. Maybe she'd buy one of those books on pleasing a man and learn some exciting moves.

Ruby sighed after checking her account—nothing but junk mail. Ever since she had logged into the Big Girls, Don't Cry! chat room, she had been getting all sorts of strange E-mails with subject headers like "Spear Britney," "Oops, I lost my panties!" or "Fat Chicks Take It up the Ass." As she quickly deleted the unsolicited mail, her phone rang.

"Ruby Waters," she said into the receiver.

"I'm so depressed," Jeremy replied.

"Why?"

"That video with Enrique Iglesias and Whitney Houston is on, and I can't stop thinking about Carlos."

"Who?"

"Carlos. You know, the guy from Honduras I met a couple weeks ago."

"I thought he was just a one-night stand."

"I guess he was, but damn, he was so hot. . . ."

"Wait a minute. What happened to Gary, the guy that was taking you to football games?"

"I didn't tell you? Get this—he's decided he's straight."

"Straight?"

"Yeah, a straight guy that likes to suck dick and—" Jeremy said before cutting himself off. "You should see this. I told you they're playing the 'Could I Have This Kiss Forever' video on VH1? Whitney Houston is pretending she knows how to speak Spanish."

"Maybe she does know how to speak Spanish," Ruby argued.

"Yeah. I bet she knows how to say 'Give me my crack!' in Spanish."

Ruby laughed. "You're terrible."

"I know, but, like I said, I'm depressed."

"You and me both. I haven't heard from Preston in almost a week."

"Not a good sign," Jeremy replied. "He hasn't been in the office?"

"No, he's traveling. He's probably got a woman in every city he goes to."

"Have you called him?"

"No, just E-mails."

"Well, maybe he isn't checking his E-mail or he's having trouble with it."

"Yeah, and maybe Liza Minnelli's husband's straight."

"Don't you be hate'n on Liza," Jeremy said. "Why don't we meet for a drink after work, and we can wallow in our depression together?"

"Thanks, but I can't. I have to meet Wanda. We're conducting a sting of sorts."

"A sting?"

"Yeah. Channel 6 is taping a feature tonight on plus-size models, and I'm supposed to help Wanda oust the woman highlighted in it."

"And how are you going to do that?"

"Well, you won't believe this, Jeremy," Ruby began and then told Jeremy how she and Wanda planned to bust Denise, and show her for the liar that she was.

The Sting

"Hurry, hurry," Simone said as she ushered Ruby and Wanda into the studio. "You don't have much time. She's down the hall, third door on the right. If anyone asks how you got in here, just say you got separated from your tour group or something."

"Okay," Wanda said.

"Good luck," Simone offered and hurried away from the girls and back toward her office. Security was very tight at the station, and she didn't want anyone to know she had let Ruby and Wanda in the building.

"You ready?" Wanda asked Ruby as they walked down the hall.

"I think so," Ruby replied. She was nervous, but the past few days had given her a new sense of boldness, and she was eager to help Wanda.

"Okay, I'll wait here," Wanda said, staying to the side of the doorway. "I hope you're right about her."

"Well, we're about to find out," Ruby said before taking a deep breath, knocking on the door, and immediately letting herself in. "Hello. You're Denise Proctor, right? How are you? Good, good. I'm Lola Patola from wardrobe. We have much work to do to get you ready for the taping," Ruby said quickly and authoritatively.

"What?" Denise asked. She had just spent an hour having her

hair and makeup done by one of the studio stylists, and they had given her a tailored black suit to wear for her interview.

"We need to get you changed," Ruby said.

"Changed? This is the suit they gave me."

"Who gave you?" Ruby questioned.

"Ah . . . Jackie, I think her name was."

"Oh, Jackie, silly girl, that Jackie. No, no, no. We've made a change in the direction of the feature on large-size models."

"You have?" Denise asked.

"Oh yes. We're focusing it on the latest fashion frenzy for big girls—the plus-size bikini!"

"The what?" Denise said with a look of relative horror as Ruby pulled out a hanger with a flower-print bikini attached.

"Oh yes. You must change, hurry you don't have much time."

"Ah . . . no . . . I don't think . . ."

"Do you not like this bikini? We have others I can show you."

"Don't you think I would look much smarter in this suit?" Denise replied with agitation. "Surely, no one expects me to be interviewed in that."

"Of course they do. Now get out of that suit and show some skin," Ruby ordered.

"Really. I don't think it's a good idea. I'd really much rather wear the suit."

"I'm afraid that's not an option. Mr. McFarland gave me strict instructions to get you fitted into a bikini."

"Ah . . ." Denise stammered. She was clearly panicked about wearing the bathing suit. "I just don't think . . . really . . . I can't . . ."

Before she could say anything further, Wanda barged into the room. "Okay, Denise," she said. "Why don't you tell us the real reason you don't want to wear the bikini?"

"Wanda? What are you doing here?"

"Exposing you for the fraud that you are."

"What?"

"We know why you don't want to wear the bikini," Wanda

said. "Because you can't, can you? Because you're not really fat!"

"Oh, that's ridiculous," Denise said, stepping away from the girls. She was trying to remain composed, but she was plainly flustered.

"Is it?" Wanda asked. "Ruby's seen you—she's seen you twice. Two times you swiped parking spaces from her."

"Once in the city and once at the airport," Ruby added, thinking back to two times when a thin woman took parking spaces that were rightfully hers—one time when Ruby was in a hurry to meet Wanda to show her the house, and another when Ruby was trying to park the car at the airport to have a food fest at Legal Seafood. It was Denise who had disregarded Ruby and stolen her parking spaces right from underneath her. "I saw you get out of the car," Ruby said. "I remember that colored braid mixed in with your 'do and you had that brooch on," Ruby continued, pointing to Denise's Joan Rivers bumblebee pin. "I'm not sure what you have under that suit today, but it wasn't there when you brazenly pilfered my parking spaces."

"Ah . . . ah . . ." Denise was stumbling, trying to think of something to say.

"The jig's up, girlie-girl," Wanda said. "Admit it, you're . . ." Wanda added, stepping in closer to Denise. "You're . . ." she said again, getting up in Denise's face. "You're *skinny!*"

"Okay! Okay!" Denise yelled. "I'm skinny, damn it! I tried making it as a mainstream model and couldn't get any work. Pretty skinny girls are a dime a dozen. I couldn't get any jobs as a thin model, but attractive fat women with sex appeal and self-esteem were so rare it was easier to make it as a plus-size model," she said, really starting to unravel. "I tried to gain weight. I ate and ate, but I couldn't put on any pounds. God damn my fast metabolism! Then I saw this *Friends* episode where they made Courteney Cox look fat, and I figured if they could make that emaciated twig look fat . . ."

Ruby and Wanda just looked at Denise as she spilled her guts, almost as if it were a relief to finally have her lies out in the open.

"You have no idea what it's like, disguising yourself as a fat woman for ten hours a day. It's misery . . . pure misery. I was so hot some days I thought I might melt."

It was all suddenly making sense. Why Denise was always complaining to the manager about how warm the store was, why she was always fanning herself and wiping her brow, why she had an unusually thin face—and maybe, to some extent, why she had been such a bitch. Who wouldn't be, wearing the equivalent of a ski suit under her clothes all day.

"How? How did you do it?" Ruby asked in awe of this woman who was going to great lengths to have something Ruby spent her life wishing she could get rid of. "How do you go from being so thin to . . ."

Denise sniffed and wiped a tear from her eye. "Have you seen Harvey Fierstein in *HairSpray*?"

"The Broadway show?" Wanda asked.

"Yeah. My uncle worked for the costumer that did his fat suit to play Edna Turnblad—he hooked me up."

"Girl, you're nuts," Wanda said, matter-of-factly and put her hand on Denise's shoulder. As awful as Denise had been to her, Wanda couldn't help but feel sorry for her—the bitch was fucked-up. "What were you thinking? How long did you really think you could keep this up?"

"I never intended on keeping it up for long. I had it all planned. The media loves a weight-loss story. I figured I'd get a buzz going as a large-size model. Then I'd lose the fat suit and make-up some story about how I lost so much weight, get endorsements . . . claim I lost it on Weight Watchers or using Slim Fast, or be the new Jared for Subway . . . but, I guess it's all over now."

"Not necessarily," Wanda said.

Denise looked up at her.

"I'll make a deal with you."

"A deal?" Denise asked as she wiped her eyes again.

"Ruby and I will keep your secret."

"You will?"

"Yes, under one condition."

"What?"

"You give up this interview and concede it to me."

Denise knew she had no choice but to agree.

"Here comes the bubbly," Ruby said as she popped the cork from a bottle of champagne and starting pouring it into three glasses. It was after midnight and she, Wanda, and Simone were sitting in the living room celebrating their ouster of Denise Proctor.

"Can you believe that skinny wack-job?" Wanda asked the other girls.

"Actually, I can," Simone replied. "There are people out there that will do anything to get what they want. But let's not talk about Denise," Simone added, before she lifted her glass. "To the next hottest thing in the modeling world."

The girls lifted their glasses and took a sip of their sparkling wine.

"When do you think they'll reschedule the taping?" Wanda asked Simone.

"Probably not for a few weeks."

"Gosh, Wanda, you'll have men coming out of your ears after the piece airs," Ruby said.

"And that would be a problem *how*?" Wanda inquired with a laugh.

Ruby giggled with her before asking, "Do you *ever* think of settling down with one guy?"

"Oh, I don't know. Maybe one day, but I bore so easily, especially in the bedroom. I like variety."

"I so agree," Simone chimed in. "But I guess you can date one guy and just keep trying new things with him . . . spice things up every once in a while."

"Yeah, that's what all the psychologists and talk show hosts say, but I'm not sure I buy it. I don't know about sex with the same guy over and over again. Even if you do try to liven things up with a little role-play or leather. I mean, it's like chicken, you know. You can liven it up with spices and sauces. You can Kiev it or cacciatore it, but in the end, it's still freakin' chicken. I don't know about you guys, but sometimes I need a steak or some ribs with hot sauce."

Mmm . . . some ribs with hot sauce, Ruby thought as she laughed with the girls and took another sip of her champagne. It was so fun to sit and relax with her friends, women she was extremely anxious around only weeks earlier. She remembered how uncomfortable she had felt the first time they went out to dinner together the day Wanda and Simone had moved in. As she laughed with her roommates, it seemed almost surreal to not feel nervous and inferior around them—to know that they liked her for who she was and would always listen to what she had to say. It was a great feeling to be comfortable around two women who seemed so self-assured and confident. Things were looking up for Ruby Waters. She had a new look, new friends, and was starting to develop some confidence. Now, if only Preston DaSilva would complete the package and give her a call and ask her out again.

The Asshole Down the Hall

Ruby was having a terrible day. It had been a couple of days since she and Wanda busted Denise, and more than a week since she had heard from Preston. She'd E-mailed him twice and left a message on his voice mail, and he still hadn't contacted her. On top of that, one of the customer service reps whom she supervised couldn't handle a nasty beneficiary, and Ruby had to listen to him rant and rave about some unpaid claims for almost half an hour. It was amazing to Ruby. Working in health care, she realized how clueless people were about the whole system. Everyone wanted top-notch care, but no one wanted to pay for it. The same people who wouldn't think twice about dropping six hundred dollars on a blouse at Neiman Marcus raised holy hell if they had to spend so much as dime on an X ray or some laboratory tests. They wanted to have procedures that cost thousands of dollars and pay nothing more than a ten-dollar copay, and when they had to actually fork out some cash for the sake of their health, Ruby and her customer service team were on the front line of hearing all about it. She'd been called everything from a lying bitch to a health-care hoarding whore. Of course, there were beneficiaries with valid issues, and there were often times that Ruby thought CrustiCare should have covered treatments that were regularly denied, but today she was in no mood to listen to a caller whine about how CrustiCare kept denying his claims for an uncovered procedure.

"No, Mr. Knitter. I don't need their Web site address. I'm sure they're a reputable organization, but hydro-colonic cleansing simply isn't covered under your benefit plan. I'm sorry."

"But she was certified!"

Certified in what? Ruby thought. Shoving a hose up someone's ass and turning the faucet on? "I'm afraid it doesn't make a difference, Mr. Knitter. You just don't have any coverage for that particular procedure."

"I'll have you know that colonic irrigation cleans out years of toxins and waste lining the walls of the colon. It says so right here in the brochure."

What a crock of shit, Ruby thought, no pun intended. "That may be, sir, but there's just nothing I can do."

"Look, you fucking bitch, I can't afford to pay for this treatment. I've paid my premiums for years and now that I actually need care, you won't cover me."

"Sir, I'm afraid there is nothing more I can do. I'm sorry," Ruby said and hung up the phone. Her boss always told her that once callers started using profanity, she and her staff were free to terminate the call. Ruby had never hung up on a caller before, but she was changing, and she wasn't as willing to take shit (once again, no pun intended) off people as she used to be.

It felt good to hang up on Mr. Knitter. A month ago, Ruby would have just continued to listen to him rant and rave until he tired himself out and hung up on his own, but now, she was feeling a bit more self-assured. If only Preston would return her E-mails or her phone message. She knew he was busy, but couldn't he make time to return a call to someone he had literally been inside of a few days earlier?

She was about to document her call with Mr. Knitter, when she saw *him* walk by her office door. Ruby's mouth went dry and her heart sank in her chest—Preston was in the building. Had he been in the building all day and not bothered to say anything to Ruby? What should she do? Should she go by his office and say hello or wait for him to come by hers? She didn't know what to do, but it was getting close to the end of the workday. If she didn't approach him right then, she might lose her chance. For all she knew, he would be traveling again the next day. She couldn't stand the waiting anymore. Even if he told her to go to hell, at least she'd have some closure.

She got up from her chair, took a deep breath, and headed toward Preston's office.

"Stay calm, Ruby," she said to herself on her way down the hall. She knew that if she stopped, for even a second, she'd lose her nerve.

"Hey," she said, trying to sound breezy as she poked her head in his door.

"Ruby. Hi," Preston said. "How are you?"

"Good. Just thought I'd say hi," she replied awkwardly. "I sent you a couple messages . . . never heard back."

"Oh yeah. I'm sorry. Gosh I've been so busy."

"Too busy to return an E-mail?" Ruby questioned, hearing the desperation in her voice, sounding like one of the jilted whores on *The Bachelor*. She didn't know exactly why, but she could feel her eyes starting to well up. Maybe she could tell by the way he was looking at her that she was a nuisance—another fat girl he'd fucked that was going to take some effort to get rid of.

Preston got up and closed the door. "Sit down, Ruby," he said.

Ruby lowered herself into a chair and tried to keep the tears from running down her face. She knew what he was going to say.

"Look, I'm sorry if you thought there might be more between us than the fun we had the other night, but that's all it was."

"No, no. I didn't think anything . . . just fun," Ruby said, using all the strength she had to keep from blubbering all over his desk.

"I'm sorry, Ruby. I have a girlfriend back in New York," Preston said, pointing to a picture on his desk. It was of him and some size-four brunette.

"That's your girlfriend?" Ruby questioned. "She's so skinny. I thought you liked . . . you know . . . big . . ."

"I do. God, Ruby, you're gorgeous! But I can't actually *date* someone . . ." Preston said, letting his voice trail off, not wanting to finish what he was about to say.

"Oh," Ruby said, as if a lightbulb had appeared over her head. "I get it. Us fat girls, we're okay to fuck, but that's it. You don't actually want to be seen in public with us."

Preston was silent. He just looked down at his desk, diverting his eyes from Ruby.

"I guess it kind of makes sense now," Ruby added, getting up from the chair and turning to leave.

"Ruby," Preston called behind her, but she kept walking. She was determined to make it to her own office before she let herself cry. She wasn't going to be the fat girl sobbing in the office hallway. Who was she kidding? Nothing had really changed. So she looked prettier and had snazzier clothes and, maybe over the past few days, she had even been holding her head up a little bit higher, but she was still fat. She was still Big Fat Ruby Waters trying to get out of sight before anyone saw her cry. As she walked back to her office she could only think of two things—how she was going to keep the tears from gushing before she made it behind closed doors, and what she was going to eat as soon as she was done crying—a run to Kentucky Fried Chicken was what was coming to mind. She'd get a bucket—a whole bucket of fried chicken—just for herself.

When she made it inside her office she was about to close the door behind her when Alan approached.

"Hey," he said with a smile before really getting a look at Ruby. "Are you okay?" he asked, changing his demeanor after seeing her eyes, swollen with the tears she was determined to keep back in public.

"Yeah," Ruby said, sniffling. "Having some allergy issues today," she lied.

"Really? I hear the pollen is coming out early this year."

"That must be it," Ruby said, wishing he would just leave, so she could get down to business.

"You've been busy lately. I haven't seen much of you."

"Yeah. Just have a lot on my plate right now I guess."

"Listen," Alan said, seeming anxious. "I've got tickets to this jazz concert thing at Wolf Trap tomorrow night, and . . ." he struggled a bit to get the words out. "I guess I was wondering if you might want to come. Maybe we could grab a bite to eat beforehand?"

"Ah . . . " Ruby replied, wiping a hint of tear that was starting to escape her eye. "What?"

"You're busy? That's okay . . . maybe some other time."

"No, no," Ruby responded, sniffling. "I'm not busy. I'd love to go," her tears fading into a look of surprise.

"Great!" Alan said, his stance immediately relaxing as if he had been deathly afraid that Ruby would say no. "Then it's a date."

Ruby let out a quick breath, startled by what Alan had said. A date? Had he just asked her out on a date? "Yeah, I guess it is." Ruby felt a slight smile come across her face.

"So we'll work out the details later?" Alan asked, and turned to head back to his desk.

"Okay," Ruby said. As Alan walked away, she closed the door behind him and sat down behind her desk. Suddenly, Preston was little more than an asshole down the hall. She'd been asked on an actual date. So what if Alan wasn't the debonair Preston DaSilva. Alan was cute and nice, and Ruby had fun with him. He had even seemed nervous—like he was afraid Ruby would reject him. He was so happy when she said yes. She felt like Joanie Cunningham the day she finally relented and decided to go out with Chachi.

Ruby thought about the look on Alan's face when she agreed to go out with him. Then she thought about how *she* had prompted that look—Ruby Waters had made his day by accepting his invitation. Then she put her head in her hands and stopped fighting the tears. She cried—she cried like a baby, and it felt fantastic.

Out in the Open

When Ruby came in the house Doris was sitting on the sofa in the living room. Taco was curled up next to her, and they both seemed to have a keen interest in the antics of SpongeBob Squarepants, which was blasting at full volume from the television.

"Hello," Ruby said.

"Hi," Doris replied, barely taking her eyes off the television. "That squirrel on *SpongeBob* . . . Sandy, I think her name is. Is she one of those *lesbians*?"

"What?"

"Well, look at her. She's always karate chopping everything, and you wouldn't even know she was a girl if it wasn't for that flower on her helmet."

"Yes, Mother. I am *so sure* that the squirrel on *SpongeBob* is a lesbian. Jerry Falwell should be protesting it any day now."

"No need to get smart," Doris said, not appreciating Ruby's sarcasm.

"You asked," Ruby said.

"Well, I'm not watching any *lesbian* squirrel," Doris said and changed the channel. She clicked the remote a few times and eventually landed on a commercial with Lauren Hutton talking about menopause and the value of hormone replacement therapy.

"Goodness gracious! On the television talking about the *change of life*! Why, in my day, she would have been taken out in the woods and shot," Doris said, before turning to Ruby. "You're not doing that hormone replacement therapy, Ruby, are you?"

"Mom, I'm *thirty-two*."

"Yes, but I read somewhere that large women go through *the change* earlier."

"Whatever, Mother," Ruby said. She was in such a good mood, and she wasn't about to let Doris's nonsense bring her down. It had been an exhausting day. It was amazing how quickly one's emotions could change. She had gone from feeling like an absolute wreck after being rebuffed by Preston to feeling hopeful and giddy after Alan asked her out.

"The girls home?" Ruby asked.

"I haven't seen Wanda, but Simone's upstairs, puking I think."

"Puking?"

"Yeah. It's almost six o'clock. That's usually when she does it," Doris said as if she was stating that Tide was on sale at the Safeway.

"What do you mean? That's when she does it? Does what?" Ruby had been so caught up in herself and her new clothes and her new hair and Preston and Alan that she had forgotten all about Simone and her hope chest full of junk food.

"Purges. It's usually about six o'clock when she purges," Doris said again, as if what she was saying was of no significance. "How else do you think she stays so thin?"

"How long have you known about this?" Ruby asked Doris.

"I don't know, a while."

"Why didn't you tell anyone?" Ruby asked.

"It's not my place to get involved in something like that. Besides, it works. Look how good she looks."

Right then it hit Ruby. Doris really believed that what Simone was doing was okay—that anything was okay, as long as it kept you thin. It was a wonder she'd never encouraged Ruby to start shoving her finger down the back of her throat.

"No!" Ruby said.

"No, what?"

"No. It's not okay!"

"What's not okay?" Doris asked.

"What Simone is doing, it's not okay. It could kill her. Is it worth dying for, Mother?"

"What's the matter with you, Ruby? Is what worth dying for?"

"Being thin?"

"Of course not," Doris replied.

"Really? But it's worth badgering me my entire life to try to make me something I'm not?"

"What are you talking about? Are you on dope?" Doris asked, surprised by Ruby's sudden brashness.

"I'm talking about my whole life, how you have harassed me about my weight and my eating for thirty-two years."

"I don't harass you. I'm just trying to help. I want you to be happy."

"Do you think, Mother . . . do you think, that maybe, just maybe, it's possible to be a big girl and be happy?"

Doris was silent for a moment as she thought about Ruby's question.

"I think it is, Mom. More and more, I'm starting to think it is, but it would sure help if you would just get off my back and accept me for what I am."

Doris looked at Ruby for a few moments. "Ruby, I've always accepted you . . . embraced you for what you are. I just want the best for you and being overweight makes life so hard and . . ."

"No, it only makes life hard if we let it," Ruby said.

Again, Doris was silent.

"I know you're trying to help, but look at me, Mother. You've hounded me about my weight for my entire life and *look at me*!" Ruby said again. "I'm still fat!"

Doris did as she was instructed and looked at Ruby. "I know. I know," Doris said as a sudden look of guilt and shame came over her face, and for the first time, Ruby understood what it was all about it. Whenever Doris looked at Ruby she felt as if she had failed as a mother; Ruby could see it in Doris's face. Doris felt as though she had failed to help her daughter have a life as a happy thin person.

"You didn't fail, Mom," Ruby said.

"What?"

"You didn't fail. It's not your fault I'm fat, and your personal mission in life does not have to be seeing that I lose weight. Aren't you tired, Mom? I know I am. I'm so tired of trying to fit a mold that isn't for me. You have to let it go."

Doris stared at Ruby and her look of failure and shame seemed to change to one of intrigue and consideration, as if she were really starting to think that Ruby had a valid point. "I'll try, Ruby."

"I hope so," Ruby said. "I really do," she added and headed for the steps. It was all so ridiculous. Half the world was starving and spoiled Americans could do nothing but obsess about being thin. While millions of children were going to bed hungry, Doris was hounding Ruby to eat less, the television was overloaded with ads about ways to lose weight, people were taking dangerous diet pills, and women like Simone were so desperate to be thin, they were forcing themselves to vomit. Insanity! It was all insanity!

When she reached the top floor Ruby knocked on Simone's bedroom door.

"Yes?" Simone called.

"It's me," Ruby said. "Can I come in?"

Simone opened the door. "Hi," she said with a smile. "What's up?"

"Ah . . . nothing. How are you?" Ruby asked.

"Good, just getting ready to go to work."

"Okay, well, I won't keep you. I just wanted to . . ."

"What?" Simone asked.

"Simone, I know," Ruby said, just wanting to get it out in the open.

"Know what?"

"About the hope chest and what's in it."

"What?" Simone said, suddenly looking embarrassed and panicked.

"You know what I'm talking about. I'm sorry if it's none of my business, but I think you need some help, Simone."

"What? Don't be silly," Simone said, backing away from Ruby.

"It's okay. It's nothing to be ashamed of, but you can't keep doing it."

"Doing what? I'm not doing anything," Simone said, diverting her eyes from Ruby, looking down at the floor.

"You're bingeing and purging, Simone, and it could kill you."

"What? That's ridiculous," Simone said, obviously agitated.

"No, Simone. No it isn't."

Simone sat down on the bed. "How did you know?" she asked, still looking at the floor.

Ruby sat down beside her. "You know what a busybody Doris is." Of course, Ruby failed to mention that she, herself, had been snooping around Simone's room the week before.

"It's really not a big deal. It's just something I do to keep my weight in check. I don't do it that often."

"Simone, you're an educated woman. You know how dangerous this is—what it can do to your health."

"Of course, Ruby, but, really, I only do it every now and then. Honestly, it's really not that big of a deal. It's nothing to worry about."

"Simone, I'm sure if you really thought about it you'd realize you need some help. There are programs. I'm sure we can find one that can help you," Ruby said, and as she was saying it, she realized the irony of the situation—how the tables had turned. Here Ruby was in a designer suit, with trendy hair and stylish makeup consoling Simone, beautiful famous Simone. For once, Ruby was the one that was holding it together and able to offer assistance. For once, she wasn't the one that was a mess, she was the strong one, the one who was going to take care of things.

"I can't go into a program. The moment I checked in it would be on the cover of every local newspaper."

"Well, maybe you can go somewhere outside the area."

"How could I do that and still keep my job?" Simone asked,

even though she really didn't have any intention of entering any program.

"I'm not sure, but we'll figure something out," Ruby said.

Then, suddenly, Simone had an idea. It was out there, but it just might work. Not only would it get Ruby off her back, but it might help her career take off as well.

"My Daughter This and My Daughter That"

It was just after one o'clock on a Saturday afternoon when Ruby arrived home. She'd been out running a few errands to get ready for her date with Alan.

"Hello," an elderly black woman, who was sitting on Ruby's sofa, said as Ruby came through the front door.

"Hi," Ruby said, wondering who the stranger was. Maybe she was Wanda's mother or an aunt or something.

"I'm Mrs. Jenkins. I live across the street from Doris. You must be Ruby."

"Yes. It's nice to meet you," Ruby said, approaching Mrs. Jenkins and extending her hand. "What brings you into the city?"

"I just came to take Doris to lunch."

"Really?" Ruby said, suddenly realizing how surprised she sounded to hear that Doris was going to lunch with Mrs. Jenkins. "That's so nice of you," she added, trying to sound more subdued.

"The last few times we talked, she said she was feeling better and would enjoy another visit."

"I didn't know you two had been talking."

"Oh, we talk every day. I keep her up to date on all the latest gossip."

"Really?" Ruby said, again failing to hide her surprise.

"Yeah, I've missed having our morning coffee together, but at least we were able to keep in touch by phone. My grandchildren keep trying to get me using that E-mail nonsense, but I'm too old for that foolishness."

"You two have coffee together in the mornings?" Ruby asked, astonished to learn of her mother's friendship with Mrs. Jenkins. She'd heard Doris talk about "that nice colored woman" across the street a time or two, but Ruby just assumed they exchanged greetings at the mailbox or something. She had never known her mother to fully socialize with anyone of color.

"Almost everyday since I moved in a few months ago. I bore her with stories about my grandchildren and she brags all about you."

Ruby let out quick laugh. "Brags about me? You've got to be kidding."

"No. I've heard all about how you're an independent career girl and manage an entire customer service department on your own."

"Mom said that?"

"Sure. She told me how you were doing so well, you didn't even need any alimony from your former husband. She's always talking about you and what great care you take of her. I think it's fantastic the way you drive all the way from the city to check in on her once a week."

"Really?" Ruby asked for the third time, truly shocked by Mrs. Jenkins's words.

"Of course . . . she never stops talking about you. All I hear is 'my daughter this and my daughter that.' And she's always talking about this house."

"Yeah, she hates this house and the neighborhood."

"What? Are you kidding? All Doris talks about is how her daughter bought a historic home in the city and renovated it from top to bottom. When I came by to take her to lunch a couple of weeks ago she gave me the grand tour. She's very proud of you, Ruby."

Ruby just looked at Mrs. Jenkins with a dumbfounded smile. She vaguely remembered Wanda telling her that a Mrs. Jenkins had taken Doris to lunch the day of her explosion when Simone had appeared at the top of the steps in Doris's little black dress, but the day had been so crazy she'd forgotten all about it.

"Hi, dear," Doris said to Ruby as she emerged from the den. "I see you've met Mrs. Jenkins. We're going to go to lunch."

"Would you like to join us?" Mrs. Jenkins asked Ruby.

"Oh thank you, but I have to get ready for a date," Ruby said, as if she had dates all the time.

"Ready?" Mrs. Jenkins asked. "You don't need to get ready. You're pretty just the way you are. Isn't she Doris?"

"Of course, but you know she'd be so much prettier if she'd lose some . . ." Doris started to say before she stopped herself. "Actually, you're right," Doris said to Mrs. Jenkins before looking at Ruby and smiling. "She does look pretty just the way she is."

"Are you sure you can't join us?" Mrs. Jenkins asked again.

"Yeah, you two go and have a good time. I'll be here when you get back," Ruby said and walked them to the door. She watched Mrs. Jenkins help Doris down the steps and saw the two of them walk down the sidewalk, chatting as they strolled toward the street corner. Ruby wondered what they were saying. Was Mrs. Jenkins going on about her grandchildren or was Doris bragging about Ruby? Ruby decided that Doris was, in fact, bragging about her.

Coming Clean

Simone waited off camera while Charlie Parker made her introduction. "We close tonight's newscast with a special announcement from my coanchor, Simone Reyes. She's been an integral part of the Channel 6 team, and we've all grown to know and love her during her time with us. Now, in a bold step, Simone has decided to share a personal decision with us in hopes of helping others."

Charlie had done the eleven o'clock newscast on his own, and Simone had been waiting on one of the side sets. She was seated in a soft leather chair wearing a simple Yves Saint Laurent beige pantsuit when the cameras turned to her.

"Thank you, Charlie," Simone responded to his introduction. "Tonight all my viewers are going to see me in somewhat of a different light. For more than a year you've watched me anchor the news with my friend Charlie and bring all the top stories into your living room. After much thought, I've decided to bring your attention to something more personal than many of the features we've highlighted on this program. Starting next week, Channel 6 will be airing a six-part series on eating disorders. Of course we've done segments on eating disorders before, but what's different about this series is that not only will it be narrated and covered by me, it will also be about me and my own struggle with an eating disorder."

Simone could hear the quiet gasps and see the mouths of

cameramen and crew members drop open. "Yes. I've suffered from bulimia for years and have decided to seek treatment through a program offered by a local hospital and document my journey through therapy," she said, remaining calm and professional through the entire announcement. "You might ask why I'm being so public about this. Why didn't I take a brief leave of absence or vacation and quietly enter a program outside the area? Of course, I could have done that, but, instead I decided . . . *refused* to be ashamed of my illness. No one would expect me to be embarrassed about having arthritis or diabetes. Why should it be any different for bulimia? I wanted to bring this disease out of the closet and hopefully help others through my own experience. Starting Monday, I'll be bringing a weekly report about bulimia, my experience with it, and my treatment to overcome it. I hope you will plan to watch the documentary, and additional information about bulimia and other eating disorders has now been posted on our Web page. So," Simone said and paused for a moment, "I hope you will tune in to the series, and I thank you for your time this evening."

Simone took a deep breath as the cameras went back to Charlie for him to do a final wrap-up. She unclipped her microphone and calmly walked off the set. All in all, she thought she had done pretty well. She had remained poised and articulate without sounding cold and unfeeling. She thought about working herself up during the announcement to make it look like she was holding back tears, but eventually decided against it. The more she thought about it, the more she figured a heartfelt but dignified message was what she wanted to deliver.

Of course it would be great if her announcement helped others and brought much needed attention to eating disorders, blah, blah, blah, but Simone had other intentions when she pitched her bulimia series to the producer of the Channel 6 news. Ruby had sparked the idea days earlier and, so far, it appeared to be working exactly as planned. Simone had leaked word of her announcement days before the broadcast, and the city was already abuzz with her plans go public about her illness. Just as she had hoped, Simone was no longer the talk of just Washington, D.C. She was making headlines nationally as the beautiful anchorwoman who was so brave and selfless to risk her career to bring attention to bulimia. Oprah Winfrey's people had already contacted her about appearing on an upcoming show, as had *Access Hollywood* and *Extra*. Simone had finally found it—bulimia had wreaked havoc on her life, but at the same time it was going to be her ticket out of boring local news and into the national spotlight of talk show and tabloid television.

Good-Bye

Ruby had just gotten home from the mall and she was exhausted. Shopping for attractive large-size clothes had seemed so much easier with Wanda there to guide her. She couldn't keep going to Saks to fill her wardrobe. If she did, she'd need to have five more roommates to avoid going bankrupt. She'd gone back to some of her old standbys: The Answer, Lane Bryant, Dress Barn. But once she'd had a couple designer suits from Saks, everything else paled in comparison. She decided she'd rather have a few outfits that she looked really good in rather than a bunch of clothes of lesser quality. She'd spent the day perusing the plus-size clothes at Bloomingdale's and Nordstrom and managed to find a couple sale items she liked. She was putting her new clothes in the closet when Wanda called her from downstairs.

"Ruby," Wanda called. "Warren's here."

Shit. There had been so much going on in her life that Ruby had forgotten all about Warren and the night they had spent together a few weeks earlier. "Okay, I'll be right down."

Ruby closed her closet door, took a deep breath, and headed downstairs.

"It was nice to meet you, Warren," Wanda said and excused herself when Ruby reached the bottom of the steps.

"Hey," she said with a smile.

"Hello," Warren said, looking surprised. "Wow, Ruby. You look . . . ah . . . different."

"Good different?"

"Certainly. What transpired . . . how did . . . ?"

"I just got some new clothes and a haircut and some new makeup . . . nothing really."

"It definitely flatters you."

"Thank you, Warren. So what brings you by?"

"I was in the vicinity and thought I'd inquire as to whether you would like to accompany me for an evening meal."

Ruby took a minute to decipher what Warren had just said. "Oh, dinner," she concluded. "I'm sorry. I told Mom I'd take her to the IHOP in Arlington, but you can join us if you want."

"No," Warren said immediately. He knew that Doris had never forgiven him for cheating on her daughter and certainly didn't want to have dinner with her scowling at him the entire time. "Maybe we can share a meal another time. Or perhaps an outing to the cinema?"

"Ah . . ." Ruby stammered. She wasn't sure what to say. She sensed that Warren had taken their night together as an invitation for them to get back together and now, more than ever, Ruby was not interested. "Sure, we can do that, but Warren?"

"Yes."

"I guess I have to say that it would just be as friends," Ruby said, feeling terrible for letting Warren down. She knew it was ridiculous. After all, he had cheated on her during their marriage and left her for another woman, but she couldn't help but look at him, with his big glasses and his awkward demeanor, and feel sorry for him. She had been let down by so many people in her life, and she hated to make someone else feel the way she had felt so many times.

"Sure . . . sure, that's all I anticipated. I wasn't seeking . . ."

"Of course," Ruby said. "Why don't you call me next week, and we'll set something up," she added, sensing, for some reason, that this might be the last time she would ever see Warren.

"I'll do that," Warren said, even though he and Ruby both

knew that he wouldn't. "You look visually stunning. Really, you do."

"Thank you."

"Good-bye, Ruby."

"Bye," Ruby said and kissed him on the cheek.

Never!

"It's been one of the most defining experiences of my life," Simone said to Randy Jarvis, who was seated across the table from her at Chef Geoff's in D.C. They were both wired with microphones and a cameraman was filming their conversation. Simone had been attending an outpatient eating disorders program for three weeks, and they were filming one of her updates. Simone figured that showing a clip of her eating a meal at a local restaurant would help show people how she was recovering.

"Can you tell us a little bit about your program and where you are in your treatment?"

"I'd be happy to, Randy. My treatment consists of a team of medical, nutritional, and mental health professionals. They're helping me learn healthy ways to eat and to control my weight. I'm learning that good food and a healthy diet will not make me fat, and I'm learning to understand and manage the situations that caused me to binge in the first place. I attend a support group and meet with my treatment team regularly."

"Any medications?"

"Not at this time. I've been responding well to the work we've done, but there are medications that can be helpful to people with eating disorders, and I'd encourage patients to discuss the option of medication with their treatment team."

"So, where are you in terms of your recovery at this point?"

"I'm feeling good. I feel like I'm doing the right thing. I can eat a reasonable amount of food and know that it's okay."

"And we've just had a meal together. Do you mind if I share with the audience what you've eaten?"

Simone laughed. "I guess not."

"So just now, you've finished a Caesar salad, a grilled chicken breast with green beans and mashed potatoes, and some raspberry sorbet."

"Yes," Simone said, feeling very silly, knowing that the entire contents of her lunch was going to be revealed to the viewing audience.

"Can I ask you . . ." Randy said, hesitating for a moment and taking a Barbara Walters kind of pose. "People are going to wonder . . . you know . . . will you keep this lunch down?"

"Of course," Simone said. "I can't say that I'm cured as I think my recovery will last a long time . . . perhaps a lifetime. But, yes, I feel I can honestly say my bingeing and purging days are over."

"Okay," Randy said and signaled for the cameraman to stop taping. "That was great, Simone."

"Thanks. I'll meet you back at the studio to work on production. We'll tie this footage with the tape of one of my group sessions," Simone said and got up from the table.

She left the restaurant and retrieved her Mercedes from the parking attendant. When she was about halfway back to the studio she spotted a Subway sandwich shop—one she had been to many times—one, because she loved their Italian Cold Cut Sub, and two, because the bathroom was private and had a loud hand dryer to muffle any embarrassing sounds.

She pulled the car into a metered space about a block from restaurant, pulled her scarf and sunglasses from the glove compartment, and quickly made her way to the entrance. She hurriedly walked past the counter and down the back hall to the ladies' room. Once inside the bathroom, she closed and locked the door behind her. She turned the faucet on and pushed the big button on the hand dryer. Then, in a twelve hundred dollar Versace suit and a pair of Prada shoes, she knelt down on the sticky bathroom floor while holding her hair back with one hand, leaned over the toilet bowl, and shoved her middle finger down the back of her throat.

Was Randy insane? she thought as her lunch spewed out of her mouth and she inhaled the foul smell of bile. How on earth could he, or anyone, expect her to eat that big lunch and still look the way she looked? They were crazy! All of them—her doctor and her therapist and that silly nutritionist she had been working with for the past few weeks—nuts, they were just plain nuts! This was the only way. This was the only way Simone Reyes was going to stay thin and beautiful and make it to the top. Besides, really . . . what was the big deal? It wasn't like she binged and purged *every* day. She only did it a couple times a week. And it wasn't like she was some sickly toothpick of a woman. She was a healthy-looking size six. She wasn't like those silly girls on the ABC After School Specials. She was Simone Reyes, and she was beautiful. She'd been fat, and she wasn't going back to that. Never! She was never going back to that!

Without Incident

Ruby was in a hurry, but figured she had just enough time to swing by McDonald's and grab a quick dinner before going to the Channel 6 studio to watch Wanda tape her interview for the story about large-size models. It had been a few weeks since she and Wanda exposed Denise for the thin waif that she was, which resulted in a postponement of the feature so Wanda could be used as the lead model.

It was almost six o'clock and there seemed to be a bit of a dinner rush. When Ruby walked into the restaurant there was a crowd of people congregating in front of the counter. Lately, it seemed like no one knew how to form lines anymore. Half the people waiting for service thought they were supposed to form separate lines in front of each register, while the other half seemed to think they were supposed to wait in one communal line and then step up to the first available cashier—the result was chaos, cranky customers, and unnecessary waits for Value Meals. It took Ruby almost ten minutes to finally get up to the counter and place her order.

"Hi. Let me get a Big Mac, a large fry, and a large Coke . . . oh, and an apple pie," Ruby said quickly, hoping it wouldn't take the cashier long to gather her order. She only had about a half hour to get to the station. Ruby watched as the young man gathered her food. God, she hoped the fries were hot. When he'd placed everything on her tray she hurried to the drink station, filled her cup with ice, and placed it under the Coke dispenser. Inhaling the smell of hamburgers and grease, she made her way to a table in the corner, sat down, and popped open the cardboard box which housed her dinner. She took a big bite and looked at her watch. She'd have to eat fast if she was going to make it downtown before Wanda got on camera. The fries weren't as hot as they could've been, but they were okay. By quickly alternating between Big Mac bites and French fry consumption, she was able to finish her entire meal in less than ten minutes. She'd take the apple pie with her and eat it in the car.

Ruby got up from the table, dumped her tray, and headed to her car. She backed out of her parking space, and as she waited to pull into traffic, she slipped a portion of the apple pie from its container and took a bite. It was all right, but God how she missed the apple pies McDonald's used to serve years ago—the ones they deep fried, the ones that always burned your tongue when you took the first bite. What on earth made them think anyone would want silly baked pies over ones fresh from the grease of a deep fryer?

Once Ruby was able to get on the road and head into the city, she took another bite of the pie and another. It was mere seconds before the pie was nothing more than a crumb or two left in the container. She was about to set the empty box on the passenger seat when, all of a sudden, like a lightning bolt, it hit her.

What the fuck had just happened? she thought to herself as she reviewed the last half hour. Had she really just walked into a McDonald's, ordered her food, and eaten it with no drama—no voices tempting her to order three Big Macs and two large fries and a chocolate shake, no conflicting voices berating her for even being in a McDonald's in the first place?

The more Ruby thought about it, the more amazed she was. She had simply, with little thought other than that she was in hurry, walked into a fast food restaurant, placed her order, and eaten it with no guilt, no internal anguish, no struggle. She hadn't looked around her to see if anyone was staring at the fat girl who had no business in a burger joint. She hadn't even considered going through the drive-thru to avoid any stares. For a moment she felt like she was in the *Twilight Zone*. She had spent her entire life being self-conscious and battling food. To have had even a brief moment of relief—a brief moment where she had just eaten without incident, without thought, without guilt was huge—huge because it had never happened before.

Ruby smiled as she turned into the parking garage at Channel 6. She knew that she had been changing over the past few weeks—she had been feeling more confident, more attractive, but today she felt powerful, or at least less defenseless. For once in her life, she had controlled food, it had not controlled her. Okay, a Big Mac and fries wasn't exactly the leanest meal she could've had, but just the fact that the thought hadn't even occurred to her to order *two* Big Macs or *two* large fries, was a victory. Of course her battle with food, and inner voices, and herself was far from over, but positive things were happening. If she could have one meal without drama, why not two, or three, or all of them? If she could have a solid half hour where she wasn't self-conscious, where she didn't feel like people were staring at her fat self, maybe she could stretch that into an hour, two hours, a full day. More and more Ruby was having something she hadn't had in a long time—hope. And no longer was her hope about one day being thin. It was about hoping that the more she worked, the more time went by, the more she would come to accept herself and like herself for what she was, the more she would stop having the equivalent of World War III in her head every time she ate a morsel of food, the more she would just relax and let go and be happy.

Ruby looked at her watch as she got out of the car and hurried toward the building. She only had a minute or two before Wanda's taping was scheduled to start. Cameramen had been at the house a few days earlier filming Wanda's home life, and they were going to film one of her fashion shows the following week, but today was the actual interview. In the end, all the film would be collapsed into a three-minute story on large-size models and run on the six and eleven o'clock news.

"Hi," she said to Wanda when she finally made it into the studio. "Sorry I'm running late. Did I miss anything?"

"No, we haven't started yet."

"Nervous?"

"A little. Do I look okay?"

"Okay? You look fantastic. You're going to knock 'em dead," Ruby replied as a middle-aged man approached them.

"Hello, I'm Steve," he said, looking at Ruby and Wanda. "Goodness, I didn't realize we were interviewing two models today. I thought it was just one."

Ruby looked around. Two models?

"We'll need to get you a chair and a microphone," he said to Ruby.

"Me?" Ruby said with a laugh. "A model? Oh no, I'm not a model."

"Oh?" Steve said, truly looking surprised. "Gosh, you're so pretty and put together. I thought you were," he added before walking away and repeating under his breath, "I thought you were."

Epilogue

"You look fierce!" Wanda said to Jeremy as they hovered on the sidewalk off 17th Street waiting for Ruby to arrive. It was early evening a few days before Halloween and the annual high heel drag race had finally arrived. Jeremy had abandoned his search for a formal gown after Simone offered him her cat woman gear. He'd spent the afternoon getting ready and planned to have the hottest costume in the race. He was in heels and full makeup, wearing a high-styled red wig, leopard print spandex pants over his padded hips, two bird seed–filled sacks under a tight black top, and a thick gold belt. He completed the ensemble with Simone's pair of cat ears and tail.

"You look fantastic!" a man said to Jeremy as he walked by. Jeremy relished the compliment, thinking he was the hottest Cat Woman since Julie Newmar, until the stranger elaborated. "You've got Peggy Bundy down pat."

"Peggy Bundy?" Jeremy asked Wanda as the man walked away.

"Yeah, you know. From *Married With Children*. I guess you do look a little bit like her with the big red hair and the leopard print pants."

"I do not. I'm Cat Woman," Jeremy said, plainly annoyed. He hadn't spent three hours primping to look like a trashy Chicago housewife.

"Okay, okay," Wanda said only to appease Jeremy. Her mind

wasn't really on the race anyway. She had so many other things to think about. The Channel 6 piece on plus-size models, of which Wanda was the star, had run a week earlier. An agent from a prestigious modeling agency in New York happened to see the story and had contacted Wanda. She sent him her portfolio, and he later invited her to come to New York to meet with him. She was due to leave the following week, and if all went well, she would be signed by the agency.

"Hello," Simone said to Wanda and Jeremy as she made her way through the crowd with a camera crew following. She'd volunteered to cover the event for Channel 6 months ago. She thought she might even report from the scene in her cat outfit, but after the incident with Eric and his mother, Simone had no interest in ever wearing the costume again and gave it to Jeremy. "Do you guys want some camera time?" she asked.

"You bet," Jeremy said before Wanda could answer.

Simone signaled the cameraman to start rolling and put the microphone up to her chin, before reporting. "I'm here at the annual Halloween High Heel Race on Seventeenth Street, taking in all the outrageous costumes. Standing next to me is local model Wanda Johnson. What do you think of all the men in such fabulous costumes?" Simone asked Wanda, putting the microphone up to her for a response.

"Well, as a model myself," Wanda said, using the free publicity for all it was worth, "I'm impressed with the creativity and the detail of the outfits."

"And standing next to Ms. Johnson is Jeremy Burke. You look great! How long did it take you to put this look together?"

"Several hours, but if you want to look good, you have to put in the time," Jeremy replied as a young woman walked by, looked him up and down, and smiled. "Cool outfit," she said. "*Married With Children* was one of my favorite shows."

"I'm *Cat Woman*," Jeremy yelled behind her.

Simone laughed. "I heard that," she said, knowing that interviewing her friends while covering a story probably wasn't the most professional thing to do, but she didn't care. Ever since she made the announcement about her eating disorder Simone's phone had been ringing off the hook. Everyone wanted to interview the courageous newscaster who had let the public into her personal life to help others. She'd done some of the major nationally syndicated radio shows, a brief interview with *Access Hollywood,* and *Cosmopolitan* planned to run a feature on her. But Simone was most excited about her planned appearance on *Oprah* the following week. She was finally on her way—it was just a matter of time before Simone landed a permanent gig in the national spotlight. There were rumors of her own talk show, and a production company had approached her about making a made-for-TV movie about her story. Her days of reporting boring local news would soon be replaced with the glamour and excitement of Hollywood, and Simone could barely contain herself. She finally had what she wanted—excitement, beauty, and fame. A part of her knew something was terribly wrong with what looked like a perfect picture from the outside, but she refused to think about it. If she wanted to make it to the top, she had to make sacrifices—"taking care of things" on her knees in the bathroom every now and then was one of those sacrifices. She wouldn't let it get out of control. She'd been doing it for years, and it really hadn't caused her any major problems. So what if the enamel on her teeth was being stripped away, she had a constant sore throat, and was plagued with stomach cramps that could one day kill her? She was beautiful—she was a success, and success didn't come easy; people who understood that were the only ones that made it. And Simone was determined to make it.

As Simone wrapped up her interview with Wanda and Jeremy, Ruby finally made her grand entrance. Alan had dropped her off near the event and then went to park the car. He and Ruby had been dating for more than a month. In fact, Alan had already started talking about them seeing each other exclusively, but Ruby wasn't ready for that. She'd gone to the Living Large event again and had met two other men that she was interested in—Jim was a real estate agent and Tom was a financial advisor. Of course, she liked Alan too, but she was starting to realize that she didn't have to jump aboard the first ship that came into her harbor. She had choices, and she was going to take her time before making any serious relationship decisions.

"Oh my!" Wanda said when she caught sight of Ruby coming toward her. "Look at you!"

"Hi," Ruby said, shivering from the October chill. The temperature was in the high forties, but Ruby wouldn't even considering wearing a coat. Tonight was the night she unveiled her special dress. She'd taken Doris's little black dress to a tailor near her office and asked for a copy to be made in her size. It had cost Ruby a small fortune to have the dress made, but it was worth every penny. Besides, Ruby's money problems would be over in a few more months once she received her settlement from Slim & Trim. They had counted on the "meek fat girl" to be too embarrassed to cause a ruckus about them unethically using her picture in their commercial, but Ruby hired a lawyer to take them for anything she could get, and rather than going through expensive court proceedings and being exposed for fraudulent advertising, Slim & Trim had agreed to pay Ruby a sizable sum of money.

Ruby felt glamorous and chic in her new dress. Even if it wasn't the real thing, Ruby had finally gotten to wear Doris's infamous little black dress, and she felt beautiful in it. It was a happy day for her—she was thrilled to be walking around town with confidence in a beautiful dress, but she was just a tiny bit sad as well. She felt like a chapter of her life was coming to a close. Wanda would soon be moving to New York, and Simone would be returning to her house in Georgetown in another week or two. Ruby knew they would remain friends, but it wouldn't be the same once the three of them were no longer under one roof. She remembered the day Wanda and Simone had moved in, and she had sat in her bedroom with a feeling that having two new roommates was going to shake up her life—she couldn't have been more right. She'd grown more as person over the past few months than she had in her whole life. She was accepting herself more and more every day, and forcing other people in her life to do the same. She no longer hated Fat Ruby. In fact, she no longer thought in terms of Fat Ruby and Thin Ruby—she was just Ruby.

Before Ruby had a chance to exchange any further greetings with her friends, the race marshal signaled for all the drag queens to assemble at the starting line. Simone and Wanda wished Jeremy good luck. Ruby was about to do the same, but as Jeremy started to walk toward the starting line, Ruby chased after him, having a sudden urge to do something wild.

"I think I might run too," Ruby said. Of course, she wasn't a drag queen, but it was called the High Heel Race and she *was* in high heels—that had to count for something.

"Sure," Jeremy said with a surprised smile as the two of them lined up with all the men in outrageous costumes and high heels. Ruby braced herself as the marshal lifted the cap gun.

"On your mark! Get set!" he called, before pulling the trigger.

As the gun shot into the air, Ruby was off, racing down 17th Street on a crisp fall evening with a slew of men in drag. She didn't feel self-conscious with her boobs shaking and her hair blowing in the wind. She wasn't even worried about any skinny bitches watching from the sidewalk, mocking the fat girl in the little black dress. Ruby just ran—she ran with a big smile on her face, and it was the most fun she'd ever had.

Please turn the page for an exciting sneak peek of
Patrick Sanchez's debut novel
GIRLFRIENDS
now available at bookstores everywhere!

Wickedly witty debut novelist Patrick Sanchez introduces a memorable trio of urban twentysomething females who are searching for the perfect job, the perfect apartment, the perfect man—or woman—all the while asking themselves and each other . . .

WHAT'S A NICE GIRL LIKE YOU
DOING WITH A LIFE LIKE THIS?

Okay, there are worse things than bringing your gay hairdresser as your date to your ten-year high school reunion. Yet after grudgingly witnessing yet another acquaintance's triumphant nuptials, assistant bank manager Gina Perry has hit an all time low . . . or so she thinks. Next thing she knows, her mangy mutt Gomez has soiled the carpet again, she's been robbed at knife point by a drive-through customer, and she's had a drunken one-night stand. So what's a gal to do? Forget about finding Mr. Right and keep an eye out for Mr. Maybe . . .

Cheryl Sonntag's already found him, but the clock is ticking for her commitment-phobic boyfriend. This chic, sexy African-American gal isn't about to waste any more time on a guy who devotes all his energy to working out, waxing his chest hair, and trying to cure himself of imaginary diseases. It's time to turn to Plan Z: the personal ads . . .

Who needs men? Not Linda Collins! Super-organized, sensible, and doomed to spending eternity—or at least the next forty years—as a Senior Customer Service Representative, Linda's perfectly content to be otherwise occupied while her heterosexual pals scour the clubs and classifieds for husband material. Now she's landed the Latin lesbian lover of her dreams—or so she thinks . . .

Before you can say loser, Gina, Cheryl, and Linda are up to their earrings in a series of romantic and professional mishaps. Luckily, the hapless trio lives by that age-old adage: when the going gets tough, the tough turn to blond highlights, margaritas . . . and girlfriends!

Princess Charming in a World of Toads

Gina and Linda were at one of their regular haunts, a dance club called Rumors, one of many in a cluster of bars and nightclubs in downtown Washington, D.C., that were known as "meat markets" for young professionals. In fact, the entire neighborhood was jokingly referred to as the "herpes triangle." On weekends these clubs were filled with D.C.'s singles—mostly young men and women who were employed by the federal government or had jobs with government contractors. Aside from the young crowd, there were always a few middle-aged businessmen searching for a little love while their frumpy wives thought they were working late. Gina spent more time than she cared to admit at these bars, hoping to find Mr. Right or at least Mr. I'll-Do-for-a-While. But even in her worst moments of desperation, she never dreamed of getting involved with one of the old farts with the tight starched dress shirts—shirts so tight you could almost hear the buttons screaming *Help me! I can't hold on!* She would *never* talk to one of those guys. Not until she met Griffin anyway.

Gina was standing against the bar, waiting for Linda to come back from the restroom. The bartender had just handed her a rum and Coke, and as she reached in her purse to grab some cash, a short, balding man intervened and paid for her drink. He must have come straight from work, because he was wearing the remnants of a business suit—no blazer or tie but those formal creased pants that look really awkward when worn without the rest of the suit. Of course, the shirt was too tight, especially around the belly. And the icing on the cake—he was wearing some ridiculous baseball cap that had "The Big G" printed on the front of it. Gina smiled, not knowing quite how to react. The kind of smile that said thanks for the drink. I'm flattered. Now get lost. She sipped the drink and smiled again, wondering how long she had to stand there. Hoping he wouldn't make her talk to him, she scanned the bar for Linda, wishing she'd come back soon.

"I think you're absolutely beautiful," the pudgy little man said with a hopeful smile.

Of course you do. Fat, ugly guys always think that, Gina thought, returning his smile, and again hoped that if she just stood there without saying anything, he'd go away.

The bald, potbellied man persisted. "And your name is?"

"Hi, I'm Gi—Mary," Gina replied, feeling obligated to say something to him. As much as she wanted to just ignore him and walk away, she couldn't do it. He was truly pathetic; she just couldn't be rude to him. Besides, there was no harm in chatting with him for a minute or two and then saying she had to go find her friend or run to the restroom or whatever it took to get away from him.

"Mary, what a pretty name. I'm Griffin," he said, pulling a pack of cigarettes from his pocket, lighting up, and offering one to Gina.

Gina shook her head. Short, fat, bald, *and* you smoke. How *do* you keep the women away? "Yeah, my mother's name was Mary, and her mother . . ."

She almost said "And her mother too" but caught herself before the lie seemed too ridiculous. It wasn't so much that she was afraid to give out her real name. She just got a kick out of making one up, especially around guys like Griffin, whom she knew she would never really be interested in. Just as she was thinking of a good occupation to tell the loser (maybe a nurse or, what the hell, how about a personal assistant to Laura Bush), Linda emerged from the crowd. Gina gave her *the look,* and Linda immediately went into action. She frowned and put her hand to her forehead before telling Gina that she had a headache and wanted to leave.

Gina turned to Griffin, not remembering his name. "Oh, ah . . . ?"

"Griffin," he replied.

"Griffin, my friend really isn't feeling well. I think we have to leave."

"I'd be happy to take you home if you'd like to stay for a while."

"Oh, I need to go anyway. I have an early day at the White House tomorrow."

"The White House?"

"Yeah, it was nice to meet you."

"Can I call you?"

"Sure," Gina said as she walked away, hoping he wouldn't have the guts to ask for her phone number.

"Mary," Griffin called. "Your phone number?"

Gina kept walking pretending not to hear, and fortunately Griffin didn't persist.

Gina and Linda hit the street.

"Where should we go now?"

"I don't know, Linda. There are so many trolls out tonight. Here a troll, there a troll, everywhere a troll troll." Gina was getting frustrated. It had been months since she'd met anyone who even remotely interested her.

"Why don't we go over to the Phase?" Linda suggested, referring to Phase One, a bar near Capitol Hill.

"The Phase? That's clear across town. Besides, what are the chances of me finding a man there?" Gina said, exasperated.

"Would you forget about finding a man for once in your life and just try to have some fun? Come on, we'll have a few drinks, and dance, and maybe *I'll* get lucky."

"All right, Linda, let's go." Gina was feeling a little resigned anyway. Maybe just relaxing and getting stoned drunk was what she needed.